JOIN THE READERS WHO CAN'T
PUT SIMON LELIC'S
GRIPPING THRILLERS DOWN . . .

'An intricate and powerful thriller' **TANA FRENCH**

'What a read! It's proper clever. Loved it' **STUART TURTON**

'Clever and atmospheric' **MARK EDWARDS**

'bloody good read and the very definition of unpredictable'
JOHN MARRS

'Skilful and compelling' *OBSERVER*, **THRILLER
OF THE MONTH**

'A brilliantly tense tale' **ARAMINTA HALL**

'marvel: intricate, complex and utterly gripping' **ALEX LAKE**

'Expect twists aplenty' *WOMAN'S WEEKLY*

'Simon Lelic just gets better and better'
DERVLA McTIERNAN

'A chillingly complex, well-crafted web' **JANE CORRY**

'A skilfully-woven mystery that oozes with tension'
T M LOGAN

D0785850

ABOUT THE AUTHOR

Simon Lelic is the author of seven highly acclaimed thrillers: *Rupture* (winner of a Betty Trask Award and shortlisted for the John Creasey Debut Dagger), *The Facility*, *The Child Who* (longlisted for the CWA Gold Dagger and the CWA Ian Fleming Steel Dagger), *The House*, *The Liar's Room*, *The Search Party* and *The Hiding Place*. He has also written The Haven series for younger readers, twice shortlisted for the CrimeFest awards.

SIMON LELIC

THE
HIDING
PLACE

PENGUIN BOOKS

PENGUIN BOOKS

UK | USA | Canada | Ireland | Australia
India | New Zealand | South Africa

Penguin Books is part of the Penguin Random House group of companies
whose addresses can be found at global.penguinrandomhouse.com.

First published 2022

001

Copyright © Simon Lelic, 2022

The moral right of the author has been asserted

Typeset by Jouve (UK), Milton Keynes
Printed and bound in Great Britain by Clays Ltd, Elcograf S.p.A.

The authorized representative in the EEA is Penguin Random House Ireland,
Morrison Chambers, 32 Nassau Street, Dublin D02 YH68

A CIP catalogue record for this book is available from the British Library

ISBN: 978–0–241–99032–2

www.greenpenguin.co.uk

Penguin Random House is committed to a
sustainable future for our business, our readers
and our planet. This book is made from Forest
Stewardship Council® certified paper.

For Sarah, Barnaby, Joey and Anja

Ben Draper wasn't ready to die.

He knew he'd done some bad things. Some very bad things. But surely he didn't deserve *this*.

It was only supposed to have been a game – a stupid game he hadn't even wanted to play.

And now he was lying here bleeding, scrunching up his eyes at the pain in his arm.

He wanted to wail, to call for help, but he couldn't be sure who would reach him first. And there were footsteps close by. He could hear them. Meaning it was crucial he didn't make a sound. He couldn't run any more either, not in the state he was in, and not without drawing attention to himself.

His only chance was to squash in tight, and to hope that the monsters passed him by. To trust the shadows, and to pray. *Please God, if you're really out there, keep me hidden. Keep me safe.*

Please let me never be found.

Twenty-two years later

Friday 18 October, 3.17 p.m.

'Why do I suddenly feel underdressed?'

Robin Fleet took his eyes momentarily from the road. Nicky was in the passenger seat beside him, her gaze turned to the window as the main building came into view. Fleet had to admit it was impressive. After they'd passed through a set of manned entry gates, the route from the road had taken them up a private drive long enough that it had seemed it would never end. There were thick banks of trees on either side, impossibly green in spite of the fact that it was already mid-October. Eventually the drive had swept left, the wall of trees receding as though someone were pulling back a curtain.

'Seriously, boss, you could have warned me. If I'd known we were heading anywhere quite so fancy, I would have worn my string of pearls.'

Fleet's eyes were back on the tarmac. 'Do you even own a string of pearls, Detective Sergeant?'

He couldn't recall seeing Nicky in a pair of heels, let alone a set of pearls. Pearl necklaces and impractical shoes would for her fall into the same category as tiaras and sequinned dresses: fine, for seven-year-olds and princesses; completely useless for anybody living and working in the real world. As a rule, Nicky wore black trouser suits and Converse trainers, and in Fleet's opinion looked all the better for it.

'I do, as it happens,' Nicky said, in answer to Fleet's question. 'My grandma left it to me. An apology for my mother, I always thought.'

'Well,' said Fleet, 'pearls or not, I don't think either of us is going to exactly blend in. It's probably only because we're coppers that they didn't ask to check our bank balances at the gate.'

The drive had turned into gravel. Fleet swung the Insignia around a fountain and followed the signposts to the visitors' car park, before pulling into a space between two Range Rovers. He and Nicky stepped out of the car, and together surveyed the building looming over them. There was a huge central clock tower above the main entrance, and crenellated red-brick walls stretching to each corner of the building. The windows were arched and leaded, and ivy crept artfully around the main entrance, an elaborately carved set of wooden doors set atop a sweep of stone steps. Looking at the storybook setting, it would have been easy to forget why they were there.

There was a tall, severe-looking man waiting for them just inside the entranceway. He was dressed in black, from his robes to the suit he wore beneath them. The only flash of colour was the crimson knot of his tie and the piercing blue of his eyes. He was most likely in his early sixties, Fleet guessed, but like the building he was standing in, showed his age without appearing in any way decrepit. Facially, he was like a stone carving of himself, reminding Fleet of one of the presidents on Mount Rushmore.

'Detective Inspector Fleet, I presume,' the man said. 'I was told to expect you. I'm Adrian Harris, headmaster.'

Fleet offered his hand. 'Pleased to meet you, Mr Harris. This is my colleague, Detective Sergeant Nicola Collins.'

Harris glanced at Nicky and nodded cursorily. Fleet caught Nicky's expression, and he could tell she'd immediately taken against the man. Too aloof, too supercilious, too dismissive of anyone who wasn't in authority. *Probably a chauvinist, too,* Fleet heard her thinking.

The headmaster extended an arm, directing them across the entrance hall and towards a doorway off to one side. The hallway was as impressive in its way as the building's facade. There was a vaulted ceiling, and a thick green carpet running up a central oak staircase, with a gleaming gold carpet rod on each step. On the wall opposite the entrance, completely dominating the room, was a wooden engraving of the school's coat of arms: a snake on one side, a dove on the other. *Sicut serpentes, sicut columbae,* read the Latin inscription – evidently the school's motto.

'I have to say, when news reached me about what had been found, I imagined sirens wailing and helicopters buzzing overhead,' Harris said. 'I am thankful that you and your colleagues instead opted to exhibit some discretion.' His eyes dipped, as though he was taking in what Fleet and Nicky were wearing. He seemed to think they'd ditched their uniforms solely out of consideration to the school.

He directed them through the door, marked *Staff only* in gold-leaf lettering.

'This is not the most direct route,' the headmaster said, as he led them down a corridor in what appeared to be the administrative area of the building. 'But at this stage of proceedings, it would not do to attract undue attention. In an environment such as this one, rumours spread quicker than measles. We're already having to act to discourage some of the more gruesome ones. The line we're taking with the pupils is that a site has been discovered of potential historical interest.'

They passed from the corridor into a kitchen, and a dozen workers dressed in white turned their way. Harris ignored them all, ushering Fleet and Nicky towards an emergency exit sign on the far side of the room. Fleet was beginning to feel like a call girl being smuggled through the back entrance of a luxury hotel.

The emergency exit took them outside, into a service area at the rear of the building. From here they could see the full extent of the enormous campus. There were football, rugby and hockey pitches off to Fleet's left, all perfectly flat even though the campus itself was on a hill with the main building perched at the top. Thirty or forty metres down the slope, almost directly opposite them, was what was unmistakably the school's chapel, although Fleet had seen cathedrals that were less impressive. Beyond the chapel was a dense line of trees, marking the boundary of a wood that seemed to stretch out of sight.

Harris was several steps ahead. He had veered from the path leading towards the chapel, on to the grass. 'We'll need to cut through the woods,' he explained, as he waited for Fleet and Nicky to catch up.

A cheer went up from behind them, and Fleet guessed one of the players on the hockey pitch had scored a goal. He turned just long enough to see that not all of the pupils on the sidelines were watching the game. Several were facing Fleet's way, and he felt their eyes on his back as he followed Harris towards the trees.

The woods were even thicker than Fleet had expected. From the moment he stepped beneath the canopy, he might almost have been in the forest on the outskirts of his home town. He shared a glance with Nicky, and he could tell she was experiencing the same sense of déjà vu he was. *At least it isn't raining*, he told himself.

They walked another hundred metres or so before Fleet spotted the tents that had been set up by the forensic teams.

They'd been pitched in a clearing, on the southern side of the chapel. Where the trees thinned, they were replaced by stone markers jutting drunkenly from the earth.

'Is this a graveyard?' said Nicky, at Fleet's shoulder.

'A long-neglected one, I'm afraid,' the headmaster acknowledged. 'It was overgrown and ignored even before the old chapel was demolished and the new one built further up the hill.'

Fleet raised his head, and realised the trees between the abandoned graveyard and the existing chapel were much younger than those they'd walked through. 'Why was the old chapel knocked down?' he asked.

'After the fire, there wasn't much left of it,' Harris said.

Fleet looked at him blankly.

'The fire?' Harris repeated, in a tone he might have used on a pupil who'd evidently forgotten a lesson that had been covered in class the previous week. 'In 1921. It completely decimated the entire school. We have some literature available on the subject if you are interested?'

'Thank you, Mr Harris,' Fleet said, ignoring the offer. 'We'll find our way from here.'

The headmaster had obviously expected to escort Fleet right into the middle of the crime scene – perhaps even to stand beside him while Fleet's colleagues outlined what they'd found. Harris appeared to wrestle for a moment with his displeasure at someone else exerting their authority on territory he clearly considered to be his own.

'Certainly,' he replied stiffly. 'You will of course let me know if there is anything more I can do. As I mentioned, your discretion in this matter is appreciated. We have to be mindful of safeguarding our children. And, naturally, the reputation of the school.'

Fleet caught Nicky's eye. They turned away, leaving Harris standing watching them from the edge of the graveyard.

A PC was stationed on the perimeter, and he nodded Fleet and Nicky through. There were one or two scenes of crime officers milling about in the cordoned-off clearing, but most of the activity appeared to be happening inside the tents. There were three: two staging areas, Fleet guessed, and one larger structure covering up whatever had been found. He looked around for the person in charge, then paused when he heard a noise he hadn't been expecting. It was singing, he realised. High and sweet, and drifting melodically from the chapel.

'Rob? Jesus Christ, Rob. When the hell did you get so fat?'

Fleet closed his eyes at the sound of the approaching voice.

'No, wait, let me guess,' the voice went on. 'It was when the divorce came through. I went through the same thing myself. Your wife leaves you, and all of a sudden Deliveroo becomes your mistress. But hey, you've got to get your hugs from somewhere, am I right?'

'Randy,' said Fleet, turning, and with as much of a smile as he could muster. 'I didn't know this was one of yours.'

'It wasn't supposed to be,' said Randolph Green, snapping off a latex glove and extending a hand. 'But Kathleen called in sick, so now it is. Lucky for you, old friend.'

They shook hands, and Fleet gestured towards Nicky. 'Do you know Detective Sergeant Nicola Collins?'

'Sure, I know Nicky,' said Randy, giving Nicky's hand a pump, too. 'What's the story, Detective Sergeant? He's got fatter and you've got thinner. Has Rob here been stealing your lunch money?'

Nicky smiled – with genuine warmth, Fleet noted. 'And pulling on my pigtails,' she answered.

Randy grinned. He was a big man himself, a match for Fleet in height if not in weight. It had been several years since Fleet had worked with the forensic pathologist, but Randy in fact looked trimmer than ever – despite being more than a decade Fleet's senior.

'We were told you'd found a body, Randy,' said Fleet, drawing in his stomach. 'I didn't know it was because you were out here digging up graves.'

'It certainly does look that way, doesn't it?' said Randy, casting around. 'But wait until you see what we've *actually* found.' Once again he looked Fleet up and down. 'Although it's going to be a bit of a squeeze, I'm afraid.'

Fleet frowned, and Randy tipped his head. 'Come take a look-see,' he said.

They followed the pathologist to the main tent. There was nothing inside but a hole in the ground – and a stone stairwell in the shadows leading down.

'What on earth . . .' said Fleet. He turned to see Randy watching him.

'Did Harris tell you about the fire? That the site of the chapel had moved? Well, most of what look like grave markers in this corner of the clearing are actually bits of debris from the original chapel. We had to move a few slabs to find the staircase, but we're assuming this was the entrance to the old crypt.' Randy held out a hand, and smiled ghoulishly. 'Step into my world, my friends.'

Once they were appropriately kitted out, Fleet and Nicky followed Randy down the narrow stairwell. Both men had to duck and turn sideways, but Nicky was so slender there would have been space for her double at her side.

'Did nobody know this place was here?' said Fleet.

'Apparently not,' Randy replied. 'It looks as though the entrance got blocked up when the old building collapsed, and it clearly hadn't been disturbed in years. Although someone obviously found out about it at some point.'

When they reached the bottom of the steps, the chamber opened out, and Fleet was able to stand upright. There was no daylight in the crypt, but the space was being illuminated by powerful LEDs, allowing Fleet to survey the scene before him. The room was perhaps seven or eight metres square. The walls were made of stone, as was the floor. There were Latin inscriptions on some of the stones, and markers to show where people had been buried. The words were so faded it was hard to tell who or when, but the vault appeared to be centuries old at least – older even than the gravestones outside.

'A site of potential historical interest,' Fleet muttered, recalling the way the headmaster had described the place. Harris must have used the description in Randy's presence, too, because the pathologist gave an irritated snort.

'I tell you, that man has been buzzing around us like a fly around a dead body. Talking of which . . .' he added, with a macabre leer.

There were two white-suited SOCOs in a corner of the room. One was on her hands and knees, while her colleague peered over her shoulder. From her evident concentration levels, and the careful sweeping of her hands, she might have been searching for a dropped contact lens.

When the SOCOs saw Randy approach, they moved to one side, allowing Fleet to see what they'd been examining.

It was a bag of bones. Literally.

Half buried in a pile of loose earth were the frayed remains of what looked like a hessian sack, and a skeleton curled in a foetal position. The skeleton was small. Child-sized.

Fleet cleared his throat. 'I don't suppose there's any chance these remains are as old as those tombs?' he asked Randy, not moving his eyes from the body at his feet.

'We can't be sure yet,' Randy replied. Fleet glanced and saw the intense fascination in the pathologist's eyes. Randy must have spent hours staring at the remains already, but now that he was looking at the skeleton again, it was as though he couldn't bring himself to look away. It would have been like a jigsaw to him, Fleet knew. The most intricately illustrated storybook. 'But I would imagine that the chances are slim,' the man concluded.

'What makes you say that?' asked Fleet, finally turning fully.

Randy stood up straight. 'Because we also found this,' he said. He passed Fleet a see-through bag. It contained a piece of material. A badge, in fact: a stitched version of the coat of arms Fleet had seen on the wall in the school's entrance hall.

'We're fairly certain it's from his blazer,' said Randy.

'*His?*' said Fleet, looking up.

'The subject is male, almost certainly. Between twelve and sixteen years of age, would be my guess. And I checked with our friend, Mr Harris. Apparently this particular version of the coat of arms has only been used on the pupils' blazers since 1984. Which doesn't prove anything conclusively, of course, and we'll be able to tell you more in due course, but for the time being . . .' He finished the sentence with a shrug.

Nicky moved in to get a closer look at the coat of arms.

'*Sicut* . . .' she read aloud, but then stumbled. 'Does that say *serpent*?' she said, pointing.

'*Sicut serpentes, sicut columbae,*' Fleet quoted, even though the second portion of the motto was illegible. 'Wise as serpents, innocent as doves. It's from the Bible. Matthew . . . something or other.'

'10:16,' put in Randy. 'I didn't know you were a scholarly man, Detective Inspector.'

Fleet turned the badge over in his hands. He dropped on to his heels, and peered more closely at the remains. Nicky hunkered down beside him. There was a distant sound of a bell ringing, presumably in the tower at the front of the school. It was almost certainly ringing for the hour, but it felt as though it were tolling for the dead.

'Do you think it's our boy?' said Nicky softly. 'Do you think it's Ben?'

Fleet looked at her, then back at the body. 'I think we should probably warn Mr Harris that things are about to get a lot less discreet.'

Ben – January 1997

(Four months before his death)

Ben saw the children watching him as he stepped from his father's car.

There were three of them, two boys and a girl. One of the boys was leaning against a tree, arms folded across his chest, while the other two simply stood there staring.

'Ben? Are you listening to me, Ben?'

His dad was talking to him across the roof of the Aston Martin, hissing in that way he did when he wanted to yell but he knew there would be people watching. Those kids by the tree. Other eyes through the windows of the building. A great big, ugly, old thing, looking like something from one of those stupid period dramas his stepmother loved to watch on TV. One look at it and he could tell his dad had been suckered. Again.

'I mean it, Ben. This is your last chance. Three schools in three years. Do you think anyone else is going to want to take you if you get kicked out of a fourth? You'll be stuck in some inner-city comprehensive, and believe me, you wouldn't last a single morning in a place like that.'

Ben wasn't so sure. He had a feeling an inner-city comprehensive would suit him just fine.

'Now wait here while I go and tell them we've arrived. Don't move a muscle, do you understand me?' His dad turned, hesitated, turned back again. He leaned in close to the car, dropping his voice and raising a finger. 'Do not. Fuck. This. Up.'

Ben glared at his dad's back, silently daring himself to raise two fingers. A hand fell on his shoulder. He gave a start in spite of himself, and turned. It was the girl from the tree, the boys now standing either side of her, the taller of the two with his arm around her. The girl was dark-haired, pale-eyed, gorgeous. The boy Ben took to be her boyfriend was dark-haired, too. The other was blond, and an inch or so shorter than Ben.

The girl extended her hand. 'It's Ben, isn't it? We heard you were arriving today.'

Ben felt his eyes narrow. 'You did?' His hand had moved of its own accord, and the girl's fingers closed around his. Her skin was soft, but surprisingly cold, and she held on to Ben's hand long enough that he began to feel slightly uncomfortable, particularly with the girl's boyfriend staring at him so intently.

'Callum here overheard the headmaster talking to your new head of house,' the girl explained, gesturing minutely to the boy with his arm around her waist. 'Apparently, the headmaster described you as a *troublemaker*.' The girl's eyes sparkled mischievously, and she uttered the word with obvious relish.

Ben didn't know whether to be offended or proud.

'I'm Melissa, by the way,' the girl went on, before Ben could decide. 'This is Callum, as I said, and that's Lance.'

'Cool car,' said Lance, the blond one, as he eyed the Aston.

Ben shrugged, affecting nonchalance. 'I'd rather have had the money when the old man dies.'

Melissa gave a squeal of delight. Lance grinned. Only Callum continued to look at him oddly, and Ben suddenly had a feeling that the boy could somehow see inside him: past the bravado, and the fear, and straight to the parts of him he always tried to keep hidden.

'What did they want?' said Ben's dad, after he'd emerged from the main building. He watched Melissa and the others suspiciously as they drifted across the car park towards the school.

Ben shrugged. 'Nothing much,' he said. 'Just saying hello.'

His father's eyes tightened even further. 'To *you*?'

Ben felt a familiar knot of rage balling within him. He could even feel it in his face: little flowers of heat that bloomed on his skin whenever he got angry, no matter how hard he tried to suppress them.

His dad, as ever, didn't even notice. Didn't care about Ben one way or another: not what he felt, nor what he did. All his dad cared about was money – of finding new ways to lose it, basically – and his only concern when it came to Ben was not having to get involved. This, the increasingly familiar routine of dropping Ben off at a new boarding school, was the closest they ever came to father-and-son time. In fact, Ben had been keeping count, and the hour and a half they had spent in the car driving out here was the most time he and his dad had spent alone together in the past twelve months. And it had been clear from his father's demeanour – the frosty silence, the muttered curses at almost every other driver they'd encountered – that he'd resented every second.

He was still staring after Melissa, Callum and Lance. 'They look like trouble,' he declared, which almost made Ben laugh. His dad, passing judgement, when every single relationship he'd ever forged, whether in business or in his personal life, sooner or later turned to shit.

'You stay away from them, do you hear?' his dad insisted, oblivious to the irony. 'Besides,' he added, 'you're not here to make friends. You're here to get an education. Is that understood?'

Ben didn't bother replying. He didn't need to. There were some things he understood perfectly.

They were at the mortuary, waiting on Randy.

The pathologist had apparently been caught on a phone call, and one of his juniors had shown them into what she'd called the *bereavement room*. 'There's no one else in there,' she'd told them. 'And it's more comfortable than anywhere else I can offer you. If you get bored you can always look at the fish.'

Fleet had assumed the name was some kind of departmental joke, but the room turned out to have a sign on the door. And as well as a fish tank gently bubbling in one corner, there were artificial flowers in a dusty vase, and washed-out floral prints on the pale green walls. They'd gone for calming, Fleet supposed, and had ended up with cloying. All that was missing were the panpipes.

'Jesus,' said Nicky, glancing around. 'I think, if I was grieving, this place might tip me over the edge. I wonder how many people have drowned themselves in that fish tank?'

'At least there's a coffee machine,' said Fleet. 'Want one?'

But before he could figure out the correct sequence of buttons, Randy blustered into the room.

'Christ on a Harley, Rob. You might have warned me I'd be getting a phone call from the PCC.'

Fleet glanced at Nicky. 'The commissioner?' he said. 'What did he want?'

Randy ran his hands through his hair. He wore it long, bordering on unkempt, and Fleet suspected he dyed it. It was possible he even had a weave. Randy was in his early fifties

17

now, but he'd never made any secret of the fact that he considered himself a catch. Three wives down, he was clearly reluctant to let that status go. To be fair to him, he'd been something of a rock star in his younger days, at least in the world of forensic pathology. He'd quickly earned a reputation as the country's foremost authority on knife wounds, at a time when knives were becoming as essential an accessory as mobile phones, and he'd been a star performer in the witness box. He dazzled juries with his monstrous self-confidence, and intimidated junior barristers with his complete lack of deference and his caustic wit. But as with his tarnished looks, the gloss on his reputation had faded. Over the years, he'd stepped on too many toes, blasted too many of his contemporaries' opinions, for his eminence to endure. These days, even though he was undoubtedly a first-rate pathologist, he tended to be the one most SIOs hoped they didn't get.

'What do police and crime commissioners ever want?' Randy said, grinning now and flapping a hand dismissively. 'Job security.'

Once again Fleet looked at Nicky. Given what they now knew about the case, they had expected interest from above. But Fleet for one hadn't expected it to manifest so quickly.

'Which makes me wonder,' Randy went on, his beady eyes arrowed, 'what is it about a corpse that has been hidden for twenty-two years that has got our elected overseer in such a flap?'

'Twenty-two years?' said Nicky. 'Does that mean you have a positive ID?'

From the way Randy was looking at them, Fleet suspected he would hold out to have his question answered first. As well as being a prima donna, Randy was a notorious collector of gossip. He didn't spread it (as far as Fleet knew) but he loved to hoard it, the way he reportedly hoarded fine wines and – so the rumours went – his own press clippings.

But he evidently had a soft spot for Nicky.

'I do, my dear,' he conceded. 'We're waiting on DNA, but dental records confirm that subject 32710 is indeed one Benjamin Draper.'

'And the cause of death?' said Fleet.

Randy looked at him archly. He folded his arms.

Fleet sighed. 'Come on, Randy. You know we can't go into details. Especially given that we hardly know yet what we're dealing with ourselves.'

'I'm not after details, Detective Inspector. Just . . . titbits. I think you can afford to toss a few of those my way, particularly after I just spent twenty minutes convincing the commissioner that it was too early to draw any firm conclusions – when the truth is, I have my conclusions all ready for you and your lovely assistant.'

'Twenty minutes?' said Fleet. 'Really, Randy? I doubt the commissioner spends that long each day talking to his wife.'

Once again Randy grinned. 'I'm rounding up.'

Christ, he was a pain in the arse. But even Nicky appeared to be covering a smile. Hard as it was to believe, it appeared she actually *liked* the man. There was no way, otherwise, she would have allowed the *lovely assistant* comment to pass.

'If it makes it any easier on your conscience,' said Randy, 'how about I toss out a few theories and you just let me know whether I'm hot or cold? First off,' he persisted, before Fleet had a chance to respond, 'Beaconsfield College is one of the top three co-educational boarding schools in the country. Which means everyone who sends their children there is either very rich or very powerful. Moreover,' he went on, raising a finger, 'privilege, as we know, perpetuates privilege.

Meaning the children who attend Beaconsfield often become rich and powerful themselves. Not always, of course. Some are so messed up by the whole public school/boarding school thing, they end up living in a squat and overdosing on heroin before they reach twenty-five. But let's assume that, for the most part, the opposite is true.

'Now,' he continued, beginning to pace, 'if Ben Draper was fourteen when he died, and it is now twenty-two years later, that would make his surviving contemporaries thirty-six, give or take a few years to account for the age range of pupils. And if my findings show that Ben Draper was murdered . . .' Here Randy paused, smiling at his own non-committal phrasing. '*If* that appears to be the case, then that would mean one or more of his contemporaries is about to be caught up in a full-blown, front-page murder investigation.'

Randy stopped walking, and turned to show Fleet his self-satisfied smile. 'So I suppose the only remaining question is, which prominent public personality attended Beaconsfield at the same time Ben did, and was close enough to the boy to be a person of interest? Someone who is now around the age of forty, and whose potential involvement is worrisome enough that the commissioner himself deemed a lowly sawbones such as me worthy of six and a half minutes of his time?'

Fleet had been watching Randy's performance with his arms crossed. Randy, facing him, spread his.

'A name, Rob. That's all I'm asking for. We all know I'll be reading it on the front pages of tomorrow morning's newspapers anyway.'

Fleet could see Randy wasn't going to budge. It was always like this with him: a quid pro quo transaction rather than a straightforward interaction. In theory, the pathologist's role was to assist the police. To provide an impartial, professional opinion on matters beyond a copper's expertise that might help them uncover the truth about what had happened to a given victim. But there were different levels of cooperation, Fleet knew. A pathologist could be an ally – a key witness – or a thorn in the prosecution's side from the beginning, as Randy knew all too well. And actually, the man was right about one thing. The name he was fishing for would be all over the newspapers come the morning. It was probably already trending on social media.

'One name,' Fleet said. 'One name, and then we talk exclusively about Ben. No more holding back, Randy. I mean it.'

Randy's eyes sparkled with expectation.

'Callum Richardson,' said Fleet.

'Callum Richardson?' Randy repeated. '*The* Callum Richardson? The . . .' Randy paused. 'How are you supposed to refer to him these days? The TV star? The socialite? The *politician*?'

Fleet didn't watch TV, and he didn't socialise, and he'd stopped being interested in politics since he'd split up with Holly. But even he knew that Callum Richardson was all three of the things Randy had mentioned, and plenty more besides. The son of a world-famous philanthropist, he'd first come to public prominence in his twenties, when his drink-and-drug-fuelled exploits had ensured he was never far from the spotlight, and more often than not on a tabloid's front page. For a time he'd been everybody's favourite scoundrel, insulated from the newspapers' scorn by the sheer reportability of his bad behaviour, and – more importantly – his good looks. Then, in his thirties, and after his father's death, he'd reinvented himself, exploiting his considerable media presence to decry his former misdeeds and lay bare the hypocrisies and immorality of the high-flying world he'd grown up in. He'd even renounced his inheritance, dismissing his father's philanthropy as just another form of politics – but worse, because rather than being democratic, it was a flagrant attempt to buy influence in the world. Somehow, in spite of his privileged upbringing, Richardson had managed to establish himself as a voice of the people, and he used that voice to tear into the rich and powerful. He was now the anchor of the highest-rated breakfast show on television, with a personal social-media following of several million, and was rumoured to be on the verge of launching his own 'non-political' political party.

'Wait,' said Randy, as another thought evidently occurred to him, 'are you saying Callum Richardson was one of the kids who were playing with Ben when he went missing? Hide-and-seek, right? They were having a game of hide-and-seek, and Ben Draper was never found. So Callum Richardson was one of the children looking for him?'

Randy had clearly been reading up. The fact that Ben Draper had been playing hide-and-seek when he'd gone missing was the detail the newspapers had fixated on at the time. It had made good copy and attention-grabbing head-lines, at least until interest in the story faded. The problem, as far as the papers were concerned, was that there was no dead body, and no evidence of foul play. In fact, there was very little evidence full stop, which is why the investigation had stalled as well. In the end, it was assumed that Ben had simply run away. He was a troubled kid, with a troubled back-ground and a history of absconding from school. And when it came down to it, he was a nobody. His family was only moderately wealthy – at least by Beaconsfield standards – so that made them only moderately interesting. Perhaps if the names of his friends had leaked, interest would have revived later, as Callum Richardson began to make headlines of his own. But after Ben's disappearance, the school had acted quickly to dampen speculation, and also to shield its other pupils from external interest.

'Callum Richardson was one of Ben's friends,' Fleet told Randy. 'One of his only friends, by all accounts. As far as we know, Callum and two others were the last ones to see Ben alive. And that's all you're getting, Randy. As you say, you can read about the rest in the morning. I'm sure the newspapers will have plenty of titbits for you, some of which may even be true.'

Randy smiled. 'Callum Richardson,' he repeated, tasting the name as though he were swilling the first sip of one of his wines. 'My, my. That *is* a juicy morsel. It's no wonder the PCC is so interested. If it's true Richardson is making a move into politics, it's possible he'll end up being the PCC's boss one day.' He looked at Fleet. 'Meaning he'll also be *yours.*'

'Ben Draper,' said Fleet, straightening. 'Talk to me about Ben Draper. A deal's a deal, Randy.'

Randy inclined his head. 'Indeed it is. And I'll do more than talk to you. I'll show you.'

Fleet's first thought when he saw Ben's remains laid out on the pathologist's table was that the skeleton looked bigger than when he'd seen it *in situ*. In the crypt, the boy's body had been curled up. The presence of the sack that had evidently been covering him suggested he'd been arranged that way, but Fleet hadn't been able to stop himself imagining the boy lying whimpering on the ground, hugging his knees to his stomach while he listened to the footsteps of his approaching fate.

Now, seeing Ben's remains arrayed more clinically, it was

hard to associate them with the same mental image – although, even to Fleet's untrained eye, the signs of the violence the boy had suffered were obvious.

'Multiple skull fractures,' said Randy, pointing with his pen, and speaking in a tone now that was completely at odds with his usual showman's charm. As he ran Fleet and Nicky through his findings, he sounded more like a particularly uncharismatic weatherman. 'The radius is cracked on his left arm, and was never given a chance to heal, suggesting the break occurred at or around the time of death. Likewise, there are chips on several bones in his hands.'

'Defensive wounds,' Nicky muttered. She looked at Randy. 'Against a knife?'

'Against something sharp, certainly,' said Randy. 'Although it is impossible to determine what caused the break in his arm. A fall, possibly. Alternatively, the boy raised his arm to try to deflect something heavy.'

'So there's no ambiguity?' said Fleet, still looking at the cracks in the boy's skull. 'He was murdered.'

'Oh, I don't think there's any question about that,' said Randy, something like a smile creeping back into his voice. 'The question is, *how*?'

Fleet raised his head.

'The hyoid bone was fractured, too, you see,' Randy explained, once again gesturing with his pen. Every time he pointed it, he also clicked it, twice in quick succession. 'See here, at the top of the neck? I'm sure I don't need to tell you, but such breaks are exceedingly rare – except in cases of strangulation, where they occur at least fifty per cent of the time.'

Fleet looked from the neck, back to the skull.

Randy was watching him closely, seemingly reading his thoughts. 'Either one of those injuries might have killed him,

Detective Inspector. But the most logical chain of events is that, first' – he pointed to the arm and hands, *click click* – 'there was a struggle. The victim was overpowered, and was struck at least twice on the head' – *click click* – 'with blows powerful enough to crack his skull. Finally' – *click* – 'the victim was throttled. Whoever killed your boy certainly wanted to make sure he was dead,' Randy concluded. He clicked his pen one final time, then tucked it into his breast pocket.

'Jesus,' said Nicky, after a silence. She'd been standing beside Fleet as Randy had spoken, and now she circled to the other side of the table, her eyes fixed on the body – on Ben – as she moved.

Fleet had moved closer in, too. He'd removed a photograph of the boy from his jacket pocket, and he was trying to reconcile the image with all that was left of Ben now. The photo was the one that had been released to the press at the time of Ben's disappearance. The boy wasn't smiling. Not in the full, sparkly-eyed manner most newspaper editors favoured when it came to missing persons. There was only a slight curl to his thin lips, a tightness around his sea-grey eyes that could have been either wary or disdainful. It was only a headshot, but the boy's school uniform was just about visible: the lapels of his navy-blue blazer with their gold edging, and the strange, high-collared white shirt, reminding Fleet of a priest's attire. He was a good-looking kid, if not conventionally so. With his pale skin and high cheekbones, and his foppish hair almost curtaining one of his eyes, he could have grown up to be a lead singer in a nineties indie rock band. Which was doubtless the look he'd been going for, given the date the photograph would have been taken.

'How the hell did you end up with this one, Rob?'

Randy was looking over Fleet's shoulder. His voice was

unexpectedly kind, as though for once he wasn't probing for information but was simply asking as a friend. Fleet didn't have many – most of the people he and Holly had spent time with had been Holly's mates and their partners, and other than Nicky there were few people Fleet was close to on the force – and he found himself oddly moved by Randy's concern. He showed the man half a smile.

'Luck,' he said. 'Misfortune. I'm still trying to decide which. But there was an anonymous email to Crimestoppers, purporting to give details of where Ben's body was hidden. Eventually it worked its way to us – and needless to say, it checked out.'

'That's not what I meant,' said Randy. 'What I meant was, what are you doing with this case in the first place? The last I heard, after that business in the woods, you'd been . . .' Randy paused, clearly searching for a term that would tactfully describe what had happened to Fleet since the Sadie Saunders case just over a year earlier. 'Seconded,' Randy settled on.

'That's one way of putting it,' Fleet said. '*Sidelined* would probably be more accurate. I was given a desk and a stack of cold case files. It turned out Ben Draper's was among them.' Missing persons had always been Fleet's speciality, more by accident than design, and as a thinly disguised punishment for the way Fleet had conducted the Saunders investigation, Superintendent Roger Burton had decided to make things official. The problem wasn't that Fleet had failed to solve the case; rather, it was that he'd managed to make Burton look foolish in the process. As such, every one of the files the superintendent had given Fleet related to a disappearance that had never been resolved – and, more to the point, most likely never would be, as Burton would have known all too well. Just like the people who were missing – caught somewhere between life and death – Fleet had been consigned to a form of purgatory.

As for Nicky, she could easily have distanced herself from Fleet in the wake of the Saunders investigation, but she'd chosen not to. Just the opposite, in fact. She'd formally requested to be included on Fleet's team – which, counting Fleet and Nicky, was now a task force of two. When Fleet had warned her of the potential implications for her career – there was no glory in cold cases, and few happy endings – Nicky had refused to be deterred. *At least it's proper police work, boss,* she'd said to him. *And the best part is, most of the paperwork has already been filled in.* Her show of loyalty had left Fleet feeling both flattered and delighted. He and Nicky had worked together several times over the years, but largely by accident, and it was as though the Saunders case had cemented their mutual admiration. Maybe Fleet didn't have many friends, but he was proud to count Nicky among them.

'Well,' said Randy, 'I suppose cold cases are something the three of us have in common.' He looked at Ben's remains. 'Will they let you keep this one? Given who's potentially involved?'

'Are you kidding?' said Fleet, smiling grimly. 'Who else is going to want it now?'

Monday 21 October, 11.47 a.m.

Outside, Nicky had wandered off a few paces to return a call she'd missed on her mobile. Fleet perched over the wheel arch of his car, and took the opportunity to light a cigarette. The smell of the mortuary – bleach, bodies – had caught in his nostrils, and he wanted to smoke it out. Officially, he'd given up, but that was going about as well as his diet. He knew how disappointed in him Holly would have been, but seeing as they were no longer married, what Holly would have thought no longer seemed to matter.

At least, that was what Fleet tried to tell himself. The truth was, Holly's opinion remained the standard by which he judged almost everything, even if these days he had to imagine what her opinion might be.

He focused on the tip of his cigarette, and turned his thoughts back to the case. He thought of Ben, and the way his body had been hidden, and the anonymous tip-off Fleet had mentioned to Randy. Unusually for the pathologist, he'd failed to ask the most pertinent question: why had they taken the tip seriously in the first place? Sure, it had taken a couple of weeks to work its way through the system, and for a young DC to finally bring it to Fleet's desk, but when it had, and Fleet had looked back at the original file, a single line had convinced him it was worth following up. Six words, in fact, to do with the game of hide-and-seek Ben and his friends had reportedly been playing at the time of his disappearance.

It was never really a game, the sender had said.

Just that.

The message had contained directions to Ben's body, and that single, one-line postscript. Perhaps if the sender had gone into more detail, Fleet might have written it off as a hoax. Lord knew plenty of those had accumulated in the file over the years as well, and most had heavy-handedly regurgitated details that had obviously been gleaned from the press.

But this note had struck Fleet as different. Something about the message had chimed with his own natural scepticism that a group of fourteen- and fifteen-year-olds would have been playing anything as innocent as hide-and-seek. As such, he had sent a couple of uniforms he trusted out to the school. Randy and his team had quickly been required to follow.

'Boss?'

Fleet raised his head. Nicky had finished her phone call and was walking towards the car.

'That was Callum Richardson's personal assistant,' she said. 'How would you feel about a trip to London?'

'About the same as I'd feel about a trip to the dentist,' Fleet replied, as he ground his cigarette underfoot.

'Oh, come on, boss. It'll be fun. If there's time I'll take you to the zoo. And who knows? You might even get to see the Queen!'

'Why? Is she mates with Callum Richardson, too?'

By all accounts, Richardson had more connections these days than a telephone junction box. And now it seemed that, even though he was a person of interest in an investigation into the murder of a teenage boy, Fleet and Nicky were being obliged to go to *him*.

'Can't we just get the Met to arrest him and have him transferred down here?' Fleet said. 'Even if he's not tied up in Ben's murder, he's got to be guilty of something. Just look at the man's history. Setting aside all of which, no one his age gets to be as influential as he is without breaking a few rungs on their scrabble for the top.'

'He's the same age as you, isn't he?' said Nicky.

'Exactly,' Fleet replied.

'Well, if you prefer, I'll go by myself.' Nicky fluttered her eyelids wistfully, and gazed towards the sky. 'Callum Richardson. Just the two of us alone in a room.'

Fleet was only ninety per cent certain that she was joking. 'Callum Richardson, Detective Sergeant? Really? I wouldn't have put him down as your type.'

'It's true that he's a bit too pretty for me. And I don't think I'd make much of an It girl. But there are about ten billion other reasons I'd be willing to try to make it work between us.'

Fleet smiled, in spite of himself. 'He renounced his inheritance, remember? And launching your own political party can't be cheap. I wouldn't be surprised if he's already down to his last few million.'

'That should still keep us going for a while.' Nicky ran her hands down her hips. 'Maybe I should dig out my blues. Do you think he'd be partial to a girl in uniform?'

'Maybe we can ask him when we see him. When is he deigning to fit us in?'

'Friday,' Nicky replied.

'*Friday?*' It was currently Monday morning. And although someone like Callum Richardson might not appreciate the urgency of the situation, given that Ben had already been waiting for twenty-two years, the reality was that every minute counted. From the moment that crypt had been opened, the clock had started ticking. Evidence was degrading, suspects had been forewarned – and, perhaps, forearmed. On top of which, there was the pressure that was already starting to come down from the powers that be, as Randy's phone call with the police and crime commissioner attested.

Unless, of course, the delay was a deliberate ploy on Richardson's part. Maybe he felt he *needed* four days' grace.

'Apparently he's travelling at the moment,' said Nicky. 'Filming somewhere on location, and after that he's picking up some gong. But he's managed to find a slot for us when he gets back. At zero-nine-fifty.'

'Zero-nine-fifty?'

'That's ten to ten. In the morning. I googled it.'

Fleet was almost afraid to ask how long Richardson had set aside for them. Not that he intended to pay the slightest bit of attention to the man's schedule once he and Nicky had got their feet inside the door.

Nicky turned her head once again to the sky. It was a warm, beautiful morning, the sky a freshly born blue. Summer had been cool and wet, but the autumn had so far been doing its best to make up for it. 'So what do you fancy doing in the meantime?' Nicky said. 'It would be a shame not to make the most of this lovely weather.'

Fleet removed his weight from the bonnet of the car. 'Ben's family is the immediate priority,' he said. 'Now that we have a positive ID, we need to get to them before the press does. After that, we'll take another trip into the countryside.' Beaconsfield College was a forty-minute drive from the city – not all that far from Fleet's home town, as it happened. 'We talk to the headmaster, other members of staff. And obviously the rest of Ben's friends.'

Fleet opened the car door, and made to get inside. He stopped, turned back to face Nicky.

'The school is at the heart of this,' he said. 'Whatever happened to Ben started and ended there.'

Ben – January 1997

(Three and a half months before his death)

A book slammed on to the table, jolting Ben from his thoughts. He'd been gazing through the lead-crossed window, at the clouds and the swirling rain, imagining all the other places he might be; the other people, had his life turned out differently, he might be with.

But now Mr Cavanagh was looming over him, the fingertips of one of his hands resting on the book he'd just dropped on to the surface of Ben's desk.

'Will you be gracing us with your attention today, Mr Draper?'

'I ... uh ...'

There were titters around the room. Ben glanced, and saw nineteen pairs of eyes glinting as they looked his way.

'*Uh?*' echoed Cavanagh. 'Perhaps at your previous school you were able to communicate in grunts and groans, Mr Draper, but at Beaconsfield you will find you struggle to make yourself understood. And I, for one, do not speak Neanderthal.'

There were more titters, and Ben felt himself flush.

'Perhaps you could direct your attention to the question on the board, Mr Draper. What is *your* opinion on the matter? In English, if you please,' Cavanagh added.

Ben turned towards the whiteboard at the front of the class. In big, blood-red letters, the words *What is 'history'?* had been scrawled and circled.

Which at least clarified what lesson this was. In his daze, Ben had been struggling to remember.

'Um . . .'

Cavanagh rolled his eyes theatrically. He was playing to the crowd now. 'Uh, um. Um, uh,' he parodied. 'Stand up, Mr Draper.'

'Huh?'

This time Cavanagh did not need to give a signal. The rest of the class laughed of its own accord.

'Stand *up*, Mr Draper. Surely you *understand* English, even if you struggle to speak it.'

Slowly, Ben rose to his feet. The pupils all sat at individual desks, and he'd chosen a seat in a corner of the room furthest from the front. He'd been trying to keep a low profile, but all of a sudden he felt horribly exposed – as though he were on the edge of something and about to fall off.

'What. Is. History. Your opinion please, Mr Draper.'

Ben knew that, whatever he said now, the other kids would only laugh. Even if he got the answer right – and there was precious little chance of *that* – Cavanagh would make out that it was wrong. He wouldn't let Ben sit down until he'd been thoroughly humiliated. It was how it seemed to work here at Beaconsfield: the teachers would pick on one or two students per class, and use them to set an example. It had happened at previous schools Ben had attended, but here the students seemed almost to expect it. And it was always the same kids the teachers singled out – and Ben, since his arrival, had apparently gone straight to the top of their list. It was obvious to everyone that he didn't belong here. He wasn't posh enough, rich enough, *clever* enough.

'Well, Mr Draper? We're waiting.'

'History is . . .' Ben glanced at the faces turned his way – at the smiles and expectant sneers. 'History is a waste of fucking time,' he pronounced, and folded his arms.

There were gasps. Whispers. One person laughed, but mainly out of shock, it sounded like.

Cavanagh remained impassive. 'Very eloquent, Mr Draper. I'm sure your mother and father would be proud. Perhaps you could use your new-found command of the vernacular to explain to them why you will be spending every evening of your first full week at Beaconsfield in detention.'

Ben blazed. Not at his sentence – he couldn't care less about that – but at the very mention of his mother.

'And no doubt your classmates will demand an explanation as well. Thanks to you, Mr Draper, everybody in this class is now required to deliver to my desk by nine o'clock tomorrow morning a two-page essay on the etymology and historical usage of the profanity that so coloured your response. Single-spaced, if you please,' Cavanagh added, to groans from the rest of the class.

Cavanagh turned to walk back to the front of the room, and immediately Ben was struck on the cheek by a balled-up piece of paper, thrown from somewhere in Cavanagh's blind spot. Ben spun, looking for the person responsible, but every single one of the other kids in the class was glaring at him, meaning it could have been anyone.

In the corridor after the lesson was over, it got worse. One boy bumped him with his shoulder, and then a foot from behind hooked one of Ben's ankles, sending him sprawling. His books skidded across the floor, and as he landed amid the laughter, Ben saw another boy deliberately veer to trample on them. By the time Ben was back on his feet, the culprits had disappeared among the crowd of leering faces. Not that it mattered who was responsible – clearly *no one* wanted Ben here, any more than he'd ever been wanted *anywhere*.

That evening, he returned to his dorm to find his bed

sheets sodden. He felt the dampness with his fingers, and when he raised them tentatively to his nose, he immediately gagged.

'Who was it?' he raged, spinning. 'Which one of you did it? Which one of you pissed on my bunk?'

He was met by a roomful of faces doing their best not to smile. The dozen or so other boys in the dorm were sprawled nonchalantly on their beds, or huddled in corners playing cards. They all knew who'd done it. They must have. But the silence was clearly the only answer Ben was going to get.

He dropped what he was carrying on to the floor – his books, after all, were ruined anyway – and took three angry steps towards the centre of the room. 'I said, which one of you did it? You better tell me or I'll . . . I'll . . .'

'Ben?'

He whipped around at the sound of the voice. Callum and Lance – the two boys Ben had met, together with Melissa, on the day of his arrival – were standing just inside the door.

'Is everything OK?' said Callum.

Ben felt his flush deepening, his rage turning to humiliation. Even though he hadn't spoken to Callum and the others since he'd stepped from his father's car, he'd seen them around campus – the three of them invariably together, always slightly apart from the other pupils. Almost two weeks into Ben's time at Beaconsfield, they remained the only people – teachers or students – who'd been even vaguely kind to him, and he'd been trying to pluck up the courage to speak to them again. They were in the year above Ben, he'd found out, which didn't help, and he didn't want them to think that he was desperate. He didn't *need* friends. He never had. But just sometimes, it would be nice to have someone on his side.

Lance had noticed the wet patch on Ben's bed. He didn't

make the mistake of touching it, as Ben had, but his wrinkled nose showed that he'd worked out what it was. He seemed to silently convey the information to Callum, who'd moved to Ben's side and joined him in looking around the room. This time, Ben noticed, the other boys all dropped their eyes.

'Come on,' Callum said, in a tone that suggested none of them were worth the effort. He placed a hand on Ben's shoulder as, behind them, Lance started balling up Ben's bedclothes. 'We'll show you where you can ditch those and get some fresh ones. And if anyone messes with *those*,' he added, addressing the room now, 'we'll help you shove them down that person's throat.'

Ben made a noise involuntarily. He managed to make it sound like a laugh, but only just. The truth was, he was so grateful, and so reassured by Callum's touch, that his first instinct had been to sob.

Tuesday 22 October, 10.49 a.m.

The woman squinted as she smoked. Her eyes never left Fleet's, even as she jutted her lower lip and exhaled towards the ceiling.

'Do I have to come and identify him?' she said at last. They were the first words she'd spoken since Fleet had told her that her stepson had been found dead.

Fleet was seated on the sofa in the woman's living room. Nicky was beside him, and he felt her shift slightly.

'No, Ms Johnson,' Fleet replied. 'That . . . won't be necessary.'

Christine Johnson, formerly Draper, ground her cigarette into an ashtray on the mantelpiece. She took her time, and Fleet had a feeling it wasn't just the cigarette she was trying to extinguish. If he had to guess, he would have said she was trying to stub out a host of unbidden memories.

'Good,' she said, when she was satisfied. 'Because if I'm honest, I'd probably have to remind myself what he looked like.' She dusted her hands and folded her arms, raising her chin defensively.

'You don't remember what your stepson looked like?' Nicky responded. She covered it well, but Fleet could tell she was shocked. Fleet was, too. He'd been moderately surprised that there'd been no photographs of Ben on display when they'd arrived at the sixth-floor council flat, but he knew as well that some people preferred to keep their grief private. His mother was one of them, as, indeed, was Fleet himself.

He'd once criticised his mother for not having any pictures on the mantelpiece of Jeannie, his younger sister, who'd committed suicide when she was a teenager, but Fleet himself didn't even keep a photograph of Jeannie in his wallet. Nor had he ever felt the need or desire to display any pictures of her at home – either in the bedsit he occupied now, or in the house he'd once shared with Holly. The difference was, unlike Christine Johnson, neither Fleet nor his mother would have needed to remind themselves what Jeannie had looked like. The image of his little sister's wide-eyed innocence was burned on Fleet's brain.

'Judge me if you want to,' said Ms Johnson. 'But it was twenty-two years ago. And that little bugger always hated me. Why should I pretend I ever cared about him?'

'You and Ben weren't close,' Fleet responded. 'Is that what you're saying, Ms Johnson?'

She gave a sniff. 'That's one way of putting it.' She lit another cigarette, and Fleet stole a glance at the photographs that *were* on the mantelpiece. They were all of her: of Ben's stepmother when she was younger. Posing on the beach in a bikini; pouting in a black-and-white close-up. She'd been a very attractive young woman. She remained attractive, in fact, in spite of the smoker's wrinkles and heavy make-up – though from the narrow range of pictures she'd selected to display, it was obvious she felt her best days were behind her. And in none of the pictures was there anyone else in shot. Fleet felt a pang of sympathy for the woman, all alone in her pokey little flat, before it struck him that his own situation was essentially the same.

'You said Ben hated you, Ms Johnson,' said Nicky. 'Why was that, do you think?'

'I was his stepmother, wasn't I? He was *supposed* to hate

me. But he hated his father, too, if that makes any difference. He hated everyone. Pushed people away. I *tried* to be nice to him, but every time I made an effort, he'd end up screaming, yelling at me to leave him alone. I said to Tony at the time, what that kid needs is some proper discipline. But Tony wasn't man enough to administer it, so he ended up making it somebody else's problem.'

'The school's, you mean?' said Nicky.

'*Schools*, plural,' replied Ben's stepmother. 'Ben got kicked out of three of them in just three years. Talk about a waste of money. Money that Tony didn't even have, as it turned out.'

'Ben's father had money troubles?' prompted Fleet.

Ms Johnson narrowed her eyes, and for a moment Fleet felt certain she would tell him to sod off and mind his own business. But after exhaling another lungful of smoke, she smiled bitterly. 'Money troubles,' she said derisively. 'What that man had went way beyond *troubles*. He wasn't just broke. He was ruined. He owed so much to so many people, there was no point trying to pay any of it off – so he kept on borrowing more. It all came to a head about a year after Ben went missing.'

'Came to a head?'

'Foreclosures, debt collectors, *death threats*. And that's when I found out myself. I tell you,' Ms Johnson added, visibly fuming, 'it wasn't the life I signed up for. I was working as a . . . a waitress at the time, and I was tricked by that fancy car of his, the suit that cost more than my entire wardrobe. He hoodwinked me, the way he'd hoodwinked people his entire life.'

Fleet registered the slight pause Ms Johnson had left before she'd described what she'd done for a living. Reading between the lines, he thought he had a fair idea of the type of establishment she might have worked in.

'In what way did your husband hoodwink people, Ms Johnson?' he asked.

Ms Johnson made a face. *Where to begin?* her expression said. 'He started off in advertising. Made something like an honest wage, I suppose. But after that, he went into investments. Property, in theory. In reality, it was all smoke and mirrors.'

'Your husband died of a heart attack. In . . .' Nicky checked her notes. '2003. Is that right, Ms Johnson?'

'Leaving me with nothing but a mortgage worth more than the house we were living in, and so many unpaid bills you could have built another house next door from just the paperwork,' said Ben's stepmother. 'That's how I ended up here. And it's why I changed my name back to Johnson. To get away from it all. I mean, even the school started sending demands for payment. Can you believe it? After what happened to my stepson while he was there?' She signalled her outrage by shaking her head. 'I would have sued if I'd been able to afford a solicitor. Although . . .' An idea appeared to occur to her. 'I could still sue. Couldn't I? If Ben's dead and someone at the school was responsible? It's not as though they're short of a bob or two.'

'We wouldn't know about that, Ms Johnson,' said Fleet. 'And we don't know *who* was responsible for Ben's death. That's why it's so important that you tell us as much about your stepson as you can.'

Ms Johnson appeared to deflate slightly, as though the momentary optimism she'd felt had gone the way of the smoke from her cigarette. 'Yeah, well. As I said, I can barely remember what he looked like, let alone much else. He was ten when I got together with his father, and he started going to prep school at eleven. And once he turned thirteen, he was boarding pretty much full-time.'

'Even over weekends?' asked Nicky.

'Who else was going to look after him? He wasn't *my* son, and Tony was never around long enough to take proper care of him. He was always travelling, or working – or hiding, if you ask me. Running away from his responsibilities. I tell you, it's no wonder Ben turned out the way he did with a father like that. What is it they say? The apple doesn't fall far from the tree.'

Ben's stepmother stubbed out her second cigarette, even more viciously than she had the first.

'Do you know of any difficulties Ben might have been having at Beaconsfield, Ms Johnson?' said Fleet. 'Any trouble he might have mentioned when he was home – perhaps problems between him and his friends?'

'*Friends?*' said Ben's stepmother, scoffing. 'Ben didn't have any friends. And I told you, the only problem Ben had was Ben. He was angry, bitter, resentful. He wound people up. Deliberately, for the most part. That's why he got kicked out of so many schools. He got into fights, swore at teachers, you name it.'

'From what age did he start behaving that way?' Nicky asked. 'His mother – his biological mother, I mean; your husband's first wife – died when Ben was seven, is that right?'

Ms Johnson reacted as though Nicky had said something funny. 'I knew you'd bring it back to that eventually. People always do. That's why Ben got away with so much for so long. The *sympathy* vote,' she added scornfully. She shook her head. 'But if you ask me, Ben's mother getting cancer had nothing to do with it. He barely even *knew* her, so how can you use that as an excuse? And anyway, the way Tony told it, Ben was trouble from the day he was born.'

Ms Johnson pulled out yet another cigarette. The last in

41

the packet, it seemed, from the way she tossed the box on to the coffee table. She clicked her lighter, and squinted at Fleet through the flame. Once her cigarette was lit, she jabbed the fiery end towards him.

'You're a policeman,' she said, blowing out smoke. 'You should know. Some kids are just born bad. And the way Ben wound people up . . . If you ask me, it's a miracle nobody murdered him sooner.'

'Well, that was edifying,' said Fleet, once they were two flights of stairs closer to ground level.

'Wasn't it just?' said Nicky. 'Restores your faith in humanity.'

Fleet veered to avoid a puddle of something on one of the concrete steps. There was a stink in the stairwell that pinched at the bridge of his nose. He glanced over the banister, and noted how far they still had to go before they reached fresh air.

'There's a perfectly good lift, you know,' he said to Nicky.

'*Perfectly good* might be stretching it,' Nicky replied. 'Personally, I'd rather not take the risk of getting trapped in a coffin-sized box that's dangling sixty feet in the air. Not in this building, anyway. Besides,' she added, 'the exercise is good for us.'

Fleet registered the pronoun. 'Very tactful, Detective Sergeant.'

Nicky turned to hide her smile.

'So what do you think?' Fleet asked when they were another flight lower.

'About Ben? I think it's no wonder he acted out. His real mother dies when he's just a kid, he's raised by a deadbeat dad – who had even less sense than money, it seems. And there were no other relatives, right? No uncles, aunts, grandparents?'

42

'None who were on the scene at the time, apparently. It was just Ben and his father. And his stepmother, of course.'

Nicky made a face, showing exactly what she thought of Christine Johnson. She was quiet for a moment, then said, 'Does that make the situation better, would you say? Or worse? You know, the fact that, twenty-two years later, there's nobody left to care. Assuming anybody really cared about Ben in the first place,' she added dourly.

Fleet wasn't sure how to answer that. And he wasn't sure if Ben having no surviving family made their job easier, or harder. Perhaps they should have been grateful that they hadn't needed to break the news to a grieving mother and father, but at least if Ben's biological parents had survived, they might have been able to offer some insight into Ben's true character, the relationships he'd forged at school . . . anything that might have provided some clue as to who might have wanted their son dead.

'Do you know what strikes me the most?' said Nicky, as they reached the bottom of the stairs. She gripped the handle of the door that would lead them outside, but hesitated before pulling it. 'How sad Ben must have been. How *unhappy*.'

Fleet nodded. He'd been pondering the same thing himself. The boy had no refuge, no place in the world he would have felt safe. And from the sound of it, it had been that way for him throughout his entire life.

'So maybe we should start there,' Fleet said. 'Not with who might have hated Ben. Rather, with how desperate he must have been to be loved.'

Ben – February 1997

(Three months before his death)

They were waiting for Ben in the corridor outside his classroom.

It was just over a week since the incident with his bunk, and although nobody had poured piss on his bed sheets again, things had otherwise got worse. The whole school seemed to have turned against him. Most of the teachers went out of their way to humiliate him, to prove to the other students that he didn't belong. And the kids who weren't sneering at him or sniggering or secretly stealing his stuff – his headphones were gone, as well as his best pair of trainers, and, this morning, his underwear – behaved as though he didn't exist, which in some ways was even worse. People walked directly towards him in the corridors, forcing him to veer out of the way. He would put his bag down on a chair to reserve a lunch seat, and return to find someone else sitting there, his bag knocked on to the floor and kicked away beneath the tables. Doors would swing shut in his face, and not even the younger kids would look him in the eye. He was being treated as though he were a parasite. An invader. A cancerous cell floating around a body, whose response was to pretend there was nothing there.

He'd been keeping an eye out for Callum and the others, but none of them were in any of his classes, and because they were older the boys both slept in a different dorm. But now here they were – Callum, Lance and Melissa – having clearly come looking for *him*.

He was just beginning to smile when someone barged him from behind.

'Hey!' growled Callum, immediately leaping to Ben's defence, and as Ben turned he saw the kid who had shoved him instantly pale. He was taller than Callum, and probably stronger, but even so he dipped his eyes and scuttled away along the corridor. Callum watched the boy go, before turning his attention back to Ben.

'Are people still giving you trouble?'

Ben glanced quickly at Melissa. He shrugged, as though it wasn't as big a deal as it felt. 'Nothing I can't handle,' he replied, hoping it sounded more convincing out loud than it did in his head. More pupils emerged through the doorway behind him, and he stepped out of the way, just in case.

Callum was looking at him intently, and Ben couldn't decide if his colour-washed eyes appeared cruel or kind.

'We were just going to head out into the grounds, hang out for a bit in the woods,' Callum said at last. 'Do you want to come?'

Delight bloomed in Ben's stomach, and he couldn't stop it from showing on his lips. But then he remembered: he had another lesson. Ms Kennedy, who was almost as bad as Mr Cavanagh.

'I can't,' he said, not even attempting to hide his disappointment. 'I've got Latin.'

Callum's mouth curled at one corner. 'So? The three of us have got double-period English.'

Ben looked at the others, who were smiling in the same way Callum was. Ben, after a moment, smiled back.

'So, what's your story?' Callum asked him.

They'd settled on the ground at the edge of what Ben had

come to realise was a graveyard. It was the first time he'd ventured into the woods, even though he knew pupils were allowed anywhere in the grounds. When he'd approached the woods before, there'd been something about the ancient trees – their jagged branches and twisted trunks – that didn't look right, as though they'd grown from soil that was noxious and rotten. He felt braver in the others' company, but the graves didn't exactly help. Ben's mum had been buried – he recalled having to stand by his dad and watch her coffin being lowered into the ground – and all he could remember thinking through his tears was, what if they'd made a mistake? What if she *wasn't* dead, and inside the coffin she was screaming, begging for someone to let her out? Now, every time Ben saw a grave, that was what he thought about: his mother, trapped forever beneath the earth, and what it must feel like to be buried alive.

He shifted, turning his back on the graves as best he could, and using the movement to disguise a shiver that had nothing to do with the chill in the air.

Melissa passed him the joint she'd rolled, and he accepted it between nervous fingers.

'My story?' he said to Callum. 'What do you mean?' He took a puff of the joint because he knew he was expected to, but he didn't inhale. He'd tried weed before – it was the reason he'd been kicked out of the school before Beaconsfield, which at least made a change from truancy and fighting – and he didn't like the way it made him feel. Adrift. Untethered. Faintly sick. Precisely the sensations, in other words, he spent most of his life trying to suppress. He fake-puffed a second time, and then passed the joint to Lance.

'Your old man, for example,' Callum said. 'What does he do?'

46

Ben gave a snort. 'He doesn't *do* anything,' he replied. 'He calls himself an entrepreneur, but as far as I can tell he basically spends his time looking for new ways to lose money.'

The others laughed. Ben blinked, then smiled, pleased with himself.

'What about your mum?' asked Lance. This time Ben turned abruptly, the way he'd become accustomed to doing whenever anyone mentioned his mum, ready to defend her if he needed to. But Lance merely squinted as he smoked, watching and waiting for Ben's answer. Ben thought he'd detected a challenge in Lance's tone, but decided he must have imagined it.

'She's dead,' he said flatly. 'She died when I was seven.' He thought for a moment, then added, 'I'm not supposed to remember her, but I do. I remember everything about her.' He was surprised by his unaccustomed openness. Was it the company? Or the weed? He watched Lance pass the joint back to Melissa – Callum, Ben noted, wasn't having any – and he figured he must have taken the smoke in more deeply than he'd intended.

'Who told you that you weren't supposed to remember her?' Melissa asked him. She tucked a strand of hair behind her ear and angled her head. Her eyes, Ben noted, were as pale as Callum's, and just as difficult to decipher.

Ben shrugged. 'My dad, I guess,' he said, even though there was no guesswork about it. Whenever Ben tried to talk to his dad about his mum, his dad would do everything but sneer. *Forget everything you think you know about her,* he would say. *All you're doing is telling yourself lies. She's gone, and good riddance – that's all you need to remember.*

'No offence or anything,' Melissa said. 'But your dad sounds like a dick.'

Lance gave a splutter of laughter. Melissa flushed when

47

Ben looked at her, but when she smiled, he found himself smiling back.

'Yeah,' he said. 'I'm pretty sure that's what my mum thought, too.'

Once again, the others laughed, and inside Ben revelled in their reaction.

'Not that I'm one to talk,' Melissa said, after a moment. 'My dad's not just a dick. He's also a fucking arsehole.'

Ben half expected Lance to laugh again, but this time he stayed silent. Ben waited for Melissa to go on.

'On the one hand, he treats me like a trophy,' she said. 'Whenever I go home – whenever I'm *allowed* home – it's like I'm something to be buffed and polished. To be paraded in front of his friends. He boasts about how well I'm doing at school, how one day I'll be a doctor or a lawyer. I mean, never mind that I want to be an actress. And never mind that, the moment his friends leave, he treats me the way he treats my mum. Like I'm *worthless*. Like no matter what I achieve, it won't ever be enough.'

She dropped the butt of the joint on to the floor, and ground it into the mud with her heel. Any remaining spark would have been extinguished long before she eventually let up.

'He wanted a son, you see,' she added, glancing at Ben. 'He's never even bothered to deny it. He even told me once, said he and Mum would have tried again, but he didn't want to risk ending up with another *girl*.'

She picked up a stick that was lying near her feet, and started jabbing it into the mud. Just lightly at first, testing the resistance, before finally plunging it in so forcefully, it snapped when she tried to pull it out.

'Do you know why my father sent *me* here?' said Callum, into the silence that followed.

All Ben could do was shake his head. He'd heard Callum's father was some super-rich businessman, but other than that he knew as much about Callum as he did about Melissa and Lance.

'To *follow in his footsteps*,' Callum said. 'To become the man he thinks he is himself.' He shook his head. 'Pathetic, right?'

Ben's thoughts turned again to his own father. Until Ben had been about nine or ten years old, he'd been *desperate* for his father's approval – or even just some attention. That was before he'd realised his old man was nothing more than a two-faced liar, no more interested in Ben than he had been in Ben's mother.

'And it's the same for Lance,' Callum said. 'He doesn't belong here any more than the rest of us do. Tell him, Lance.'

'I'm here on a scholarship,' Lance said. 'The annual fees are more than my mum and dad earn put together.'

'They're ashamed,' Callum explained, looking at Ben. 'They think that Beaconsfield will make Lance better. A better person, a better prospect, a better *son*.'

Lance started on rolling another joint. He caught Ben studying him, and Ben was the one to look away.

'Anyway,' said Callum, once again breaking the silence. 'I guess the point is, you're not the only one who feels out of place here. In fact, all three of us knew it the minute we saw you.'

Lance and Melissa nodded. Ben felt his expression contort in confusion.

'Knew what?' he said.

Callum gave a smile, and Ben basked in its warmth. 'That you were one of us. That you'd need us as much as we need you.'

LENT TERM REPORT CARD

Date: 27ᵗʰ March 1997
Student name: Benjamin Draper
Student house: Churchill
Parent/Guardian: Anthony Draper

Subject	Teacher	Grade
Mathematics	Dr Nixon	F
English Literature	Mrs Shaw	C-
English Language	Mr Wrigley	D
Biology	Mr Marshall	C
Physics	Dr Craig	C
Latin	Ms Kennedy	U
Chemistry	Miss Lucas	C
Politics and Discourse	Ms Sullivan	F
Art and Design	Mr Rayner	B+
History	Mr Cavanagh	F

Comments

By all accounts, Benjamin has had a difficult start to his time
at Beaconsfield. As Benjamin's house leader, and being aware of
Benjamin's rather fraught educational background, I have followed his
development closely, and paid due regard to the inevitable turmoil
inherent in transferring from one institution to another in the middle
of a school year – particularly one as crucial as this. But Benjamin
has not helped himself. He is quick to anger and riposte. He is – or
can be – indolent and disrespectful, and he has gone out of his way
to make himself unpopular with his fellow students. In short, he is
very much his own worst enemy.

All that said, it is not Beaconsfield's policy to give up on its pupils, most especially those who have been with us for such a short period of time. And there is one minor bright spot on his report card, which we can but hope will spark a corresponding enthusiasm in other, perhaps more academic, subjects.

In sum, there is hope for Benjamin yet. Certainly there is a brain in his head somewhere. The challenge for us as teachers, and most particularly for Benjamin himself, is to feed and nurture the talent he has, so that Benjamin's tendency towards misconduct and mediocrity is allayed.

The boy has a future, if only he could bring himself to see it.

Signed: **Philip Craig**

Dr Philip P. Craig, Head of Churchill House

Fleet allowed his eyes to skim back over the list of grades. Cs, three Fs, even a U. He recalled receiving a report card that wasn't dissimilar when he was Ben's age, although the school Fleet had attended was a very different proposition to Beaconsfield. His school had been – and still was, the last time Fleet checked – a failing comprehensive, in a crumbling seaside town not twenty miles from where they were now. It was a world away, in other words, and most outsiders would probably have said that, in terms of education, he'd drawn the shorter of the two straws. But at least he'd got to go home at the end of the day.

'And this is all?' Fleet said. 'This is the only official record of Ben's progress that you have?'

They were in the headmaster's office, Adrian Harris on one side of his desk, and Fleet and Nicky in uncomfortable leather armchairs on the other. Since they'd last been at the school, the atmosphere had changed completely. Whereas before the headmaster had been able to escort Fleet and Nicky through the grounds relatively unnoticed, this time when they'd arrived, pupils had stared openly at them from classroom windows, while those who'd been outside when they'd pulled up in Fleet's car had pointed and gawped. As expected, details of what had been discovered at Beaconsfield had quickly leaked, and Callum Richardson's name had emerged in connection with the case soon after. As such, the Ben Draper investigation was now officially headline news.

There was a press pack gathered outside the school gates, and even the helicopters the headmaster had feared in the skies overhead – including one, Fleet had noticed, from the channel Richardson appeared on himself. The actual police presence on Beaconsfield's grounds hadn't much changed, but even so, Harris seemed to have interpreted the turn of events as a personal betrayal. Last time, he'd praised Fleet and Nicky for their discretion. This time, he was making them feel about as welcome as a thunderstorm at a garden party.

'That is correct,' the headmaster said, in answer to Fleet's question. 'In the end Benjamin was with us for only a very short period. As it is, you have probably seen the report card before. We of course provided a copy to your colleagues after Benjamin's disappearance, so it is no doubt already in your files.'

Fleet had, and it was, together with the statements of innumerable teachers, pupils and members of staff that were taken at the time – all of which revealed precisely nothing. The last reported sighting of Ben had been at around 3 p.m. on Saturday 10 May 1997. Callum Richardson, Melissa Haynes and Lance Wheeler told police officers that the four of them had been involved in a game of hide-and-seek in the school's grounds. But from the point Ben had gone off to hide, the evidence ran out. No one had seen anything, no one suspected anyone, and no one had expressed any concrete theory about what might have happened to Ben. There was plenty of conjecture, all of which was no doubt being revisited online and on the twenty-four-hour news channels even as they spoke.

'Detective Inspector?' said Harris, prompting Fleet. 'I am as eager as you are to get to the bottom of this tragedy, but to be honest I am unsure how else I might help. And the situation as it stands is completely intolerable. I would be failing in my responsibility as headmaster of this institution if I did not press for a return to normality as rapidly as possible. This seems unlikely to happen if the strategy is to focus on going over and over ground that has already been covered.'

Fleet sat back in his seat, considering the man in front of him. At the time of Ben's disappearance, Adrian Harris had been the headmaster of Beaconsfield for two years, which meant he'd now held the role for almost a quarter of a century. Fleet had read the headmaster's original statement, too, and the only thing he'd taken from it was how desperate Harris had been to safeguard the school from scandal. The headmaster had come across as pompous and defensive, more concerned with the potential ramifications of Ben's disappearance than with Ben's well-being – and it seemed that, despite the years that had passed, very little had changed.

'I appreciate the state of affairs is inconvenient for you, Mr Harris. There is very little I can do about the press, but for our part we will do our best to get out of your way as soon as possible. In the meantime, is there anything else you can tell us about Ben? Anything that might have perhaps come back to you over the intervening period that you've found yourself dwelling on, or that seems more important than it once did in light of the things we now know?'

Harris sighed impatiently. 'As I have told you, Detective Inspector, there is nothing I feel able to add. Perhaps it would be helpful to remind you that at the time of Benjamin's disappearance, he was one of over six hundred children in my care. And since then, almost two and a half *thousand* boys and girls have passed through Beaconsfield's gates. You will understand, therefore, why I may occasionally have been preoccupied with matters other than Benjamin Draper's whereabouts.'

Pompous and defensive, thought Fleet. Old habits, it seemed, died hard.

'So until the discovery of Ben's body,' he said, 'you accepted the idea that he'd simply run away?'

'I was satisfied with the explanation, yes. It also seemed to satisfy your colleagues, you will recall.' Harris waved a hand, almost dismissively. 'Benjamin had a history of absconding from school. Even at Beaconsfield, where he slept in the same building in which he had most of his lessons, his attendance record was woeful. When no evidence to the contrary was found, it seemed entirely logical that Benjamin had followed the same pattern of behaviour he had exhibited all of his life.'

'Forgive me, Mr Harris,' put in Nicky, 'but it sounds to me as though you didn't like Ben very much.'

Was that it, Fleet wondered? Was that part of the reason Harris seemed so indifferent to Ben's fate, and so focused on the imposition on the school? Did he not consider Ben worthy of all the time and disruption the investigation into his disappearance had already caused?

Harris moved his eyes, and then his head. 'I am not employed to *like* my pupils, Detective Sergeant, nor am I here to make friends. If you want the truth, I barely knew Benjamin, other than by his reputation.'

'His reputation as a troublemaker, you mean,' Nicky said. 'Ben was hardly classic Beaconsfield material, was he?'

'He was not. And in all honesty, if it had been up to me, he would not have been admitted. But ultimately it was not my decision. Unfortunately, in the educational sector, as in so many walks of life, money has a tendency to talk.' Harris pursed his lips. 'We may look like a wealthy institution, but I can assure you that maintaining a financial balance is a constant battle.

When I first took over as headmaster, Beaconsfield was practically on its knees.'

Once again Fleet thought of his own school. If Beaconsfield was ever on its knees, the comprehensive he'd attended was surely crawling in the gutter.

'So you were reluctant to have Ben here,' Fleet said. 'Meaning some of the staff might perhaps have felt the same way? What about the other pupils? Did they resent Ben's presence as well? His friends, for example. Callum Richardson, Melissa Haynes, Lance Wheeler. Just how close were they to Ben?'

It didn't escape Fleet's notice that Harris's expression wrinkled slightly at the mention of Callum Richardson's name. Clearly it wasn't just Ben he hadn't approved of.

'I'm afraid I would not know,' the headmaster answered. 'And I cannot presume to know the mindset of each and every member of my staff. All I can tell you is that Ben would have been treated like any other Beaconsfield pupil, with no fear or favour. As indeed my own son was treated when he was a pupil here himself.'

Fleet did his best to mask his surprise. He would never have put Harris down as a family man. And there was no wedding ring on his finger.

'Your son studied at Beaconsfield?' said Nicky. 'While you were headmaster, do you mean? That must have been tough for him. For you as well, I would imagine.'

Now the headmaster was the one to shift, as though something Nicky had said had struck a nerve.

'We did not advertise our relationship, Detective Sergeant,' Harris said. 'And we each stayed true to our responsibilities. Besides, it takes more than a crisis to prevent the wheels at this school from continuing to turn. Often, in spite of others' best efforts to the contrary.'

Interesting, Fleet thought – ignoring the jibe – that when the subject of the headmaster's son came up, one of the first words Harris had reached for was *crisis*.

The headmaster seemed to notice his curiosity. 'His mother and I divorced when he was young,' Harris explained – rather impatiently, it seemed to Fleet. 'In the end he was at Beaconsfield only for a very short time – until it became obvious that he would be better off with his mother.' The headmaster rearranged himself importantly. 'The demands of my role here leave me very little time for the challenges being a full-time parent entails.'

In other words, Fleet thought, Harris had a very clear hierarchy of priorities – and Beaconsfield was right at the top.

'Other than you, Mr Harris,' Fleet said, 'are there any members of staff still working at Beaconsfield who were here when Ben was a student? This Philip Craig, for example, who wrote Ben's report.'

'No,' said Harris. 'Dr Craig died from a stroke several years ago. And since Mr Berkley, our head of geography, retired last year, I am the last one remaining at their post.'

He spoke as if he were a soldier at a time of war, Fleet noted.

'Although . . .' the headmaster added, with a barely hidden scowl. 'I suppose there is also Father Steiner.'

'Father Steiner?'

'The school chaplain. He's been here almost as long as I have, though is something of an independent entity. He does not report to me – rather, directly to the school's board.'

Was that why Harris appeared to dislike him, Fleet wondered?

'Did Father Steiner know Ben?' Nicky asked.

'Yes,' said Harris. 'By all accounts he knew Ben quite well.'

'Could we speak with him?' said Fleet, registering the note of disapproval in the headmaster's tone. 'Where might we find him?'

'I'm afraid I have little influence over his movements. But I suggest you first try the chapel.'

'Thank you,' said Fleet. 'We'll do that. Just finally, though, and while we're on the subject of the chapel, I gather the survival of the original crypt has come as something of a surprise to you.'

Was Fleet imagining it, or did Harris stiffen slightly? The man was as rigid as a mortar board anyway, making it hard to tell.

'From what I understand,' Fleet went on, 'you were under the impression the crypt had been filled in when the chapel was rebuilt. Is that correct, Mr Harris?'

'No, Detective Inspector, it is not.' After seeming on his guard, Harris appeared to take pleasure from being able to contradict Fleet. 'It was not that I, or anyone else at the school, thought that the crypt had been filled in. Rather, we had no reason to suspect it existed in the first place.'

'You're saying it's been there this whole time without anybody connected with the school knowing about it?'

'That's the way it would seem, Detective Inspector. As I told you before, the original chapel was destroyed a full century ago. The site, including the cemetery, has long since been reclaimed by the woods.'

'And you've never come across any record of the crypt's existence in any documentation? In the school's records, perhaps.'

'I have not.'

'Or heard any rumours that it was there? Among the staff, the pupils?'

'No, Detective Inspector,' said the headmaster categorically. 'Apart from anything else, if anyone connected to the school *had* known about the crypt, they would surely have mentioned it at the time Ben went missing. There was a thorough search of the entire grounds.'

Fleet hadn't been around to witness it, but he had his doubts that the search for Ben had been as thorough as Harris seemed to think. Judging from the material on file, a decision appeared to have been made quite early on that Ben had most likely run away, and the search – such as it was – had been staffed mainly by volunteers. In this case, that had meant teachers and other employees of the school, who were likely to have been under pressure to get back to work as quickly as possible.

'So . . . and forgive the bluntness of this question, Mr Harris,' Fleet said, 'but how do you think Ben's body got there? If the existence of the crypt was as much of a secret as you claim?'

Now the headmaster reddened slightly. 'I am not *claiming* anything, Detective Inspector. I am merely stating the facts.'

'The facts as you understand them. But do you perhaps have any theories? You must have given it some thought.'

'I have had a great deal to think about these past few days, Detective Inspector,' said Harris, clearly struggling now to contain his anger. 'All I can tell you is that the woods behind the chapel are not off limits. The pupils are free to come and go there whenever their timetables allow. Meaning anyone might have discovered the entrance to the crypt and kept its existence a secret.'

'True enough,' said Fleet. 'Although as I understand it, Beaconsfield's grounds cover almost a thousand acres. Pupils are also free to go virtually anywhere within the school's boundaries they wish, are they not?'

'They are.'

'And the entranceway to the crypt was exceedingly well hidden. Meaning it would have taken quite a stroke of fortune for someone to have discovered the crypt accidentally. Do you agree, Mr Harris?'

'I suppose I would have to,' the headmaster said. He held Fleet's eye, and his look, to Fleet's mind, seemed like a challenge. 'And yet I cannot think of an alternative explanation, Detective Inspector. Can you?'

Ben – February 1997
(Three months before his death)

'There are only two things you need to know about Beaconsfield. Two things, once you understand them, that will help you survive.'

They were gathered on one of the benches overlooking the hockey pitch. Callum was balanced on the backrest, the soles of his shoes on the seat. Melissa and Lance were either side of him – Melissa sitting cross-legged, her head resting against Callum's thigh; Lance with an ankle propped on one knee. Ben hadn't seen any of his new friends since they'd skipped lessons a couple of days ago to smoke weed in the woods, and he'd been beginning to think he must have done something wrong – that Callum and the others were avoiding him. But then, at the start of break this time, they'd been waiting for him once again outside his classroom, and his fears had melted away.

Now, as he perched on an arm of the bench, he leaned forward to hear what Callum had to say. Just because he had friends now didn't mean Beaconsfield was any easier to bear. Ben hated it, hated being here. Most of all, he hated the fact that there was nowhere else for him to go.

'One,' Callum went on, holding up a finger. 'It may not look it, but this whole place is a cesspit. These blazers, these stupid shirt collars, this perfectly manicured grass – it's all window dressing. Like . . . curry. A fragrant sauce to disguise rancid meat. Or tinsel on a dead Christmas tree.'

Ben felt himself showing his confusion. It wasn't just what

Callum was saying. The way he was talking . . . he sounded more serious than Ben had ever heard him. There was an intensity to his demeanour Ben had only seen so far in flashes.

'It's rotten,' Callum said. 'Right to the core. Run by hypocrites and frauds, and funded by people who think having money gives them the right to act however they want. You know?'

Ben didn't know, not exactly, but he bobbed his head.

Of course you do, said Callum's expression. *I knew you would.* It was like in the woods: *one of us*, Callum had called Ben – when, aside from his mum, Ben had never been one with anyone.

'And the other pupils here are just as bad,' Callum went on. 'Not one of them thinks for themselves. They all just believe what they've been told: that if they pass some stupid exam, they'll have earned their privilege and power – that all the money that eventually comes their way will rightfully belong to them. Never mind that they won't have really earned *anything*.'

Something appeared to catch Callum's eye, and he tipped his head. 'Look,' he said, and they all turned to watch Mr Harris, the headmaster, striding through the grounds towards his office. As ever, he was sporting black, full-length robes that were every bit as ridiculous as the uniforms the pupils were obliged to wear. 'Harris is the perfect example of what I'm talking about. Do you know he only got the job of headmaster in the first place because his uncle is the provost?'

'The what?' said Ben, and immediately wished he'd held his tongue. He knew instinctively that Callum was smarter than him; Lance and Melissa, too, and not just because they were older. All Ben had done was make himself look stupid.

But: 'The provost,' Callum answered, without a pause, and without a trace of judgement in his tone. 'That's like . . .'

'Chair of the governors,' put in Melissa. She smiled at Ben kindly, again without seeming in any way patronising.

Even as they watched, Harris seemed to notice the four of them gathered on the bench. He stopped in his tracks, and turned as though to tell them off. Break time wasn't quite over yet, but the first bell had rung, indicating they should already be heading to their next lesson. Ben braced himself for the headmaster's inevitable rebuke – but rather than launching into a tirade and marching them back inside the school, Harris just dipped his head and walked on as though he hadn't seen them.

'Oh, and he's a coward, too,' Callum said. 'He hates me with a passion, but he wouldn't ever dare tell me off.'

Ben wouldn't have believed it if he hadn't seen it for himself. But it was true: Harris had reacted to seeing Callum just as the bigger boy who'd shoved Ben in the corridor had, not to mention the kids in his dorm when Callum had challenged them about Ben's bed sheets. Why were people so afraid of him?

'And it's not just Harris,' Callum went on. 'All the teachers here are frauds. They prance around like mini Mussolinis, acting as though they're better than anyone else, when the truth is they're either inept, stupid . . . or worse. And whenever something bad happens at Beaconsfield, the governors use their connections to ensure it never gets out. Like with Father Steiner, for instance.'

Ben had been watching Harris disappearing along the path. Not once had he even looked back. 'Father who?' Ben said, turning.

Callum glanced behind him, as though he was worried

that someone might overhear. 'Father Steiner,' he said. 'The chaplain. Everyone knows what he gets up to with the pupils he singles out for special attention. The boys, anyway.'

'The man's a predator,' chipped in Lance, with a knowing look at Ben.

Ben turned to face the chapel. 'No way. Why hasn't he been fired?'

Callum shrugged. 'Nobody's been able to prove anything, I suppose. Or, more likely, nobody cares. They're too busy watching their own backs. And that's what I'm saying. In this place, *everybody's* hiding *something.*'

Ben looked at Callum, Lance and Melissa in turn. Melissa dropped her eyes.

'You said there were two things I needed to know,' Ben said. 'What's the second thing?'

Now, for the first time, Callum smiled. 'The second thing,' he said to Ben, 'is that if you don't want to die of boredom here, you need to make your own fun.'

Ben frowned. 'What do you mean?'

'Just what I said. You like to have fun, don't you, Ben?'

'Fun as in, like, games and stuff?' Ben tried to laugh, unsure of what exactly was expected of him. 'Games are for little kids. Aren't they?'

Callum looked at Lance, and then Melissa. His smile broadened. 'Not the games we play,' he said.

Wednesday 23 October, 11.25 a.m.

Shortly after leaving Harris's office, Fleet and Nicky emerged into the central courtyard. The headmaster's room had a window overlooking the quad, and when Fleet glanced behind them, he saw Harris peering down through the glass. He was only partly visible, like a spectre half formed in the dark, though Fleet could sense his eyes watching them intently.

'Jesus,' said Nicky, catching sight of Harris, too. 'Not exactly Dumbledore, is he?' She kept her voice low, as though Harris might somehow be able to overhear.

When Fleet checked again, the headmaster was gone, as though he'd never been there at all. But they were still being watched, this time by a group of kids who were standing by the central fountain. Perhaps they should have taken the more circuitous route, Fleet thought – the way Harris had led them on day one – but the explosion of interest in the case meant time-consuming detours were a luxury they could no longer afford. As it was, Fleet had a meeting scheduled with Superintendent Burton that very afternoon, in which he would be expected to outline the investigation's progress – an update, as things stood, he would just as easily have been able to deliver in a text.

'Do you think it's genuinely all about the school for Harris?' Fleet said, once they were clear of the fountain.

Nicky frowned at him. 'You don't?'

The quad was mainly gravel, which crunched beneath their feet as they walked. The sky was bright, the air cold,

65

their breath misting into speech bubbles. Groups of pupils passed them on both sides, books clutched to their chests and eyes darting Fleet and Nicky's way.

Fleet pondered for a moment before answering. 'I don't doubt he's concerned about Beaconsfield's reputation. But maybe it's not just the school he's trying to protect. Maybe he's also worried about something else.'

'About his job, maybe? He obviously values his position. He's clung on to it long enough.'

'I might have bought that twenty-two years ago,' said Fleet. 'Right after Ben went missing, and when Harris was relatively new to his role. But he's close to retirement age. He must know he'll be stepping down soon anyway.'

'Unless he's in denial. Or maybe he's not trying to protect his position any more. Maybe now it's about his legacy. He doesn't want to be remembered as the man who was at the helm when the good ship Beaconsfield ran into the iceberg.'

Fleet bobbed his head, not entirely convinced. They walked on, towards the arch at the far end of the courtyard that led under the southern wing of the main building. As they passed from the courtyard and into the tunnel, they saw the chapel further down the slope, the spire perfectly framed by the stone archway. The hockey pitch was empty this time, as indeed were the rest of the grounds on this side of the main building, all the way to the first line of trees. Fleet didn't know whether the students had been told to stay away from the woods and the area around them, or whether they'd opted to do so voluntarily. Either way, the entire school felt eerily quiet. Even in the quad, where pupils had been crossing back and forth, there'd been no laughter, no fooling around, none of the banter Fleet would have expected, even at a school like Beaconsfield.

'Poor kids,' said Nicky, nodding her head to indicate the pupils they'd passed in the courtyard. 'I bet this place feels more like a prison now than ever.'

Fleet glanced Nicky's way, remembering something about her that he'd forgotten. 'Didn't you go to a boarding school yourself?'

'Yep. For five whole years. A place called Welton House. It was nothing like Beaconsfield, but even still . . .'

'You mean prison is what it felt like to you?'

'Prison is putting it mildly,' said Nicky. 'Boarding school scarred me for life. You can ask my therapist.'

Fleet had assumed Nicky was making a joke, but when he turned again she'd stopped walking, and was gazing up at the building that was now behind them.

'The worst thing is being sent away from home,' she said. 'I don't think when you're young you can ever really understand it. My dad actually apologised to me once, soon after he and Mum got divorced. *She's* never said sorry – which is probably why I've never forgiven her, for boarding school or anything else.'

Fleet knew Nicky was close to her father – from what he understood, Nicky's dad was in his seventies, and was still a practising solicitor, in spite of all Nicky's efforts to convince him to retire. She rarely mentioned her mum, however. Until recently, Fleet had been estranged from his own mother, and although he and Nicky had bonded in an odd sort of way over their upbringings, they'd done so without ever really having talked about the details. Now, Nicky knew all about Fleet's relationship with his mum. From the sound of it, being sent away to boarding school was at the heart of Nicky's falling out with hers.

'I was a mistake, essentially,' Nicky said. 'My mum didn't

really want children, and she's never gone to any pains to hide the fact. Even now, on the rare occasions we speak, she talks to me the way she would an old acquaintance. Someone she's half forgotten is still alive. And needless to say, she never asks about Dad. They were married for almost twenty years, but in her mind that counts for even less than having given birth to someone.'

Fleet didn't know what to say. He thought of his own mother, of how grievously he'd misread the way *she'd* acted – but it sounded as though Nicky's mother knew exactly what she was doing; how hurtful her behaviour would have been.

'Parents,' Fleet said, through a sympathetic sniff. 'Who'd have them?'

Nicky smiled weakly. They joined the track that would take them to the chapel. The chapel itself loomed over them, the shadow of the spire like a blade across their path.

'Six hundred pupils,' said Nicky eventually – just for the sake of saying something, it seemed to Fleet. 'That's what Harris said, right?'

'Right,' Fleet agreed.

'Which means . . . what? A hundred or so members of staff?'

Fleet thought of all the workers they'd seen in the kitchen, as well as the immaculately tended grounds. And Beaconsfield had a teaching ratio of eight to one, a detail that was plastered all over the school's website.

'You do realise that's an awful lot of suspects?' said Nicky, and Fleet couldn't help but smile: at the obvious futility of it, mainly. Because as Nicky well knew, it wasn't just the sheer number of suspects that they were up against. It was also the fact that most of them had scattered on the wind. After twenty-two years, and given that for most of Beaconsfield's graduates money would have been no object, they might literally be anywhere. And anyone Fleet and Nicky *could* track down – potential witnesses, for example – would by default have to be considered unreliable. Most people could barely remember what they were doing twenty-two days ago, let alone a quarter of a century.

'So what's the word from on high?' Nicky said. 'The brass must have seen the news. They surely can't believe this is just about a missing kid any more, whether Callum Richardson is caught up in things or not. Is there any chance they'll lend us some extra bodies?'

At the moment, not counting Randy and his team, it was still exclusively Fleet and Nicky's show. They had scope to rope in a few uniforms here and there, but nothing like the numbers they really needed.

'I'll raise it with Burton when I see him,' said Fleet. 'Irrespective of how he reacts, though, we're still going to be up against it. Which is why we need to keep this focused. How are we getting on with rounding up Ben's friends?'

Nicky made a face. 'Mixed,' she said. 'I managed to get hold of Lance Wheeler. No full-time employment, so I had a bit of trouble tracking him down, but it turns out he's local. From what I've gathered he graduated from Beaconsfield and basically took the first job he found, as a painter and decorator. He was here on a scholarship, meaning he had the brains for university – for Oxbridge, probably – but for some reason never applied.'

'Money, perhaps? If he was here on a scholarship, he might not have been able to afford it. And maybe, after Beaconsfield, he'd had his fill of education.'

'Maybe. Probably. Anyway, he's due into the station first thing tomorrow morning.'

'You don't think he'll turn up?' said Fleet, reading Nicky's tone.

'He said all the right things, insisted he was eager to help, but I had a sense he was playing for time. Let's just say I'll believe him when I see him.'

With the exception of Holly, perhaps, Nicky was a better judge of people than anyone Fleet had ever known. If she had her doubts that Lance would show, Fleet knew better than to get his hopes up.

'What about Melissa?' he asked.

Nicky's frown set deeper. 'The honest answer? I'm having trouble believing Melissa Haynes even exists any more. The trail after Beaconsfield just seems to vanish. Again, she graduated, though not with the grades she was predicted to get. From what I can make out based on her academic records, she started struggling the term after Ben vanished. Which tells us something, perhaps, though I'm not sure what. And so far I can't find her to allow us to ask.'

Fleet mirrored Nicky's expression. 'Keep on it. We've still got a couple of days before our audience with Callum Richardson. And given how little time we're likely to have with him, we need to go in there knowing at least as much as he does.'

Ben – February 1997
(Three months before his death)

It was the one part of the day Ben enjoyed. Actually, genuinely enjoyed. He'd never been into God – what had He ever done for him? – but he'd always loved churches. The smell, the silence, the sense of safety. The chance, for once, to be at peace.

So morning worship was a time he'd come to look forward to. Every day at eight o'clock, the entire school was made to gather in the chapel, which was big enough to seat all six-hundred-odd kids. They perched on the wooden benches, while the teachers sat along the aisles, as well as at the front near the altar. Ben didn't care about the service itself. He quite liked the bits where the chaplain read from the Bible, but then, when the headmaster took over to deliver his sermon, Ben always allowed himself to tune out. To allow his mind to drift.

It was better than sleep, in a way, because when you slept the chances were you would dream – and Ben's dreams couldn't be trusted. Sometimes they would start out OK. He'd dream of his mum, and she would hold Ben in her arms. Except then something would happen. Either his mum's embrace would become too tight, squeezing him, suffocating him, or else the opposite would happen. Ben would be trying to cling on to her, but something would start pulling her away. She would begin to dissolve, so that when Ben grabbed for her, his hands would pass right through her. And every time he flailed she would disappear a little bit more, to the point that, just before Ben finally woke, he would always be alone.

Completely, utterly alone.

But in the chapel, there was no risk that the peace would betray him. For half an hour every morning, he could just sit and take in his surroundings, enjoying the shapes and textures of the building. It was a secret he'd never told anyone, but architecture had always fascinated him. The way buildings managed to develop personalities, even though they were basically lumps of concrete. Or wood, or glass, or metal, of course. And that was the other thing he found fascinating: the way different materials could be fused together to create something completely different, like notes arranged in a song.

Harmony. That was the word. Looking at buildings – *good* buildings – gave Ben a sense of harmony.

The school itself wasn't a good building. With its dark walls and coal-black windows and its ramparts that looked like teeth, the only personality the school projected was that of an angry bully. Even the bell tower looked like a finger raised in warning.

But the chapel was different, and Ben enjoyed trying to figure out why. Rather than ugly, it looked elegant. It was like . . . like the contrast there would have been had his real mum been standing next to his stepmother. He even liked the slight chill in the air that was always there in the chapel when you first filed in. It was refreshing, like splashing your face with cold water. Cleansing, even. And being inside the chapel made you feel small. Like nothing you did or said even mattered. Some people – the headmaster, for example – would probably insist that it was being in the presence of God that made you feel that way, but Ben didn't agree. It was the *architecture* that made you think that: the vast ceiling, the stone columns, the simplicity of the building's strength.

Today, Mr Harris was lecturing them all about their

upcoming exams, even though it was February, and the exams didn't take place until June. In contrast to the way Father Steiner spoke, in tones as rich and soft as incense, the headmaster's voice was angry and intrusive. It bounced from the hard stone walls, as though the chapel itself were rejecting it. When Harris got overexcited, it would have been easier to tune out a baby's wail.

'And finally,' the headmaster said, and Ben found himself simultaneously grateful and disappointed. Grateful that Harris would at last stop talking; disappointed that the morning service would soon be over, and the rest of the day would shortly begin. 'Father Steiner has requested that two strong lads stay behind for half an hour after the service,' the headmaster went on. 'The new hymn books have arrived, and he requires assistance carrying the boxes through from the vestry.'

Ben sat up straighter. He was seated at the end of a row, with Lance and Callum to his right. Melissa was on the opposite side of the central aisle. The girls always filed in from their dormitories separately, and ended up sitting apart from the boys.

'Strong, but not too strong,' Lance whispered. 'Not strong enough that they'd be able to fight him off.'

Ben focused on Father Steiner, who was standing beside the headmaster with his hands clasped modestly in front of him. The chaplain was a short man, roughly Ben's height, with a thin face and narrow shoulders. Beneath his round, frameless glasses, he looked relatively young, at least compared to the rest of the teachers. It was the one thing he appeared to have in common with the headmaster. The headmaster was taller and broader across the shoulders, but from the neck up he looked just as fresh-faced. In a way that had nothing to do with their stature, neither man quite filled his robes.

'Do I have any volunteers?' the headmaster called. 'Or should I volunteer you myself?'

Ben looked across and met Callum's eye. There was a hand already up in the front row – and then, surprising even himself, Ben slowly raised his. He noticed Melissa glance at him from across the aisle, but he kept his eyes fixed on Father Steiner, who – from smiling at the boy in front – turned and looked Ben's way.

Ben thought back to what his new friends had told him about the chaplain – a *predator*, Lance had called him – and for the first time wondered whether it could really be true. Father Steiner didn't look dangerous from where Ben was sitting.

He didn't look dangerous at all.

It was like stepping back into his childhood. When Fleet had been growing up, even well into his otherwise unruly teens, his mother had dragged him to church a minimum of once a week. Sometimes – particularly as Fleet got older – the act had been literally that: his mother throwing back his duvet and physically pulling Fleet from his bed. She insisted that, while Fleet was living under her roof, he would obey her rules, and really the only rule book she cared about was the Bible. It had been the same for Fleet's sister, although Jeannie had gone more willingly. But Fleet had stopped believing in God around the time he'd discovered drink and drugs, and the last time he'd stepped into a church was the day of his sister's funeral.

Now, as he and Nicky entered Beaconsfield's chapel, it all came back to him: the musty smell and heavy silence, the vague discomfort and indeterminate sense of guilt.

'Shouldn't we have knocked or something?' Nicky whispered. They'd paused at the end of the central aisle, just beyond the vestibule, and there was no one in sight. The dark oak pews were laid out in front of them, the rows extending all the way to the altar. There were huge stained-glass windows along the walls, like pages of a vast and colourful picture book narrating, in this instance, the story of Christ and the apostles. In the alcoves, there were gilded statues and gold candelabras, while above them hung a vast chandelier – all of which contributed to the strangely yellow light.

'We could ring the bell,' said Fleet. 'That would probably get the chaplain's attention. But we'd be in danger of having six hundred pupils descending on us, too.'

He started towards the altar, and Nicky followed a step behind. She looked as much of an intruder as she clearly felt.

'At ease, Detective Sergeant,' Fleet said. 'I'd imagine you're not the first non-believer to step through those doors. If you need evidence, try feeling for chewing gum on the undersides of those pews.'

'Exactly,' said Nicky. 'I put my fair share of Hubba Bubba under the seats in the chapel at my old school, and now it feels like I'm back to face the music.'

Fleet turned as he walked. 'Your school was Catholic?'

'C of E,' Nicky replied. 'But to be honest it's all the same to me. I'm going to hell either way.'

They reached the altar, and still there was no sign of Father Steiner.

'What about you, boss? Didn't you grow up Catholic?'

'I did.'

'So what made you stop believing? Assuming you ever believed in the first place.'

'Oh, I believed,' Fleet told her. 'My mother made sure of that. She used to terrify me with stories about what happens to non-believers – or, worse, Protestants – when they die; what would happen to *me* if God doubted my faith. But the older I got, the more it started to sound like a fairy tale. And also like . . . Well. Like wishful thinking.'

What Fleet didn't say was that, after Jeannie died, he'd tried desperately to rediscover his belief in heaven. But no matter how hard he worked to convince himself, the conclusion he reached was always the same: his little sister was gone forever. He hadn't been there when she needed him, and there was nothing he could do to bring her back.

Fleet had noticed something on the wall behind the altar, and he circled to get a closer look.

'Seems the place could do with some TLC,' said Nicky.

Fleet looked up, around. The church was spotless, the wood well-polished and the walls relatively recently painted, and yet there were several large cracks in the plasterwork running diagonally from the ceiling. They were too high for him to touch, but in places he would have been able to reach a hand into the gaps.

'Subsidence,' came a voice, and Fleet turned. A man who could only be Father Steiner had appeared through a doorway off to one side, presumably one leading to the vestry. 'It's always been a problem, though apparently not one serious enough to do anything about. From what I've been led to understand, it's one of the perils of building on a hill. Although perhaps now we know the real reason.' He tipped his head slightly to his right. Towards the graveyard outside, and the remains of the original chapel's crypt.

Father Steiner stepped forward and extended his hand. Nicky was closest, and she shook it first.

'At the risk of sounding like a Bond villain,' said the chaplain, 'I've been expecting you. You're the detectives investigating what happened to Ben, I'm guessing.'

Father Steiner nudged his glasses towards the bridge of his nose. He was a short man, with a shiny dome of a head but a face that appeared not to have aged at the same pace as the rest of him. He must have been at least as old as the headmaster, but if it weren't for the stiffness of his movements and the slight stoop to his narrow shoulders, Fleet would estimate him to be twenty years younger. It didn't even appear as though he shaved.

'I'm Detective Sergeant Nicola Collins,' Nicky replied. 'This is Detective Inspector Robin Fleet.'

'Welcome,' said Father Steiner. 'Both of you. Please, have a seat.' He gestured towards the front row of pews.

'Thank you,' said Fleet, sensing Nicky shift slightly, 'but we're happy to stand.' Even for Fleet, entering the church was one thing; taking a pew right in front of the altar felt like a regression too far.

'By all means,' said Father Steiner. 'Although, do you mind if I sit down myself? The knees,' he explained, with a grimace.

Fleet watched as the chaplain lowered himself on to the edge of a pew, at the end nearest the central aisle. Now, under the glow from the chandelier, he really did look his age. The yellow light changed the appearance of his skin, turning it the colour and texture of a page in a library-copy paperback.

'I assume you'd like me to tell you about Ben. About what I remember from before he went missing.'

'That would be very helpful, Father,' said Fleet. 'We understand you knew him quite well.'

The chaplain appeared mildly surprised. Then he gave a small sniff, as though working out where that particular piece of information would have come from. 'It's not uncommon for our headmaster to overstate my bond with a particular student, I'm afraid. The reality is, I didn't know Ben particularly well. Not as well as I would have liked to, anyway. And perhaps not as well as I thought I did.'

The chaplain's answer raised a dozen further questions in Fleet's mind, but he waited for Father Steiner to go on.

'Ben used to come here. To help out, initially. But then, like one or two others, he found reasons to keep coming back. It happens in a place like this more often than you might think.' The chaplain gestured loosely around him, and Fleet understood that he was referring to the school itself. 'Kids feel lost, abandoned, out of their depth, and the chapel is an obvious place of refuge, whether they believe in what the Bible teaches us or not.'

'And that's how Ben felt, would you say?' asked Fleet. 'Lost, out of his depth?'

'Oh, undoubtedly. He tried to conceal it, of course. With children his age, particularly boys, it's all about hiding how you really feel. There's a misconception that, if you acknowledge that there's something missing from your life, even inwardly, you immediately become more vulnerable. So kids pretend. They make-believe. Precisely as they do when they're at play.'

The chaplain pointed over Fleet's shoulder. 'Do you know who that is?' He was gesturing towards the largest of the stained-glass windows, the one directly behind the altar. The image was of one of Christ's apostles. St Jude, if Fleet wasn't mistaken.

'I'm afraid not,' he told the chaplain, not wanting to get drawn into a discussion on theology. Or, worse, his own personal beliefs.

'Jude Thaddeus,' Father Steiner announced. 'The patron saint of lost causes. The glass was installed long before I came to Beaconsfield, but I always felt it was appropriate. A bit like those cracks you noticed before. They seem symbolic to me, too – of the pressures on the students here that go largely unseen, but that can be no less destructive if left unchecked.'

Fleet looked again at the cracks behind the altar, before

settling his gaze on the stained-glass window. It showed a man with a brown beard, his head ringed with flame. The image was dominated by greens and yellows, further adding to the jaundiced haze.

'You said Ben helped,' Fleet said, turning back to Father Steiner. 'With what exactly? Do you mean he was interested in Catholicism? That he participated in the chapel's services?'

The chaplain gave a humourless laugh. 'Oh, no. Nothing like that. I won't deny that I tried to open Ben's mind to the existence of God. One of the things missing from his life, I would have said, was faith. But I could tell he considered it nothing more than a bunch of mumbo jumbo. Much as he tried to pretend otherwise.'

'So why was he here?' said Nicky. 'Or rather, why did he keep coming back?'

'He liked to draw,' the chaplain said.

Fleet and Nicky shared a glance. Father Steiner obviously noticed.

'It's not what you expected me to say, I can tell. But Ben had a passion for architecture, and something about the chapel made a part of him sing. I'll be honest, architecture is far from my own specialist subject, but Ben and I would talk about the building – about buildings in general – and sometimes those discussions would branch into others. Conversations about God, occasionally. About family, every so often. We would rarely digress for long, because Ben was always wise to what I was doing.'

'Which was?' said Fleet.

'I was trying to get him to open up,' the chaplain said. 'Which Ben resisted, as I said, but even so I had a feeling he was pleased to be talking at all.'

'You mentioned family,' Fleet said. 'What about friends? Did you and Ben ever talk about the other pupils he was hanging around with?'

Father Steiner's expression set firm. 'We did not.'

'You sound very definite about that, Father,' Fleet said.

'Because Ben was very definite about it himself,' Father Steiner responded. 'It was one of two things he was clear on. We might speak about family in very general terms, but if conversation turned specifically to his mother or father, he would shut down. And he was just as defensive when it came to his friends.'

'Can you say why?'

Father Steiner pursed his lips. 'I expect it was because he knew I disapproved.'

'You disapproved? Of who, exactly? Callum Richardson? Melissa Haynes? Lance Wheeler?'

The chaplain seemed about to answer, but hesitated.

'Father Steiner?' Fleet prompted, and the chaplain sighed.

'I disapproved of all three of them, if you want the truth. But of Callum Richardson in particular.'

'And why was that?'

'They . . . Callum especially . . . they weren't the sort of friends I would have suggested Ben choose. They were brighter than Ben, for a start. Cannier. Their morals, to my mind, were . . . questionable. And Ben was easily led. A bit like Melissa, actually, who would have thrown herself from the bell tower if Callum had asked her to. She was besotted with him, you see. As was Lance, come to that,' Father Steiner added meaningfully.

'Romantically, you mean?' said Nicky. 'Lance Wheeler was gay?'

'Oh, I doubt it was that straightforward,' said Father

Steiner. 'They were fifteen years old. And this was boarding school. I doubt even Lance was certain whether or not he was homosexual. All I'm really saying is, even at that age Callum Richardson had his followers. Melissa and Lance were both infatuated with him, and Ben was in danger of being sucked in, too.'

'Sucked into what exactly?' said Fleet.

'Into Callum Richardson's secretive little clique. The boy had an agenda. I couldn't tell you what that agenda was, but I was always sure it served Callum Richardson's purposes and nobody else's. And I'd seen the consequences before.'

'What do you mean?' said Nicky.

'I mean, I'd witnessed other people getting hurt. More than that, I would prefer not to say. Particularly in light of . . . I would prefer not to say, that's all. I do not feel it is my place.'

'I understand your reluctance, Father Steiner,' said Fleet. 'But I surely don't need to remind you why we are asking you these questions. Ben Draper was murdered, his body stuffed into an underground chamber not fifty metres from where you are currently sitting. And I can tell you that whoever killed him went to considerable lengths to make sure he was dead.'

The chaplain, at that, went pale. Even paler in the insipid light than he already looked.

'I understand,' he said. 'I truly do. But I've said more than I should have already. If I had proof, I would have presented it long ago. And I have no wish to influence the course of your investigation now.'

Unless that's precisely what you wish to do, thought Fleet. He regarded the chaplain appraisingly. 'The headmaster didn't seem to approve of Callum Richardson either, I noticed,' he said.

'That doesn't surprise me. Mr Harris has always prided

himself on being in charge, but at Beaconsfield, Callum Richardson was a law unto himself. Nobody ever dared challenge him, because the school couldn't afford to risk losing his father's donations.' The chaplain's expression clouded. 'Although it wasn't just about the money. The other children were wary of Callum, too. They craved his approval, but at the same time, even when Callum Richardson was a teenager, there was something about him that was . . . unsettling.'

'I take it you won't be voting for your school's alumnus if he ends up standing in the next general election?' Nicky asked.

The chaplain turned to her. 'I will not. And by the way, Beaconsfield is not *my* school. I don't approve of its values. And I don't believe the pupils who study here should be sleeping anywhere but in their own homes. Boarding school, to my mind, is an unnecessary evil.' He spoke forcibly, but in something approaching a whisper, as though conscious of the blasphemy in his words.

'With respect, Father Steiner,' said Fleet, 'if you do not believe in what Beaconsfield stands for, why have you remained in your position for all these years? From what I gather, you've been here almost as long as the headmaster has.'

'I joined Beaconsfield about five months after Mr Harris did. And it's *because* I don't believe that I have stayed so long,' the chaplain said. 'There are children here – children very much like Ben – who stand to benefit from having someone sympathetic to talk to. Someone who has no interest in whether the school succeeds as an institution – only that *they* do, as individuals, in whichever capacity they choose.'

So that perhaps explained the headmaster's animosity towards the chaplain, Fleet reasoned. Assuming both men truly believed in the principles they claimed to.

'Going back to Ben's disappearance,' Fleet said. 'Did you

see Ben and his friends on the day he went missing? From what they told investigators at the time, the four of them were playing hide-and-seek in the grounds, and Ben vanished after running off to hide.'

The chaplain shook his head. 'I did not.'

'But you were here, on campus? What were your movements? You will understand, I hope, why I have to ask.'

'It was a Saturday, and Saturdays are one of the few clear windows in my week. I use them to catch up – with administrative matters, with personal ones. And with prayer. I'm something of a creature of habit, Detective Inspector. I tend to follow a daily routine.'

'Meaning you were in your quarters in the main building?'

'Meaning I was here, in the chapel, from dawn until the middle of the afternoon. As God is my witness,' Father Steiner added, with a twitch of a smile. 'But I doubt anybody else will be able to vouch for me. The day started brightly, but by late afternoon the weather was awful. And most of the children who hadn't gone home for the weekend were up at the school, meaning the grounds would have been largely deserted. I don't recall seeing more than one or two other people all day.'

'Not even after you returned to the main building?' Nicky asked.

'Not even then. I believe I went straight to my room. I remember . . . I remember feeling slightly unwell.'

There was a buzzing sound, and it took Fleet a moment to work out that it was coming from his pocket. His phone was set to silent, but even so, in the confines of the chapel the noise of the vibration felt as intrusive as a ring.

He muttered his apologies and turned away. When he looked at the screen, he felt himself frown. He knew the number, and he knew nobody would be calling him from it if it weren't important.

He accepted the call, and strode towards the vestibule, only raising the phone to his ear when he was through the first set of doors.

'Fleet,' he said.

He listened to the voice at the other end. He closed his eyes. When he opened them again, Nicky was leaning through the gap between the vestibule doors. She could clearly tell something was wrong even before Fleet had hung up the phone.

'Boss?' she said, keeping her voice low. 'What's up?'

Fleet exhaled. 'Ben's friend. Lance Wheeler. When did you say you last spoke to him?'

'Monday afternoon. I tried to get in touch with him again yesterday to confirm our appointment, but his phone just went to voicemail. Why?'

Fleet peered over Nicky's shoulder. Father Steiner was still seated on the front row of pews. His head was dipped, as though he was praying.

'Because Lance Wheeler has just been found dead.'

Ben – February 1997

(Three months before his death)

It was too heavy to lift. The books were stacked neatly inside, with not a centimetre of space wasted, but it was only once Ben had taped down the flaps that he realised he couldn't move it from the table. He stared at it, simultaneously irritated and perplexed. There was a tutting noise from behind him.

'Weren't you listening? Father Steiner *told* you to only fill them halfway.'

Isaac Sinclair reached past Ben and started pulling up the tape Ben had only just stuck down. Isaac was the boy whose hand had gone in the air before his, when Ben had volunteered to help Father Steiner. It turned out Isaac was also in Ben's dorm, which on top of the fact that Isaac was obviously a goody-goody, was part of the reason Ben had immediately taken against him. Ben didn't suspect him of being one of the boys who'd messed with his stuff, but he'd done nothing to *help* Ben. Instead, he was just as snobby and unfriendly as all the rest of them. More so, even. With his neat blond hair and blemish-free skin, as well as his perfectly knotted tie, he was like a poster boy for this entire place.

'Hey, get off,' Ben said, shrugging him away. 'I haven't finished.'

Isaac tutted again, but withdrew. Ben could feel Isaac watching him behind his back. They were in the vestry, packing up the old hymn books. It was now three days later, the two of them having agreed to come back to complete the job. Father Steiner had arranged for the old books to be sent to some charity or other – something about poor kids in Africa – and had now gone hunting for more boxes while Ben and Isaac got on with the packing. Isaac seemed to think he'd been left in charge. He obviously considered himself Father Steiner's extra-special assistant or something. Over the past few days, Ben had noticed Isaac heading in and out of the chapel pretty much every lunch break, as though he couldn't get enough of the place. Although it was clearly Father Steiner he couldn't get enough of. He made out he was all interested in Jesus and everything, but it had made Ben wonder about the stories Callum had mentioned – the *special attention* the chaplain was rumoured to give certain boys. Plus, if Isaac was genuinely only interested in learning about God, why did he shoot Ben evils every time Father Steiner paid Ben any notice?

'You do realise that even if you manage to lift it, the bottom's going to fall out?' Isaac said. 'You've packed it too full.'

'I said I'd sort it,' Ben grumbled, ripping off the tape himself. 'Jesus,' he added in a whisper, but loud enough that Isaac would hear it. He took a petty thrill from knowing that Isaac would disapprove. And God, too, probably. Wasn't blaspheming inside a church one of the worst things you could do?

'Here,' Isaac said. An empty box appeared on the table next to the carton Ben had overfilled. 'Put half of them in that one.'

'That's what I was going to do,' said Ben huffily. He ignored the box Isaac had given him, and bent down to collect one of his own.

Isaac tutted again and started sealing up his own box, even though from what Ben saw it was barely a third full, let alone half.

Isaac caught him looking, and he turned away. When Ben glanced again, Isaac was still staring.

'You're not fooling anyone, you know,' he said. 'You do realise that, don't you?'

Ben was focused on moving books from one box to the other. 'What are you talking about?'

'Whatever game it is you're playing. You're not fooling anyone.'

Ben stopped what he was doing and turned to Isaac, who started on filling another box.

'What do you mean? What game?'

Isaac shot Ben a look. 'You tell me. Why is it you're here, *really*? I know you're not interested in religion. And I know you're not the type to volunteer out of the goodness of your heart. So, what is it you're up to?'

Ben opened his mouth to answer, but found himself at a loss for what to say.

'How are we all doing?'

Oblivious to the mood in the room, Father Steiner bumbled cheerfully through the doorway of the vestry. He dropped the boxes he was carrying on to the floor, and brushed his hands together theatrically. His glasses had edged towards the tip of his nose, and he used a knuckle to nudge them higher. '*Excellent* work, Isaac,' he said as he noticed the stack of boxes at Isaac's feet.

Isaac reached for the packing tape to seal up yet another box, and Ben could see him struggling not to broadcast his pride. He was like a little kid or something. Or a puppy receiving praise for not having peed on the floor.

'Although' – Father Steiner's smile faltered slightly as he edged close enough to see over Isaac's shoulder – 'you could probably make the boxes just a *bit* fuller.' He chuckled. 'It's no wonder we were running out if the rest of them are as empty as this one.' He turned to Ben, whose pile was smaller.

But the two boxes on the table in front of him were now both exactly half full.

'Now *that's* more like it,' said the chaplain, clapping a hand on Ben's shoulder. 'Isaac, do you see? Try to follow Ben's lead.'

Father Steiner gave Ben's shoulder a gentle squeeze. Ben caught Isaac's eye. It was foolish, he knew, but he couldn't resist flashing a triumphant smile. The truth was, he didn't care about the stupid boxes, nor if he packed them better than Isaac or not. But for a second there, Isaac had made Ben think he might actually have guessed what was going on. It was the mention of a *game* that had done it – that unconscious echo of the very phrase Callum had used. But it was as Callum had said: if they were smart, and they were careful about not being seen hanging around together too often, there was no way anyone would ever know what they were planning. If they wanted to, they could get away with murder.

Wednesday 23 October, 1.55 p.m.

Fleet had smelled death before: most recently, in the woods that bordered his home town.

This time was different. Then, he recalled, the smell had enveloped him slowly, creeping towards him like mist through the trees. Now, as he stepped on to the landing outside the door to Lance Wheeler's flat, it was like wading through something viscous. The air was warm, stifling even, which didn't help. The actual scent was different, too. Out in the woods, Fleet had at first mistaken the smell for decaying foliage, but here it was sharper, more acrid, like the bins at the back of a restaurant.

Fleet stepped into the flat itself. Two SOCOs were already on the scene, prowling around at the threshold of one of the rooms. The kitchen, Fleet presumed, because the flat was barely any bigger than his bedsit, and he could see the lounge ahead of him, the bathroom on his left, and the bedroom immediately to his right. The whole place, Fleet noticed, was a tip, and it could well be the state of the bathroom that was contributing to the acerbic smell. The bed – a single – was unmade; the lounge a mess of coffee mugs and pizza boxes. Even the hallway was cluttered with junk. Several battered pairs of trainers had been kicked into a corner, and there was a bicycle missing its front wheel, as well as at least a dozen used paint cans in teetering stacks. Fleet recalled Nicky saying that Lance was a painter and decorator, and in addition to the tins of paint, there was a bundle of dust sheets, and a set of overalls draped across the frame of the bike.

On the wall beside the bathroom door there was a storage heater, and Fleet could feel it kicking out heat.

'It's like an oven in here,' said Nicky, beside him. She called to one of the SOCOs. 'Any chance we could get the temperature turned down?'

'Already asked,' came the muffled reply. 'Apparently it's on a central system, and the thermostat's broken. Nothing we can do about it from in here.'

Randy was apparently on his way over, and Fleet could just imagine the pathologist's reaction when he arrived. The heat would make his job that much harder, not least in trying to pinpoint a time of death. Apparently none of Lance's neighbours had seen him in days, meaning Nicky could well have been the last person to speak to him, forty-eight hours ago now.

'Sorry, sir. Until we get set up, that's as far as we can allow you to go.'

One of the SOCOs held up an arm to barricade the doorway into the kitchen. The kitchen was galley-style, Fleet saw, with a short run of units on either side. Even in normal circumstances, there would have been barely enough room for him to fit inside. As it was, the space between the units was taken up by Lance Wheeler's dangling body.

'Jesus,' muttered Nicky.

A stepladder had been laid sideways across the top of the wall units. Ben's former schoolmate was hanging by his neck from a leather belt that had been looped around one of the rungs. A chair was toppled over underneath his feet, and his trousers sagged below his waistline. His eyes were open. They gazed glassily into empty space.

Like the rest of the flat, the kitchen itself was filthy. There were used cooking pots on the hob, and unwashed dishes stacked in the metal sink. As for Lance, it was obvious that even when he'd still been alive, he'd hardly been in a better state himself. There was a scruffy beard covering his pale and bloated cheeks, and his hair – thin on top – appeared greasy and uncut. The waistband of his trousers was frayed, with one of the belt loops hanging loose and another missing completely. His T-shirt was equally threadbare, with a brownish tinge in places that would once have been white.

'Who was it who found him?' Fleet asked the nearest SOCO.

'The landlord,' she replied. 'A neighbour complained about the smell.'

'Boss? Take a look at this.'

It was Nicky's voice. She'd moved away, and was standing at the threshold to the living room.

Fleet turned from the scene in the kitchen, and tracked Nicky's gaze. On a desk beside the sofa there was an ancient laptop. It had the look of being permanently plugged into the wall, suggesting the battery had given out, but it was clearly drawing power from the socket, because the screen showed a blank white page and a blinking cursor. Although, as Fleet stepped forward, he realised the page was only mostly blank.

He glanced at Nicky, and then moved closer, carefully picking his way across the cluttered floor. Halfway to the desk, he stopped again. There were indeed two typed words at the top of the page. Barely even a sentence, really – but the message Lance had left them was clear.

Wednesday 23 October, 3.16 p.m.

'So you have a confession? Is that what you're telling us?'

Superintendent Roger Burton didn't look like a man on the cusp of an investigative win. He looked like someone who hadn't been sleeping, and who was running largely on coffee and cortisol. Burton was known for his fastidious diet, as well as his daily pilgrimages to the squash court, and ordinarily whenever Fleet was in the superintendent's presence, he felt like a walking NHS warning poster. But today Burton's cheeks appeared unusually gaunt, his skin worryingly grey. The man was in his fifties, so perhaps it was the years of hypertension catching up with him. Or perhaps it was the pressure of the case, together with his evident discomfort at being only the third-most important person in the room.

'We have an apology,' Fleet answered. 'I wouldn't go so far as to call it a confession. And the reality is, we still don't know what exactly Lance Wheeler thought he was apologising *for*.'

'But that seems obvious. Doesn't it?'

Both Fleet and Burton turned to face Manish Apte, the county's police and crime commissioner, who was sitting at the head of the conference table. They were in a room on the top floor of the police station, seated at one end of a table that had enough chairs around it for twenty-five. Fleet was to the PCC's right. Burton and a man named Webb – who was here, in his words, *representing the Home Office* – were to Apte's left. Nominally Apte was chairing the meeting, and Webb had barely spoken. But from the way both Apte and

Burton repeatedly glanced Webb's way, it seemed perfectly obvious that he was really the man in charge.

'I mean, given the timing,' Apte continued, 'and the fact that Wheeler was due to be interviewed first thing in the morning. If he didn't kill the Draper boy, what else would have prompted Wheeler to take his own life? Why *else* make an apology?'

And that, indeed, was the question Fleet had been wrestling with himself. On the laptop in Lance's apartment, the words *I'm sorry* had been left on the screen – seemingly Lance's last act before stringing himself up by his belt in his kitchen. As Apte had said, the explanation seemed obvious. But Fleet had been doing his job long enough to know the perils of taking things at face value.

'Detective Inspector?' Apte prompted, and Fleet realised the PCC's question hadn't been purely rhetorical. He genuinely seemed to think that, barely an hour after being presented with Lance Wheeler's body, and having come straight from the scene to this meeting, Fleet might have some definitive answers. Fleet didn't know a lot about Apte, and this was the first time they'd met, but he was aware the man had never been a copper himself. As the police and crime commissioner, he was the elected official to whom the chief constable was accountable, but in his former life Apte had been a banker.

'I would agree that the most logical explanation for Wheeler's suicide was that he was involved somehow in Ben's death,' Fleet said. 'But two typed words on a screen hardly constitute a signed confession. And from the little we know about Wheeler's personal situation, there seem to be plenty of other reasons he may have decided to take his own life.'

'Such as?' said Apte.

'Well, it was pretty obvious from the state of his flat that he was broke,' said Fleet. 'The landlord was the one to let us in, and – according to the uniforms who were with him – almost the first words out of his mouth when he saw Wheeler's body were about the number of weeks Wheeler was in arrears on his rent. And from what we've gathered so far, Wheeler was a loner. Neighbours never saw him with friends, rarely ever saw him going out. The owner of the decorating company Wheeler worked for reckoned Wheeler was suffering from depression. Said he was becoming so unreliable, he'd been considering letting him go.'

'But the timing,' Apte repeated. 'First the Draper boy's body is discovered, next Wheeler receives a phone call from your detective sergeant, and *then* the man commits suicide. Surely you have to concede that the course of events is categorical.'

Fleet tried to ignore the way Apte had described Ben. For some reason, every time anyone referred to him as *the Draper boy*, Fleet felt a flash of irritation. He'd experienced something similar when Adrian Harris, Beaconsfield's headmaster, had insisted on calling him Benjamin, in spite of the fact that, from what Fleet had learned, no one else ever had. In both cases, it seemed an attempt to strip Ben of his identity, to render his death somehow less meaningful.

'As I say,' Fleet responded, 'the timing would suggest a link of some kind. But if Wheeler was struggling already, maybe it was just the memory of his friend going missing – the realisation that Ben was really dead – that finally tipped him over the edge. Maybe that's what Wheeler was sorry about. The way things turned out.'

The PCC did everything but scoff. 'Come now, Detective Inspector. You surely don't believe that? I may not have the investigative background you do, but even to me that sounds like reaching.'

'I would prefer to describe it as keeping an open mind. At

least until we uncover evidence that points us definitively either way.'

'And in the meantime, we're in danger of looking a gift horse in the mouth. Almost overnight, this has become an extremely high-profile case. The entire country is watching, and we have a chance to claim an early win. To put this to bed before there are any embarrassing—'

'I agree with Detective Inspector Fleet.'

When Fleet turned to Webb, he couldn't be sure the man had spoken at all. He was looking down at his phone, apparently not particularly interested in what he saw there, his thumbs nevertheless chasing each other frantically across the screen. He was a thin man, not much older than Fleet, with a round head and a shabby haircut, and clothes he might very well have slept in. He was the complete opposite of Apte, in other words. The PCC was as well groomed as he was well fed. He bore a tie knot the size of a child's fist, and his thick, black hair couldn't have been more perfectly styled had it been tweezered into place strand by strand. He appeared every bit the man in charge, in other words, whereas Webb might have blown in off the street.

And yet it was the man from the Home Office who exuded a sense of authority. When he spoke, both Apte and Superintendent Burton stopped to listen.

Webb finished typing and raised his head, palming his phone the way a con man would an ace from a deck of cards. 'There is no sense rushing to a premature conclusion,' he said. 'Particularly if you are only going to have to rescind it later.'

You, Fleet noted. Not *we*. So he was clearly not here to assume any responsibility. Which begged the question, what was he doing here at all?

Instinctively Fleet trusted Webb even less than he did the

PCC. At least Apte was publicly accountable. Fleet had never heard of Webb until they'd shaken hands across the table, and he still hadn't been told what the man did exactly. Fleet's best guess was that he was a special adviser of some kind. To the home secretary? The prime minister himself? Either way, if Webb was here to represent the government, it was surely Callum Richardson's involvement in the case that had drawn him in.

'But that's precisely my point,' said Apte, looking at Webb. 'There's no reason to suspect we *would* have to rescind it. We have a chance here to demonstrate to the public that, even when it comes to a decades-old murder, the police in this county are firmly in control. After all the years of scandals and cutbacks, it would send a powerful message.'

'Which, if Wheeler is ultimately cleared of responsibility, would be in danger of backfiring,' said Webb. 'I am of course not here to interfere, but it is my belief that we would all stand to benefit to a far greater degree if, instead of anyone leaping to premature conclusions, the investigation is allowed to run its course.'

He looked at Apte meaningfully, and Apte closed his open mouth. From the expression on the PCC's face, he was clearly struggling to understand Webb's reasoning.

Fleet, on the other hand, thought he was starting to.

'Sir,' he said, focusing on Superintendent Burton. 'Given the complexity of the investigation, Nicky and I could really use some extra bodies. The killer already has a twenty-two-year head start on us. With the resources currently at our disposal, we're going to struggle to catch up.'

Had the circumstances been different, Fleet would have been able to predict precisely how Burton would react. When the superintendent had buried Fleet under a mountain of decades-old mispers, he would have had no expectation that Fleet would actually solve any – and the last thing he would have been prepared to offer was any kind of operational assistance. But the situation had evolved beyond anything either Fleet or Burton could possibly have envisaged. Ben Draper wasn't just another missing kid. He was a boy whose murderer had escaped justice for more than twenty years, and whose fate could well turn out to be the cause of the biggest celebrity scandal the country had seen since Savile – not to mention political dynamite.

The superintendent looked at Webb. Webb looked down at his phone. It was a signal of some kind, clearly – just as it was suddenly obvious to Fleet that his instincts about Webb's objective here were right, and that the superintendent had taken the hint, too.

'I believe you have the resources you need, Detective Inspector,' Burton said. 'It is crucial, given the sensitive nature of this investigation, that we proceed as we would in any other comparable situation.'

'Comparable?' echoed Fleet. 'As far as I can see, this case is utterly unique. All I'm asking for is—'

'We have to be seen to be absolutely fair,' Burton cut in. 'You can imagine how the press would spin it if they got wind that extra resources had been pumped into an investigation in which Callum Richardson is a potential suspect. It would be seen as a witch hunt. An attempt on behalf of the government to discredit a political opponent.'

'With respect, sir,' said Fleet tightly, 'isn't that exactly what this is?'

The superintendent clamped his jaw. Webb looked up from his phone, peering at Fleet from underneath his thick blond eyebrows, which were as unruly and dishevelled as his hair.

'What are you implying, Detective Inspector?' said Apte.

Fleet focused on Webb, who clearly understood precisely what Fleet was implying. Webb – and whoever he worked for – didn't want Ben's murder pinned on Wheeler, because he didn't want it pinned on *anyone*. Not yet, anyway; not while Callum Richardson was still in the frame. By keeping the investigation active, yet denying it adequate resources, Webb could ensure Richardson would continue to be linked to an open murder enquiry every time he was mentioned in the press. If it turned out that Richardson was guilty, so much the better, but in the meantime even the uncertainty – the inevitable insinuations – would be enough.

In other words, it wasn't the fire Webb was interested in. It was the smoke.

'Are you really that scared of the man?' Fleet said, ignoring Apte's question and talking directly to Webb. 'Is your boss really so afraid of having to make a fair fight to keep his job?'

Don't get into politics, Rob, the superintendent had told Fleet once. And yet the longer he worked as a copper, the more he came to understand that the real challenge was keeping politics *out*. You only had to look around the room. Burton had always been a yes man. It was the reason he had that crown on his sleeve. Apte had stood for his position as a candidate representing the ruling party, so obviously he would do whatever people like Webb told him to do – assuming he ever figured out what that was. As for Webb himself, in theory he had no authority here, and yet there he sat with his eyebrows and his phone, subtly manipulating everyone else around the table.

'That's enough, Detective Inspector Fleet,' said Burton, in

a tone Fleet recognised all too well. So far today, in spite of their mutual animosity, they'd been managing to keep things between them relatively civil, probably because there were other people in the room. But steadily they'd drifted back on to more familiar ground.

'You have been given your instructions,' Burton growled. 'I believe that will be all. Please keep me informed of any further developments. *Before* I am obliged to read about them in the press.'

Fleet stood. He looked at Apte, and then at Webb, who for the first time in the entire meeting had set his phone face down on the table. He was staring at Fleet impassively, but there was no mistaking the curiosity in his eyes.

Fleet turned back to face Burton. He hesitated for a moment, thinking of all the things he might say, then clamped his lips and raised his hand in a salute.

He had to resist slamming the door on the way out. At a set of fire doors, he gave in to the urge, but the hinges were hydraulic and he might as well have tried to slam the door through water.

In the lift he fired Nicky a text – *We're on our own* – and as he glared at the screen waiting for Nicky's reply, his phone vibrated in his hand. *Randolph Green*, read the caller ID, and after checking he had enough signal, Fleet swiped to answer the pathologist's call.

'Randy?'

'Rob. Can you talk?'

'Randy, it's . . . it's not a good time. And I'm probably just about to lose reception. Can I call you back when I get to the car?'

'Do that. I'll wait by the phone. But make it quick, Rob. You're going to want to hear this as soon as possible.'

Ben – March 1997

(Two months before his death)

Ben was tucked away in a corner of the library, a sheet of paper and a book on the history of Beaconsfield spread out on the table before him. He'd been sketching an image of the old chapel, the one that had burned down in the fire, and that had stood near the graveyard he'd visited with Callum and the others. The old building hadn't been as grand as the new one, but to Ben's eye it was prettier, like the contrast between a parish church and a cathedral.

'That's pretty good,' said a voice, and Ben gave a start. He'd been so involved in what he was doing, he hadn't noticed Callum approach.

'Oh, thanks, I . . .' Ben tried to cover the piece of paper with his hands, but Callum reached across and pulled it free. He sat down on the seat next to Ben's, so close that their knees were touching, and held up the drawing in front of him.

'More than *pretty* good, actually,' he said.

Ben flushed – half with embarrassment, half with pride. He never showed anyone his drawings, least of all Callum. Ben would have thought Callum would consider drawing stupid. Or not stupid, as such. Inconsequential.

Callum set the drawing to one side. 'So, how's everything going?'

Ben blinked. 'Fine. I guess. I mean . . .'

'Because I heard what happened this morning.'

Callum had been smiling pleasantly, and even though the

shape of his lips didn't change, his eyes, always pale, turned cold.

'This morning?' said Ben.

Callum waited.

'Oh, you mean in the physics lab. It was no big deal. I mean, I guess I might have overreacted, but—'

'*Overreacted*,' Callum echoed. The smile fell from his face. 'You started a fight.'

Ben swallowed. At first he'd been glad to see Callum. They hadn't actually spoken in almost a week, because Callum had made it clear from the start that Ben and the others shouldn't be seen together too often. But Ben had done everything he was supposed to do, and more besides, and he'd been hoping that Callum would be pleased. Pleased enough, maybe, that Ben would be able to convince him that there was no need for them all to remain so far apart.

But there was no way Ben would have dared to raise the subject now.

'I didn't *start* it,' he tried to explain. 'He was talking shit about my *mum*. He called her a whore. A *slut*.' Even as he recalled what the boy had said – a boy he didn't even know – Ben flushed with unsatiated rage.

'So you shoved him. And in the process earned yourself another full week of detention.'

'Yeah, but . . . what was I supposed to do? I mean, everyone heard what he said. I'm not going to just sit there and—'

Callum's hand shot out and seized one of Ben's fingers. Ben was too surprised to react, and before he'd registered what was happening, Callum was wrenching his finger against the joint, forcing it towards his wrist. He was about to cry out – in shock, in pain – but Callum's other hand reached around Ben's neck and clamped across his mouth.

'*Shut up and listen to me,*' he hissed.

Wide-eyed, Ben saw Callum check around the room. But there was nobody watching them. They were as tucked away as it was possible for them to be, with the other pupils all facing in the opposite direction. It was the reason Ben had sat here in the first place.

'Are you listening?' said Callum, his breath damp against Ben's ear.

Ben did his best to nod. He tried to speak, to say yes, yes, he *was*, but all that came out was a muffled moan.

'I helped you,' said Callum. 'And you promised you'd help *me*. Didn't you?' He removed his hand from across Ben's mouth, but if anything tightened his grip on Ben's finger.

'Yes!' said Ben. 'I—'

'*Lower your voice.*'

'OK, OK! Just . . . let go of my finger, will you? *Please.*'

'I will once you've answered my question.'

'I said already! *Yes!* I said I'd help! I did!'

'So why are you so determined to *fuck everything up*?' Callum released his hold and Ben collapsed forward, whipping his arm away and cradling his throbbing hand in his lap. The pain was white-hot, so intense he almost couldn't feel it at all.

'I'm sorry, Callum, it won't . . . it won't happen again, I promise!'

Callum was regarding Ben coldly. But then his expression seemed to alter, as though more than anything he was disappointed that Ben had let him down.

'I thought you wanted to be our friend,' Callum said. 'To be *my* friend.'

'I did! I do!'

Callum shook his head. 'Well, if that's true, you've got a funny way of showing it. You do realise that if you get yourself expelled, it's all over? Everything we talked about. Everything *you* said you wanted.'

'No, I know, I just . . . I'm sorry, Callum. Really! I just . . . I didn't think. I got so angry, and—'

Callum raised his hand, and for a moment Ben thought his friend meant to hit him. But then Callum's hand settled on his shoulder, and gave it a gentle squeeze.

'I know this is hard for you. I *do*. You're the one doing most of the work, and most of the time you're having to do it on your own. Which is tough, right? Particularly in a place like this.'

'It is! And actually that was something I wanted to—'

'But you understand why it has to be this way,' Callum interrupted. 'Don't you?'

Ben, reluctantly, gave a nod.

'If they see us together too often,' Callum explained, 'there's a chance they'll figure out what's going on. You need to be like . . . like what's his name. The kid in your dorm who's always hanging around the chapel. Father Steiner's *favourite*,' he added meaningfully.

'Isaac,' said Ben. 'His name's Isaac.' Just the mention of Isaac made Ben uncomfortable. Isaac's only friend at Beaconsfield seemed to be Father Steiner. Ben was just *pretending* to be alone, but even so, most of the time, he *felt* it, which made him wonder if he and Isaac weren't actually the same.

'But it's just for the time being,' Callum consoled him. 'OK?' He squeezed Ben's shoulder again, and this time Ben was grateful for his touch. 'After this is over, we'll be able to hang out all the time. I *promise*.' Now Callum grinned: that warm, winning smile he had, that always made Ben think he should go on TV.

Callum had been flicking through the pages of the book

Ben had been copying from. After a moment he stopped, then squeezed Ben's shoulder one final time. He got to his feet.

'In the meantime,' he told Ben, 'keep your head down. And if you get another urge to lose your temper, try to remember what's at stake here.'

He slid *A History of Beaconsfield College* closer to Ben, then turned and headed for the door.

Ben's eyes dropped to the pages that were spread before him – the pages Callum had clearly wanted him to see. It was the chapter in the book about the fire, and an image of Beaconsfield in flames.

Wednesday 23 October, 7.17 p.m.

> Nicky? It's me. Sorry to call so late, but . . . Well, you're going to want to hear this. I had a call from Randy.

> *About Lance Wheeler? That was quick. Even for Randy.*

> No, he . . . he hasn't had a chance to conduct a full examination. It'll be a day or two before we get his post-mortem report. But he gave me a heads-up.

> *On what?*

> On what he's expecting to conclude. Nicky, listen: it wasn't suicide.

> . . .

> Nicky? Are you still there?

> *Yes, I . . . Shit. What the hell does that mean? I mean, I know what it means, but . . . Shit. Was he sure? How could he tell?*

> Sure enough to pick up the phone. He said something about the ligature. The marks on Lance Wheeler's neck.

> *Jesus. I mean . . . Jesus.*

> Quite.

> *So what do we do? Have you told Burton?*

> I . . . No. They're playing games, Nicky. Burton, the PCC, the Home Office. This isn't about Ben for them. For one reason or another, it's all about Callum Richardson. Which, to be fair to Randy, is why he called me. I guess he must have seen the politics coming before I did, wanted to give me a chance to stay a step ahead.

> *Good old Randy. I know you think he's a pain in the arse, but his heart's in the right place. Did you know he's friends with my dad? Randy's the one who stuck up for me when I told Dad I wanted to be a copper. Dad said if I wanted to work with the law, I should be a solicitor, like him. Randy's the one who convinced him I had a mind of my own.*

> Well, I definitely owe him. But we're not going to be able to keep this to ourselves for long. The way I figure it, we've got a day or so to work out what exactly we're dealing with here, before Randy has to file his report and someone higher up leaks it to the press. Which, the way everyone seems to feel about Callum Richardson, I guarantee they'll do.

> *Christ. Once the press starts working everyone into a frenzy, this whole investigation is going to be like fishing in a whirlpool.*

> Quite. The good news is, I managed to get our interview with Richardson pulled forward to midday tomorrow.

> *How did you manage that?*

> I spoke to Richardson's solicitor, threatened to call in a favour with the commissioner of the Metropolitan Police and have a bunch of squad cars turn up outside Richardson's home address. After first tipping off the press, of course.

> *Do you even know the commissioner of the Metropolitan Police?*

> Never met her before in my life. But listen, Nicky. While I'm talking to Richardson, I want you to stay on Melissa.

> *Anything you say, boss. Do you think . . . if Randy's right . . . do you think she's in danger?*

> To be honest, I don't know what to think. But we need to bring her in while we still can.

> *That's going to be easier said than done. But don't worry, boss, I'll think of something.*

> Thanks, Nicky. Stay in touch.

> *Will do. Oh . . . and, boss?*

> What's up?

> *Just, when you see Callum Richardson . . . play nice.*

Thursday 24 October, 11.43 a.m.

London. The question Fleet always asked himself whenever he was obliged to visit was, *why?* Why would so many people willingly do it to themselves? It wasn't as though it was cheap. It wasn't good for their health. It was nine million frantic pairs of feet scrabbling for a spot on the same hamster wheel – one that had been designed for half that number, and that was so clogged it regularly stopped spinning.

Except: the museums. The theatres. The libraries. The cafés and the restaurants and the shops. That was what Holly had always countered with on those rare occasions when she would try to convince Fleet to go with her on one of her visits. And the crowds, she used to say, were the point. If you are tired of London, you are tired of life, ran the adage, and Holly was a firm believer in it.

To be fair, it wasn't as though Fleet liked his own city much either. It was just as clogged, and almost as expensive, and if it had any notable museums, Fleet had never visited them. He might have chosen to live in the country, he supposed, but the countryside didn't have home delivery, and Fleet was a terrible cook. The seaside reminded him too much of home. Of growing up and losing his sister. Which left . . . what? A hut on the side of a mountain somewhere? But then there would be snow to deal with, and men of Fleet's height and weight didn't need anything else to slow them down.

So maybe it wasn't just London. Maybe it *was* life that was the problem. Or maybe not life as such, but life without

Holly. Because Fleet knew that, were she to ask him to, and it was the only thing that was stopping them being together, he would move to London in a heartbeat.

He dodged a passer-by's umbrella, and only narrowly avoided stepping into the path of a motorcycle courier. His foot landed in a puddle instead, soaking him to his sock. It had started raining just as his train pulled into Waterloo station, and was now coming down with a vengeance – as though the weather had realised it was late for the season and was frantically trying to catch up.

By the time Fleet found the building he was looking for, the downpour had begun to ease, but too late to make any difference to the state of his overcoat and suit. He had enough of a window before the interview was due to start to find a bathroom and tidy himself up, but as soon as he stepped into the lobby of the glass-fronted building, he found himself face-to-face with a chirpy-looking receptionist seated behind the mahogany front desk. *Lattey and Lawe*, read the gleaming brass lettering on the wall behind her.

'Detective Inspector Robin Fleet,' Fleet told the woman, as he discreetly tried to shake himself off. 'I'm here to see Callum Richardson. He's a client of yours, I belie—'

'Detective Inspector,' the receptionist chirruped, interrupting him. 'Mr Lawe and Mr Richardson are expecting you. I'll take you right through. Would you like me to hang up your, um, coat?'

Fleet's overcoat was heavy from the rain, and when the receptionist rounded the desk to take it from him, her arm sagged under its weight. To her credit, her smile only faltered momentarily.

Callum Richardson and his solicitor were waiting for Fleet in a ground-floor conference room. The solicitor, the appropriately named Mr Lawe, rose when the receptionist showed Fleet inside. Callum Richardson, Fleet noted, did not. He was seated on one of the expensive-looking leather chairs, pushed back from the table, with an ankle propped on one knee and his hands linked in his lap. Beneath his dark, swept-back hair, he was scowling like a moody teenager, and his right thumb was drumming furiously against the knuckle of his left. It was a marked contrast to the dynamic, forceful persona Richardson projected on his morning television show. Whenever Fleet had happened to catch it, Richardson was invariably holding forth, haranguing his guests and pontificating to his audience.

'Detective Inspector Fleet?' said Lawe. 'A pleasure to meet you. I'm Herbert Lawe, and this is my client, Mr Richardson.'

Fleet shook the solicitor's proffered hand. He nodded at Richardson, whose only response was to uncross his legs.

'Please,' said Lawe, 'take a seat.'

There were six chairs around the circular table, and Lawe had gestured Fleet towards one directly opposite Richardson, whose pristine navy suit put Fleet's to shame. In between them on the surface of the table was a tray of china coffee cups and a plate of pastries, but otherwise the room was almost bare. There were no phones, no TV screens. The windows were frosted, and when the door had closed behind Fleet, he could tell from the noise it made that it was probably soundproof. It was like being shown into an airlock.

'Can I get you anything? Tea? Coffee? A towel, perhaps?' Lawe's tone suggested he was attempting to lighten the mood. Neither Fleet nor Richardson smiled.

'Thank you for agreeing to be interviewed so promptly, Mr Richardson,' Fleet said as he settled on his seat. The chair was cantilevered, and for the briefest of moments as he sat down, he was worried it might not take his weight.

Richardson leaned forward, and spoke with the intensity of someone who'd so far been struggling to hold his tongue. 'For the record, Detective Inspector, and before you go any further, I want you to realise if you don't already that this entire investigation is a charade.'

Lawe was halfway towards sitting, and Fleet caught his look of alarm. The solicitor had a worried air about him anyway, from the lines on his forehead to the colour of his hair: it was grey all over, even though Lawe couldn't have been more than five or six years older than Fleet.

'It's bullshit,' Richardson continued. 'Plain and simple. And if your superiors think they're going to intimidate me, you can tell them they've got another think coming. All my life there have been people out to get me, and not once have I ever backed down from a fight.'

'You think someone is out to get you, Mr Richardson?' said Fleet. He kept his voice even, but immediately he was thinking about Lance Wheeler. About his body swinging by his belt. If Melissa was in danger, who was to say Callum Richardson wasn't, too? On the other hand, Richardson didn't exactly strike Fleet as the vulnerable type.

Richardson scoffed as he reclined in his chair. 'Oh, please. You work for Manish Apte. Am I right? And Apte is a stooge – a political appointment with no more backbone than a jellyfish. He'll do whatever his paymasters tell him to do.'

'Manish Apte is a civilian, Mr Richardson. Neither he nor his political associates have any direct authority over the course of active police investigations.'

'Is that a joke, Detective Inspector? Or are you stupid enough to actually believe that?'

'Callum, please—'

Richardson held up a hand to silence his solicitor. 'Apte is a Tory. The Tories are more afraid of me than anyone. They see my transition into politics as a direct attempt to muscle in on their constituents. The longer I'm associated with any kind of criminal proceedings, the better it is for them all round.'

Fleet looked at Lawe, who'd apparently given up attempting to intervene. His look of resigned despondency suggested he knew full well how much success he was likely to have trying to limit what Richardson chose to say.

'Just look at the timing if you really need convincing,' Richardson insisted. 'My party is a fortnight away from its official launch, and has already attracted more financial backing than any other anti-establishment political organisation in recent history. And suddenly the police decide to respond to an "anonymous" tip about something that may or may not have happened twenty-two years ago? They're literally going around digging up skeletons, for Christ's sake.'

'I can assure you, Mr Richardson,' Fleet said, 'it happened. Ben Draper was murdered. I've seen his skeleton myself.'

'I'm not disputing the fact a boy was killed,' Richardson countered. 'What I'm telling you is that Ben Draper isn't the only victim here.'

'Maybe not,' Fleet responded. 'But for the time being at least, he is the only victim I care about. And Ben Draper wasn't just a boy, Mr Richardson. He was your friend. And by your own admission twenty-two years ago, you were one of the last people to see him alive. So let's talk about that. Shall we?'

The silence crackled. *Play nice*, Nicky had urged Fleet, and he was aware the interview hadn't exactly got off to the most

113

auspicious of starts. Richardson fixed Fleet with a look he usually reserved for people like Manish Apte when he was interviewing them on television; for politicians and public figures who'd crossed whatever moral line Richardson and his producers had decided to draw that day.

'So,' said Fleet, opening his notebook. 'Tell me about Ben, Mr Richardson. How would you characterise your relationship with him?'

He looked at Richardson evenly. From his expression, Richardson seemed to be seriously considering refusing to answer. But at a nod and a hopeful look from Lawe, he recrossed his legs and drew back his shoulders.

'There was no relationship, Detective Inspector. The truth is I barely knew Ben, and frankly I'm struggling even to remember what he looked like.'

It was a line Fleet had heard so frequently over the past few days, it was losing its power to surprise.

'All I can recall about Ben is that he was, frankly, a loser,' Richardson said. 'Nobody liked him. I may have felt sorry for him, and we might have involved him once or twice in our games, but that doesn't mean he and I were friends.'

Even though Fleet suspected Richardson was doing what any politician would in the circumstances, and attempting to distance himself from events, Fleet wasn't entirely certain he was lying. In the original witness statements, there did seem to be a lack of consensus about just how close Richardson had been to Ben. Some interviewees professed to having seen them hanging around together; others insisted Ben had spent his entire time at Beaconsfield on his own.

'By *we*,' said Fleet, 'I assume you are referring to Melissa Haynes and Lance Wheeler. You remember them, I presume, Mr Richardson?'

Fleet was watching for some reaction when he mentioned Lance's name, but Richardson didn't so much as twitch.

'Of course I do,' he said.

'And these games you mention. Do you mean games like the one you were playing at the time Ben went missing? Hide-and-seek, I believe. Is that right? Would you be able to talk me through it?'

It was an easy opening, and Richardson clearly couldn't resist. 'It really is quite straightforward, Detective Inspector. One person hides and the other people try to find them.'

Fleet ignored the sarcasm. 'I would have thought a group of fifteen-year-old kids would have been a bit beyond playing hide-and-seek.'

Richardson shrugged. 'What can I tell you? It was boarding school. We had to find something to do.' He paused for a moment, then added, 'If you didn't want to die of boredom, you needed to make your own fun.'

'So Ben was the one hiding? And the rest of you were looking for him? You, Melissa and Lance? I have to say, that sounds less like a game to me – more like a hunt. In the version I remember playing, everybody hid, and only one person started off looking for them.'

Another shrug. 'Call it what you like. It doesn't really matter. Because as you know, we never found him.'

'Where exactly were you looking for him?'

'We'd agreed to stick to the southern section of the campus, and the woods were the best place to hide, so for the most part we searched for Ben there. From what I recall we started off at the lake.'

There was a small lake where the woods on the campus were at their thickest, Fleet knew. At first, when fears for Ben's safety were at their height, there was a suspicion he might have accidentally drowned. But it had taken a pair of divers barely half a day to search the shallow water, and they'd found nothing connected to Ben except a pair of his old trainers. One of his dorm mates later confessed to having thrown them in there several weeks earlier – as a joke, he claimed, which investigators at the time had taken as proof that Ben was being bullied, increasing the likelihood in their minds that he had run away.

Fleet checked his notes. 'You claimed in your original statement that you left the main building with the others, including Ben, at around two-thirty p.m. None of you were seen all afternoon, until you, Melissa and Lance were spotted near the entrance to the main building at just before six p.m.'

'If you say so, Detective Inspector. I don't recall the precise timings.'

'At what point did Ben disappear?'

'The last we saw of him was when he went off to hide. So a count of sixty after we reached the lake.'

'And you kept looking for more than three hours? On a day very much like today, from what I understand.'

'We looked for some of that time. Not all of it. The rest of the time we sat and smoked. We decided fairly quickly that Ben must have cheated. That he was probably already back inside.'

'And yet you didn't think to raise the alarm when he failed to show for dinner that evening. It was one of his teachers in the end who reported him absent, wasn't it? But not until the middle of the following morning.'

'You would know better than I do. I've told you the extent of my involvement in what happened.'

Richardson was regarding Fleet coolly, and maybe it was just the man's youthful demeanour, but once again Fleet had the sense that he was dealing with an obnoxious kid: one who knew he'd done something wrong, but was aware, too, that there was nothing anyone could do about it.

'Where did you go when you went inside, Mr Richardson?'

'To be honest, I don't remember. Probably to Melissa's room.'

'Boys were allowed in the female dormitories, were they?'

'No,' answered Richardson. 'They were not. But you know what they say about rules. And we couldn't hang out in the boys' wing. Lance and I were in a dorm of twelve, but the girls' rooms were smaller. Melissa had a double, and her roommate was hardly ever around.'

'So, for a large portion of the day of Ben's disappearance,' said Fleet, 'the only people able to confirm your whereabouts were your two closest friends. The people who, along with you, were the last ones to see Ben alive.'

'Now wait just a minute, Detective Inspector,' interjected Lawe. 'My client is here voluntarily. We even agreed to reschedule several of his urgent appointments in response to your request to expedite this interview. We did not do so in the expectation that you would present us with slights and insinuations.'

Richardson once again held up a hand. 'It's fine, Herb. He's only doing what he's been told to. *Just following orders.* Isn't that the phrase, Detective Inspector?'

His smile was a deliberate provocation. Fleet had seen Richardson goading interviewees on his TV show in a similar manner. He would say something inflammatory, or even deliberately insulting, just to get a rise.

'And anyway,' Richardson went on, when Fleet failed to react, 'it was a weekend, meaning the school was half empty. And it's a large campus. I doubt anyone who was there that day could claim to have an alibi for the entire twenty-four-hour period.'

Fleet tapped his pen against his notebook.

'Have you stayed in touch, Mr Richardson? With Melissa Haynes. With Lance Wheeler.'

'I can't say that I have. We'd drifted apart even before we'd finished school.'

'So you haven't seen or spoken to either of them since you graduated?'

'My client has already answered that question, Detective Inspector.'

Fleet continued to look at Richardson.

'No, Detective Inspector. I have not seen or spoken to either Melissa Haynes or Lance Wheeler since the three of us graduated from Beaconsfield. Is that categorical enough for you?'

'Perfectly,' said Fleet. 'Thank you. Although I am curious, too, about your impressions of their relationships with Ben. Did they feel the same way about him as you did?'

'You would have to ask them, Detective Inspector. Assuming you are able to find them. Personally I wouldn't know where to even begin looking for them.'

'There's no need to worry about that, Mr Richardson. We've already tracked them down.'

Fleet was again watching Richardson closely, and for the first time – unless Fleet was imagining it – Richardson betrayed a flash of unease.

'Well,' he said, 'there you go then. You can ask them yourself. Although, if you want my *impression* . . . I would have to say that, whereas I was largely indifferent to Ben, the others actively disliked him. Lance was . . . resentful. He . . . Well. He didn't like the idea of Ben muscling in on our group.'

Fleet recalled what Father Steiner had told them about Lance; his suggestion that Lance might have had feelings for Richardson that went further than simple friendship.

'Muscling in on your *group*?' Fleet echoed, emphasising the final word.

Richardson sneered. 'On *me*, then, if you prefer. He never came out and admitted the way he felt about me, but I don't think either of us was in any doubt. As for Melissa, she was always friendly to Ben's face, but the truth was, she didn't appreciate his hanging around with us either. She was always the jealous type.'

'Again, do you mean jealous in a romantic sense, Mr Richardson? Melissa was your girlfriend, wasn't she?'

'She was, and yes, I do. It took me a little while to realise it, but Melissa wasn't exactly stable. She had . . . daddy issues, I suppose you could call them.' Again, there was a sneer audible in Richardson's tone. As before, Fleet thought about what Father Steiner had said, about Richardson having had *followers*, and it was becoming clearer to Fleet how someone like Richardson might have taken advantage of his friends' devotion. How easily he might have preyed on their weaknesses.

'Between you and me,' Richardson went on, 'Melissa and Lance had some rather outlandish ideas. That's one of the reasons the three of us drifted apart.'

'What kind of outlandish ideas?'

'Well, for one thing, they were obsessed with trying to get Beaconsfield shut down. They said . . . they said that, if they could have, they would have burned the place to the ground.'

Fleet blinked. 'Excuse me?'

'Beaconsfield had been destroyed by a fire once already, and they regarded the incident as their . . . inspiration.'

'Why on earth would they have wanted the school closed down?'

Richardson paused for a moment before answering. He tilted his head. 'Where were you educated, Detective Inspector? A state comprehensive, I would imagine. Which I don't mean to sound in any way disparaging.'

And yet he managed to make it sound exactly that.

Fleet allowed his silence to be his answer.

'Well,' said Richardson, 'if you've never been to boarding school yourself, it would be hard to comprehend quite how dispiriting it can be. To be shown – not just told – that your parents don't want you around. Melissa in particular felt like she was being punished. For who she was. For what she wanted to be.'

'What do you mean?'

'She had ambitions to become an actress. Either an actress or a photographer. Her father was determined that would never happen. She was to be something *respectable*. Something he could brag about to his friends. He was a bit of a control freak, by all accounts. I know for a fact he used to hit Melissa's mother. It wouldn't surprise me if he hurt Melissa physically as well.'

There was something knowing in Richardson's expression that Fleet didn't care for. 'What about Lance?' he asked.

'Lance was at Beaconsfield on a scholarship. It was so far away from the world he grew up in, it was as though his parents had sent him away to a different planet. He didn't adjust particularly well.' Richardson gave a sniff, whether in sympathy or contempt, Fleet couldn't tell.

'So you can understand, Detective Inspector, why Melissa and Lance hated Beaconsfield as much as they did. The school became a symbol to them: a physical representation of everything that was wrong with their lives. With their entire existence, in fact. Some days it would be all they talked about.'

Fleet thought back to his conversation with Nicky. She'd described boarding school in very similar terms, he recalled.

'Are you suggesting it ever turned into more than that?' Fleet asked. 'Into more than just talk, I mean.'

'Again,' said Richardson, 'you would have to take that up with Melissa and Lance.'

Fleet couldn't escape the feeling that he was being played somehow – nudged down a path that Richardson wanted him to follow.

'Would you be willing to provide a DNA sample, Mr Richardson?' said Fleet, changing tack. 'Purely to allow us to eliminate you from our investigations, of course.'

He didn't think it worth mentioning how unlikely it was that any workable DNA traces would be recovered from the crypt where Ben's body had been found. The scene of Lance Wheeler's murder would hopefully prove a different matter, but as the news of his death was still to get out, it was only his killer who would know to be concerned.

'Gladly,' said Richardson, apparently without hesitation. 'Anything I can do to help.'

'And it would be helpful to have an itinerary of your movements for the past week. If it's not too much trouble.'

This time Richardson narrowed his eyes slightly, as though puzzled by the request. But once again he didn't demur. 'I'll ask my assistant to print it out for you.'

Richardson's solicitor glanced ostentatiously at his watch. 'As you know, Detective Inspector, my client has other appointments he needs to get to, but there is one final matter we would like to raise before we wrap things up.' Lawe reached below the table. He produced a laptop and set it on the surface, opening the screen and angling it towards Fleet. The computer whirred into life, and an image became visible of what looked like CCTV footage on pause.

The solicitor set the video playing, and Fleet leaned closer. The footage was low-quality but full-colour, and showed what appeared to be somebody's lounge. There was a large sofa wrapped around a coffee table, and a pale, thick-piled rug on the dark wood floor. The camera had been set high in a corner, so that most of the room was visible. The time on the screen showed 01.43, and the date was 5 October.

'What am I looking at?' said Fleet, as the time continued to tick by.

Even as he spoke, a figure entered the room through a door in the top left corner of the screen. Their face was covered by a balaclava, and they were dressed all in black.

'My client's sitting room,' said Lawe, in answer to Fleet's question. 'Mr Richardson was travelling at the time, and there were contractors carrying out renovations, meaning security wasn't as tight as it would normally be.'

'If you want proof that someone is *out to get me*, Detective Inspector, then here it is,' put in Richardson. He sounded angry, just as he had when he'd spoken shortly after Fleet first entered the room.

Fleet watched as the figure in black slowly circled Richardson's living room. They were taking their time – as though they were looking, but not for anything in particular. Nothing was disturbed, nothing touched. The figure moved with an eerie calm, as though it was their own room they were surveying, not somebody else's.

Fleet's eyes flicked again to the date stamp in the corner. Ben's body was discovered on 18 October, but the 5th felt significant in Fleet's mind for some reason, too. And then he remembered: it was the date the anonymous tip about the location of Ben's body had been received. The information had taken almost two weeks to work its way through the system.

The figure on-screen moved closer to the position of the camera. From the casual nature of their movements, they seemed unaware there was anything monitoring them – but when the figure looked up, it was directly into the camera. Whether they'd only just spotted it, or they'd known it was there all along, there was no way to tell. But one thing was clear: they weren't afraid. They didn't run, didn't hide. In fact, even though it was impossible to tell through the balaclava, Fleet had the distinct impression that, whoever it was, they were smiling.

Lawe hit pause on the recording. 'The intruder is caught again on another camera in an upstairs bedroom, but this is the clearest shot we have of them. By our estimation, they were in my client's house for at least seventeen minutes.'

'Was anything taken?' said Fleet, still studying the screen.

'Not that my client has been able to determine.'

'So all they did was have a look around?'

Richardson made a disgusted noise. 'You see, Herb, I told you it would be pointless to report it.'

Fleet turned. 'You didn't tell the police you'd had a break-in?'

'No, I did not.'

'Given his public profile, my client decided reporting the incident would cause more problems than it would solve,' explained Lawe. 'But now, in light of everything that has happened since, and given the entirely unsubstantiated rumours about Mr Richardson's involvement in—'

'Let's not beat around the bush, Detective Inspector,' Richardson interrupted. 'You're here because you've been tasked with uncovering something to connect me to Ben's murder. You won't find anything, I assure you. But clearly you're not the only person who's looking.'

Fleet frowned. 'How can you be sure the break-in is connected to the investigation?' he said, even as the image of Lance Wheeler hanging from his belt flashed once again in his mind.

'Because the intruder also left this,' Richardson replied, and he reached across the table to tap the keyboard. The screen switched to a different window. In place of the CCTV footage, there was a photograph. It was a picture of a sheet of paper, entirely blank except for a single typed sentence right in the centre.

Your turn to hide, the note read.

Thursday 24 October, 3.41 p.m.

Nicky was searching for street numbers. None of the properties she passed appeared to have any.

She wondered how the local postmen managed. Although, it was entirely possible they avoided this end of town completely. Nicky wasn't afraid of physical confrontation. Given her sex and her size, she'd become accustomed to having to put large, mouthy blokes in their place – felons and fellow police officers, both. She'd also been taking kickboxing lessons twice a week for the past six years. But even she felt slightly uneasy walking around Blackhawk on her own, in spite of the fact it was the middle of the afternoon. It was one of the most deprived neighbourhoods in the city, and a focal point for pimps and pushers – as far away from Beaconsfield as it was possible to get and still be within a twenty-mile radius.

89 Blackhawk Rise, read the destination she'd entered on Google Maps, and as far as Nicky could tell, she was standing right at the sharp end of the little red pin. But just ahead of her, the row of dilapidated bungalows came to an end, making way for a larger building set back from the road that had clearly at one point been a church. It was nothing like the chapel at Beaconsfield, however. This building looked more like a block of Lego that had been fished out from amid the cobwebs under the sofa. It was squat, with a flat roof and an inelegantly tapered bell tower that appeared to be missing its bell.

Nicky checked the map again, wondering whether the

address would turn out to be yet another dead end. So far today, her search for Melissa Haynes had taken her to three different corners of the city – the only remaining clues to her whereabouts that Nicky had been able to uncover being the places of residence Melissa had given on past benefits application forms. The first two addresses had turned out to be squats, and no one Nicky had spoken to had ever heard of Melissa – at least as far as they were willing to admit to a representative of the local constabulary. The third address had taken Nicky to a detached mock-Tudor mansion on a leafy street in one of the city's poshest suburbs, on the route out to Beaconsfield itself. Again, nobody there had professed to ever having heard of Melissa Haynes, and this time Nicky had believed it. The house was so far removed – literally, metaphorically – from the life Melissa clearly inhabited, that Nicky figured Melissa must have either plucked the address at random, or been making a joke at the expense of whichever poor sap had processed her income support claim at the local Jobcentre.

Either way, for Nicky it had been a wasted trip, and now she was down to the last address on her meagre list. If Blackhawk failed to check out, she would be back to square one. There were no more leads, no more hints as to where Melissa might be. Even Melissa's parents had apparently lost touch with her. Her father had died in 2015 – killed in a car wreck on his way home from the pub – but her mother lived in Somerset, and Nicky had spoken to her on the telephone. Veronica Haynes had claimed she hadn't seen her daughter since Melissa left home at the age of eighteen, almost two decades ago now. And Nicky had believed that Melissa's mother was telling the truth even before the woman dissolved into tears. The whole conversation had left Nicky feeling distinctly unsettled, and not just because she'd resorted to assuring Melissa's mother that her daughter was almost certainly fine – something Nicky was becoming less convinced of by the hour. As she'd hung up, she'd also found herself thinking about her own mother, comparing her situation with Melissa's. The truth, Nicky had realised, was that she was jealous. Not of Melissa's troubles, obviously – Nicky wouldn't have wished Melissa's circumstances on anybody. Rather, it was the reaction of Melissa's mother that Nicky coveted: the knowledge that, whatever had transpired in the past, she still cared about her daughter in a way Nicky's mum had never cared about her.

She turned her attention back to the former church, forcing herself to focus on the matter at hand.

Perhaps the church was another squat. Given its condition, it was about all the building looked good for. And maybe this time someone inside would own up to having heard of Melissa.

There was no gate, just an open driveway, gravelled and overgrown with weeds. Nicky almost didn't bother with the front door, fully expecting it to be locked and bolted, and she was already veering to head around back when she spotted a postcard-sized sign beside what appeared to be a recently installed doorbell. *Shining Light charitable foundation*, read the notice. *Please ring for assistance.*

She pressed the bell, which continued to buzz for the second or two she held her finger on the button. After a moment, she heard the door being unbolted, and took a step back. Experience had taught her to give people a little space before introducing herself as a police officer on their doorstep.

'Can I help you?'

The man who'd opened the door was tall, youngish and neatly dressed, with a collar and tie poking out above the neckline of his jumper. He was the exact opposite of what the building had led Nicky to expect.

'Good afternoon,' she said, showing her ID. 'I'm Detective Sergeant Nicola Collins. Are you . . . Is this . . . What *is* this place?' She was able to see over the man's shoulder, and the corridor beyond looked warm and welcoming. And the building clearly extended further back than Nicky had realised. She could see all the way through to a yard at the rear, which from the brief glimpse she was able to steal, appeared far better tended to than the front part of the building's exterior.

'We're Shining Light,' the man said, as though it were obvious. Then, at the flicker of confusion on Nicky's face, he smiled. 'It's kind of cheesy, I know. But I guess it doesn't matter much what we call this place. It's what we do here that counts.'

'Which is what exactly?'

'We're a community. A shelter for the homeless, basically, but also quite a lot more than that. We—' The man interrupted himself with a frown. 'What do you want, Detective Sergeant? If you don't know what this place is, why are you here?'

'I'm looking for a woman called Melissa Haynes.'

The man's face fell. He glanced behind him, then turned back and opened the door wider.

'In that case,' he said, 'you'd better come in.'

The man led her along the hallway, past a pokey-looking office and into a room with space for at least a dozen people to sit comfortably on the ragtag assortment of sofas and armchairs. There was a pool table at one end of the room, and a large, wall-mounted TV at the other. Nothing looked new, but it all appeared clean and well cared for.

'You probably noticed the size of my office on the way through,' the man said. 'This is about the most comfortable place for us to talk. And we should have some privacy. Most of the companions are still at work.' He offered his hand. 'My name's Zack, by the way. Zack Lawrence. I'm the manager.'

'*Companions*, you said,' Nicky responded, shaking the manager's hand. 'Is that what you call the residents here?'

'Right,' said Zack. 'We . . .' He seemed to notice the sound from the television, which was tuned to one of the news channels. Zack had perched on the arm of a sofa, and he scanned the seats around him for the remote control. When he found it he pointed it at the TV, but hesitated before hitting any of the buttons. Nicky turned to see what had caught his attention. The face of Callum Richardson filled the screen. He was stepping from the back seat of a car, holding up a hand and smiling tightly in response to the barrage of questions from the waiting members of the press. Normally it would have been Richardson asking the awkward questions, and he didn't appear best pleased about the reversal of his position.

After watching for another couple of seconds, Zack hit a button on the remote and the screen went blank. His expression when he turned to face Nicky was one of disgust.

'I take it you're not a fan,' Nicky said, tipping her head towards the television.

'Hardly,' said Zack. 'The man's always been a snake as far as I'm concerned. He represents the complete opposite of everything this place stands for. To be honest, I wouldn't be surprised if what people are saying about him is true.'

'What are people saying?'

'You know. That he was involved in what happened to that poor kid. Apparently, Callum Richardson was one of the last people to see him alive.'

Nicky wondered if Zack would make the connection between the story and her presence here, but the manager simply tossed the remote control back where he'd found it. 'You said you were looking for Melissa,' he said. 'Is she in trouble?'

'That's partly what I'm trying to discover,' Nicky replied. 'Is she here? Do you know where I might find her?'

Zack shook his head. 'I haven't seen her in days. Three, to be precise. That's why I've been so worried.'

'Is she a . . . companion here?' Nicky asked, recalling the term Zack had used.

'Not exactly. To be a full-time companion, the rules are pretty strict. No drink, no drugs. Melissa, she . . . she's never quite managed to fulfil the criteria.'

Which Nicky interpreted as being a delicate way of saying Melissa was an addict.

'But we have a few rooms for temporary residents,' Zack went on. 'People who are working towards becoming full-time companions. At the moment there's only space for three or four at a time, but hopefully that will change once we find the money to finish the renovations.' The manager's tone suggested it was more an aspiration than an imminent prospect. 'Anyway, temporary residents are only supposed to stay for a week or two, but this last time, Melissa ended up staying for almost a month.'

'This last time? You mean she's a regular here?'

'Everyone who stays here is a regular, Detective Sergeant. Homelessness is like quicksand. Once you're in, it's almost impossible to climb out. Believe me, I know from personal experience.' Zack gave a lopsided smile. 'So yeah, people show up here, move on, then turn up again days, weeks, months later. We try to help as many as we can. We offer shelter, help finding work, even counselling right here on site. But there's a limit to how much of a difference we can make in terms of the overall problem.'

'So Melissa was here and then she left? Did she give a reason? Say anything about where she might be going? It really is very important that I find her.'

'No, she just left. Disappeared, I suppose you could say. Sometimes that happens, but in the past Melissa's always made sure to say goodbye. *Checking out*, she'd call it, and I'd always pretend to present her with her bill, ask her if everything had been to her satisfaction. It was kind of like our little joke.' Zack smiled fondly, and it was clear he had a soft spot for Melissa. It was even possible his feelings went deeper than that. 'But this time she just vanished,' the manager went on. 'Left everything she owned in her room. Which isn't much, but even so, it's one of the things that struck me as strange. When all your worldly possessions fit into a single carrier bag, you tend to guard those possessions with your life.'

'Did you report her as missing?' Nicky asked.

'To the police, you mean?' Zack's expression suggested he thought Nicky might have been making a joke. 'With all due respect, Detective Sergeant, I think you know as well as I do how that conversation would have gone. They don't send people like you out to look for people like Melissa unless . . .' He frowned. 'Why *are* you looking for her? You still haven't said. And really, I don't want to cause Melissa any problems. Any more than she already has.'

'I just need to ask her a few questions,' Nicky said, attempting to sound reassuring. 'For her sake as much as anyone else's.'

Zack was looking at her dubiously. 'Yes, well,' he said at last. 'It's like I said. She was here, and now she's not. I'm not sure what else I can do to help.'

'Might I perhaps be able to take a look in Melissa's room?'

Zack bridled. 'Well, I . . . I'm not sure that would be—'

'I only want to help,' Nicky insisted. 'Truly. And I won't disturb anything, I promise. You can stand right beside me the whole time I'm in there.' She gave the manager her sweetest smile. That was something else she'd learned over the years she'd been a police officer: being a woman made almost everything harder, but sometimes, in certain circumstances, it paid off.

Zack continued to hesitate. But in the end his expression softened, and he sighed. 'Follow me,' he said.

The manager led the way from the recreation room straight out into the neatly tended yard. The main building appeared to be U-shaped, with a squat, single-storey extension having been built on either side of the original church. One of the wings had been boarded up, however, and was in a similar state of disrepair as the church had appeared to be from the street. It was the only blot on what would otherwise have been an attractive open space, with benches scattered around the perimeter and geraniums flourishing in the late autumn sun.

Zack took her through another doorway, back inside. 'The guest wing,' he said wryly, as they entered a corridor in the extension where the renovations had obviously been completed. There were three plain doors on either side. 'Melissa's room is the one at the end.'

He produced a set of keys from a trouser pocket, unlocking the door and gesturing Nicky in ahead of him.

The corridor had been windowless and gloomy. Melissa's room, in contrast, was refreshingly bright. There were dried flowers in a vase on the windowsill, and pictures of seascapes on the walls. Oddly, and perhaps only because boarding school was on her mind, it reminded Nicky of the room she and a girl called Sarah Sullivan had shared at Welton House. Their bedroom had become like a sanctuary to Nicky – the only place in the entire school that had felt even vaguely like home.

She took a few exploratory steps around the room. 'These are her things?'

'Everything that isn't the furniture or the flowers,' said Zack.

The manager had been wrong. Melissa wouldn't have needed a carrier bag for her worldly possessions. The stuff on the little desk and the bedside table would probably have fitted in her pockets. There was a splayed paperback with a title Nicky vaguely recognised from her classics class at Welton: *Oedipus at Colonus*, with letters underneath the title in Ancient Greek. Beside it were a chewed biro and an open notepad, the pages full of frantic-looking doodles, completely filling the space. There was a holey-looking cardigan in a heap; and on the bedside table, a cheap digital watch and a tarnished silver necklace. The charm was a mask with a face set in a frown. An empty link was beside it, suggesting the mask was likely to have been one of a pair: Thalia and something, Nicky recalled, the twin faces of Greek drama. But the mask representing comedy was missing. All Melissa had been left with was tragedy.

Nicky looked more closely at the notebook. She used her own pen to turn the pages, idly scanning the doodles – until her eyes suddenly snagged.

The manager seemed to realise she'd spotted something, and edged closer.

'Do you have a computer here?' Nicky asked, turning. 'Access to the internet?'

Zack appeared slightly surprised. 'Sure. You can use the laptop in my office if you—'

Nicky shook her head. 'Not for me. For the residents.'

'Oh, I see. Yes, there's a workroom off the main corridor, next door to the counsellor's office. There are only two computers, both pretty ancient, but good enough to allow the companions to search for jobs.'

'Would Melissa have had access?'

The manager shrugged. 'I lock the room at night, but anyone can use it during the day.'

Nicky looked again at the page in the notebook. At what she'd spotted written down amid the scrawls. She raised her head. 'Did you see Melissa using either of the computers before she disappeared?'

Zack frowned as he tried to remember. 'I can't . . . No, wait. I did see her in there. A couple of times, actually. Including on the day before she left.'

Nicky felt a fluttering in her stomach – whether sickness or excitement, she couldn't tell. 'Show me,' she said.

Ben – March 1997
(Two months before his death)

Ben was alone in the southern transept. He was trying to draw again – the chapel's beams, the pattern of the parquet, the shadows that pooled below the arches along the aisles – but his finger hurt so much he was finding it hard just to hold his pencil. And anyway, his heart wasn't in it. He kept thinking about Callum, and how cross he'd been, which was nothing compared to how angry Ben was with himself.

He flexed his hand, and tried adjusting the pencil in his grip, but when he lowered it to the notepad again, the pencil slipped, scarring the page with a jagged streak before landing with a clatter on the floor. Ben cursed, and reached to retrieve it, but caught his finger on the seat of the bench and felt the pain carry all the way to his elbow.

He started to cry. He couldn't help it.

He was such an *idiot*. Why did he always have to mess everything up? What was *wrong* with him?

It was no wonder nobody wanted him around. Not even his father. As for his mum . . . Who was to say she'd wanted Ben around either? Ben had told himself that she did – that she *must* have – but he didn't know, not for certain. Sometimes, even though Ben knew it made no sense, he thought it might have been his fault she'd got ill in the first place. That it was because she hadn't loved him more that she'd failed to survive.

'Ben?'

Ben whipped his head towards the sound of the voice.

Seeing who it was, he hastily turned away again, swiping at his eyes with the ends of his sleeves.

'I hoped I might find you here. I . . .' Father Steiner was moving closer. Two steps from the corner of the nave, he stopped. 'Ben? Is everything all right?'

'I'm fine. I got some dust in my eyes, that's all. When I bent to pick up my pencil.' Once again Ben ducked towards the floor and, using his left hand this time, retrieved the pencil that was still lying underneath the bench. He wiped his eyes again on the way back up, before holding the pencil aloft to prove his story.

'Oh,' said Father Steiner. 'I see. Well, I'll leave you alone. If you'd like me to. I didn't mean to interrupt.'

Ben didn't reply, and the chaplain lingered.

'Is there . . . is there anything you would perhaps like to talk about?'

For a moment Ben hesitated. There was something he wanted to ask: a question that had been on his mind for as long as he could remember, and that he thought perhaps the chaplain might be able to answer. Ben wanted to know what happened when someone died; whether there was really a chance you would ever see them again. But Father Steiner wasn't the friend he was pretending to be, Ben reminded himself. Probably he'd tell Ben anything he thought Ben wanted to hear.

'No,' Ben said, focusing on his drawing. 'Thank you.'

He didn't look up, but he could tell Father Steiner hadn't moved.

'It's just, you seem upset,' the chaplain said at last. 'Did something happen? In class maybe? Or between you and your friends?'

Involuntarily Ben raised his head, and a look of understanding passed across the chaplain's features.

He edged closer. There was space on the bench beside Ben, but after seeming to hesitate for a moment, Father Steiner took a seat on the bench opposite. He looked at Ben across the width of the transept, two or three extended arms' lengths between them.

'What are you drawing? May I see?'

It was an uncomfortable echo of what had happened with Callum in the library. 'I'm not really drawing anything. Just . . . fragments. And nothing's turning out right, anyway.'

Succumbing to a wave of frustration, Ben scribbled angrily over everything he'd been sketching, then tossed his notepad on to the bench beside him. What was the point? Even if he could do it properly, drawing wasn't going to change *anything*.

He glanced and caught the chaplain's expression of concern. But when Father Steiner saw Ben looking, he smiled kindly. 'Lacking inspiration, perhaps?' he suggested. 'We all have days like those, I'm afraid.'

Ben didn't reply. He felt tears building once again behind his eyes.

'Ben?' said the chaplain softly. He leaned forward, linking his hands and resting his elbows on his knees. 'This may not really be my place, but . . . will you allow me to give you a piece of advice? The children I've noticed you hanging around with. Callum Richardson. Melissa Haynes. Lance Wheeler. They're not . . . they're not the kind of people you perhaps think they are.'

Ben felt himself bridling, and the chaplain obviously noticed it, too. Father Steiner held up his hands.

'All I'm trying to say is, there are other pupils at the school who would perhaps make you happier. People like . . . like Isaac, for example. You're both . . . thoughtful. Compassionate. And you could both use a proper friend of your own age.'

'I'm not looking for any more friends,' Ben said. *Least of all Isaac*, he added in his head. Callum was his friend. Melissa and Lance, too. Isaac was just a sad, pathetic loser, and Ben wasn't going to let himself turn into the same thing.

'I'm not trying to interfere,' said Father Steiner. 'I just think that if you and Isaac were to spend a bit more time together, you'd find you have an awful lot in common.'

As if on cue, a door opened somewhere in the nave. There were footsteps, and Ben could tell even before Isaac appeared from around the corner who it would be. When Isaac reached the transept and noticed Ben, he abruptly stopped walking.

'I have to go,' Ben announced, standing up.

'Already?' said Father Steiner, looking disappointed. He looked from one boy to the other.

'I've got lessons.'

'But . . . it's lunchtime,' said Father Steiner. 'And anyway, there was something I wanted to give you. That's why I came here hoping to find you. Just . . . give me a moment. Half a moment. I'll be right back, I promise.'

Before Ben could respond, Father Steiner swished off towards the vestry, touching Isaac's arm in greeting as he passed. Isaac looked at Ben suspiciously – *what are you doing here?* – and then trailed after the chaplain, once again reminding Ben of a sad little puppy. It made him think of all the rumours about Father Steiner, too, and Callum referring to Isaac as the chaplain's *favourite*. Was that why Father Steiner wanted Ben and Isaac to be friends? So Ben would become one of his 'favourites', too?

A few moments later, Father Steiner reappeared on his own.

'Here,' he said, holding something aloft as he strode back. His footsteps echoed in the refrigerator air.

'What is it?' said Ben, curious in spite of himself.

'It's a book,' said Father Steiner, stopping in front of him and holding out the book with both hands. He was slightly out of breath, and he smiled through parted lips. 'I thought . . . Well. I thought you'd be interested.'

Ben read the title. *The World's Greatest Cathedrals*. The chaplain was turning the pages, showing Ben some of the photographs inside.

'It's yours to keep. Assuming you want it. I found it at a charity bookshop at the weekend. It's in excellent condition, and some of the photos are magnificent.'

He closed the book and held it out again. Ben accepted it gingerly.

'I . . . Thanks.'

'You're very welcome. You will show me if you decide to make sketches of some of the details in the photographs?'

'Sure,' said Ben. 'I guess.' He tucked the book under his arm and made to head towards the vestibule. Three steps along the aisle, he stopped, an idea occurring to him.

He turned back.

'Father Steiner? I don't suppose . . . Could you write in it? Just . . . I don't know. *From Father Steiner* or something? It would . . .' Ben shrugged. 'It would mean a lot to me.'

The chaplain's smile broadened. 'I'd be delighted to,' he said. He patted his robes, as though frisking himself to try to locate a pen.

Ben produced one from his blazer pocket. 'Here,' he said.

The chaplain took the book and the pen, and moved to sit down on the nearest pew. He tapped the pen against his chin, gazing up towards the altar, then bent towards the open pages. '*Dear Ben,*' he spoke aloud, as he wrote. '*I hope this book serves to offer you some inspiration. Fondly, Father George Steiner.*'

He finished with a flourish, then folded the pen into the book, and passed them both back to Ben.

Ben opened the book and looked down at the inscription, pleased. And Callum, he knew, would be pleased, too.

Thursday 24 October, 9.45 p.m.

Fleet's first thought, when he saw the figure slumped outside his bedsit's door, was of the intruder in the CCTV footage from Callum Richardson's living room, their hollow eyes staring up at the camera. *Your turn to hide*, said a voice in Fleet's head, and he felt a cool prickle at the base of his neck.

'Hello?' he said.

Whoever it was raised their head.

'Rob? Is that you?'

It was late, and the bulb in the communal hallway barely added to the feeble light seeping in through the window from the streetlamp outside, meaning Fleet could see the figure's silhouette and nothing more. Yet he would have recognised that voice anywhere.

'Holly? Jesus. You almost gave me a heart attack. What are you . . .'

But he got not further. His ex-wife had clambered to her feet and into the light, and before Fleet could finish his sentence, she started to cry.

'Here,' Fleet said, as he handed Holly a mug of tea. He was out of milk, so he'd added a spoon of sugar instead. Holly accepted it without appearing to notice.

'Thanks,' she said, and she smiled at him weakly, cradling the cup in both hands.

Fleet touched her cheek with the backs of his fingers. 'You're freezing. How long were you sitting out there?'

'Not long. A couple of hours?'

'A couple of *hours*?'

'I went for a walk, and it started to rain again, and by that point I was closer to here than I was to home, so . . .'

'You walked here all the way from the house?'

'It's not that far.'

'It's five miles. And it's dark outside. And you're not even wearing a coat.' Fleet moved his hand to Holly's arm. 'Jesus, you're wet through. Here.' He took off his suit jacket and draped it around his ex-wife's shoulders.

She looked up at him, and tears welled again in her eyes. 'I'm sorry,' she said. 'I shouldn't have come here. I didn't mean to. I just . . . when I started walking, I wasn't really thinking about where I was heading. Or . . . I don't know. Maybe I was.'

'There's no need to be sorry. You can come to me whenever you want. Always. You know that.' Fleet sat down on the sofa beside her. She leaned into him and he wrapped her in his arms.

Christ, it felt good to hold her. She fitted perfectly, just as she always had.

'I've been stupid, Rob. So, so stupid. And I didn't know where else to go.' Holly shook her head. 'Rob, I . . .' She pulled away, looked down at the liquid in her cup.

'Tell me,' Fleet urged. 'Whatever it is, you can tell me.'

'I've been seeing someone,' Holly replied – quickly, as though ripping off a plaster.

But the pain, for Fleet, bloomed. It was like something solid swelling in his chest, pushing against his lungs, his windpipe, his heart.

'I'm sorry,' Holly said. 'I should have told you. I just . . . I didn't know how to. And I didn't know whether it meant anything, or . . . or whether it was just a . . . a . . .' Her sentence trailed off.

'Why would you have felt you had to tell me?' said Fleet. The words, to his ear, sounded petulant. He hadn't meant for them to come out that way. 'We're divorced, Holly. It's your business who you see.' And then something clicked, and the pain in Fleet's chest turned to something sharper. 'Did he hurt you? Is that why you're here? If he hurt you, I'll—'

'He didn't hurt me. Rob? Honestly, Rob, he didn't. Please, sit back down.'

Fleet hadn't noticed getting up. Holly's hand caught his wrist and pulled him towards her.

'He didn't hurt me,' she repeated, looking him straight in the eye. 'He left me, but he didn't hurt me. That is, we left each other. We only saw each other for a couple of months. Three. I thought I liked him. I did like him, but not . . . not as much as I told myself I did. And it turned out he was never really serious about me.'

'What do you mean?'

Holly put her mug down on the table. She looked like she was about to cry again, but rolled her lips between her teeth as though to stop herself.

She took a breath.

'I'm pregnant, Rob. I'm going to have a baby. And I've never been so scared in my whole life.'

He'd switched on some lights, found Holly a change of clothes. Just one of his old shirts and some woollen socks. He had nothing else he could offer her that she wouldn't have slipped right through.

He made her another cup of tea – two sugars this time – and turned on the electric fire.

'You can stay here tonight. If you'd like to. I mean, there isn't much space, but . . . but you can have the bed. I wasn't planning on doing much sleeping tonight anyway.'

Holly didn't argue. She glanced around the room. As well as the bed, the two-seater sofa and the coffee table, there was a kitchenette with a breakfast bar. The electric fire was underneath the mantelpiece, where a real fire would once have been. On one side of the chimney breast there was a built-in wardrobe, containing Fleet's suits, and on the other a television, which he never watched. The nicest part of the room ordinarily was a large bay window, but Fleet had covered it with the curtains when he'd turned on the lights.

'Is this where you've been living?' said Holly. 'This whole time?'

She meant since the divorce, Fleet presumed, but actually he'd first started renting this place at the beginning of their trial separation. Which meant he'd been here . . . two years now. It was one of six bedsits in the converted Victorian semi. Fleet could easily have afforded something better, but he knew that moving somewhere else would be as good as an admission: that it was really over. That Holly was gone from his life. The bedsit felt temporary, and more than a small part of him wanted desperately to cling on to that feeling.

'It's just a place to sleep,' he told Holly. 'I'm barely here.'

She frowned at him, a flash of the Holly he'd been married to. She knew that if he was barely at home, it meant he was working too much.

'Where's all your stuff?' she asked him. 'There's no way it would all fit in that wardrobe.'

When Fleet had moved out, he'd left almost everything behind except his suits and his razor. Not that he'd ever had much. His old records, a few shelves of books, a couple of drawerfuls of clothes. But he hadn't wanted any of it. It was Holly who'd boxed it all up for him, once the divorce had been finalised. Not because she was trying to remove all trace of him, she'd insisted. Rather, because it was too painful to keep stumbling on reminders of what they'd once had. Ironically perhaps, it was only because of the issue of children that they'd agreed to split up in the first place. Holly wanted kids and Fleet didn't. Couldn't. Not after Jeannie. When she'd killed herself, Fleet had been the closest thing she'd had to a father, and he'd never been able to forgive himself for failing in that role; for not even having a clue what his little sister had been going through. As for Holly, Fleet loved her too much to deny her the thing she craved most from life, just as she cared too much for him to ask him to pretend to be something he could never be.

'It's all still in boxes,' Fleet said. 'I put them in storage. To be honest, I think I'm paying more each month just to keep them dry than I am for this place.'

Holly didn't smile. She tended not to when it came to matters of Fleet's well-being.

'What did you mean when you said you weren't planning on sleeping?' she asked him, still frowning.

'Nothing, Sprig.' He used his old nickname for her almost without realising. 'It was just a joke. It's been a long day, that's all.'

Holly's frown tightened. 'You've got that look about you, Rob. That haunted look. What are you working on? If you were to tell me what it was, would I disapprove?'

'You might,' Fleet replied. He smiled. 'If I were to tell you.'

He even missed this. Holly's protective side. The unusual thing was that she hadn't already guessed what Fleet was caught up in. Ben's murder was all over the news. It was Fleet's patch. And his train ticket to London was beside his wallet and keys on the breakfast bar, where he'd automatically emptied his pockets when they'd come in. Holly knew full well how much he hated the place, meaning it wouldn't have taken a lot for her to make the connection to Callum Richardson had she known the basic details of the case. That she seemed not to suggested that, for once in her life, she was out of touch with what was going on in the world. Although that was perhaps less surprising, given what had evidently been going on in her own life.

'It smells of smoke in here, Rob,' Holly said. 'What happened to you giving up? And that hob looks as though it's never been used. Are you eating properly? You know takeaways aren't good for you. Most curries are nine parts cooking oil, and pizza is basically carbohydrates and cheese.'

'Now you're making me hungry,' said Fleet, smiling again. In truth, more than anything he wanted a cigarette, but he knew how Holly would react to *that*. And that was without even taking into account her . . . condition.

He'd been standing by the breakfast bar, and as before he took a seat beside her on the sofa. She nestled into him, and his arm moved naturally once again around her shoulders.

'Have you decided . . . I mean . . . Have you thought what it is you're going to do?'

Holly's voice, when she answered, was a whisper. 'That's all I've been thinking about. Every second of every minute since I found out.'

Fleet waited. 'And?' he prompted gently.

'And I'm going to keep it.' Her voice remained quiet, but there was no mistaking the decisiveness in her tone. In truth, Fleet had never expected her to say anything else.

Holly's hands, he noticed, had crept to her belly.

'It's all I've ever wanted, Rob. I mean, not *all* . . .' She glanced up at him. 'I don't mean . . .'

'I know, Sprig.' He stroked her hair. 'I know what you mean.'

She looked down at the place she was covering with her hands. 'It doesn't even matter to me that it's half him. Because it – she, he – is *all* me. And I'm going to love it so much, Rob. So, so much. More than enough to make up for him not being there.'

'Is that what he said? That he won't be there?' Fleet felt that same sharpness in his chest that he'd felt when he'd thought Holly might have been hurt. Not quite as insistent, perhaps, but just as fierce.

For a moment Holly didn't reply, and it was obvious there was something else she was reluctant to tell him.

'He's married. With three kids of his own. I didn't know, Rob. I swear to God, I didn't know. I met him at my yoga class, and he never once wore a wedding ring. And he never gave the slightest *hint* when we were together that he had a family. I mean, he . . . he gave me his business mobile number rather than his private one, but he said that was because he was more likely to answer it. And the times we . . . we . . . the *three* times we . . . because that was all it was, Rob. Three lousy times. And they *were* lousy, I promise you. It . . . it was nothing like . . . like we . . .'

'Holly . . .'

'But it was never at his place. We never once went back to his place. There was one time we stayed at a hotel, but again that was because of work, he said, because he had to stay overnight in the city, so he . . . we . . .'

'Holly. Stop. Just stop.'

She was crying again. She shook her head. 'I should have known. Shouldn't I. Should I have known? *Did* I know? I just . . . I can't . . .'

'Shh. It's all right, Sprig. It's all going to be all right.'

She shook her head again, more forcefully this time. 'You don't know that. *I* don't know that! All I know is, I want to keep it, I *will* keep it, but I can't help thinking about work, about how I'm supposed to manage with work, and about . . . about childcare, and . . . and all the . . . all the things you *have* to think about. I mean, it's not a . . . not just a . . . It's a baby, for Christ's sake. A *child*. And I . . . I just . . .'

Unaccountably, Holly laughed. But it was a desperate, hollow laugh, that afterwards only made her cry harder.

'And it's my last chance, Rob,' she said, between sobs. 'I'm forty-one. Meaning I can't help thinking this is my very last chance.'

Fleet gathered her to him. He let her cry. He wanted to say something, but he didn't know what, so instead he just continued to hold her. After a while her crying eased, and her breath deepened, and Fleet realised she'd fallen asleep in his arms. Just as she used to do every night when they were in bed together. It was enough to make Fleet feel drowsy, too, in spite of what he'd said to Holly about not planning on sleeping, and when he closed his eyes he found himself struggling to open them again. It was morning when he finally did, and Holly was gone, leaving Fleet wondering if he'd dreamt the whole thing.

Ben – April 1997
(Four weeks before his death)

Ben sat awkwardly at the end of Melissa's bed.

It was his first time in a dorm that wasn't his own, let alone the girls' wing, let alone *Melissa's* room. He knew the others came here sometimes, but so far they'd never asked him to go with them. But this time they *had* asked him, and Ben knew he should have been pleased. Ecstatic, even. This is what he'd wanted after all: the four of them hanging out together. Instead, he found himself wishing he was somewhere else. Anywhere else. Doing anything other than what they were planning.

Ben was the only one sitting. The others were making preparations: discussing props, backgrounds, lighting. Melissa clutched her camera the whole time, and Ben's eyes kept drifting towards it as though it were a loaded gun. And she hadn't even taken off the lens cap yet.

'Is this . . . is this really necessary, do you think?'

After what had happened with Callum, Ben didn't want to be the one to raise any objections, but as he waited he found he couldn't help himself.

The others turned.

'It's just . . . I mean . . . don't you think it's a bit . . . dangerous?'

Lance gave a snort. It was barely audible, but Ben heard it clearly enough. He focused on Callum.

'All I'm saying is, we've got the book now. The one I asked Father Steiner to sign? That's got to count for something, right?'

When Ben had brought the book to Callum just over a week ago, it had been as though their argument in the library had never happened. Callum had been delighted, smiling down at the inscription with something like greed.

'And the other thing is, everybody's seen me,' Ben went on. 'Isaac in particular sees me in the chapel all the time. So . . . so that's enough. Isn't it? If I just keep doing what I've been doing. That's got to be enough.'

'I told you,' said Lance, before Callum could respond. 'I told you he wouldn't go through with it.'

Ben looked at Lance, and this time there was a definite sneer.

'Seriously, Cal,' Lance went on. 'Let me do it. I knew I should have done it from the start. He's just going to mess everything up.'

'No!' Ben protested. 'I didn't say I wouldn't do it! I was just . . . just asking, that's all. Just . . .'

'The book's not enough, Ben,' said Callum. His tone was reasonable, almost gentle. The way a parent would speak. A proper parent. 'You know it's not going to be enough.'

Ben dropped his head. 'No,' he agreed. 'No, of course not.'

'But there's no danger,' Callum insisted. 'You're the *victim* here, remember?'

Something about the way Callum said the word caused Ben to look up.

'Would it help if we left you and Melissa alone?' Callum said. 'Just the two of you. So you can . . . get on with things.'

Now Ben swallowed. He wasn't sure if being left alone with Melissa would make things better, or worse.

Callum picked up his blazer from where he'd tossed it on the chair beside Melissa's bed. 'Come on,' he said to Lance. 'Let's leave the artists to their work.' He winked at Ben, and steered Lance towards the door. Lance resisted for a moment, then snatched up his own blazer. He threw one last scowl Ben's way before trailing Callum from the room.

'Don't mind him,' Melissa said to Ben, when the two of them were alone. 'He's just jealous.'

'Jealous? Of *what*?'

For a moment Melissa smiled snidely, but just as quickly her expression returned to normal. 'Of the fact that Callum's trusting you to do this, for one thing,' she said. 'And there's the book, too. Maybe it's not enough by itself, but it could still be important. You should have heard Callum singing your praises for thinking on your feet like that. For asking Father Steiner to sign it. Lance would never have thought of that. And he *knows* he wouldn't have. That's partly what's bothering him, too.'

Ben looked towards the door, wondering what, exactly, Callum had said about him.

'He was seriously impressed, Ben,' Melissa said, as though reading Ben's thoughts. 'And, well . . . I was impressed, too.'

When Ben looked back at her, she seemed to colour slightly. A strand of hair fell across her eyes, and she used a finger to tuck it behind her ear. As she did so, Ben noticed a red mark on her wrist. It looked painful, like a burn.

'So, are you ready?' she said, and she unsnapped the cap from the lens of the camera. She turned back, and appeared to notice Ben stiffen.

She smiled again, and although Ben wasn't sure why, her expression was even more unsettling than the smile she'd showed before. 'Relax,' she said. 'I promise it won't hurt a bit.'

'So she was looking for him,' Fleet said.

'I'd say she was more than looking for him,' Nicky replied. 'I'd say she found him.'

They were in Fleet's office, catching each other up on their progress the previous day. Fleet had recounted his interview with Callum Richardson; Nicky was filling Fleet in on what she'd discovered at Shining Light.

'Lance's address was written on a notepad in Melissa's room,' Nicky said. 'His name was all over the search history of a computer she had access to. More to the point, it was all on the day the rumours about Ben's body being discovered first started appearing online. Which also happens to be the day Melissa vanished from the shelter. It's not exactly conclusive, but . . .'

'But it makes her a suspect,' Fleet said. 'She was already in the frame for Ben's murder. And now she's tied directly to Lance's. *Christ.* And there we were worrying about her safety.'

They were huddled around the screen of Fleet's computer. The CCTV footage from Callum Richardson's living room was paused at the moment the intruder gazed up at the camera. Richardson's solicitor had provided Fleet with a copy of the footage at the end of their meeting, and Fleet had already watched it so many times, he knew the precise sequence of steps the figure took as they moved towards the camera from the door.

'So do you think that's her?' Nicky said, voicing the

question Fleet was pondering himself. 'Do you think the intruder could be Melissa? Because it's hard to be sure if it's even a woman. I would guess not, but when it comes to Melissa, we don't exactly have much to compare them to.'

On the desk beside the computer was a headshot of Melissa that Nicky had managed to retrieve from Shining Light. Apparently all the residents at the homeless shelter were issued with a photo ID, and the manager had emailed the image that appeared on Melissa's pass to Nicky. He'd taken the photograph himself, with a phone that he'd described as ancient, so the quality wasn't great. But everything they had on file otherwise was twenty years out of date. If they'd been looking for Melissa based on the picture of her in the Beaconsfield yearbook, they would have walked right past her on the street. They were like before and after shots, Fleet had decided – and not in a good way.

'The clothes don't help,' Nicky was saying. 'The loose trousers, the puffy jacket.' She rewound the footage to the point the intruder was caught entering the room. 'I suppose the height could be about right, judging from the doorframe. Zack Lawrence, the manager at the shelter, reckoned Melissa was almost as tall as him, which would make her close to five-nine.'

Nicky allowed the footage to continue, and then paused it once again when the intruder was looking directly into the camera. Fleet focused on the figure's eyes, which were shadowed by the outline of the balaclava. It wasn't even possible to make out their precise colour. Melissa's were blue, and those in the footage could have been anything from grey to light brown.

'Do you think we could get the tech guys to have a look?' said Nicky. 'See if they can clean it up a bit?'

Fleet exhaled. 'You know what it's like down there. They'll have a backlog, and thanks to the powers that be, we'll go straight to the bottom of the pile. By the time they get to us . . .'

Fleet paused. *It will probably be too late*, he'd been about to say. But where had that thought come from? Too late for *what* exactly?

An alert sounded on Fleet's phone. He pulled it from his pocket, hoping the text might be from Holly. He'd sent her a message first thing – *Did you get home OK? Call me. Any time* – and he'd yet to hear back.

But the text wasn't from Holly, it was from Randy, letting Fleet know that he would be submitting his autopsy report on Lance Wheeler later today. His opinion hadn't changed, he said, but more had come to light that Fleet would probably want to discuss. He'd be at the school all day if Fleet wanted to meet him there.

'Send the techies a copy anyway,' Fleet instructed Nicky. 'You never know, we might get lucky. But my hunch is we've got as much from the footage as we're going to, at least in terms of making a definitive ID.'

He moved towards the window, leaving Nicky staring at the screen. Fleet's office was on the first floor of the building, six storeys below Superintendent Burton's. While Burton enjoyed a view across the city, with a corridor between the buildings all the way to the docks, Fleet's panorama extended approximately twenty feet, as far as the rusting fire escape of the apartment block next door. But that was fine by Fleet – he knew Burton had probably assigned him the office as further punishment for what had happened during the Sadie Saunders affair, but the superintendent didn't know about

Fleet's less than cosy relationship with heights. It wasn't something Fleet tended to advertise, as – for the most part – it didn't affect his ability to do his job. And anyway, there was nothing he could do to change it. He'd been afraid of heights for as long as he could remember.

'Tell me again what Callum Richardson said about Melissa?' Nicky said.

Fleet turned to face her. 'He said she wasn't stable. And that when she was at Beaconsfield, she and Lance Wheeler were obsessed with trying to get the school shut down. That they would have burned it to the ground if they could have. And he intimated that it had been more than just talk.'

Nicky stood up straighter and folded her arms. 'He didn't just come out and say it? Why not, I wonder? If there was something he wanted you to know, why bother playing games?'

'That seems to be a bit of a pattern,' said Fleet grimly. 'Don't you think? And besides, since when have you known a politician to talk plainly about anything? Particularly one as slippery as Callum Richardson.'

Nicky gave a sniff.

'So what do you think?' she said, after a pause. 'Forget what Richardson told you for the moment. Just in terms of Melissa. She was friends with Ben. She was one of the last three people to see him alive . . .'

'That we know about.'

'Right. That we know about. So from the moment we found out that Ben had been murdered, she was already joint top of the list of suspects. And now there's a trail directly connecting her to Lance Wheeler. Plus,' Nicky went on, 'it's clear something went wrong in her life at some point. You remember her grades? They dipped almost immediately after Ben went missing, and from what I've been able to find out, it's been pretty much downhill for her from there. She's living on the streets, estranged from her family. She was clearly damaged by something. Haunted by it, maybe?'

'Maybe,' Fleet agreed, playing devil's advocate now. 'But you went to boarding school, you know what it's like. How was it Randy put it? Some people are so messed up by the experience that they end up overdosing on heroin before they reach twenty-five. You said Melissa was an addict, right?'

'That's what the manager of the shelter told me.'

'So maybe . . . I don't know. Maybe she was just unlucky in life. Maybe it was Ben going missing that scarred her, particularly if they were genuine friends, and she was only reaching out to Lance because she felt she needed to reach out to *someone* after finding out what really happened to Ben. Someone who would understand how she was feeling. Maybe we only *think* she's gone to ground, when really . . .' Fleet stopped himself, but he could tell Nicky knew what he'd been about to say. Maybe Melissa's body would be the next one they discovered, and this time it *would* be suicide.

'Apart from all of which,' Fleet said, 'we still can't rule out Lance Wheeler as Ben's killer. Everything you just said about Melissa could apply to him as well. He hadn't fallen as far as Melissa, perhaps, but considering his potential when he was younger, he wasn't exactly living up to expectations. So maybe, over all these years, he was struggling to come to terms with something he did, too.'

'But if Lance killed Ben, who killed Lance? Unless Randy was wrong about it not being suicide. With the timing, and the note Lance left, it would certainly tie things up nicely. It could even be Lance in the CCTV footage.'

Fleet thought of Randy's text, and wondered what else the pathologist had discovered. But he'd also made it clear that his primary conclusion hadn't changed.

'I'd say the chances of Randy being wrong are pretty slim,' Fleet said. 'But we know Lance was struggling financially. Possibly he was in even more debt than we realise. Perhaps he was killed because of *that*, and the timing in terms of Ben is coincidental.'

From nowhere, Fleet heard Manish Apte's voice. *Come now, Detective Inspector. Even to me that sounds like reaching.*

'There's another possibility, of course,' said Nicky. 'Ben's friends have always presented themselves as a group. They stuck to the same story, claimed the same alibi. So maybe Melissa and Lance killed Ben together. When Melissa heard Ben's body had been discovered and realised the truth would come out, she went looking for Lance because she was worried he would talk.'

'Or the other way round. *She* wanted to confess, and Lance didn't.'

'Either way, they end up arguing. It gets heated, one of them threatens to tell all, the other is determined to stop them . . .'

'And Callum Richardson?' said Fleet. 'He's got an alibi for the entire timeframe surrounding Lance's death. I checked, and two hundred people saw him walk on stage in a London hotel and pick up an award. But if Melissa and Lance were involved in what happened to Ben, there's every chance all three of them were. If we're to believe Father Steiner, Richardson was always the ring leader.'

He looked across the room towards the computer screen, then at the wall behind his desk. On a noticeboard almost the size of the wall itself, Fleet had pinned pictures of every one of the missing souls in the files Superintendent Burton had personally delivered to Fleet's desk the morning he'd moved into his new office. There were husbands, wives; mothers, fathers; sons, daughters. All had been missing for years. Some, decades. Fleet had spent hours staring at them. He'd found that if he focused on the same picture long enough, he would start to imagine the pain behind their eyes. The fear that they would remain lost forever. And the chances were, Fleet knew, that was the way it would be.

In the centre of the display was a photograph of Ben, where Fleet had moved it at the start of the investigation. At first the boy's expression had struck Fleet as disdainful, he recalled. But now more than anything Ben seemed afraid. His lips were drawn tight; his eyes, if anything, were slightly wide. In the image he was posing for a school photographer, but even then, it seemed, he'd been reluctant to drop his guard.

'I believed him, you know,' Fleet said. 'Callum Richardson, I mean.'

'About what in particular?'

'I don't think he knew that Lance Wheeler was dead, for one thing. Least of all that he was murdered. And I think Richardson genuinely feels he's the victim of some conspiracy. That Manish Apte and all the rest are out to get him. To discredit him before he has a chance to damage them in the polls.'

Nicky smiled sardonically. 'Well, in that sense he's got some justification. But . . . and don't take this the wrong way, boss . . . but lying is what Callum Richardson does for a living. As a pundit. As a politician. And the reason he's so popular is that he's so bloody good at it.'

Fleet had already told himself a thousand times not to blindly trust his instincts – at least when it came to Callum Richardson. It hadn't escaped him, for instance, that there was a possibility the CCTV footage was fake. The intruder, the timestamp, the note: everything. It could explain why Richardson hadn't reported the break-in at the time it was supposed to have happened, and perhaps why he'd stalled on submitting to an interview with Fleet. And there was no question Richardson had the resources. Just as he had the resources, probably, to have somebody like Lance Wheeler killed, even if he hadn't been directly involved himself. Perhaps *that* was the reason Melissa went to ground: after looking for Lance and finding out what had happened to him, she was worried that she would be next.

It sounded outlandish, like something out of a political thriller – about as likely, in fact, as Richardson's contention that the establishment had set the whole thing up in order to frame *him*. But Fleet wasn't naive. He knew that it wasn't only in places like Russia that people were murdered for political reasons. Even if the footage proved real, for example, Richardson might still have ordered Lance's death. If Lance had been the person in the footage, say, and Richardson had somehow found out that his former schoolmate had been the one behind the note.

Your turn to hide . . .

Whatever the truth, Fleet had been relying on his intuition for the vast majority of his career, and it was a hard habit to talk himself out of. And there was one thing he was sure of in his gut: Callum Richardson was at the centre of things somehow. Maybe Fleet had believed the man, but he certainly didn't trust him.

'You know what I keep coming back to?' Fleet said. 'The anonymous tip. Why now, after all these years? Ben was dead and buried. Who benefits from dragging everything up, almost a quarter of a century after whatever happened?'

There were so many dangling threads, it was hard to know which to grab and start tugging. And there was something else that was nagging at Fleet: that feeling he'd had before, that they were somehow up against a ticking clock.

Nicky sat down on the edge of Fleet's desk. 'So what now?' she said. 'Do we go back to Burton and the brass? Ask them for permission to conduct a full-scale search for Melissa? Get the news outlets on board, social media, everything?'

Fleet was already shaking his head. 'As soon as we let the brass in on what we know, this whole thing is going to spiral out of our control. They want the stink, remember? The whirlpool. It's going to be hard enough finding Melissa as it is. Pass that photograph of her around among the uniforms, but keep it low-key.'

'Whatever you say, boss. Although if we let Burton know what we think we're dealing with, there's a chance we'll get those extra bodies we asked for.'

'There is. There's also a chance they'll give the whole investigation to somebody else. Somebody who's happy to play along with their political games. Besides, it's not just Melissa I'm worried about. It's everyone and everything connected to the case. As soon as this thing escalates, there's going to be so much noise around Callum Richardson, it's going to drown out everything else. No,' Fleet said, shaking his head again, 'Burton can wait until he gets Randy's report. In the meantime, we've got a window of opportunity. I say we use it. Agreed?'

'Agreed,' Nicky said. She smiled wryly. 'So long as I don't have to be there to watch when Burton decides to skin you alive. He's not going to like the fact that you held things back from him, you know.'

'I doubt it will make much difference to how he feels about me either way,' Fleet said. 'You may have noticed I'm on his shit list already. His latest gripe is the number of bodies that are going to be sucked into policing Ben's memorial service. Somehow that's my fault, too.'

'Ben's memorial service?' said Nicky. 'When's that happening?'

Fleet had received word about the memorial service on his way back from London the previous day. With everything that had been happening since – with the case, with Holly – he hadn't yet had a chance to think about it, let alone to brief Nicky. It had clearly been playing on Burton's mind, however. Fleet had received a message from the superintendent complaining about it first thing.

'They're hosting it at the school a couple of days from now,' Fleet said. 'It was the headmaster's idea, apparently. A publicity stunt as much as anything, if you ask me. Harris probably thinks that, by letting the press snap a few pictures of mourners filing into the chapel, they'll decide the story has run its course and move on. Leave him and his precious school alone.'

'Fat chance of that,' said Nicky. 'Especially once word gets out that Lance Wheeler was murdered, too. The newspapers aren't going anywhere, not while Callum Richardson's connected to the story.'

Which, again, was exactly how Manish Apte and his paymasters wanted it. For an instant Fleet was tempted to leave the lot of them to their games: Burton, Apte, Webb. Harris and Richardson, too.

But then Fleet's eyes settled once again on the picture of Ben. Even from the way Fleet had positioned his picture on the board, with clear space between Ben and the other images, he looked alone. Forsaken, even. And Fleet was determined he wouldn't remain that way.

'Stay on Melissa,' he told Nicky. 'The way it's looking right now, she's the key to this case.' He unhooked his coat from the back of his chair.

'What are you going to do?' Nicky asked him.

'Randy suggested we talk. I'm going to try to catch up with him at the school.'

Fleet hesitated. He thought of the crypt, and of the way Richardson had spoken about the fire.

'And while I'm out there,' Fleet said to Nicky, 'I think I'll take the headmaster up on his offer.'

Ben – April 1997

(Four weeks before his death)

'You! Boy! Stop!'

It was getting towards dinner time when Ben finally left Melissa's room. He'd assumed the others would still be in the corridor outside, but there was no sign of them, or anyone, when Ben slid into the dark stone passageway. He was glad in a way that he didn't have to face them, and it made sense that they wouldn't have wanted to linger in an area of the school that was supposed to be off limits to boys. But Ben was disappointed as well that they hadn't thought to wait for him. Apart from anything, he never liked walking the school's corridors on his own, particularly once the sun was beginning to set and the shadows seemed to take on a life of their own. But probably Lance had been in a strop, and had stormed off, with Callum doing his best to console him. The idea that Callum had chosen Lance over Ben gave rise to a pang of jealousy.

And something else occurred to Ben as well. If Callum and Lance had left the corridor the moment they'd departed Melissa's room, it meant Ben and Melissa had been alone. Properly alone. In her *bedroom*. The realisation was both thrilling and oddly terrifying. He knew there was no chance of anything ever happening between the two of them, but even so, it was nice to daydream; to think about what might have happened if, for example, he'd dared to be as bold as Callum always was. And it was perhaps because Ben's mind was on things other than what he was doing, where he was, that he failed to notice the headmaster coming up behind him.

'I said, *stop*. This is the *female* wing, young man. You had better have a very good explanation as to why—'

Ben spun just as the headmaster's shadow fell over him. When Harris realised who he'd caught, he stopped mid-sentence, and his features creased in obvious disgust.

'*You*. I might have known.'

Ben swallowed. The headmaster appeared ghostly in the murky light, and his eyes blazed with fury.

'How disappointingly predictable,' he said. 'What were you doing? Peering through keyholes? *Stealing?* Empty your pockets.'

'What? No, I wasn't—'

'I said, *empty your pockets.*'

There was nothing in Ben's pockets except a folded piece of paper with his timetable on (he *still* hadn't managed to remember it) and a few coins. When Ben held out his palms, he could read the headmaster's disappointment in his snarl. But after a second or two, his expression turned to one of triumph.

'So, spying, then. *Peeking*. You dis*gust*ing child. Your father shall hear of this. The disciplinary board, too. Given your woeful record, I would not be surprised if this proves to be the final straw. I shall certainly be recommending suspension at the very minimum.'

Harris grabbed Ben by the upper arm, his strangler's fingers pinching Ben's bicep.

'Hey! Get off me! I wasn't doing *anything*!'

Harris gave a snort. 'I can imagine precisely what you were doing. I even saw you, bending to look through that door.'

'What? That's a lie!' Ben's own fury gave him strength enough to break free. The headmaster's grip left a burn on his arm, but Ben barely felt it as he whipped around to face him. 'I wasn't *peeking*. I wasn't doing anything. I *told* you!'

'Really?' said Harris. 'Then perhaps you could explain how I happen to have found you in the girls' dormitories in the first place.'

Ben opened his mouth to reply, but from struggling to contain his righteous anger, he didn't know what to say.

Harris's smile spread like melting butter. 'You *have* no excuse because there *is* none. You are a liar and a reprobate, Benjamin Draper, and you have no business being at an institution as prestigious as Beaconsfield. As I am sure the board will agree when I present them with the facts.'

Harris tried to grab him again, but Ben backed away. He knew the headmaster was right. There *was* no excuse for Ben being here. The girls' dorms were in the east wing of the school, as far from the boys' dorms as it was possible for them to be, and nowhere near any of the classrooms. Still, it wasn't fair, what Harris was accusing Ben of. He didn't steal. Since Ben had arrived at Beaconsfield it was other kids – *richer* kids – who stole from *him*! And he wasn't a perv, either. The idea of Ben spying had probably only crossed Harris's mind because he was here to spy on the girls himself.

'*You're* the liar,' Ben found himself saying. 'I wasn't doing anything, and if you try to make out I was, I'll . . . I'll tell everyone I followed you and caught *you* looking through keyholes!'

Harris flushed with indignation. 'How *dare* you,' he hissed. 'I am the *headmaster* of this school! Your threats and filthy insinuations will not save you, young man. But rest assured, I will be certain to mention them when I make my report.'

Ben knew he'd crossed a line. Suspension was the best he could hope for now. Expulsion was far more likely. He thought of what his father would say – of how furious he would be – but it wasn't his father's reaction that worried him. Rather, it was the prospect of letting Callum down. Of proving that what Lance had said about Ben was true. And it was the thought of Callum – of what *he* would do in these circumstances – that drove Ben to say what he said next.

'You won't tell the board. You won't tell *anyone*.'

The headmaster stood up straight. He was a full head taller than Ben, and he looked down his nose at him with an outright sneer. 'I most certainly shall.'

'Oh, no, you won't,' Ben said. 'Because my friends will back me up. Lance Wheeler. Melissa Haynes. *Callum Richardson*. We'll all say we saw you, and then it'll be four against one.'

Now, for the first time, a flash of doubt crossed the headmaster's features. Ben knew Harris was afraid of Callum – of losing his father's contributions to the school, probably – and Ben wasn't sure if it was that or the threat itself that was causing the headmaster to have second thoughts. Either way, he could tell he'd said the right thing.

'You're a joke,' Ben pressed, on a roll now. 'You act like you're so superior, but really you're as afraid as everyone else. It's like Callum said: you're a phoney. A fraud. You don't belong here any more than I do, and you're terrified someone's going to find out.'

For a moment Ben was worried he'd pushed too far. There was such a look of hatred in Harris's expression, Ben felt sure the headmaster would decide to risk it all – his reputation, Callum's father's contributions to the school – just for a chance to make Ben suffer.

But in the end Harris said nothing, and Ben knew he'd won. He turned away, giddy with anger and adrenalin. In that instant, he realised what it must feel like to be Callum – to know that he could get away with *anything*.

Friday 25 October, 10.55 a.m.

Adrian Harris was surprised to see him. All the more so when Fleet, on stepping into Harris's office, reminded him of the offer he'd made the first time the two of them had met. But the headmaster recovered himself quickly, and rose rather stiffly from his leather chair, before escorting Fleet to the library himself.

'Is it just the fire you are interested in reading about, Detective Inspector?' There was a curiosity in the headmaster's tone that went deeper than a desire for an answer to his question.

'For the time being, I think. Thank you, Mr Harris. I recalled you mentioning you had some literature available on the subject.'

The headmaster showed Fleet to a table right in the centre of the room. There were no children around. It was midmorning, and Fleet presumed they must all be in lessons. Other than Fleet and the headmaster, the only other person in the library was the librarian, a short, frail-looking woman with a stare that was several degrees chillier than the room itself.

The headmaster's leather soles resounded on the parquet floor as he perused the stacks. It didn't take him long to find what he was looking for, and by the time he'd returned to the desk, he already had the book spread open to the relevant pages. He set the volume on the table, and Fleet found himself looking at an image that reminded him of a Turner painting of the burning of the Houses of Parliament. Art wasn't ordinarily Fleet's thing, but in the past Holly had dragged him around various exhibitions, and once in a while a painting would strike a chord. Turner's images of London aflame had been among them: the vicious swirl of the reds and oranges; the white so intense you could feel the heat. According to the caption in the book, there were no surviving photographs of the fire at Beaconsfield, and the painting had come to represent the most famous recorded image of the event. It was beguiling enough even to Fleet's eyes. What would a teenager have made of it, he wondered? Especially if they'd hated the school as much as Callum Richardson claimed Melissa and Lance had.

'Is there anything else I can help you with, Detective Inspector?'

Fleet flicked a few pages ahead, and saw that the story of the fire was narrated over an entire chapter. The volume itself was the size of one of Holly's cookery books. *A History of Beaconsfield College*, read the title at the top of the page.

'No, thank you, Mr Harris. This will be ample.'

'Very well, then. You may leave the book with Ms Cole, our librarian, when you are finished. She will ensure it is returned to the shelves in the correct place.'

Fleet didn't doubt it. He glanced again towards the woman at the front of the room. Even though she was busy at some task on her computer, Fleet had the impression she was watching his every move.

'In the meantime,' Harris went on, 'I shall leave you to it.'

Fleet allowed the seconds to pass, then looked up.

The headmaster was still standing over him.

'Is there something on your mind, Mr Harris?'

The headmaster came as close as Fleet had so far seen him to smiling. 'There are many things on my mind, Detective Inspector. As I am sure there are on yours.'

It was an invitation for Fleet to reveal what those things might be – what he was doing *here*, in the library, rather than out chasing suspects or interrogating witnesses or whatever else the headmaster imagined would be more appropriate for a man of Fleet's calling.

'You will have to forgive me, Detective Inspector,' Harris said, when Fleet didn't respond. 'But this is my first experience of being so intimate with the progression of an active police investigation. I admit I am curious as to your … methods.'

Now Fleet was the one to smile. 'It's just a little research, Mr Harris. I'd have thought you would approve. It's not often you'll find a policeman in a library, after all.'

'No,' said Harris, mirroring Fleet's expression with a curl of his lips. 'I don't suppose it is. Perhaps that is why it strikes me as curious. Far be it for me to instruct you on how to do your job, but … Well. I would have thought that, given the circumstances, you would have more urgent lines of enquiry to pursue.'

The man was genuinely unsettled, Fleet realised. Was it just idle curiosity? Irritation, perhaps, that Fleet was poking his nose into the history of an institution Harris had come to view as his own. Or was it something more than that?

'Thank you again for your assistance, Mr Harris. I won't keep you. I know you must be busy. Even more so than usual, I'd imagine.'

Harris tightened his eyes.

'Ben's memorial service?' Fleet clarified.

'Ah.' Harris's expression seemed to cloud slightly. 'Yes. I must admit the service is proving more time-consuming to arrange than I had foreseen.'

'Oh?'

'Yes, it . . . it seems to have turned into something slightly grander than I originally envisaged. There will now be several high-profile guests in attendance. Numerous trustees of the school. Various alumni. Including Callum Richardson.'

Fleet noted the headmaster's evident distaste, and recalled what he'd learned from his conversation with Father Steiner. For a man like Harris, it must indeed have been galling to have to kowtow to a student, even one whose father was as rich as Callum Richardson's. Twenty years on, the headmaster's resentment clearly lingered.

As for Richardson's decision to attend the memorial service, Fleet wasn't surprised. It was a perfect PR opportunity. A chance for Richardson to show the public that he was facing up to what had happened, and was as devastated as anyone else. If he played it correctly, it was even possible that *he* would emerge looking like the victim. It only served to reinforce Fleet's suspicion when he'd first heard the memorial service was to take place. It was nothing to do with mourning Ben, and everything to do with polishing reputations that had in one way or another been tarnished by his death.

'I would imagine that Mr Richardson and the school's trustees are looking for the same thing you are, Mr Harris,' Fleet said.

'And what is that, Detective Inspector?'

'Closure. Something that will make this whole sordid matter go away.' It was a deliberate provocation, but Fleet couldn't help himself.

The headmaster's expression darkened. 'Well,' he said. 'Given the lack of progress on other fronts, that is perhaps entirely understandable.' He looked at the book, then back at Fleet, making no attempt to disguise the implied affront.

Fleet just smiled again.

The headmaster drew back his shoulders. 'I presume you will be attending the memorial service yourself, Detective Inspector?'

'I will,' Fleet replied. The truth was, he hadn't yet made a conscious decision one way or another, but really there was no question that he wouldn't go. It struck him that he and Nicky might be the only people in attendance genuinely there to represent Ben.

'Then I shall see you there,' the headmaster said stiffly, and he turned away.

Fleet allowed him to take a step towards the door. 'If not before, Mr Harris,' he called out after him.

There was a glitch in Harris's movements, a dip of his chin towards his shoulder – and then he was gone.

It took a while for Fleet to settle into his task. He was irritated by his own irritation, and his failure not to rise to the headmaster's provocations. In general, there were very few people in the world Fleet found himself actively disliking before he'd really had a chance to get to know them, but Adrian Harris was unquestionably one of them. In many ways, the headmaster reminded Fleet of Superintendent Burton, indeed of almost every senior police officer Fleet had ever worked under – unless that said more about Fleet's relationship with authority than it did about anything else. And with Harris there was something else at play, too. The man was hiding something, Fleet was sure – for the sake of the school, was Fleet's initial instinct, but maybe there was more to it than that. Fleet had a feeling that he was somehow underestimating the man. Or, perhaps, that he was judging him precisely the way the headmaster wanted him to.

He returned his attention to the book, and forced himself to begin reading. He wasn't sure what he was looking for exactly, but Callum Richardson had been very clear in describing the fire as Melissa and Lance's inspiration, and there was obviously *something* he wanted Fleet to find out – though whether it would help Fleet get any closer to identifying Ben's killer was another matter entirely.

The fire, it turned out, had been set deliberately. Fleet had so far assumed it had been an accident, but eyewitnesses reported seeing flames emanating first from the library – which, given that the main building of the school had been refurbished to the exact specifications of the original structure, meant somewhere very close to where Fleet was sitting now. By the time the blaze had been brought under control, the southern wing of the school had been completely gutted, as had several of the outbuildings – including, of course, the original chapel. The weather conditions were largely to blame for the way the fire had spread, apparently – the high winds and uncharacteristically dry summer – as well as the slow response of the fire brigade, which was still depleted following the huge loss of manpower the country as a whole had suffered during the First World War.

In the end, seventeen people were wounded – three severely – and two people lost their lives. One was a firefighter, the other a teacher who'd evidently become trapped while attempting to direct the children under his care to safety. It was tragic, but the death toll might well have been far worse – if, instead of starting during the day, for example, the fire had happened at night, when six hundred children were asleep in their dorms. Even for Fleet, reading about the fire a century after the event, it was an outcome that didn't bear thinking about.

Once he'd read the chapter from start to finish, he turned back to the image of the school ablaze and wondered what it was he was missing. For all Richardson's hints and insinuations, there seemed no obvious connection between the fire that had almost destroyed Beaconsfield a hundred years ago and whatever had happened to Ben. Fleet had half hoped he might find some reference to the survival of the original crypt, accounting for the fact that someone had later discovered its existence, but there was none. The fire had occurred almost exactly a century ago, which at first Fleet thought might be significant, except the anniversary related to the discovery of Ben's body, not to the murder itself. The only detail that did strike a chord was the fact that whoever had set the fire had never been caught, meaning whoever had killed Ben wasn't the first person connected with the school to have effectively got away with murder.

After skimming the chapter one final time, Fleet started flicking through the rest of *A History of Beaconsfield College*. As he did so, another image caught his eye – this time a face peering out at him from one of the pages. It was Callum Richardson himself, he thought at first, before dismissing the notion as a trick of his mind. He'd only seen Richardson's features in somebody else's because the man was so prominent in Fleet's thoughts. And yet when he leafed back to the page that had caught his attention, he saw the resemblance was indeed uncanny. And the caption beneath the image explained why: the man in the photograph was Callum Richardson's father.

Fleet knew from his conversation with the school chaplain that Richardson senior had contributed financially to the school, but he'd failed to understand how large those contributions had been. It was no wonder the headmaster had been so worried about crossing James Richardson's son. It turned out that not only had Richardson senior been a Beaconsfield alumnus himself, he'd also rescued his alma mater from financial collapse, single-handedly restoring it to its former glory. An entire chapter in *A History of Beaconsfield College* was devoted to him – more pages even than to the fire. For James Richardson, clearly, the success of the school he'd attended as a young man had turned into a labour of love. He'd even bequeathed Beaconsfield a substantial portion of the inheritance that would otherwise have gone to his son – an inheritance, Fleet recalled, that Callum Richardson had later renounced.

All of which made Fleet wonder: what effect did his father's association with Beaconsfield have on how Callum Richardson viewed the school? Richardson had told Fleet that Melissa and Lance had been obsessed with trying to get the school shut down – but was *he* the driving force behind their hostility? It would seem to fit with the general pattern of their friendship. And when it came to Richardson's relationship with his father, he clearly had issues of some kind. The drink and drugs he'd been so fond of in his twenties spoke to that: an early sign, perhaps, of his determination to turn his back on his family, which he later demonstrated so publicly.

On the other hand, if Richardson *had* felt the same way as Melissa and Lance, why had he drawn attention to their animosity towards the school in the first place?

Fleet left the library no clearer in his thoughts than when he'd walked in. He made his way back to the front of the school, passing through the entrance hall with the huge wooden engraving of Beaconsfield's coat of arms, and out into the grounds, before taking the long way around the building towards the woods.

As he wove his way through the trees, he passed members of the forensic team carting equipment back towards the vans he'd spotted in the car park. In the clearing on the southern side of the chapel, the tents had already been dismantled. When Fleet made it known he was looking for Randy, one of the SOCOs pointed him towards what now resembled an open grave, and – within – the narrow stone staircase leading down.

He found the pathologist alone in the crypt. All but one of the portable LED units had already been taken away, leaving Randy standing in an eerie half-light, his back to Fleet and his eyes seemingly on the corner in which Ben's body had been discovered. If Fleet hadn't known better, he would have said that Randy – brash, egotistical Randy, who liked nothing better than to listen to himself holding forth – was silently and discreetly paying his final respects.

'Not getting sentimental in your old age, are you, Randy?'

The pathologist turned. He squinted against the single beam of light, then grinned when he realised it was Fleet who'd spoken.

'I suppose I must be,' Randy said. 'But don't spread it around, for Christ's sake. I've got a reputation to protect.'

Fleet moved next to the pathologist.

'Hell of a final resting place, don't you think?' said Randy.

Fleet glanced around. With everything but the last remaining light already removed, the crypt now looked like nothing more than what it had become: a dank, dark hole in the ground, abandoned and forgotten about for almost a century. Whoever had put Ben here had decided, consciously or otherwise, that he hadn't even deserved his own burial plot.

'You know,' said Randy, 'people always assume that pathologists are these cold, clinical automatons. Devoid of empathy, impervious to emotion. And maybe sometimes we have to be. It makes being married a hell of a lot easier, I can tell you that.' He sniffed, then said what Fleet had immediately started thinking. 'Then again, maybe that's why I also ended up getting divorced three times.'

Now Randy smiled – rather sadly, Fleet thought.

'Anyway,' the pathologist went on, 'it's not true. Oh, I know I make jokes, and I know *some* people think I can be a royal pain in the posterior . . .' There was an emphasis in there, a pause at the end of the sentence, that made it clear who Randy was referring to. 'But when you spend hours alone with someone's remains laid out in front of you on a metal table, it's hard not to start thinking about the person they once were. Or, when you're dealing with a kid, who they might have become.'

Randy was right: he could be a pain in the posterior. But Nicky had been spot on, too. Randy's heart was indeed in the right place.

'Apparently Ben used to draw,' Fleet said. 'He wanted to be an architect.'

The two men looked at the spot on the floor anew. Neither of them spoke for a moment. There seemed nothing more to be said.

Eventually, Randy turned away. 'Well, that's us all done and dusted,' he said. 'When Mr Harris holds his memorial service in two days' time, there'll be nothing left to show we were ever here. Get the lights on your way out, would you, Detective Inspector?'

Without so much as a glance behind him, the pathologist headed towards the narrow stone staircase, stooping slightly as the ceiling began to slope. Fleet watched until Randy's feet rose level with his eyeline. He took one final look around, suppressing an involuntary shiver, before picking up the last remaining LED unit and following Randy up towards the daylight.

'So there's no doubt?' Fleet said to Randy once they were back above ground. The clearing was now almost empty, leaving only a muddy mass of footprints among the chipped-teeth gravestones. As Randy had said, by the time the guests started gathering in the chapel for Ben's memorial service on Sunday morning, there would be no indication that a crime had ever been committed in the building's shadow. One sharp downpour, and even the footprints would dissolve into the mud. Adrian Harris, it occurred to Fleet, was likely scanning for clouds at that very moment.

'In terms of Lance Wheeler, you mean?' said Randy. 'No, there's no doubt. My report will conclude that Mr Wheeler died from asphyxiation, and not from the belt around his neck. The man was strangled. The marks on his neck couldn't have been clearer had his killer dipped their hands in paint.'

So suicide was off the table once and for all. Even though

Fleet had known what Randy was going to say, he couldn't help but feel a measure of frustration. The idea of Lance taking his own life had been the only part of the case that had come close to making sense.

'And there was a hell of a tussle, by the way,' said Randy. 'Lance Wheeler didn't go quietly. Which is partly what I wanted to talk to you about. As far as murders go, it was messy as hell. There was a struggle, he took a blow to the head, and eventually he was strangled. His hyoid bone was fractured.' The pathologist looked at Fleet meaningfully. 'Any of that sound familiar?'

And there, perhaps, went another theory, that Lance's death was unconnected to Ben's. The similarity between the two murders was yet another link tying them together.

'So you think they were killed by the same person?'

'If they weren't, whoever killed Wheeler did a hell of a job replicating Ben Draper's murder. Of course, I'm a pathologist, not a psychologist,' Randy went on, 'but if you were to ask my opinion . . .' He left a pause, which somehow seemed to make clear that he would give his opinion whether anybody asked him to or not. Now that they were above ground, it was notable how the pathologist's usual personality had reasserted itself. '. . . I would have to surmise that neither murder was particularly well planned. In all likelihood, they weren't planned at all. Which is good news, on the one hand, because it makes it unlikely that you're dealing with a psychopath. On the other, the killer is clearly highly volatile. And it would take an extraordinary effort of will to throttle someone with your bare hands. To look your victim in the eye as they suffocate. And, what's more, to do it twice.'

Fleet took a moment to contemplate what Randy had said. Apart from all the other implications, it seemed to put

Callum Richardson further in the clear. A professional acting on Richardson's behalf would almost certainly have been more clinical.

'Based on the physical evidence,' Fleet asked the pathologist, 'do you think Lance's killer could have been a woman?'

Randy's smile showed he knew exactly who Fleet had in mind. 'I don't see why not,' the pathologist said. 'If the blow to the victim's head incapacitated him, as I believe it would have done, the killer need not have been that strong. Although there's the position Wheeler was left in to consider. If you'll forgive the pun, a body is a hell of a dead weight. To kill a man and then string him up *would* have taken strength. Or, at least, determination.'

Fleet thought about what Randy had said before, about the effort of will it would have taken to manually strangle a person to death. Moving the body afterwards, regardless of how heavy it was – and Lance, if anything, had struck Fleet as being underweight – would surely have been child's play in comparison.

'Although, on the subject of the position of the body,' Randy went on, 'that's something else you may wish to ponder. The killer must surely have known that the true cause of death would come out. Not as quickly as I discerned it, perhaps, but even a third-rate pathologist would have spotted the signs of violence eventually. So why bother trying to make it look like suicide if it was obvious from the start it wouldn't stick?'

It wasn't something Fleet had so far considered, but the answer came to him immediately. 'To buy themselves time,' he said.

Randy had evidently already reached the same conclusion. He tipped his head in acknowledgement.

But why, Fleet wondered? Time for *what*? Even more than before, he had the sense events were building up to something. That the game that was mentioned in the anonymous email was still going on.

Fleet held out his hand for Randy to shake. 'Thanks, Randy. I know you didn't have to go out on a limb for me the way you have.'

'You know me, Detective Inspector,' Randy said with a glint. 'I've always been a sucker for an underdog.'

Fleet smiled wryly.

'There is, however, just one final thing I wanted to mention before you head off to solve this thing,' said Randy.

'Oh?' said Fleet.

'Whether or not you feel it's important, I'll leave up to you. But our friend, Mr Wheeler. I've never seen a liver so damaged in someone so young.'

'You mean he drank?'

'To excess. Quite regularly, I would say. And although it will be a while before we get the toxicology report on his blood, I'm expecting it to prove a heady cocktail. Amphetamines, marijuana, barbiturates: my guess is that Lance Wheeler was a regular consumer of everything and anything he could get his hands on.'

Given Lance's apparent trajectory after leaving Beaconsfield, Fleet wasn't exactly surprised. But there was clearly something significant about the extent of the man's substance abuse that Fleet was missing.

'All I'm trying to say,' Randy concluded, 'is that just because Wheeler's death wasn't suicide, doesn't mean he wasn't trying to kill himself.'

Friday 25 October, 2.47 p.m.

Melissa Haynes was a ghost. She was the key to this case, just as Rob had said, but Nicky was running out of ideas about how to find her. How did you track someone who left no footprints? Who had no digital presence, no assets, no friends or family? And more to the point, perhaps, how did someone end up that way in the first place? *Why?*

It was desperation that led Nicky to call the manager of Shining Light. She'd left him a stack of business cards, and he had assured her he would ask around among the other residents and get back to her if any of them had any clue as to where Melissa might be. That he hadn't been in touch suggested he'd had about as much luck as Nicky had – but when Nicky spoke to him over the phone, it turned out the call was worth making after all.

'I suppose there is one person you could try,' Zack Lawrence told her. 'I mean, I doubt very much she'll talk to you, or I would have suggested you speak to her before. But maybe, given the circumstances . . .'

Nicky wrote down the name and address the manager gave her. She thanked him, and, ten minutes after hanging up the phone, was on her way through another October squall to the other side of the city. She found the building she was looking for down a cul-de-sac, at the end furthest from the main road. The sign on the doorway, however, seemed to indicate the building contained a dental surgery, which wasn't the type of practice Nicky was looking for. She was about to buzz anyway when a woman's voice spoke from behind her.

'Can I help you?'

The rain had stopped, and the woman was lowering an umbrella. She was in her early fifties, Nicky guessed, with greying blonde hair and a wary smile.

'I'm looking for Susanna Fenton,' Nicky said. 'The psychotherapist? I was told she worked in this building.'

'I'm Susanna,' the woman said. 'Are you looking to make an appointment?'

'Not as such.' Nicky showed the woman her ID. 'I'm Detective Sergeant Nicola Collins. I was hoping to have a quick word.'

Susanna Fenton's smile immediately faltered. Nicky was used to people reacting guardedly whenever she announced herself as a police officer, but her intuition in this case was that Susanna had likely had dealings with the police before. Maybe Melissa Haynes wasn't the first client of hers to get themselves in trouble.

'The manager at Shining Light passed me your details, Ms Fenton. It's about one of the residents there, who I understand you were seeing.'

'I have a number of clients at Shining Light, Detective Sergeant. I volunteer there once a week, and submitting to counselling is one of the conditions of residency.'

'So I understand,' said Nicky. 'This client in particular is potentially in a great deal of trouble. I hesitate to use the phrase, but it would be no exaggeration to say it is a matter of life and death.' She indicated the door behind her. 'Could we perhaps talk inside?'

Susanna led Nicky up to a small but cosy room on the first floor of the building. They passed the dental surgery on the way, and Nicky tried not to wince at the high-pitched drilling noise that was seeping from the other side of the closed door. Inside the psychotherapist's office, the two women settled on opposite sides of a narrow desk. There was a pretty Georgian window behind Susanna's chair, and through it Nicky could see that another heavy downpour was bearing in.

'Before you go on, Detective Sergeant, I feel I have to make clear that I would never betray a client's confidence. Everything discussed in therapy is strictly private, meaning there is likely to be very little I'll be able to tell you.'

'I understand, Ms Fenton—'

'Susanna, please.'

'I understand, Susanna, but I'm not asking you to betray your client's confidence. I'm merely asking you to help me find her. Melissa Haynes is in trouble. She's either in danger herself, or represents a significant danger to others.'

Susanna stirred uncomfortably, and Nicky wasn't sure if it was because the psychotherapist had her doubts about Nicky's assessment, or it confirmed some pre-existing suspicion.

'May I ask how long you've been seeing Melissa?' Nicky asked.

Susanna appeared to consider this for a moment. 'About six months, on and off.'

'On and off?'

Again Susanna left a slight pause. 'Melissa isn't a full-time resident at Shining Light. A *companion*, they're called. She typically stays at the shelter for days, sometimes weeks, at a time. While she's there, she's permitted – encouraged, even – to make use of the charity's resources.'

'Including the service you offer? I believe you even have your own office at the shelter, is that right?'

'That's correct.'

It was clear Susanna was going to weigh each answer she provided very carefully, and limit her responses to conveying only as much information as was strictly necessary.

'How many sessions have you had with Melissa?'

'I would have to check my notes, but I would estimate . . . nine or ten? A dozen at the very most.'

'And have they been productive, would you say? I'm not asking you to betray Melissa's trust,' Nicky added quickly, when she saw the expression that was forming on Susanna's face. 'But she is in trouble, as I said. Very real trouble. I'm simply asking you for information that will help me to ensure her safety.'

The psychotherapist appeared to wrestle with herself internally. 'It took Melissa some time to fully engage,' she conceded. 'I think . . . I think she has struggled throughout her life with knowing who to trust. Which is entirely understandable given . . . Well. Given her background.'

Meaning that was as far as Susanna was prepared to go.

'I realise this is tricky for you, Susanna. But are you able to reveal *anything* about the sorts of things you discussed with Melissa? The events that you feel were at the root of her troubles, in particular. From what I've found out myself, it all started to go wrong for her in her teenage years. Would you agree?'

Now Susanna appeared distinctly uneasy. 'Detective Sergeant—' she began, but Nicky held up a hand.

'Please, Susanna,' she urged. 'This really is incredibly important. For Melissa's sake as much as anyone else's. We are investigating something that happened at Melissa's school when she was a pupil there – something we believe she was caught up in – and unless we fully understand what happened back then, we won't be able to protect her now.'

Once again the psychotherapist seemed to struggle with the ethics of what Nicky was asking her to do.

'I will not recount word for word what Melissa told me, Detective Sergeant,' Susanna said at last. 'Even if I were minded to, you wouldn't be able to rely on whatever I told you as being objectively true. All I will say is' – she paused, as though giving herself one final chance to hold back – 'is that Melissa has spent her life wrestling with the memory of something she claims she did.'

Nicky's ears, at that, pricked up.

'It is my belief,' Susanna went on, 'that Melissa has, in effect, been punishing herself – and trying to come to terms with her sense of guilt.'

Was that it, Nicky asked herself? Was that as good as Melissa making a signed confession to Ben's murder herself?

'And that, Detective Inspector,' Susanna concluded, 'is as much as I'm prepared to tell you. I've already shared more than I feel comfortable with, and it's only because I believe you when you say you are trying to help Melissa that I've spoken to you at all. Is she . . . is she all right?'

Now it was Nicky's turn to prevaricate. 'The honest answer is, we don't know. Which is why it's so important that we find her. She disappeared from the shelter several days ago, and nobody has reported seeing her since. Would you have any idea about where she might have gone? Any friends she might have mentioned, or family members? I know she was estranged from her parents, but a cousin maybe, or . . . or anyone at all. A place, even. Somewhere she might have mentioned that you know she associated with feeling safe.'

Susanna sighed. 'My sense is that Melissa has never truly felt safe, Detective Sergeant. Anywhere; with *anyone*. If she had access to the sort of refuge you seem to be referring to, I think her life would have turned out very differently.'

It was a fair point, and it made Nicky think about her conversation with Melissa's mother – about the fact that Melissa had cut herself adrift from her family almost the moment she'd left Beaconsfield and reached adulthood.

'Just one final question, Susanna,' Nicky ventured, aware of the response it was likely to provoke. 'In your professional opinion, would you say Melissa Haynes is capable of violence? Either to herself – or to others?'

The shutters came down. 'I will not answer that, Detective Sergeant. Nor am I trained to. I am a psychotherapist, not a clinical psychologist.'

Nicky nodded her understanding. She sighed inwardly, and made to get up from her chair.

'Although . . .' Susanna added, and Nicky paused halfway to standing. 'If my experience in life has taught me anything, it's that we are all capable of violence if pushed to it. Melissa is no more the exception to that rule than you or I.'

Outside, the clouds had turned the colour of coal. Nicky stood in the doorway of the building for a moment, knowing the heavens would open the minute she started up the cul-de-sac towards her car. And anyway, she was unsure where to head once she was back behind the wheel. She'd reached a dead end, literally. It was as Nicky had told herself: Melissa was a ghost. She'd lived her life that way for the past twenty years, and if she didn't want to be found now, Nicky was always going to be chasing after shadows.

Suppressing her frustration, she raised the collar of her jacket and headed back towards the main road. Sure enough, halfway to her car, the rain began to fall, so hard and so fast that Nicky was soaked through within seconds. The wind had picked up, too, and the noise of the deluge was such that she almost didn't hear her phone when it started ringing.

Her car was still some distance away, so she ducked into another doorway. She was expecting the phone call to be from Rob, and she braced herself to deliver her bad news: that, in terms of Melissa, and as things stood, there was nowhere else for them to go. But the number on the screen was one Nicky didn't recognise.

'Hello?' she said into the mouthpiece, raising her finger to her other ear to block out the sound of the rain.

There was silence on the other end of the line. Either that or the connection had been lost. Nicky stole a glance at the screen to check the reception. The display showed four full bars. She was about to speak again when she heard a voice sounding faintly through the speaker.

'Nicky?'

Nicky strained to hear. 'This is Nicky,' she responded. 'Who is thi—'

But somehow she knew the answer before she'd even finished asking the question.

'I heard you were looking for me,' said the caller. 'Please . . . I need your help.'

Ben – April 1997
(Three weeks before his death)

Ben wanted to be there when Melissa developed the pictures. For one thing, he had a vague notion he might be able to stop her seeing any that were too embarrassing. For another, after his run-in with the headmaster in the girls' wing he was as eager as he'd ever been to get on with things. He couldn't wait to see Harris's face when it was over. Ben would teach *him* for accusing him of lying. For treating him like something he might have scraped off the sole of his shoe. And the same went for everyone else at Beaconsfield, too. One way or another, they would *all* be made to pay, just as Callum had promised.

Ben peered through the glass-panelled door to make sure the classroom was empty. Melissa had assured him it would be. The school day had finished hours ago, and photography club only met on Mondays and Wednesdays. Sometimes members used the darkroom at the rear of the classroom to work on their projects, but only if they had permission, and Melissa had checked to make sure the rota was clear. If anyone caught *her* here, she would claim she'd asked Mr Garfield and he'd simply forgotten. Mr Garfield, who ran the photography club, was a pushover, apparently. According to Melissa, she had him wrapped around her little finger – something Ben, knowing Melissa, could well believe.

As he approached the back of the classroom, he saw that the red light on the wall outside the darkroom was on, suggesting that, even though Ben was early, Melissa was already inside. The door to the darkroom was ajar, meaning she hadn't started work yet on developing the photographs, and there was no chance Ben would ruin the negatives by blundering in. He reached to open the door wider – and then stopped when he heard voices filtering out from the darkness inside.

'—not what we agreed. I told Ben it would be just me and him.'

'So what? I'm not staying long. And if he gets here before I leave, we'll tell him there was a change of plan.'

It was Melissa's voice Ben had heard first, and if he wasn't mistaken she was talking to Lance. Arguing with him, rather.

'That's not fair. You saw how nervous he was. That's why I said we'd develop the pictures together.'

'What do you care how he feels? If I didn't know better, I'd say you were actually starting to *like* him.'

Ben recoiled. What was *that* supposed to mean?

'At least I'm making him feel wanted. Seriously, Lance. It's like you're actually *trying* to drive him away. What are you even doing here, anyway?'

'I've got a right to be here, haven't I? I thought I was part of this, too.'

'Yeah, well, that's what we thought as well. But you haven't exactly been acting like it lately.'

Lance muttered something that Ben didn't catch. Careful not to make a sound, and wary of the extra light that would leak into the darkroom, he opened the door a fraction wider.

'And anyway, that's exactly my point,' Lance was saying. 'We were supposed to be doing this together. *Deciding* on things together. Why do I get the feeling that Callum's decided everything for us?'

'Because he has! Callum's the one who figured everything out. Who came up with the idea in the first place.'

Once again Lance said something Ben didn't hear. He pressed himself closer to the gap in the door, and one of the hinges gave a creak. For a second nobody spoke, and Ben was worried the others had realised he was listening in. But then he heard Lance's voice carrying through the darkness. He spoke more softly than he had before, but somehow his words seemed more urgent.

'You know there's more to it than you think, don't you?'

Ben felt himself frown.

'Melissa? Did you hear what I said?'

'Of course I heard,' Melissa snapped. 'And of course there's more to it. You know how it turned out last time. There *has* to be more.'

'And you're not worried about it? You're not worried about *what*?'

When Melissa spoke again, it sounded as though she'd turned away. 'I trust him,' she said.

Lance gave a mirthless laugh. 'Seriously?' he said. 'You *trust* him? Knowing what he's capable of?'

Melissa didn't respond.

'How's the wrist, by the way?' Lance said, his voice taking on a crueller edge.

'What are you talking about?' Melissa replied, and even Ben could tell she was stalling. He imagined her pulling her sleeve down towards her hand.

'Your wrist. I saw the mark. Did Callum give you that?'

'Don't be ridiculous. I got it . . . playing hockey.'

'You're lying. I know he hurts you. I've seen the bruises before. Make-up only covers up so much.'

'He doesn't *hurt* me. He *loves* me! And don't think I don't know what you're trying to do.'

'What am I doing, Melissa?' Lance said. 'Tell me.'

'You're trying to split us up. You're *jealous*. Don't think it isn't obvious to me and Callum how you really feel about him. You *fancy* him. And you resent me for getting in the way.'

There was another silence. Ben pictured Lance scowling, and Melissa glaring right back. In the meantime he was trying to process everything he'd just heard. Melissa's wrist. Lance fancying Callum. *There's more to it than you think* . . .

'You do realise this is exactly what he wants, don't you?' Lance said. 'Us arguing. Bickering with each other. It's how he operates.'

'You're the one who's standing there arguing,' Melissa shot back. 'Take some fucking responsibility for once!'

'But that's just it! Callum doesn't *have* to take responsibility. He can get away with anything. He always has. It's not the same for people like us. That's the other reason he wants us involved.'

'So what are you saying? You want to back out?'

'No, I—'

'Because you'd better not, Lance. I'm telling you now. You'd better not even *think* about it.'

'Or what?' Lance replied. 'You'll tell Callum? I'm not afraid of him, you know.'

'No? Well, maybe you should be.' It was Melissa talking, but Ben would never have known it if he hadn't been following the conversation. He'd never heard her speak with such venom.

'What's that supposed to mean?' Lance had clearly registered the change in her voice as well.

Melissa didn't reply.

'Melissa? I said, what's that—'

Lance fell silent. Ben sensed something pass between them: a look, an understanding . . .

'You already know,' said Lance, after a pause. 'Don't you? Callum's already told you how this is supposed to end.' He sounded shocked. Afraid, even.

'Oh, please,' said Melissa. 'Don't pretend that you don't know, too. That you haven't known from the start. You said it yourself: there *has* to be more. Why do you think we needed somebody else in the first place? Or why Callum wouldn't let *you* do it?'

Ben heard footsteps approaching the door. They were shuffling, hesitant, as though Lance were backing away. Ben cast around, looking for cover. There was a cupboard in the corner closest to him, and he ducked into the gap between the unit and the wall. The space was barely big enough, and if Lance turned his way when he stepped out of the dark-room, he would surely see him. But when Lance appeared he was shaking his head, staring back into the darkness.

'I meant what I said, Lance,' came Melissa's voice, and Ben could tell she'd followed Lance towards the threshold. 'If you don't want to be a part of this, fine. Go tell Callum. See what he says. But if you go blabbing to anyone else, I swear to God . . . it won't just be Callum you'll need to be afraid of.'

Sicut serpentes, sicut columbae.

Fleet was in the car on his way back from the school, and the words kept playing in his head. It was like the line of a song that had snagged.

Sicut serpentes, sicut columbae.

He could picture the engraving of Beaconsfield's coat of arms in the building's entrance hall, and see the motto that was inscribed beneath it. 'Wise as serpents, innocent as doves' was how he'd initially translated the Latin, but there was another possible translation as well, he knew – substituting *wise* with *cunning*.

As he squinted through the rain that was hammering the Insignia's windscreen, it occurred to Fleet that maybe he'd been thinking about things the wrong way round. He'd gone to the school intent on finding out more about the fire, but maybe it wasn't the blaze itself he should be focusing on – rather the fact that whoever started it had got away with it without being caught. Maybe *that* was the source of inspiration Callum Richardson had been referring to.

Fleet turned the wipers up to high, and indicated to turn right, on to the road that would take him back towards the centre of the city. He tapped his thumb against the steering wheel.

So what scheme might someone who'd been planning to get Beaconsfield shut down have come up with – something as destructive as a fire, but that would allow them to proclaim their innocence? Arson itself would surely be too risky. Maybe the culprit had got away with it a hundred years ago, but these days there was very little chance that someone setting a building ablaze would not be caught. And a fire, somehow, did not feel subtle enough. Not *cunning* enough, particularly if Richardson himself had been involved.

Sicut serpentes, sicut columbae.

Cunning as serpents, innocent as doves.

Unless *innocence* was the key . . .

Fleet swung the Insignia towards the kerb. A horn blared from the car behind, and continued until the vehicle drew level. Fleet vaguely registered the gesture the driver was making through his window, but Fleet's attention was already on his phone. He was scanning his emails, searching for a list he knew he had somewhere but had so far paid very little attention to. The focus of the investigation had been on the people who'd been at Beaconsfield at the same time Ben was. The pupils, the staff. They'd had no reason to consider the circumstances of anyone who might have left the school before Ben had arrived.

Until now.

Three names immediately jumped out. It was mainly a question of timing. Fleet googled them all, and soon enough narrowed the list down to a single name. *Richard Hewitt.*

A phone call and a short wait later, Fleet had an address. He entered the location into his satnav, and – checking carefully this time before pulling into traffic – turned the Insignia around.

It wasn't the kind of place Fleet would have wanted to end up in. Then again, he doubted anyone else was particularly pleased to be here either. After thirty seconds standing in the lobby, Fleet could tell the staff were overworked and under-paid, and the patients dour and demoralised. And those were just the ones who weren't already confined to their beds.

'Can I help you, honey?'

Fleet turned towards the receptionist. He moved out of the way of an attendant manoeuvring an elderly lady in a wheelchair, and shook off the rain as he approached the front desk. He introduced himself and held up his ID.

'What kind of hospice is this exactly?' he asked.

'What kind?' The woman behind the counter beamed. She looked like a larger, more cheerful version of Fleet's mother: how his mum would have perhaps ended up looking if she'd smoked and gone to church less, and instead had eaten more cake. 'The underfunded kind, honey. But other than that we take all sorts. Cancer, stroke, Alzheimer's, motor neurone. What particular flavour are you looking for?' She said this last with a sparkle. Fleet had a sense she'd used the line before, and enjoyed it every time.

'Actually, I was hoping to talk to a man called Richard Hewitt.'

'Old Dickie?' The woman arched an eyebrow. 'Well, what-ever you want to speak to him about, I can promise you he didn't do it.'

Now Fleet was the one to raise his eyebrows.

'Come with me,' the woman said. 'I'll show you what I mean.'

She led Fleet along a corridor that was beige from floor to ceiling, and they eventually came to a stop at the threshold of one of the rooms. Most of the doors they'd passed had been open, and Fleet could tell that every room was identi-cal, save for the unique array of medical equipment that had been prescribed for each occupant. In Richard Hewitt's room, as well as the bed, television and a chair for visitors, there was an IV stand and an oxygen tank. Hewitt was hooked up to both.

'Dickie? You've got a visitor, honey!' the receptionist half yelled.

Hewitt's eyes were closed and he didn't respond. The rhythm to which his oxygen mask misted and then cleared again seemed to confirm he was asleep.

'You see what I mean?' Fleet's escort said to him. 'It's a good day for old Dickie if he can make it outside into the garden. Mostly he's lucky if he has the strength to get up to pee.' There was genuine compassion in the woman's voice, and Fleet had yet to see the smile disappear entirely from her face. If the rest of the staff here cared as much as she did, maybe this wouldn't be such a bad place to end up in after all.

'What's wrong with him?' Fleet asked.

But before the woman had a chance to answer, another voice cut in.

'Who the hell are you?'

Fleet and the receptionist both turned.

'Are you a reporter? Because if you are, you can get out of my father's room *right now*.'

'Mrs Leigh . . .' the receptionist began, even as Fleet reached for his ID.

'I'm with the police, Mrs Leigh,' he said, as the woman who'd appeared in the doorway – slim, fair, about Nicky's age – strode into the room. She moved directly to her father's side and rested a hand protectively on his shoulder. She peered intently at Fleet's identification, but rather than seeming reassured, her eyes grew a fraction tighter.

'Perhaps I'll leave the three of you to get acquainted,' said the receptionist.

Fleet nodded his thanks, and waited until she'd made herself scarce.

'Mrs Leigh—'

'What do you want, Detective Inspector?'

Fleet had the impression the woman had about as much time for the police as she did for members of the press. 'I was hoping to speak with your father,' he said. 'But, well . . .' He glanced at the man in the bed.

'My father's in no condition to speak to anyone,' said Mrs Leigh. 'As I'm sure you can see.' The pause she left felt laden with reproach. 'What's this about, anyway? I swear to God, if it's something to do with what's going on at that school . . .'

'I'm afraid it is,' Fleet confirmed. He held up a hand, cutting off Mrs Leigh's reply. 'But not in the sense I'd imagine you're thinking. No one suspects your father of being involved in a crime, Mrs Leigh. Rather, I was hoping he might help us solve one.'

There'd been a break in the weather, and Fleet suggested they talk outside. Angela Leigh led the way to the hospice's garden. It was lush and overgrown, and a welcome contrast to the prim fastidiousness of Beaconsfield's immaculately tended grounds. One or two patients and their carers seemed to be considering following them out, but for the time being Fleet and Richard Hewitt's daughter had the space to themselves.

'From what I understand,' said Fleet, 'your father taught drama at Beaconsfield College for fifteen years. And then he left, in March 1996, just over a year before Ben Draper went missing. It was rather an abrupt departure, I believe.'

Angela gave a sniff. 'My father dedicated his career to that school. To those *kids.*' She spoke the word with obvious bitterness. 'And his reward was being hounded from his job. He had a stroke six months later, two more over the next ten years. For the past decade, Detective Inspector, my father has been virtually bed-bound.'

They were ambling along a path that cut diagonally across the lawn, and abruptly Angela stopped walking. 'How old do you think my father is? If you don't already know, have a guess.'

Fleet didn't know, but he would have estimated from the brief time he'd spent in the same room as the man that Richard Hewitt was in his early eighties. Late seventies, at least.

'He's sixty-seven,' Angela said, sparing Fleet from having to answer. She seemed to take some grim satisfaction from Fleet's evident surprise.

'That's what being falsely accused does to a person,' Hewitt's daughter went on. 'He never got over it. Could never comprehend why someone would make up such *lies*. Someone, moreover, he'd taken under his wing.'

She smiled without a trace of good humour. 'Although I've always considered it ironic. You know, that a child my father mentored to become an actress should use the talent he helped her develop to end his career. Because that's the thing,' she said. 'My father wished nothing but the best for her. Before Melissa Haynes accused him of sexual assault, he always used to say she had a *gift*.'

And there it was. There'd been no names mentioned in any of the newspaper reports Fleet had discovered when he'd been searching the internet in his car, but it had been clear that immediately prior to Hewitt's departure, there'd been some form of scandal at the school. The timing had fitted perfectly – Melissa and the others would have been fourteen, in their second year at Beaconsfield – and in line with Callum Richardson's insinuations, it seemed precisely the type of scheme a group of disaffected teenagers might have come up with. A teacher disgraced, parents panicked about the welfare of their kids . . . it wouldn't have been out of the question that Beaconsfield would end up closing. Its reputation, at the very least, would be in ruins. And all the while the accuser herself would remain insulated from blame.

And yet the school had survived. Hewitt had ended up losing his job, but the stories had come to nothing and Beaconsfield had ridden out the waves.

'What happened exactly?' said Fleet, as they resumed walking. 'An accusation was levelled against your father—'

'A *false* accusation.'

'A false accusation,' Fleet amended. 'And he ended up losing his job. But he never faced any criminal charges, did he?'

'It would have been better if he had,' said Hewitt's daughter. 'At least then he would have had a chance to present his side of the story. To expose that lying bitch for what she was.' She flushed, and Fleet couldn't tell if it was anger or embarrassment. 'Sorry, I . . . I just get so mad when I think about it. Even after all this time. I mean, I was eight years old when it happened, and most of the details I only heard about when I got older, but my entire family has been dealing with the consequences ever since.'

'But if the allegation was never proved, why did your father end up losing his job?'

'A *compromise* was reached,' Angela said, making it sound like a dirty word. 'Another member of staff came forward and basically refuted Melissa Haynes's story. And from what my mother told me, Melissa's parents *knew* she was lying – but of course they couldn't back down. So they agreed not to press charges on the condition my father lost his job.'

'Who was the member of staff who came forward?'

'I've no idea. All I know is he or she was the only person who did, and that it ultimately made no difference anyway. Not to Dad.'

'Did he try to fight it?'

'Fight it *how*? If he left quietly, the school said, he would at least be able to get a post somewhere else. If he caused a fuss, the details of the accusation would be made public, and then, even if he was cleared, there wouldn't be a school in the country who would go anywhere near him. And he would have lost his job at Beaconsfield anyway. There's no way they would have kept him on with a cloud like that hanging over his head. The school had a *reputation* to protect,' she added scathingly.

Fleet thought of Adrian Harris, who would have been Beaconsfield's headmaster at the time. But only just. If he was wary of exposing the school to scandal now, after twenty-four years at his post, what must he have been like then, when he was still trying to prove himself worthy of the role?

'And Beaconsfield's a private school, remember,' Angela said. 'It wasn't as though Dad had a union or anything to back him up. So he basically had no choice but to hand in his resignation, and hope he could get a job somewhere else. Except it turned out that no other school would go near him anyway. After what happened at Beaconsfield – after what Melissa Haynes did to him – my father never worked again.'

They'd reached the far end of the garden, and they turned back to face the building. Like Angela, Fleet imagined, he was picturing her father lying bed-bound inside.

'He should be enjoying his retirement,' Angela said. 'Playing with his grandkids. He has six, you know. Three of which are mine.' She looked skyward for a moment, and raised a finger to one of her eyes. Then she turned to face Fleet with the same steely anger in her expression that she'd displayed when she'd first walked into her father's room.

'And that's everything, Detective Inspector. That's the entirety of my father's story. Meaning that, whatever happened to that boy whose body they found, Dad had nothing to do with it. He never even *met* him.' She scoffed and shook her head. 'Not that I'm surprised you're here. As soon as I saw the headlines, I knew that someone would turn up eventually. Either a journalist or somebody like you, looking to dredge up old lies.'

'I can assure you, Mrs Leigh, I—'

Fleet's phone buzzed in his pocket, but before he could check who was calling, Richard Hewitt's daughter held up a hand. 'Please, Detective Inspector, do me the courtesy of not patronising me. The police didn't help us before, and I'm not naive enough to believe that you're here to help now.'

Fleet held his tongue. He wished there was something he could say to mitigate the imposition of his visit, but the reality was, Angela was right. In terms of what had happened to her father, the damage was already done.

'So if you don't mind,' Hewitt's daughter said, beginning to move away, 'I would be grateful if you and your colleagues could please leave my family in peace.'

Fleet was back in his car by the time the rain began to fall again. It turned out the call he'd missed was from Nicky, but when he tried to phone her back, it went straight through to voicemail. He raised his eyes to the building outside, and his thoughts returned to his conversation with Richard Hewitt's daughter.

So that was what Callum Richardson had wanted Fleet to

find out. Melissa Haynes had been involved in a scheme to engulf Beaconsfield in scandal – one that had cost a man his career, but had ultimately fallen short of what it had set out to achieve.

Was the implication that Ben had been dragged into something similar? It would explain the unlikely friendship between Ben and the others. In Fleet's mind, there'd always been something odd about their association. By all accounts Ben had never made friends easily, and Melissa, Lance and Callum had been as close-knit as they come. How did a boy with a backstory like Ben's slot neatly into a group like theirs – unless they invited him in? It wouldn't have been hard to entice him. To make him feel valued, after Ben had spent his entire life believing that not even his father wanted him around. Fleet thought of what Father Steiner had told them: that Callum and the others were brighter than Ben, cannier. *And Ben was easily led* . . .

But then what happened? The others had a plan that involved Ben, but somehow Ben ended up getting in the way? Or something went wrong? But how did a plan to bring down a school end up with a boy lying forgotten in an unmarked grave, with no word about his fate leaking out for the best part of a quarter of a century? And why, after all that time, would someone choose to make an anonymous tip-off to the police – or be in a position to in the first place?

And then there was the game. Hide-and-seek. Where did *that* come in?

Whatever the truth, and whatever Callum Richardson's real intentions were in directing Fleet towards Richard Hewitt, one thing was clear in Fleet's mind: it was more important than ever that they find Melissa. If Angela Leigh's story was to be believed, Melissa was cold, calculating, and willing to sacrifice whoever it took to achieve her ends – all of which made her far more dangerous than Fleet and Nicky had realised.

He picked up his phone to try Nicky one more time, but once again it went straight to voicemail.

Friday 25 October, 5.27 p.m.

The clouds had closed like a lid upon the city, and the rain had resumed its steady fall. It wasn't quite dark when Nicky arrived at the docks, but even so the streets were deserted. The gutters overflowed, blocked by leaves and litter, and a cruel wind cut in from across the sea.

If there was a part of the city more destitute than Blackhawk, then this was it. A mile up the coast, a former shipyard had been developed into an indoor multiplex, boasting a cinema, bowling alley and upmarket gym. Here, though, a dying industry was still clinging on, and a block inland from the cranes and container ships it was just squat, sad-looking houses, most of which were probably worth less than the mortgages that had been taken out to buy them. Some had been abandoned and boarded up, including the building Nicky pulled up outside.

She checked her phone before stepping from the car. She'd tried to reach Rob to let him know where she was heading, and when he'd failed to answer she'd contemplated leaving him a message. But then it had struck her that it was probably for the best that she hadn't got through. If Rob knew what she was doing, he'd almost certainly tell her to wait, or at the very least to call in for a pair of uniforms to go with her. Melissa, though, had asked her to come alone. Begged her, practically, and Nicky didn't want to do anything that might spook her. To Nicky's ear she hadn't sounded like a killer – she sounded genuinely terrified. There was the possibility she was faking, but in Nicky's experience nobody was that good an actor.

Now, the display on Nicky's phone told her she was in one of the many dead spots that blighted the city, meaning there was nothing she could do about contacting Rob anyway. Like it or not, she was on her own.

Not for the first time, she marvelled at Melissa's change of circumstances: from the hallowed halls of Beaconsfield and a vista of opportunity before her, to an area of the city in which hope was in as short supply as beauty was. Rumour had it that the council planned to raze this entire block, probably to make way for another multiplex. The house Melissa had directed Nicky to had apparently once been a squat before all the residents had left, fearful the building was about to come down on their heads. Melissa had only gone back there in desperation, she'd told Nicky over the phone, and she didn't plan on being there for long. She was afraid to stay in one place, but at the same time she was running out of places to go. Hence why in the end she'd called Nicky. She'd heard through one of the companions at Shining Light that Nicky had come looking for her, and word was that Nicky was somebody she could trust.

'Melissa?'

Ridiculously, Nicky felt an urge to knock on the front door, in spite of the fact it was half boarded over and scrawled on with graffiti. She pressed her nose to one of the windows alongside it, but those on the ground floor had been covered with metal shutters, and the perforations were too small to see through. She turned to the door again, and realised the padlock that had been sealing it shut had been prised apart. When she gave the door a tentative push, it creaked open on rusty hinges.

'Melissa? Are you there? It's me, Nicky.'

The residents may have left some time previously, but the smell of human occupancy remained. The plumbing in the building had clearly given out years ago, and the floor in the hallway was strewn with rubbish. The stink wasn't quite as pungent as the stench they'd encountered at Lance Wheeler's flat, but even so it was an uncomfortable reminder of what they'd found there. Nicky couldn't help but worry that she was already too late.

'Melissa?' she called again, and waited for some indication that she'd been heard. But the silence remained as thick as the fetid air.

She stepped into the hallway, and right away there was a groaning sound behind her. She spun, just in time to see the front door swing shut.

'*Shit.*'

What little light that had been coming into the house from the recently awakened streetlamps was immediately extinguished. In the sudden darkness, Nicky's instinct was to head back outside and find a way to call through for that backup. She knew she was taking a risk coming here on her own, and that however Melissa had come across on the phone, she was still a suspect. But Nicky could just imagine the reaction down at the station if word got out that she'd failed to bring in a key witness just because she'd got spooked by the dark – all the sexist, misogynistic bullshit she'd have to deal with once again, after all the years she'd already spent proving her worth. And Rob wouldn't have turned back. Maybe if he was obliged to climb a ladder, he might hesitate momentarily, but even his phobia of heights wouldn't stop him from doing his job.

Nicky switched on the torch on her phone, and slowly began to pick her way into the gloom. Two steps further along the hallway, her foot came down on what felt like a glass bottle, and her ankle twisted beneath her. She swore again, and berated herself for not bringing a proper torch. She wasn't even sure how much battery life she had left on her phone. When she checked, the bar was just under half-way full, which in theory was more than enough. But it was an old phone, and the battery had a habit of giving out when it still had a quarter of a charge remaining.

The better news was that she now appeared to have a signal. Only a single bar, but it was something. She decided to fire Rob a text – but before she could open the app, she heard the unmistakable sound of movement, and then a noise like someone catching their breath.

'Melissa?'

The shuffling sound stopped. 'Hello?' came the reply from up ahead. It was Melissa's voice, Nicky was certain, and she sounded just as petrified as she had on the phone.

'It's me, Melissa. It's Nicky. I'm alone, just like I promised.'

Melissa, in response, gave a whimper. Nicky couldn't tell whether it was desperation or relief.

'Melissa? Where are you? It's safe to come out. Whatever trouble you're in, I guarantee we'll be able to set things straight.'

From what Nicky could tell, the house seemed to have a fairly standard layout. Living room at the front, dining room in the middle, and then what would once have been a kitchen at the far end of the hall. There was also a staircase ahead of her and to the left, but it looked to be pretty much impassable. A discarded mattress covered the bottom steps, and further up there was a tangle of wires and broken banisters.

'Melissa?'

Nicky continued along the hall. Both the living room and

dining room appeared to be empty, and she stopped at the threshold of the kitchen.

'Melissa? Are you in here?'

The kitchen went further back than Nicky had anticipated. The room seemed bigger than the rest of the downstairs combined, and Nicky's torch beam barely penetrated to the furthest wall. Unlike the living room and dining room, the kitchen was cluttered with old furniture: a table, overturned chairs, and another mattress propped against one of the walls, not to mention the kitchen cabinets themselves. It was an obstacle course, in other words – and the perfect place for someone to hide.

'Melissa, I—'

Abruptly, Nicky's phone started ringing. The chime shattered the heavy silence, and Nicky was so startled that the phone slipped from her hand. She fumbled to catch it, and as she did so, everything seemed to happen at once. There was a noise, like a piece of furniture being shoved to one side, and then movement in the corner of Nicky's eye. A shadow darted towards her. It seemed to grow as it closed in, and dimly she realised it was a figure raising something above their head.

'Melissa, wait—' Nicky started to say, but she was too late even to lift an arm. Something heavy struck her on the temple. She'd shifted at the last second, lessening most of the impact, but still the blow rattled her skull. She staggered, dazed, and her legs buckled beneath her. Her phone clattered off to one side, leaving the torch beam jutting uselessly towards the ceiling. On her hands and knees, she tried to crawl, but something grabbed her leg and pulled her round, and she found herself staring blearily towards the torch beam. And then the darkness seemed to envelop her, and a pair of hands closed around her neck.

Ben – May 1997
(One week before his death)

Ben crouched nervously in the shadows of the staircase. His eyes swept the entrance hall, from the arched window over the doors, aglow with moonlight, to the huge wooden engraving of the school's coat of arms directly above him. It was the same coat of arms that appeared on his blazer, and it always gave Ben the creeps. On one side of the image there was a bird, which Ben had heard from somewhere was supposed to be a dove, but to his mind looked more like a crow. Its single dead eye stared out coldly. Facing the bird, there was a snake. It was coiled around a tower, which Ben had always presumed represented the school, and the snake appeared to be laughing as it *squeezed*.

There was a creak, a noise like a footstep on a floorboard. After a moment, the sound repeated. It seemed to be coming from the darkened corridor off to his right. Ben edged forward to try to see if somebody was approaching – and then jumped when a voice sounded directly behind him.

'Where do you think you're going?'

Ben spun. Seeing who was there, he clutched his heart.

'*Lance*. You scared me. I thought I heard you coming the other way.' Ben peered over Lance's shoulder. 'Where are the others?'

'Keep your voice down, for Christ's sake,' Lance hissed, dragging Ben back into the corner. 'The others aren't coming. Callum didn't see the point in all of us taking the risk of getting caught. So it's just me,' he added sourly.

'Just you? But—'

Lance leered. His face seemed to warp in the pallid moonlight. 'What's the matter? Were you hoping Callum would hold your hand? Or *Melissa*, maybe?'

Ben couldn't think how to reply. He swallowed.

Lance checked the space around them. 'Did anyone see you leave your dorm?'

This time Ben shook his head. When he'd slipped from his bed, there'd been the usual stirrings from the other bunks, but if anyone had noticed him leave, they would have assumed he was going to the toilet.

'They better not have,' Lance warned, and his eyes hardened.

Ben swallowed again, and Lance flicked his head.

'Come on. Let's get this over with.'

Even during daylight hours, the school felt cold and inhospitable. At night, when the rest of the occupants were asleep, it was like creeping through a nightmare. The floorboards protested every footstep, and the corners seemed to crawl with shadows. At one point Ben stopped and turned, certain he'd felt a breath on his neck. But the corridor behind them was empty.

'Is this the quickest way?' Ben whispered to Lance's back. As far as Ben could tell, they were taking the long way around, via the wing of the building that was closest to the woods. When Ben looked through one of the windows towards the trees, he saw their ghostly silhouettes, as well as his own ashen reflection looking back at him.

'No,' Lance replied, without turning around. 'But if we go the most direct route, we pass Harris's room, and rumour has it the man never sleeps.'

Ben recalled his last encounter with the headmaster, in the

passageway outside Melissa's room. He felt nothing like as bold as he had then. And he knew as well that, were the headmaster to catch him prowling the corridors again, even the mention of Callum's name wouldn't be enough to save him.

They climbed a winding stone staircase, and when they reached the top Lance slowed his pace.

'Which room is his?' he hissed to Ben.

Ben was scanning the corridor ahead of them. They were actually here. They were actually going to do this.

'Ben,' said Lance impatiently. 'Which room is Father Steiner's?'

Ben dug his hand into his pocket, and pulled out the key he'd swiped from the chaplain's jacket the previous week. 'The fob says *Rowan*. Whatever that means.'

'They're tree names,' said Lance. 'Look.'

They were passing a door labelled *Blackthorn*. Opposite was another marked *Ash*. From behind it, Ben could hear a teacher snoring. It sounded like someone sawing wood, and the noise carried so clearly, Ben was convinced it would rouse the entire floor.

Lance seemed unperturbed, and crept on.

Rowan was exactly halfway along the passageway, they discovered, as far from an escape route as it was possible for it to be.

Lance gestured for the key and, when Ben passed it over, immediately slid it into the lock. They knew the room would be empty, because Father Steiner was away for the entire week, but Ben had a sudden fear that there might be someone waiting for them inside. Isaac maybe, was his first thought, even though he'd seen Isaac asleep in his bunk as he'd crept from his dorm. But if not Isaac, then perhaps one of the teachers. Or even the headmaster himself . . .

For a moment Lance seemed to struggle, as though the key wouldn't turn. It was possible that, rather than issuing Father Steiner with a spare, the caretaker had changed the lock. But then there was a click, and the sound of a bolt drawing back. Ben knew he should be pleased – he had a feeling that, if the key hadn't worked, Lance would almost certainly have blamed *him* – but instead he felt his stomach fall. There was no backing out now.

'After you,' said Lance.

Ben's first thought when he entered the room was that the chaplain was asleep on the bed. In addition to the shape of the bed covers, like a man lying curled up on his side, it was the smell that convinced him. He recognised it from the vestry, from all the times Father Steiner had stood close. It was a dusty, slightly unwashed musk, tinged with incense and coffee, and the chaplain carried it with him wherever he went.

But as Ben's eyes adjusted to the gloom, he saw the bundle on the bed was just a pile of blankets. And there was enough light from the bulb in the corridor to show him the rest of the room was empty, too.

He felt a rush of relief – which vanished instantly when Lance closed the door behind them and switched on the overhead light.

'Are you crazy?' Ben spluttered. 'Someone will see!'

'Relax, would you? Everybody's asleep.' All business now, Lance strode past Ben, deeper into the room.

'But . . .' Ben's eyes swept the doorframe for gaps, but it seemed to be sealed tight. 'What about the window?'

'What about it?'

'The curtains aren't even drawn!'

'So draw them! Jesus Christ, Ben, get a grip, would you?'

Ben stood rooted, terrified of being spotted from the grounds.

'For fuck's sake,' Lance muttered, and he crossed to the window himself. But rather than drawing the curtains, he faced Ben and jabbed a thumb towards the glass. 'See?' he said. 'Nobody's going to be outside at this time of night.'

'But . . .' Ben repeated, and even to his ear it sounded like a nervous stutter.

Lance rolled his eyes, and whipped the curtains across. 'There. Satisfied? Now let's get on with what we came here to do. The longer you stand there bleating, the greater the chance someone will *hear* you.'

Lance went back to what he'd been doing. As well as the bed, the room contained a wardrobe, a chest of drawers, a reading chair by the window, a bedside table and a desk. Lance seemed to be scouring the desk's cluttered surface.

'What are you doing?' Ben asked him.

'Never you mind,' Lance replied. After a moment he turned. 'Well?' he said, when he saw Ben still standing in the same spot. 'Don't you have something to be doing, too?'

Ben's hand went to his back pocket. 'Right,' he mumbled. 'Sorry.'

Lance was obviously looking for something, but Ben had no idea what. After a moment Lance seemed to feel Ben watching him, and his chin dipped towards his shoulder. Ben turned hastily away, and moved towards the chest of drawers.

He took the photographs Melissa had developed from his back pocket.

'Put them in with his underwear or something,' said Lance snidely.

Ben opened the topmost drawer. It was full of Father

213

Steiner's pants and socks, and ordinarily Ben might have scrunched his nose up in disgust. But he was too focused on what it was he was about to do. Even though he'd known exactly why they'd come here, and they'd been planning this part for weeks, Ben wasn't sure he'd ever really believed things would get this far.

He risked a glance over his shoulder. Lance was continuing his search of Father Steiner's desk. But as Ben watched him, Lance stopped moving, as though he'd found whatever it was he'd been looking for. Once again his chin moved towards his shoulder, and Ben quickly turned away.

He looked at the photographs in his hand. He was deliberately holding them face down.

Just do it, he told himself. *Just do what you came here to do.*

This time when he considered the contents of the drawer in front of him, he allowed his expression to curl into one of disgust.

He deserves it – remember? And Harris deserves it, too. This whole stinking place does. It's real – the loneliness, the humiliation, the shame – so why shouldn't this be, too?

'Ready?' said Lance, from behind him.

Ben reached into the open drawer, and turned back to face Lance empty-handed.

'Ready,' he said. 'Let's go.'

Second murder linked to 'boy in the crypt' killing

- *TV star Callum Richardson knew both victims*
- *Questions raised over police bias*
- *Elite private boarding school faces parent backlash*

A murder enquiry has been launched after a second former pupil of Beaconsfield College was found dead, less than a week after the remains of Ben Draper were discovered on the school's campus.

The body of Lance Wheeler, 38, was found in a one-bedroom flat he was reportedly renting, on Wednesday afternoon. Sources say suicide was initially suspected, but an autopsy report obtained by this newspaper states categorically that Wheeler was murdered, prompting police to reclassify the investigation.

The two victims – killed twenty-two years apart – are rumoured to have been friends during their time at Beaconsfield, and police refuse to rule out the possibility that the crimes are linked.

'It is clearly too early to draw any firm conclusions,' a spokesperson said. 'At this stage we are very much keeping an open mind.'

Pressed to comment on fears that others associated with the school may be in danger, the spokesperson declined to respond directly.

'There are absolutely no grounds for public concern, or for undue scaremongering,' the spokesperson said.

Television presenter Callum Richardson, himself a former acquaintance of both victims, has in the meantime criticised the leaking of the report on Wheeler's death, calling into question its timing.

'You have to ask yourself, why now?' Richardson said. 'I'm on the brink of launching a movement that promises to shake the political establishment in this country to its core. And all of a sudden a story is concocted – before the facts of each case are fully known – that is almost perfectly engineered to engulf me in scandal.'

It has long been widely known that Richardson was a pupil at Beaconsfield at the time of Ben's disappearance. It was only after Ben's body was discovered last week, however, that information emerged suggesting Richardson was one of the pupils who'd been playing with Ben in the moments before he went missing.

Richardson has since admitted that he was also friends with Wheeler during his time at Beaconsfield, and that both he and Wheeler were among the last people to see Ben alive.

At an impromptu press briefing held outside the studio of his television production company, Richardson did not pull any punches. In a typically combative performance, he accused Manish Apte, the Conservative-backed police and crime commissioner for the police force that is running the two murder enquiries, of directly engineering what Richardson described as a 'smear campaign'.

'If Manish wants to go on record refuting that, I'm more than happy to keep a slot on my show open for him on Monday morning,' Richardson added.

The police and crime commissioner could not be reached for comment.

Meanwhile, the school at the centre of the deepening scandal has issued a statement attempting to reassure parents and staff, insisting that pupils are being shielded from any potential impact on their well-being, and that lessons and school routines will continue as normal.

'What happened to Benjamin Draper was a tragedy,' the statement reads, 'and everyone at Beaconsfield College wishes to express their deepest condolences to Benjamin's family. We can confirm that Lance Wheeler is an alumnus of this school, but so far we have not been contacted regarding the circumstances of his death, and do not feel it appropriate to issue any further comment at this time. We will, however, continue to offer our full cooperation to the police.'

A memorial service for Ben had been scheduled to take place in the school's chapel on Sunday morning, and a spokesperson for the school has confirmed that the event is to proceed as planned. Attendance will reportedly be by invitation only, and the grounds will be closed to the general public.

Callum Richardson is expected to be among the guests.

- *Coming, ready or not . . . A children's game turns deadly.* TURN TO PAGE 5 for the full background on Ben Draper's 'hide-and-seek' disappearance

- *Callum Richardson: Pundit, politician . . . prime minister?* Will scandal derail a divisive figure's attempts to take charge of the country? TURN TO PAGE 9

Saturday 26 October, 10.21 a.m.

'How long have you known, Detective Inspector?'

When Fleet was finally admitted into Burton's office, the superintendent was reclined in the seat behind his desk, his hands braced against the arms of his chair and an array of printed newspapers on the surface before him. One, Fleet noticed, was open to the same story he'd skimmed himself in between pacing the waiting area outside. He'd ended up tossing the paper aside in frustration.

'Well?' said Burton – but when Fleet tried to speak, he held up a hand. 'And do me the courtesy of not trying to deny it. I know you're chummy with Randolph Green, and I know full well that he would have had a quiet word with you about the real cause of Lance Wheeler's death well in advance of submitting his report.' The superintendent leaned forward. 'Didn't I instruct you right at the start of this to keep me abreast of any developments? *Before* I read about them in the press? So if you have any misconceptions that I'm going to permit you to remain in charge of this investigation, and you've come here to grovel for forgiveness, you can—'

'She's missing, Roger.'

Burton frowned at the interruption. 'What?'

'Nicky. DS Collins. She was chasing up a lead and now she's gone. So spare me the rollicking for the time being, would you? I'm here because I need your help.'

*

Burton listened as Fleet told him what he knew – which, in terms of the past twenty-four hours, was frustratingly little. The last time Fleet had seen or spoken to Nicky had been in his office, just before he'd headed out to Beaconsfield. He'd left Nicky to her own devices, confident that if anyone could track down Melissa Haynes, she could.

'And she clearly found something, Roger. I've been trying to get in touch with her since late yesterday afternoon. I even swung by her flat first thing this morning, but she wasn't home. None of her neighbours have seen her since she left for work yesterday morning.'

'What about her boyfriend's place? Did you try—'

'She doesn't have a boyfriend. I called her dad, but he hasn't heard from her either. And before you ask, there's not a chance in hell she'd be at her mum's, and she doesn't have any other family that I know of.'

The superintendent's frown set deeper.

'She would never just go off-grid like this,' Fleet insisted, as he paced in front of Burton's desk. 'She'd call, or text, or find some other way to let me know what she was doing.'

'Unless she wasn't able to,' Burton countered. 'You said she was following up on a lead. So maybe she *had* to go off-grid in order to—'

'Roger, please,' said Fleet, turning. He'd already been over every scenario he could think of in his head, and there was simply no explanation as to why Nicky would have failed to check in that didn't involve her being in some sort of trouble. 'You know me, and I know Nicky,' he told Burton. 'And we both know I wouldn't be in here if I wasn't one hundred per cent convinced that something was wrong.'

Burton's expression tightened a fraction. 'You mean you have a *feeling*,' he said disparagingly. Fleet was well aware that the superintendent wasn't one to indulge his subordinates when it came to judgements that weren't based on stone-hard facts. Fleet's theory was that it was because Burton had never really had an instinct for the job himself. The *real* job, that is. When it came to politics and back-room manoeuvring, Burton's instincts were as honed as his squash-court backhand.

'The reality is, DS Collins has been out of contact for less than a day,' Burton said. 'Her day *off*, I'm guessing. You do realise it's the weekend, don't you? Is DS Collins even scheduled to be working today?'

'Probably not,' Fleet conceded. 'But then again, neither am I. Nor you, I would imagine. And Nicky and I haven't exactly been punching out every day at five on the dot. It's been just the two of us – remember? A lot's happened over the past twenty-two years for us to try to catch up on.'

Burton visibly bridled. 'So this is my fault? Is that what you're saying? Because I'm not going to sit here and—'

Fleet couldn't hold his temper in any longer. He slammed a palm on to the surface of Burton's desk. 'For Christ's sake, Roger!'

Burton bit down. His fingers tightened on the arms of his chair.

Fleet dropped his head, and breathed into the silence.

'Do you really think I hold anyone to blame but myself?' he said, looking up. 'Yes, I admit, I'm pissed off. At you, and Apte, and all the others. At Webb in particular, that—' Fleet cut himself off, shaking his head instead of voicing what he really thought of the man from the Home Office, whose plots and subtle manipulations had ensured that Fleet and Nicky were caught in the middle of a political pissing contest in the first place.

'But I'm Nicky's commanding officer,' Fleet said. 'Meaning *I'm* the one responsible for her safety. I shouldn't have let her go off on her own, not after it was clear to me that something else was going on ... something bigger than a decades-old murder.'

He stood up straight.

'Which is exactly what I'm trying to tell you: it's all connected, Roger. Ben's death. Lance Wheeler's. Nicky going missing. I don't know how exactly, but I'm *sure*. And now a police officer's life is at stake.'

Burton made a face then, and Fleet could tell he was trying to convince himself that Fleet was being overdramatic. But there was a crease of uncertainty as well.

'Tell me,' the superintendent growled. 'What exactly would you have me do?'

'Give me the resources I asked for,' Fleet said. 'We need every spare body on the search for Nicky, and after that we need to find whoever's behind this. The politicians have had their fun. They've stirred up a shitstorm, and done everything to make sure Callum Richardson is at the centre of it. But now they need to let us do our jobs.'

'You seem to be assuming that this investigation remains yours to run,' Burton responded. 'You disobeyed a direct order, Detective Inspector. I can and will not tolerate insubordination.'

'Fine,' said Fleet. 'Once Nicky's safe, you can punish me however you see fit. But in the meantime, you know I'm the one with the best chance of finding her. It's going to take days for whoever you bring in to replace me to get up to speed. Which I realise would suit Webb and the rest of them just fine, but we're talking about a double murder here, Roger. A killer who's evaded capture for twenty-two years. Who, if you want my opinion, isn't done with killing yet.'

Burton looked up then. Fleet held his gaze, trying not to think about the implications of what he'd just said for the chances of them finding Nicky alive.

The superintendent dragged both palms across his face. The man that emerged appeared thin and grey, and for the first time since Fleet had entered the office, it struck him that Burton looked even worse than he had when Fleet had last seen him. The previous time, Fleet had put it down to the stress of meeting with Apte and Webb, but there was clearly something else eating at him. Whether it was the same sense of guilt that was gnawing at Fleet, he couldn't be sure. Burton was in his office on a Saturday morning, and it hadn't even crossed Fleet's mind to try the superintendent at home, so maybe it was simply the years of overwork catching up with him. But for the first time, Fleet wondered if it might actually be something more serious.

'Do you know what your problem is, Detective Inspector?' Burton spoke to the surface of his desk, then raised his eyes, and for all his wan appearance, there remained a steel to his demeanour. 'Your problem is, you've got no idea what policing actually *is*. Oh, you think you do. You think it's simple. Right versus wrong. Innocent versus guilty. You just follow that damn *intuition* of yours and assume everything will turn out fine.'

The superintendent made no attempt to disguise his scorn. Fleet, in response, held his tongue, knowing that whatever Burton had to say, there was no sense in interrupting him until he'd got it off his chest.

'What you've never seemed to comprehend, Detective Inspector, is that politics *is* policing. Do you think I like kowtowing to some scruffy, jumped-up millennial who can't put his phone down for more than three seconds? Or knowing that, when he ends up as political roadkill – which he inevitably will – somebody else just like him will scurry out of the nearest hole to take his place?'

The superintendent left a silence, almost like a dare, and then sniffed when Fleet continued to say nothing. He raised his hand to his face again, this time pinching at the bridge of his nose.

'I'm sick and tired of it, if you want the truth. I'm sick of the politics, the politicians. And I'm sick of people like you coming in here and telling me what I should and should not do. As though you have any idea . . . *any* of you . . . of the things, the *pressures*, I have to try to . . .'

He allowed the sentence to trail off, as though deciding he was wasting his breath. He flapped a hand.

'Do what you have to,' he said dismissively. 'I just hope you realise how much it's going to cost me. How much it's going to cost this entire constabulary. The powers that be are going to see it as us letting Richardson off the hook.'

'If it makes you feel any better, Roger,' Fleet said, 'you're doing the right thing.'

Burton scoffed, and sat back heavily in his chair. 'There's nothing you can say that's going to make me feel better, Detective Inspector.' He waved a hand again. 'You've got what you came for. Now get the hell out of my office.'

Saturday 26 October, 9.15 p.m.

They'd narrowed the window of Nicky's disappearance down to sometime after five o'clock on Friday evening.

The trail until that point was becoming clearer. After Fleet had left Nicky in order to catch up with Randy at the school, she'd spent several hours at her desk – focused on the hunt for Melissa, judging by her computer's search history. In the middle of the day she'd made a phone call to Shining Light. Fleet had called the number himself, and the manager, Zack Lawrence, confirmed he'd spoken to Nicky and suggested she contact Melissa's counsellor. He'd repeated the address he'd given to Nicky, and when Fleet had paid a visit to Susanna Fenton, too, Melissa's therapist had recounted the conversation she'd had with Nicky almost word for word. Fleet wondered if Nicky had interpreted what the psycho-therapist said the same way he had. Nicky didn't know everything Fleet did – about Melissa's role, in particular, in ending a man's career – but nothing Susanna Fenton had said reduced the likelihood, in Fleet's mind, that Melissa was the killer they were looking for.

At 4.49 p.m., Nicky had tried to call Fleet – at the point he'd been wrapping up his conversation with Richard Hewitt's daughter – and soon after that her car had been captured on a traffic camera. She hadn't been driving towards the police station, and her flat was in the opposite direction entirely. Fleet's best guess was that Nicky had for some reason been heading towards the docks, a fact borne out by the last location signal generated by her phone.

But that was where the trail – and the signal from Nicky's phone – went dead.

The only other clue they had was a call Nicky had apparently received shortly after leaving the psychotherapist's office. Fleet's colleagues had identified the number, but it wasn't connected to a contract, nor did it appear in Nicky's contacts. Whoever had been calling, Nicky had spoken to them for just over a minute, and it was shortly after the call had ended that Nicky's car was pictured heading south. Were the two events connected? Fleet assumed they had to be, and he had a theory about who it was Nicky had spoken to – but assumptions and educated guesses had got them no closer to finding out what had happened to Nicky after that.

Now Fleet was sitting at his computer in his office, waiting for news from the teams out searching for Nicky's car, and desperately trying to figure out where to direct the hunt next. Burton hadn't stinted on resources – as well as the uniforms on the streets, they had bodies scouring traffic cams and rounding up CCTV footage, as well as techies looking at the data from Nicky's phone – but so far the past twenty-eight hours remained a blank.

Was it her, Nicky? Was it Melissa who called you? What did she say to you? And what was it you wanted to say to me?

If only Fleet had answered the phone when Nicky had tried to get hold of him. If only he'd given her clearer instructions about not approaching Melissa alone. Even before Fleet had spoken to Randy and to Richard Hewitt's daughter, Melissa had been their prime suspect. Nicky had suggested intensifying the search for her sooner. If only Fleet had listened, and at least *tried* to convince Burton to give them the resources they would have needed.

There was a knock at the door, and it was only then that Fleet realised his head was in his hands. He sat up straighter.

'Sir?' said a PC, leaning into Fleet's office. 'You've got a visitor.'

The officer moved aside, and Holly appeared in the doorway.

'Sprig. What are you doing here?' Fleet rose from his seat as his ex-wife came into the room. She didn't say anything. She just crossed the floor and wrapped Fleet in a hug. Fleet wasn't sure there was anything he'd ever needed quite as much.

'Is there any word?' said Holly, stepping back.

Fleet had texted Holly earlier in the day to let her know that Nicky was missing. Doing so had gone against his better instincts, particularly given Holly's condition. But in addition to the full-blown search, Burton had authorised an appeal for information to the general public, meaning Holly would have found out anyway, and would have been furious with Fleet for not telling her.

'We're doing everything we can,' he said. 'We'll find her, Sprig. We will.'

It didn't escape Fleet that he was as much trying to reassure himself.

Holly took hold of his hands. 'I know you will,' she told him, with a certainty Fleet wished he shared.

Holly glanced at Fleet's desk, which was covered in paperwork and printouts. There were also two untouched cups of coffee, which someone must have brought him at some point, though Fleet could not have said when.

'When did you last take a break?' Holly asked him. 'I bet you haven't eaten all day.'

Fleet smiled tiredly. Holly was right, but food was the last thing on his mind.

'I had a sandwich an hour or so ago,' he lied.

Holly obviously took pity on him, because she pretended to believe him. 'Well,' she said. 'You still look like you could use a break. Come on. Let's get some air.'

'I can't, Sprig, I have to . . .' Fleet didn't finish the sentence, but instead gestured uselessly towards his desk.

'You can,' Holly insisted. 'And we don't have to go far. You never know, a fresh perspective might help.'

After letting the other officers involved in the search know where he would be, Fleet led Holly to the lifts, and together they rode to the rooftop.

The roof was where Fleet and others in the building came to smoke. It wasn't Fleet's preferred option. But he was better on the roof than he would have been on a ladder, and when the choice was between smoking up here or *not* smoking, it was barely a choice at all.

Out of habit he'd wedged a cigarette between his lips and readied his lighter even before they'd reached the door leading outside. It was only when he cupped his hands and brought the flame to the tobacco that he remembered he was supposed to have given up.

'Go ahead,' Holly told him, when she noticed him stall and glance her way. 'You look like you need it.'

Still Fleet hesitated, his eyes this time going to Holly's midriff.

Holly smiled. 'I'll stand upwind.'

They made their way past a group of younger officers vaping beside an air conditioning unit, and towards a private corner of the rooftop. Without consciously realising it, Fleet had taken them to the side of the building that faced towards the docks.

He lit his cigarette, and then tilted his head and exhaled towards the sky. Above them, the moon was a ghostly scimitar among the stars.

'Are you warm enough?' Holly asked him. She was still wearing her coat, but Fleet had left his suit jacket in his office. The breeze this high up was strong enough to sweep the smoke away, and there was a chill in the autumn air – a gentle hint of the approaching winter. But Fleet was numb to everything except the sickness in his gut.

'I'm fine,' he said.

He gazed across the rooftops towards the docks, the lights on the cranes visible in the distance. Below them, cars clogged the surrounding roads, and pedestrians trickled in and out of the neighbourhood restaurants and bars, as though this were a normal Saturday night.

'Is that where she was when she went missing?' Holly asked. 'Somewhere out towards the docks?'

Fleet must have been staring more intently than he'd realised.

'It's where she was last headed,' Fleet told her, tearing his eyes from the horizon. 'But the truth is, by now . . .' *She could be anywhere*, he didn't need to add.

Holly looked where Fleet had been looking. She gave a shiver.

'Jesus, Sprig, I'm sorry. Let's go back inside. I should have taken the hint.' Fleet hastily stubbed out his cigarette on the guard rail in front of them.

'No, it's fine,' Holly said. 'I'm not cold. I was just . . .' She glanced towards the distant cranes. 'I'm not cold,' she repeated. 'I promise.'

Even so, she wrapped her coat tighter. Whether consciously or not, she kept her arms crossed over her stomach.

'How are you feeling?' Fleet asked her.

'Me?' Holly responded, sounding surprised.

Fleet's eyes dipped again towards her belly.

'Oh. I mean . . . fine. Physically. Just a bit embarrassed I came to you in such a state when you and Nicky were dealing with *this*.'

'You weren't to know. And anyway, it was good to see you. It's always good to see you.' Fleet looked at the cigarette packet he'd started fiddling with in his hands.

'It's been good to see you, too,' Holly agreed.

Fleet's eyes met hers and then rebounded.

'Listen, Sprig. I've been thinking.'

'About what?'

Fleet turned to face her. 'Just . . . and don't take this the wrong way . . .'

Holly's expression tightened a fraction, and Fleet considered whether he would be better off holding his tongue. It was none of his business, after all. He had no right to interfere. Even though his intention was to help, there was no guarantee Holly would see it that way, and after what had amounted to a small detente, he risked pushing her further away again.

On the other hand, he'd already pushed her so far they'd ended up divorced, meaning he could hardly make things worse. And Holly knew he had her best interests at heart. Didn't she?

'I was wondering . . .' Fleet ventured. 'Just, whether you'd given any more thought to . . . you know. To the baby. To what you intend to . . . That is, to whether you'll . . .'

'To whether I'll keep it?'

'Right,' said Fleet, wary of the flatness to Holly's tone.

'I told you already that I will, Rob. Nothing's changed. And to be honest, if there's something you were planning to say on the matter, now's probably not the best time.'

'No, I know. But it's important. It's a big decision. And I didn't want you to feel you had to make it on your own.'

'I appreciate that,' Holly answered, sounding distinctly unappreciative. 'But I *am* on my own, Rob. And while I realise I have nobody to blame for that but myself, it also means I have a right to make my own choices. I'm a big girl. I'm perfectly capable of thinking through the implications of my actions, you know.'

Fleet turned slightly away, rubbing his eyes with his fingertips. Already this was going precisely as he hadn't meant it to. He felt an urge to light another cigarette, but he knew that would only rile Holly further.

'Look, Holly . . .' *Holly*, this time, he noted, not *Sprig*. Which part of his subconscious mind had decided *that* would help the situation? 'I'm just worried about you, that's all. About the thought of you doing this all by yourself.'

'Are you saying you don't think I should keep it? That I won't be able to cope?'

'No! That's not what I'm saying at all. I just—'

'Because it sounds as though that's what you're saying,' Holly interrupted. 'Jesus Christ, Rob. You *know* I've always wanted a baby. More than anything else in the world. You've known that since the day you met me, practically, and you're sure as hell aware of it now.'

They were getting dangerously close to replicating the same argument they'd had on and off for years: the one that always led them around in circles, and that had eventually caused them to agree to separate. It was the only path they'd been able to identify that offered them a way out of the endless loop.

And yet here they were, being drawn right back in again. Fleet could see it happening, and he knew he should say something to diffuse the tension.

Instead: 'That sounds an awful lot like an accusation,' he said.

'An accusation? In what way is it an *accusation*?'

'This idea that I've always known that having a baby is exactly what you wanted. That it was my fault for somehow not understanding how much it meant to you.'

'Oh, please,' said Holly. 'Don't let's start all of this again. Not now.'

'We never had the conversation, Holly,' Fleet said, aware he was being disingenuous. 'When we met, you said you were focused on your career. You were very definite about that.'

'I said *for the time being* I wanted to focus on my career! That's not the same thing, and you know it!'

Holly threw up her arms and turned away. Immediately she turned right back again.

'Besides,' she said, 'what the hell business is it of yours? I mean, you do realise what's going on here, don't you?'

Fleet narrowed his eyes. 'What?'

'You're trying to *fix* me. You're frustrated because you can't help Nicky, so instead you're—'

Holly stopped talking. Her face fell, as though she'd heard through Fleet's ears what she'd just said.

'Oh, Rob. I'm sorry. Really, I'm so, so sorry. I shouldn't have said that.' She reached out, but her hand stopped centimetres short of Fleet's arm.

His jaw had clamped shut, and he swallowed painfully.

'It's fine,' he said.

'No, it's not fine. Forgive me, Rob, please. I had no right to . . . to even come here in the first place, I . . .'

'I'm the one who had no right,' said Fleet.

'But—'

'Holly, really. Forget it. Forget I even brought it up. It's like you said. Now isn't the best time. It obviously isn't, because I completely messed up what I was trying to say to you.'

Holly's expression dissolved into a smile. 'You're trying to look out for me. That's all. I *know* that, and still I allowed myself to get angry.'

'No, it's . . . it's not that. I mean, yes, it is, but also . . .' Fleet sighed. He took hold of Holly's outstretched hand. 'Look. All I was trying to say—'

But he got no further.

There were voices in the background, and Fleet turned to see Sean Bevan, the young DC who'd brought the anonymous email that had started all of this to Fleet's attention in the first place, talking to the uniforms by the air conditioning unit. As one, the uniforms pointed Fleet's way, and when Bevan spotted him in the corner, he immediately hurried over.

'Sir,' he said, breathless. His freckled skin was flushed, the colour of his cheeks clashing with his ginger hair.

Fleet glanced at Holly. 'What is it, Sean? Is it Nicky's car? Her phone?'

'Sir, it's . . . it's both. One led us to the other. I'm not sure which we found first, but—'

'Where?' Fleet cut in.

The DC tipped his head towards the docks without breaking eye contact. 'A block from the shore. The car was parked outside an abandoned house. DS Collins's phone was on the floor inside. But, sir . . .'

Fleet braced himself. There was more, clearly. And whatever Bevan still had to say, it obviously wasn't good news. 'Spit it out, Sean. Did they search the house? Is Nicky . . . Did they . . .'

'The house was empty,' said Bevan, and Fleet closed his eyes momentarily with relief. But when he opened them again, the DC was still staring at him apprehensively. The officer's eyes flicked towards Holly, who had tucked in tight beside Fleet.

'You can speak freely, Sean,' Fleet reassured him.

'Yes, sir.'

Bevan appeared to be gathering himself, and Fleet waited for him to go on.

'Sir, they . . . they found something else as well. Not in the house. In the water.'

Fleet closed his eyes again. He knew what was coming now, and he knew there was no escaping it, but it was the only thing he could do to hold it off.

The DC kept speaking.

'They found a body. And they think . . . that is, they say . . . They say it's her, sir. They say it's Nicky.'

Ben – May 1997
(Five days before his death)

Ben saw Callum talking to Lance up ahead. Before they could spot him approaching, he turned on his heels, heading back the way he'd just come. He knew he would probably be late for class, but he preferred the idea of being humiliated by Mr Cavanagh again to being cornered by Callum and Lance. They would want to know where he'd been, why he'd been avoiding them for the past two days. And then Ben would have to lie, and Callum, he knew, would see through him in an instant.

He turned the corner, relieved to have escaped unnoticed – and came face-to-face with Melissa.

'Ben. *There* you are. We've been looking for you all over.'

Ben tried to keep the anxiety from his face. 'You have?' He glanced behind him, half expecting to see Callum and Lance closing in on him from the rear. Did Melissa know they were right around the corner? 'Sorry, I . . . I've been catching up on work and stuff.' He laughed nervously. 'I just realised it's only four weeks till the exams.'

Melissa smiled. 'Oh, I wouldn't worry about the exams.' She lowered her voice to a whisper. 'I mean, who knows? Maybe none of us will end up having to sit them.' She smiled again, conspiratorially this time.

Ben did his best to smile back.

'Listen, Ben.' Melissa placed a hand on Ben's arm, and guided him towards the side of the corridor. They ended up tucking into a stone alcove around one of the windows, slightly removed from the steady stream of pupils. 'Are you OK? We've been worried about you. That is . . . *I* have.'

Melissa allowed her hand to trail down Ben's arm, until her fingertips were resting lightly below his elbow.

'I'm fine,' said Ben. 'Really. I was just . . . I'm late for class, that's all. It's Cavanagh again, and he hates me enough as it is.'

Melissa appeared to be studying him intently. 'You're not . . . I don't know. Having second thoughts or anything. Are you?'

'No!' Ben replied, a bit too quickly. 'What makes you say that?'

Melissa shrugged coyly, but her eyes never left Ben's. For the first time, he noticed a dark patch on her skin at the point her jaw met her earlobe. In the light from the window, Ben could see she'd tried to cover it with make-up, but either she'd missed a patch, or the bruise was deep enough that it continued to show through.

'It's like I said,' she replied. 'We haven't seen you around. And Lance, he . . .'

Ben screwed up his eyes. 'What about Lance?'

Melissa shrugged again. 'It's nothing. Just Lance being Lance, probably. You know what he's like. But he thought perhaps . . . he said he wasn't sure you'd gone through with it. The other night.' She looked over her shoulder. 'You know. With the photos.'

Ben showed his indignation. 'But he was there. He *saw* me. I put the photos where I said I would, right at the back of the—'

Melissa gestured for Ben to lower his voice. She glanced around, and Ben caught a flash of that bruise again. It made Ben think of what Lance had said to Melissa in the darkroom:

I know he hurts you. And it made Ben think of the time Callum had hurt *him*.

'So we're OK?' said Melissa, turning back. 'I can tell Callum there's no need to worry?'

'Of course,' Ben replied. He felt an urge to move a hand to his back pocket, but caught himself and linked his fingers in front of him. 'Why would Callum need to worry?'

Melissa's smile broadened. She touched Ben's arm again. And then, out of nowhere, she leaned forward and kissed him on the cheek. When she pulled back, she looked up at him through her eyelashes and rolled her lips. 'Don't tell Callum I did that, will you?'

Ben swallowed hard. He shook his head.

Melissa gave him one last smile. 'Meet us tonight,' she said. 'Eight o'clock. In the common room. If you get there first, find some seats in a corner.'

This time Ben nodded. He watched as Melissa turned away, and then raised his hand to his cheek.

She'd kissed him. Melissa had kissed him.

It was what he'd wanted. What he'd fantasised about since the day they'd met.

And yet all he could think about was what he carried in his back pocket, and the fact that Melissa's lips, when they'd touched him, had been deathly cold.

Fleet stood staring over the inky water. The sun was hours from rising, but there was a morbid glow cast by the lights over-looking the team of officers gathering evidence further along the dock. If anything, from where Fleet was standing twenty metres away, the fuzzy light made the water appear even more impenetrable – as though it were holding something back.

'How are you doing?'

Fleet turned to see Randy approaching along the walkway. He'd removed his coveralls as far as his waist, and was reaching into his suit jacket pocket. As he came to a standstill at Fleet's side, he lit two cigarettes, and then silently held one out for Fleet to take.

Fleet reached for it, grateful. 'I didn't know you smoked.'

'Neither did my ex-wife,' Randy replied. He sucked and then exhaled theatrically. 'She wasn't happy when she found out, I can tell you. Her solicitor tried to claim medical damages as part of the divorce settlement. Said I'd aggravated her asthma.'

'Which ex-wife was this?'

'Contestant number three. She was right, I suppose. It's a disgusting habit. Now I only smoke to spite her. And when I feel I really have to.'

They stood in silence until their cigarettes were finished. Randy stubbed his out on a nearby mooring. He joined Fleet in staring at the coal-black water.

'It's good news, you realise,' he said at last. 'I mean, not for Melissa Haynes, obviously.' He glanced back at his colleagues working along the dock, then turned to face Fleet more fully. 'But it wasn't her, Rob. It wasn't Nicky. There's no reason to believe she isn't alive.'

As if in answer, the water lapped at the wall of the dock, making a gurgling noise that to Fleet's ear sounded a lot like a laugh. It wasn't Nicky, that was true. The officers first on the scene had been too quick in connecting the discovery of a woman's body with the proximity of Nicky's broken phone and abandoned car. But that didn't mean the divers wouldn't discover another body when they started searching the harbour in a few hours' time.

'Tell me about Melissa,' Fleet said to Randy.

'Rob . . .'

Fleet raised his eyes from the water and turned his gaze on the pathologist.

Randy read the look, and gave a sigh. 'She was strangled, exactly like Lance Wheeler and Ben. I won't know for sure until I see her lungs, but it's my feeling that was what killed her, not the water. At a guess . . .' The pathologist hesitated, perhaps anticipating Fleet's reaction – knowing that, whatever fate Melissa had suffered, Fleet wouldn't be able to help imagining it befalling Nicky, too. 'At a guess, she was choked to death, before her body was tossed into the harbour.'

For a second or so, Fleet was convinced he was going to be sick.

'Anything else?' he managed to say.

Randy was eyeing Fleet concernedly. 'Again,' he said cagily, 'I'll need more time with her. But it was apparent right away that her body had been treated like a pin cushion. And some of the track marks on her inner thighs were recent. Days old, at most. Possibly hours.'

Fleet scowled at the water.

A fresh perspective. That was what Holly had suggested he needed, and she'd been more right than she'd realised. Now that their lead suspect had been found murdered, everything Fleet had thought he knew about the case had just been flipped on its head.

'Who's doing this, Randy?' he asked in frustration. 'Who took Nicky? Because assuming she's ... that she's not already—'

'She's not,' said Randy categorically. 'If she were dead, that would make it my fault, because I'm the one who encouraged her to become a police officer in the first place. And frankly, although my ego is considerable in size, I'm not sure it's robust enough to take the hit.'

Fleet gave a smile in spite of himself. It quickly faltered. 'The point is, the only way I'm going to find her now is to solve this case.'

This time Randy didn't argue.

'Maybe we were wrong,' Fleet went on. 'Maybe it's not just one person we're looking for. Maybe whoever killed Lance and Melissa isn't the same person who killed Ben.'

Randy seemed to consider this for a moment, then shook his head. 'I'm rarely wrong, Detective Inspector, as I've told you before. And that's not just my ego talking. When it comes to forensic medicine, it's a statistical fact. If it wasn't the same person who killed all three victims, I'll eat my proverbial hat.'

It wasn't the answer Fleet wanted to hear. Or maybe it was. *Christ.* He didn't know *what* he wanted to hear. This whole case was as inscrutable as the water below his feet.

'There's no question in my mind that Melissa Haynes, Lance Wheeler and Callum Richardson were all guilty of something,' Fleet said, thinking aloud. 'Richardson wears his lack of remorse like a badge. It's almost as though he *wants* people to be aware of what he's capable of, just so long as he knows he can't be caught. And as for Lance and Melissa, you said it yourself, Randy. Lance was on his way to drinking himself to death. Melissa was killing herself with drugs. Their entire lives since Beaconsfield have been an exercise in self-flagellation.'

'So Richardson then?' said Randy. 'That's who you're left with.'

Fleet had long ago reached the same conclusion himself. 'I think he's ruthless enough,' he agreed. 'Particularly if it was a question of saving his own skin. But just from a practical standpoint, how could Richardson have done it? He's got an airtight alibi for Lance's murder. And when it comes to Melissa, I can't quite see him prowling around the city's slums.' He looked towards the houses in the streets beside the docks. 'Richardson could have paid someone to kill Lance and Melissa, of course, but if he hired a so-called professional, I'd say he'd be entitled to ask for his money back.'

Fleet was thinking of what Randy had said about the messy nature of the murders, as well as the fact Lance's 'suicide' had been so poorly staged. As for Melissa, Randy had already told Fleet that her body had likely been in the water less than twenty-four hours before it had washed up alongside one of the busiest walkways in the docks.

'Unless the killings were deliberately sloppy,' the pathologist suggested. 'To throw you off track.'

Again, it was something Fleet had already considered, but he couldn't bring himself to buy it. His instinct was that Randy had been right the last time they'd spoken. The person they were looking for was highly volatile. It was *passion* that was driving them – rage, impotence, obsession – not money. The irony being, Richardson in that sense would have been a perfect candidate. His whole career seemed powered by fury.

'The killer isn't a professional,' said Fleet. 'For whoever's behind this, it's deeply personal.'

The two men stood in silence. After a moment, Randy took out his packet of cigarettes again. Fleet declined with a gesture. He kept his eyes fixed on the surface of the water, an ache building behind his frown.

'So if it's not Richardson,' Randy said, lighting his second cigarette, 'it must be somebody else entirely. Someone who's punishing all three of them? For something they did? The murder of Ben Draper being the obvious infraction. Except we just agreed that whoever killed Lance and Melissa also killed Ben.'

'You agreed that,' said Fleet, his frown deepening. 'All of a sudden I'm not so sure. Unless—'

Voices were raised further along the docks, and Fleet and Randy turned. A news van had pulled up beside the police cordon, and a pair of uniformed officers were busy trying to prevent a camera crew breaching the perimeter.

After watching the commotion for a moment, Randy turned back to Fleet and cocked his head. 'Unless what? Don't keep me in suspense, Detective Inspector.'

'It's nothing. I . . .' Fleet watched the news team for a moment longer, his thoughts slowly crystallising in his head. *You never know*, came Holly's voice, *a fresh perspective might help.*

'Rob?' Randy prompted. 'What's on your mind? You've got a look like my first wife used to get just before she decided it was time to redecorate.'

Fleet turned to him. 'We've been looking for a killer,' he said. 'But maybe, all along, we should have been looking for another victim.'

Randy narrowed his eyes. 'You mean three isn't enough for you?'

'No, I . . . Shit.' Fleet had started frisking himself to try to find his mobile, and realised he must have left it in his car. 'Can I borrow your phone?'

The urgency of Fleet's tone seemed to convince Randy to hold off for the time being on further questions. He handed Fleet his mobile, unlocking it with his thumbprint as he passed it over.

Fleet dialled and held the phone to his ear. As he waited for someone to pick up, he tapped his hand against his leg.

'Sean?' It was the same DC who answered as had broken the news to Fleet on the roof of the station about the washed-up body. 'Listen,' said Fleet. 'I need a pair of uniforms sent to Callum Richardson's house. Richardson, that's right. A protective detail. Richardson's probably not going to like it much – he trusts the police about as much as he trusts the prime minister – but tell them not to take no for an answer, even if it means sitting in the car outside Richardson's front door.'

Fleet looked at Randy, who'd raised an eyebrow. The pathologist was probably thinking along the same lines Fleet was: that when Burton heard about what Fleet had just authorised, he was likely to burst a blood vessel.

'And once you've done that,' Fleet continued down the phone line, 'take another pair of uniforms out to the school with you . . . To Beaconsfield, right. You're looking for a man named Steiner. Father George Steiner, the school chaplain . . . Yes, I know what time it is. If he's asleep you'll have to wake him up. But I want him in an interview room by the time I get back to the station.'

DC Bevan ran over what he'd been asked to do, and Fleet nodded.

'And one more thing, Sean . . .' Once again Fleet met Randy's eye. 'When you approach Father Steiner, use caution.'

Ben – May 1997

(Three days before his death)

Ben had been carrying the photographs around with him for days now – since, instead of slipping them into Father Steiner's drawer as he'd pretended to, he'd palmed them into his back pocket.

Now, in the old graveyard in the woods behind the chapel, a place he'd only come to because he knew few people in the school ever did, he sat with the photographs spread out before him.

What had he been thinking?

In most of the pictures he was pretending to be asleep. He'd only had to remove his shirt, and his bottom half was covered by a blanket, but the suggestion from the way Melissa had composed the photographs was that he was completely naked. The story they told was of a young, innocent boy tenderly being immortalised by his lover. Slowly, he appeared to be waking up – before smiling, and then reaching for the person behind the camera, urging them to join him on the bed. It had been easy enough pretending when it was Melissa he'd been looking up at – Ben recalled how his body had betrayed his genuine excitement, which he'd awkwardly had to conceal from her – but now Ben saw the photos as they were intended to be viewed, he felt physically sick. Partly it was imagining Father Steiner gazing down at him, in line with the story he and the others had set out to construct. Mainly, though, his revulsion was with himself.

In his defence, he'd never expected things to go this far. It was a fantasy, he'd thought. A *game*, just as Callum had referred to it himself. And for a time it *had* been fun, imagining that the fate of the entire school lay in their hands. Although, really, for Ben, the bigger draw had been the sense of belonging. The invitation the others had offered him to be part of their world. But that had been a fantasy, too, it turned out – as much of a sham as the story they'd set out to construct.

It was Melissa's kiss that had sealed it in Ben's mind. The fact that she'd kissed him in the first place, for one thing. And then the feel of her lips against his skin when she had.

What do you care how he feels? If I didn't know better, I'd say you were actually starting to like *him.*

Lance had spelled it out in the darkroom, and Ben had been in denial of the truth ever since. Melissa had only ever been pretending. She was better at it than Lance was. Almost as good as Callum. But all three of them had been lying to him from the start. That was why he always had such trouble finding them when *they* didn't want to see *him*. The idea of the four of them not being seen together too often was just an excuse. Although Ben wasn't completely stupid. He knew it was Callum and the others protecting themselves as well. If anything went wrong – if they got found out – they could wash their hands of him. Pretend that they'd never really been friends in the first place. Which, of course, they hadn't.

To think, Ben had spent most of the past four days trying to convince himself that he was wrong. He'd even considered going back to Father Steiner's bedroom on his own, at a time he knew the chaplain would be in the chapel. Maybe if he planted the photos the way he was supposed to, he told himself, the others *would* like him. Maybe . . . maybe it had all been a test, one he'd come so close to passing.

But that kiss. Melissa's lips . . .

He was kidding himself, he'd realised. *Again*. And now he was decided. He would get rid of the photographs once and for all, and then this whole thing would be over. He could go back to being him. *Just* him. The way it had always been, and the way he knew now it would always be. It wasn't so bad. In fact, in many respects it was easier. At least when the entire world was against you, you always knew exactly where you stood.

Ben wiped his eyes.

He gathered the photos together in a pile, and tried to focus on how best to get rid of them. He might have burned them if he'd thought to bring a lighter – if he'd been careful, he could probably have swiped Callum's – although there was a risk someone passing would see the smoke. He could venture deeper into the woods and throw them into the lake. But what if they washed up on the shore? Better, Ben thought, to bury them. To let them rot beneath the earth, exactly like the bodies in the surrounding graves.

He cast around, ignoring his instinctive unease and searching for the ideal spot. Under one of the slabs he was sitting on would be perfect. Nobody would ever find them there.

After checking the clearing to make sure he was alone, he set the pile of photographs to one side, and bent to lift the nearest stone. But it was lodged in tight, almost as though it had been cemented to the ground.

He tried another, smaller slab, and this one came up surprisingly easily. Too easily for Ben's liking. He needed something heavier, like ... *there*. The largest of the slabs was cracked, meaning even if he couldn't lift the whole thing, he would probably be able to prise up the part that wasn't wedged into the earth.

Straddling the stone, he tried to work his fingers into the

crack. It was already several millimetres wide, and when he felt a slight draught, he wondered if he could simply post the photos through, three or four at a time. There was clearly a cavity of some sort underneath. Plenty of space, probably, for a handful of photographs.

But when he turned to pick up the photos to start sliding them through, something made him stop and turn back.

Tentatively, he peered more closely at the stone beneath his feet. He licked his fingertips, then hovered them a centimetre or so above the crack. Immediately his fingers felt cold. There was: there was a definite draught. Meaning . . . what exactly? The stones in this corner of the clearing weren't the same as the markers on the graves. If anything, they looked more like the slabs on the floor inside the chapel.

Ben stood up straight. He took in the position of the graveyard in the clearing, and the chapel fifty metres or so further up the hill. The space between was filled with trees. But not trees like the ones elsewhere in the woods: the gnarled chestnuts and impossibly tall oaks. The trees between the graveyard and the chapel were younger, and Ben already knew the reason why. He'd studied enough pictures of Beaconsfield through the ages to know that the younger trees had been planted on the site of the original chapel. That was why the graveyard was here in the first place, and it was partly because of the graveyard that the chapel had been moved. Whoever had rebuilt the school had wanted the new chapel to be bigger, better, and the only option short of exhuming all the bodies in the cemetery was to position the new building further up the hill.

All of which meant that the stones beneath Ben's feet had probably come from the original building. And if there was a cavity somewhere below them, that meant . . .

With something between trepidation and excitement, Ben dropped on to his hands and knees, and tried to peer through the crack. He worked his fingertips into the gap, the way he had before, and this time pulled with all his strength. But it was no use. The slab didn't shift.

Frowning, Ben stood upright again, and surveyed the cluster of stones at his feet. The slab was maybe half a metre wide and twice as long, and one end seemed to disappear into the slope. After stealing another glance around the clearing, he took a step forward, positioning one of his feet on the grass, and the other on the slab beside the crack. He raised his knee, then stamped down with his heel. He stamped again, and again, and again – and all at once there was a sound like a gunshot echoing through the trees.

Ben stumbled backwards on to the grass, almost falling, so startled was he by the noise. He fully expected to see one of the teachers, or even the headmaster himself – the noise he'd heard somehow the sound of their fury. But there was no one, and when Ben looked back at the slab, he realised the rifle sound had come from the slab splitting further in two.

He bent towards the stone, and this time when he wedged his fingers into the crack, the larger portion of the slab moved easily. He had to wiggle it a bit to break the grip of the weeds that were clinging to its corners, but within a few minutes he was able to lift it and slide it to one side. And what he saw underneath took his breath away.

The slab had been resting on what at first glance looked like a wall buried underground. But quickly Ben realised it was an archway. An *entrance*. Below it, a set of steps sheared off into the darkness. He'd discovered the old chapel's crypt!

There was some debris at the top of the stairwell, most of which he'd probably displaced himself, but the opening was wide enough, and the steps clear enough, that Ben could easily climb down inside.

Almost in disbelief this time, he looked around the clearing again. Did anyone else know the crypt was here? Ben didn't think so. He couldn't see how that would be possible, not with the entrance covered over the way it was.

No, the crypt was *his*. It was his own private discovery. Not Callum's, not Melissa's, not Lance's. His own. A private place, just for him. A *hiding* place.

When he dropped on to his hands and knees again and peered inside, he could just about make out the bottom of the stairwell. The vault beyond looked several metres wide at least, but there was no telling how far it extended back.

'Ben? Is that you?'

Quickly, Ben scrabbled to his feet.

'Father Steiner,' he blurted. 'What are you doing here?'

The chaplain was beside the trees, near the pathway that ran down the hill from the chapel. As he edged closer, Ben used a heel to try to move the slab he'd dislodged back into place, but it was too heavy to shift.

'I was just about to ask you the same question,' Father Steiner said. 'I thought I heard someone setting off firecrackers. Did you hear anything? Or see anyone?'

Father Steiner turned to look deeper into the woods, and Ben used the opportunity to move away from the entrance to the crypt. The opening was only half a metre or so wide, and from across the clearing would almost certainly look like a shadow, but if the chaplain moved much closer, there was a chance he would notice the hole.

'Now that you mention it,' Ben said, 'maybe I did hear something. But I thought it came from up near the school. It sounded like a . . . a clash of hockey sticks or something.'

This time the chaplain twisted his lips. 'I suppose it could have been that. With all the trees, sounds do tend to echo out here.'

Ben seized on the opportunity to change the subject. 'Actually, Father Steiner, I was just on my way to see you.'

'You were?'

'Yes, I . . . I thought I might show you some of the sketches I did. From the book you gave me? You said you wanted to see them.' Ben had dumped his school bag on one of the gravestones when he'd first arrived in the clearing, and he picked it up and started rummaging inside. But before he could find his sketchbook, the chaplain frowned again and peered over Ben's shoulder.

'What's that?'

'What?' said Ben, consciously not turning around. His heart was hammering in his chest.

'That. On the floor over there, beside those stones.'

Ben had no choice but to look where Father Steiner was pointing.

'Did you drop something?' the chaplain asked him.

Realising what Father Steiner had spotted, Ben's eyes widened in horror. The photographs. He'd left them piled on one of the slabs.

Before Father Steiner could take another step, Ben rushed to gather them up. 'Oh, right, thanks.' He stuffed the photographs in his pocket. 'My timetable,' he explained, patting the seat of his trousers. 'I can never seem to commit it to memory.'

Father Steiner continued to frown. Was he close enough that he'd been able to make out the image in the topmost photograph? Or had something else caught his eye among the stones?

'Father Steiner?' Ben said, stepping into the chaplain's eye-line. He'd pulled his sketchbook from his bag.

Father Steiner's gaze flicked back to Ben.

'Did you want to take a look?'

The chaplain seemed to hesitate for a moment, then hoisted a smile. 'It would be a privilege,' he said.

Ben started to open the sketchbook, then had a better idea. 'Would you mind if I showed you in the chapel? If there is somebody else around, I . . . I'd rather they didn't see.'

The chaplain laid a hand on Ben's shoulder. 'Of course. I understand completely.'

They started to move off together, along the path Father Steiner had arrived by. The chaplain kept his hand on Ben's shoulder the entire way, his grip only tightening once – when he paused at the edge of the clearing and looked back towards the entrance of the crypt.

Sunday 27 October, 8.37 a.m.

Back at the station, Fleet stood beside DC Bevan as they watched the chaplain pace the perimeter of the interview room.

'Did he give you any trouble?' Fleet adjusted the angle of the monitor slightly to reduce the glare from the sunlight that was cutting through the blinds.

'Not in the sense I think you mean,' Bevan replied. 'He was still half asleep when he answered his door, and there were a few grumbles after that about the timing. Said something about having to prepare for his sermon. But other than that he's been as good as gold since we brought him in' – the DC checked the clock on the wall – 'just under two hours ago. It's only in the past thirty minutes or so he's started pacing.'

Fleet wasn't surprised. The memorial service for Ben was due to start at ten o'clock, and Father Steiner was no doubt getting twitchy. Which was exactly the way Fleet wanted him.

'Have you offered him coffee? Something to eat?'

'Um, no, sorry, I—'

'Good,' said Fleet, cutting off the young DC's apology. He stood up straight, and took a sip from his own mug. Despite having been awake for the past twenty-seven and a half hours, and having averaged probably four or five hours' sleep a night since the Ben Draper investigation had begun, Fleet didn't feel tired. But he didn't feel sharp, either. Anxiety about Nicky kept cutting in on his thought processes, welling in him unexpectedly and knocking him off balance. Speed was of the essence, he knew, but he was also painfully aware of the potential consequences of rushing headlong in the wrong direction entirely.

When he entered the interview room, Father Steiner was in the corner furthest from the door, midway through one of the laps he'd been making around the table.

'Detective Inspector Fleet,' he said, turning, and sounding simultaneously anxious and relieved.

'Thank you for making yourself available, Father Steiner.'

The chaplain baulked slightly at Fleet's frosty demeanour. 'Well, I . . . I didn't feel as though I had much of a choice.'

Fleet took a seat, and he stared at Father Steiner until the chaplain moved warily to do the same.

'I have to stress,' Fleet began, 'you are here voluntarily, meaning you are free to leave whenever you wish. It is also your right to have a solicitor present.'

'A solicitor?' the chaplain echoed, halfway to sitting. Some of the colour drained from his features.

'Do you need a solicitor, Father Steiner?'

'What? No, I . . . No, of course not.'

Fleet laid out the files he'd carried in with him, on his side of the table. 'Let's start with Callum Richardson,' he said. 'When we spoke last time . . . That is, me, you and Detective Sergeant Nicola Collins – you remember her, don't you, Father Steiner?'

'What? Yes. Of course I do. And I . . . I saw the news. That she . . . that she may have . . .'

'She's missing,' said Fleet. 'But we'll find her. Don't you worry about that.'

The chaplain closed his open mouth.

'Going back to Richardson. Last time we spoke about him, you weren't completely honest with us. You told us you'd been worried about Ben being sucked into, quote, *Callum*

Richardson's secretive little clique. You said you'd seen the conse-quences before, and that you'd witnessed other people getting hurt, but you were reluctant to explain what you meant.' Fleet had been consulting his notes, and now he looked up. 'Tell me about Richard Hewitt, Father Steiner. The teacher who lost his job after being accused of sexually assaulting a pupil. I presume that was who you were referring to?'

The chaplain blinked. 'Well . . . yes,' he said. 'I suppose I was. But as I believe I also said to you at the time—'

'I remember what you said,' Fleet interrupted, not even bothering to look at his notebook this time. 'You said you had no proof. By which I presume you meant proof of Cal-lum Richardson's involvement in the allegations that were levelled against your colleague. And yet you knew precisely how close Richardson was to Melissa and Lance. So when Melissa Haynes came forward to claim she'd been assaulted, you immediately suspected that she was lying – and that Richardson had for some reason put her up to it.'

'I didn't just suspect her of lying, Detective Inspector,' said the chaplain defensively. 'I *knew* she was. Richard Hewitt was a thoroughly decent man. He put his *soul* into teaching. So for Melissa Haynes to fabricate some story, just for the sake of stirring up trouble . . .'

'Is that what you believed she was doing? Stirring up trouble?'

'To be honest I have no idea what would have motivated her to make up such lies. But I knew Callum Richardson was vindictive and malicious. And I knew Melissa had a difficult upbringing. Perhaps not in a conventional sense, and obvi-ously I'm no psychoanalyst, but you only had to look at the nature of her relationship with Callum.'

'What do you mean?'

The chaplain pursed his lips. The impression he gave was of a man wrestling with himself over whether it would be ethical for him to continue. It was the same act he'd performed last time, and Fleet, frankly, was getting tired of it.

'What I mean, Detective Inspector, is that Melissa was suffering, as so many children at boarding school do, from intense feelings of abandonment. She craved the love of her parents. Probably of her father in particular, given the way she latched on to Callum. And he . . . he treated her poorly. Bullied her, you might say. Psychologically, certainly. Possibly physically, as well.'

'Did you have evidence of this?' Fleet asked.

'No, I didn't. If I had, I would have done my utmost to put a stop to it.'

Fleet took a moment to think. Father Steiner was right: he wasn't a psychoanalyst. And even assuming he was spot on about the nature of Melissa's relationship with Richardson, it didn't alter the point Fleet had set out to make.

'But you were able to put a stop to Melissa's allegations against your friend, weren't you? Would that be going too far, would you say? To describe Richard Hewitt as your friend?'

The chaplain raised his chin. 'I admired Richard, both professionally and personally. I would consider it an honour to describe myself as his friend.'

'So you came forward yourself,' said Fleet. 'Even though, as you pointed out, you didn't have any evidence to contradict Melissa's claims, nor to verify Richardson's involvement. So what did you do? Did you lie? Make something up to get Richard Hewitt off the hook? Is that why you were so cagey with us before?'

The chaplain reddened. 'I didn't *lie*. I just . . . I told the board what *actually* happened. Melissa claimed Richard cornered her backstage one evening after drama rehearsals and attempted to force himself upon her. The way Richard told it, *she* came on to *him*, to try to coax him into doing something she could hold against him. I just ... I verified his version of events, that's all.'

'Meaning you presented yourself as a witness? When in fact you didn't witness anything?'

Father Steiner's flush deepened to the colour of shame.

Fleet didn't wait for him to answer. 'The point is, you got in Melissa's way. In Callum Richardson's way. Because I tend to agree with you. I think Richardson was probably behind the whole thing. It's my belief Richardson and the others were trying to engineer a scandal that would have forced Beaconsfield to close. Or at the very least destroyed the school's reputation. And I think, when their first plan failed, they decided to try again. With a different scheme, this time. A different victim.' He looked at Father Steiner meaningfully.

The chaplain gave the impression that he was struggling to catch up. And then he appeared to grasp the implications of what Fleet was saying.

'You mean ... me? But ... why? *How?*'

'We've just established *why*. As for how, it would be my guess they would have tried something similar to what they'd attempted before.' Although, even as Fleet said it, he was aware it didn't sound quite right. If their plan hadn't worked the first time, it was unlikely they would have tried the exact same thing again. There was Ben, of course, and the role he played – but was that the only thing that had been different?

'You said Ben used to hang around the chapel, that you suspected he was never really interested in religion,' Fleet went on. 'Even Adrian Harris seemed to think that the two of you had become close.'

'Yes, but . . . that doesn't mean anything! Adrian's always been oversensitive when it comes to my relationships with certain pupils. And Ben liked to draw! He came to the chapel because of the architecture! To talk as well, yes, but he and I . . . we were . . .'

'Were what? Friends? You thought he trusted you. And who knows, maybe in the end he did. But that's not why Ben first came to you. He came to you because Richardson and the others put him up to it. Didn't it strike you as strange that Ben hung out with them in the first place? That they'd allowed him into their *little clique*?'

'But that's . . . that's what I said to him. I told him. I tried to warn him . . .'

'They promised Ben friendship, and in return convinced him to play a part. To get close to you, or at least to make it *look* as though you and he were close, so that others, when the time came, would believe whatever story they chose to tell.' Fleet paused for a moment to let what he was saying sink in. 'So what happened next? Did you discover what they were trying to do? Did Ben accidentally let something slip?'

Father Steiner was staring at Fleet, but his gaze seemed to have turned inward. 'The book . . .' he muttered.

Fleet frowned. 'What book?'

'Nothing, I . . .' The chaplain shook his head. 'I gave Ben a book. To copy from. And he . . . he asked me to write a dedication. I thought . . .'

Fleet was watching the chaplain intently. He was acting, Fleet told himself. The shock he was showing wasn't real. And yet it *looked* real. If Fleet didn't know better, he would have said Father Steiner was only belatedly grasping the truth himself, piecing it together the same way Fleet was.

'Did Ben proposition you the way Melissa propositioned

Richard Hewitt?' Fleet asked, pressing on. 'Is that when you realised that you'd been played?'

The chaplain's gaze snapped to meet Fleet's.

'I would imagine that men in your position have to contend with allegations of the sort Richard Hewitt faced all the time,' Fleet said. 'Did the idea disgust you? Did you lose your temper? Lash out, maybe, when you and Ben were alone?'

'No,' Father Steiner insisted. He was shaking his head emphatically. 'No, that's not—'

'Where were you the day Ben was killed?'

'I told you! I was ill! I was in the chapel in the morning, but then, in the afternoon—'

'What about yesterday? Last night? Where were you then?'

'Just . . . at the school! I don't know exactly, just . . . just in my room, probably. Or the vestry. I don't remember!'

'What about Tuesday last week? Were you on your own all day then as well?' As he spoke, Fleet opened one of the folders, and slid two A4 photographs into the centre of the table, where Father Steiner could see them. One showed Melissa's body lying bloated and semi-clothed on the side of the docks. The other showed Lance Wheeler hanging in his kitchen.

The chaplain's eyes widened in horror.

'It's extremely unfortunate, Father Steiner, that on the days Ben, Lance and Melissa were killed, there are no witnesses to verify your whereabouts. And God, I'm afraid, doesn't count.'

'I didn't say nobody could verify my whereabouts,' the chaplain responded, flustered. 'I said . . . I said I couldn't *remember* where I was! If you'd just . . . just give me a moment to think . . .'

'Here's what *I* think,' said Fleet. 'I think you found out what Ben was up to, and so you killed him. Maybe it was an accident, maybe not. Somehow, twenty-two years later, you realised it wasn't only Ben who was involved. Or maybe you knew all along, and it's been eating at you, the way your guilt has. So you decided to punish them. *All* of them. For Richard Hewitt, for Ben, for what they almost did to *you*.'

'No,' said the chaplain. '*No.*'

'And it was because of the guilt you were feeling that you decided to allow Ben to be found – so that instead of lying alone in the dark for another twenty-two years, he could finally be buried properly. Respectfully. Because you've known all along about the crypt, haven't you, Father Steiner?'

'What? No! How could I have?'

'For one thing,' Fleet said, 'you know the chapel better than anyone. You know its history, its heritage, its every corner, I would imagine. It stands to reason you would have known about the building it replaced. Tell me, how did you find it? Did you read about the crypt in Beaconsfield's library? Or just stumble across it when you were walking in the woods?'

'I didn't do either of those things! I told you, I . . . I had no idea it was there. *No one* did. I . . .'

Father Steiner's eyebrows came together in a frown. Instead of looking pleadingly at Fleet, he gazed down at the surface of the table.

'Father Steiner?'

The chaplain didn't respond.

'Father Steiner, you're not going to help yourself by—'

'Ben found it.'

Fleet blinked. 'Excuse me?'

'Ben found the crypt. He . . . he must have. I remember . . . I remember I came across him in the clearing. Two days, three, before he went missing. There was something odd

258

about his behaviour. I remember thinking . . . I remember thinking he'd been up to something.'

'Up to something?'

'Yes, I . . . I thought he was looking at . . . at pornography. And I thought he was acting strangely because he was embarrassed at being caught.'

Father Steiner appeared embarrassed enough by the revelation himself. But then he looked at Fleet with a sudden certainty in his eyes. 'But don't you see? *Ben* was the one who found the crypt. When I came across him, he was standing right beside the entrance. No!' the chaplain declared. 'He wasn't *standing*. He was on all fours. I thought he'd dropped something and was trying to locate it. And what you said before, about me knowing the chapel better than anyone . . . the truth is Ben knew it, too. Even if he was faking his relationship with *me*, he wasn't pretending when it came to his drawing, his passion for architecture. If he found a way into the crypt, he would have realised immediately what it was.'

As before, Fleet had the sense that Father Steiner had genuinely just made a connection that had somehow eluded him until now.

'Why didn't you mention this sooner?'

The chaplain shook his head helplessly. 'I . . . I don't know. Maybe I did, originally, but at the time Ben went missing I don't suppose it would have seemed relevant. And it's only because you mentioned the crypt . . . the woods . . . that I suddenly recalled.'

Fleet could feel his anger – his frustration – beginning to build. Not so much at the fact that Father Steiner hadn't mentioned seeing Ben near the crypt earlier – the chaplain was right, it *wouldn't* have seemed relevant that he had seen Ben in the clearing, because no one had known until just over a week ago that the crypt even existed – but rather at the growing sense he had that the chaplain was telling the truth. And if that was the case, it meant Fleet was even further away from finding Nicky than he had been before.

'It doesn't change things,' Fleet said, shaking his head. 'Even if Ben found the crypt himself, someone still blocked him inside. And in case it hasn't already occurred to you, Father Steiner, you've just given us reason to suspect that you knew about the entrance to the crypt, too.'

The chaplain's expression morphed from one of hope to despair.

'But . . . but I didn't. I just told you! I didn't *see* the entrance.'

'You saw Ben find it. Meaning you could easily have gone back to the clearing to investigate it yourself. Maybe he even told you what he'd found, and you advised him to keep it to himself. Assuming you're telling the truth about what you witnessed in the first place.'

'It is true! And the point is, if Ben found the crypt, *anyone* could have! Any of the teachers, or the pupils, or . . . or the grounds staff, or even the workmen who surveyed the site! Why *didn't* anyone find it? Either before . . . or . . . or even afterwards. If someone had, you wouldn't have had to resort to guessing all this time later. To blaming me when I didn't do anything wrong!'

From looking lost and desperate, the chaplain's expression turned to one of anger.

'Why didn't the *police* find the crypt, Detective Inspector? You knew Ben was missing twenty-two years ago. You even searched the grounds at the time! Why did it take you and your colleagues so long to do your job? You drag me from my bed, in the middle of the night practically, and you make these ... these *foul* accusations, when ... when really you should be looking at yourselves!'

Fleet could have answered Father Steiner had he chosen to. He could have said that he agreed, that the police *had* failed Ben, just as the school had, as well as his family. He could have offered excuses as to why the crypt wasn't found sooner: that the likelihood was, whoever had covered up the entrance after hiding Ben's body had made sure it was even more concealed than it had been before; that the search after Ben went missing had been half-hearted at best, and that the crypt was anyway almost the perfect place to conceal a body.

Instead, Fleet found himself focusing on the one thing Father Steiner had said that had snagged. 'Which workmen?'

The chaplain was clearly struggling to come to terms with his fury. He didn't seem to know which way to look.

'What?'

'You mentioned workmen. Which workmen surveyed the site? When?'

The chaplain shook his head in apparent exasperation. 'Just ... the workmen. The structural engineers. The ones who checked the subsidence in the chapel.'

Fleet recalled the cracks he'd seen in the wall of the chapel behind the altar. Some, he remembered, were wide enough that he would have been able to fit a hand in. *It's always been a problem, though apparently not one serious enough to do anything about,* the chaplain had said. *One of the perils of building on a hill. Although perhaps now we know the real reason ...*

'When did structural engineers investigate the subsidence, Father Steiner?'

Fleet was leaning forward in his seat, and the chaplain seemed confused by his sudden interest. From the look he gave Fleet, he was clearly expecting some sort of trick.

'I couldn't tell you precisely. Not off the top of my head.'

'But was it before or after Ben went missing?'

'Well . . . both,' the chaplain said, warily. 'The first time was just before I joined the school. Someone else came six or seven years ago, but only because I kicked up a fuss when it became obvious the problem was getting worse.' He shook his head as he remembered. 'I still don't believe either of them did their job properly. There's *clearly* an issue that needs attention – you've seen the cracks yourself.'

'So the site was investigated twice. And both times they reported that everything was fine? That nothing needed to be done?'

'As I said, Detective Inspector, I'm not at all convinced they did a thorough job. But that's apparently what they said.'

Fleet felt his frown deepen. 'Meaning you didn't actually speak to them yourself? Obviously not the first time they came, but what about the second?'

The chaplain exhaled in evident frustration. 'Look, is this really what you feel we should be focusing on? Given the circumstances. And given what you've just accused me of . . .'

'Just answer the question please, Father Steiner. Did you speak to them? Or even *see* them?'

'No, I . . .' The chaplain scrunched up his eyes as he tried to recall. 'The first time, as I say, was about two months before I took up my post. The second time I was visiting my sister. She has mobility issues, and I do my best to look in on her as often as I can. She lives in—'

'So who did?' Fleet interrupted. 'Who would have authorised the site surveys in the first place?' But even as he waited for the chaplain to respond, he was fairly sure he already knew the answer.

'Why, the headmaster, of course,' said Father Steiner. 'Adrian Harris.'

Fleet slumped backwards in his seat. He was aware Father Steiner was staring at him, but it was all Fleet could do to focus on his thoughts. He was remembering something else the chaplain had said to him the first time they'd spoken – something else that Fleet had failed to pick up on.

'He doesn't like you,' he said, raising his eyes to meet Father Steiner's. 'Does he?'

'I beg your pardon?'

'Adrian Harris. You and he don't get along. Why not?'

'Well, I . . . I wouldn't say we don't *get along*. We just . . . we don't always see eye to eye on matters of—'

Fleet was shaking his head. 'That's not it. You said something else. Last time. You said the headmaster had a habit of . . .' He tried to recall how Father Steiner had put it. 'Of *overstating your bond* with certain students. And you mentioned something similar again just now. What did you mean? *Who* did you mean?'

'Well, Ben, obviously. And . . .'

'And?' Fleet prompted. 'And who else, Father Steiner? Who was the other pupil who came between you?'

But once again Fleet thought he already knew the answer. Finally everything was sliding into place. The reason why the chapel had been neglected, the cracks in its walls allowed to widen, while the rest of the school was kept pristine. The headmaster's animosity towards Father Steiner, and his desperation for the investigation to move on. Even the length of Harris's tenure. For almost a quarter of a century, like a soldier in a time of war, Adrian Harris had been standing guard . . .

*

Two minutes later, with the name Father Steiner had given him echoing in his head, Fleet rushed from the room. He spotted DC Bevan at his desk in the open-plan office outside.

'Sean. Get Callum Richardson's protective detail on the phone. I need to talk to them right away.'

'But—'

'Just do it, Sean!'

'I can't, sir. I mean, I could, but if you like you can speak to them face-to-face. They're just downstairs.'

'Downstairs? What are they doing downstairs?'

'They got back to the station about an hour ago. Richardson sent them away. Said if they didn't leave him alone, he'd sue them and the entire police force for harassment.'

Shit, thought Fleet. *Shit*.

He checked the time. The memorial service for Ben was just about to begin, assuming Adrian Harris had decided to press ahead without Father Steiner.

'Then get me a car,' Fleet said to Bevan. 'And start praying we're not already too late.'

Ben – May 1997

(The day of his death)

Ben had been looking for a chance to return to the crypt for the past two days.

He'd made it as far as the edge of the clearing twice, but both times there'd been other kids in the woods, close enough to the graveyard that Ben hadn't wanted to risk anyone seeing him. Finally, though, it was the weekend, meaning quite a few of Beaconsfield's boarders had already left for home. The weather had turned chillier, too, and there was a forecast of rain, which should have afforded Ben the perfect opportunity to go back and investigate what he'd found – but all of a sudden he had a more pressing matter on his mind.

He couldn't find them.

The photographs.

They'd been in his trouser pocket and now they were gone.

He'd already retraced his steps around the school, visiting everywhere he'd been since the last time he remembered having them. Now he was back in his dorm, going through his belongings for what must have been the third or fourth time. He'd started with his clothes, checking every pocket, before moving on to the rest of his stuff. His bed sheets, his books, his single suitcase. Even his wash kit and the folds of his towel. His area was a mess, his meagre belongings scattered all about him, and still the photos were nowhere to be found.

'Looking for these?'

At the sound of the voice behind him, Ben froze. He was on his knees beside his bunk, and he could tell immediately that, however sick he was feeling already, he was about to feel a whole lot worse.

When he turned around, he saw that the photographs, as he'd expected, were in Callum's hand. Lance was standing next to Callum, not quite meeting Ben's eye.

'Callum, I—'

'Save it, Ben. If you're not going to be honest with me, I don't want to hear it.'

Rather than angry, Callum looked disappointed, just as he had that time in the library after Ben had been caught fighting in the science lab. Ben had told himself he was past caring what Callum thought of him, but he found himself experiencing that familiar mix of shame and self-loathing. He glanced at Lance, who still wouldn't look at him.

'What I don't understand is why you didn't just tell me,' said Callum. 'Why you felt you had to *lie*.'

Ben opened his mouth to mutter some excuse, but he knew there was no point.

Callum's expression had been set firm, but all at once it softened. 'If you changed your mind, you should have just said. We would have understood, Ben. We're not *monsters*.'

At that, Lance turned away.

Ben concentrated on Callum.

'You're not mad?' he said.

'I *am* mad,' said Callum. 'But that doesn't mean I don't understand. I said to you before, I realise how much of the responsibility for what we're doing has fallen on you.' He took a quick glance around the dorm. The room was empty, all the other kids who were still at school most likely in the lunch hall, or else taking advantage of the extra space in the common room. 'Look, let's . . . let's go for a walk or something. Talk things through. Anyone could come in here at any moment.'

Slowly Ben got to his feet, but inside he felt a flicker of uncertainty. Wasn't this how it had worked last time? Was Callum just manipulating him again? What was there to talk about, after all? It was obvious Callum was going to try to convince him to go back to the original plan, and if there was one thing Ben was sure about, it was that he no longer wanted any part of it. Making the decision had been one of the hardest things he'd ever had to do in his life, but as soon as he had, he'd realised that, actually, it had been easy.

'Where would we go?' he asked.

'Just . . . I don't know. To the woods or something,' said Callum. 'Just so we can figure out what to do now. At the very least, you owe us an explanation. Don't you think?'

Ben glanced towards one of the windows. It was barely the middle of the afternoon, but the sky was darkening already, and the rain that had been forecast surely wasn't far away. And something else was making him hesitate, too. Lance still hadn't said a word. He wasn't gloating, as Ben might have expected him to. And he didn't appear angry either, again as would have been his right. Planting the photographs in Father Steiner's room had been his responsibility as well, and Ben had made him look foolish. Unless *that* was the reason he was looking so anxious. Maybe he was in Callum's bad books, too.

'Look, I'm not going to try to change your mind,' said Callum. 'I promise. Here, take these if it will make you feel better.' He extended his arm, offering Ben the stack of photographs. 'Bring them with you. I've got my Zippo. We can burn them when we get to the woods. Forget they ever existed.'

Tentatively, half expecting Callum to whip his hand away at any moment, Ben reached. His fingers closed around the photographs, and Callum relinquished them with a smile.

'Come on,' he said, as though the matter was settled. 'Melissa's waiting for us downstairs. And if anyone asks where we're going, we'll tell them . . . we'll tell them we're bored and we're going to play a game.'

'What game?' said Ben, suddenly wary and remembering the last time Callum had invited him to play one of his 'games'.

'I don't know,' Callum responded, as though oblivious to Ben's hesitancy. 'But if we're going to the woods . . . how about hide-and-seek?'

No one did stop them to ask where they were going. They heard one or two voices drifting out of the common room on their way past, but there was nobody in the quad as they crossed towards the archway that would lead them to the rear of the building, and the grounds themselves were deserted. The air was utterly still, and though the clouds appeared to be thickening, there was no sign of any rain. Maybe they would escape a downpour yet.

Ben and Callum walked slightly ahead. After greeting Ben with an uneasy smile – which Ben put down to her embarrassment at having kissed him – Melissa fell in beside Lance, and the closer they got to the woods, the further the two of them dropped behind. Ben had the distinct impression that their eyes were fixed on the back of his head, though every time he glanced behind him, they were conspicuously looking towards the ground. There was the occasional hiss of whispered conversation, and although Ben couldn't catch what they were talking about, he was reminded of the time he'd overheard the two of them arguing in the darkroom.

'So what made you change your mind?' said Callum as they walked.

They were passing the graveyard, and Ben stole a peek at it through the trees. He hadn't even had a chance to go back and slide the slab he'd dislodged into place again, meaning the staircase down to the crypt would be visible to anyone who came within a few metres of it. To his relief, the clearing was empty, and he had a feeling that it would have been all over the school by now if someone else *had* stumbled on the entranceway. His secret was safe – for the time being, at least.

'Ben?' Callum said, glancing his way.

'What? Oh, I . . . I felt bad for Father Steiner, I guess. He's only ever been nice to me, and I . . . I wondered if the rumours about him could really be true.'

In fact, it had dawned on Ben that the only rumours he'd ever heard about the man were the ones Callum and the others had told him. Which in turn had added weight to the *real* reason Ben had changed his mind: his growing certainty that Callum and the others were using him. But he couldn't tell Callum *that*.

'Fair enough, I suppose,' Callum said, and not for the first time Ben wondered why he wasn't angrier. And where was he leading them, anyway? They were already deep enough into the woods that they could burn the photographs without anyone seeing, and there'd been none of the *figuring out* Callum had mentioned. The conversation, such as it was, had so far felt more like idle small talk, of the kind Callum always claimed he detested.

'So are we quits?' said Ben, feeling suddenly nervous. 'I mean, I'll understand if you don't want to be friends any more. And I swear I won't tell anyone if you guys decide to go ahead with the plan without me.'

'I know you won't tell, Ben,' said Callum. 'I'm not worried about that.'

They'd reached the lake. The shoreline appeared through the trees, and when they stepped from beneath the canopy on to the bank, Ben realised it had started raining without him having noticed. The lake appeared to be gently bubbling, as though a million little creatures were breathing just below the surface.

'Although you do realise,' Callum said, 'that the entire plan revolves around you? What you said just now about us going ahead without you – you understand we can't do that, don't you?'

Callum stopped at the edge of the water. The lake was only small, but signs had been posted around the shore giving warning that it was deeper than it looked. Ben had only visited it once before, and then only by accident. He didn't like it this far into the woods. Most of the trees appeared to be dead or dying, and the water itself appeared dark and gloopy – all the more so under the blackening sky.

'No, I know,' Ben said. 'I just meant—'

'I know what you meant,' Callum interrupted. 'But the problem is, we *need* you, Ben. Just . . . not quite in the way we said we did.'

From nowhere, Ben heard Lance's voice echoing from the darkroom. *You know there's more to it than you think, don't you?*

'What . . . what do you mean?' said Ben. He didn't like the way Callum was looking at him. He didn't trust the glint in his eye.

'I mean, no one would have believed you anyway,' Callum said. 'Even with the book, and the photos, and all the time you've spent alone with Father Steiner – it was never going to be enough. We've done this before, you see. Which is why the plan this time was always slightly different.'

When Ben looked around, he saw Lance and Melissa had

drifted slightly apart, blocking the most obvious pathways back into the trees. Lance's hand was behind his back.

'Look, I . . . I've changed my mind,' Ben said, edging towards the water. 'It was just the photos that were making me nervous. I . . . I overreacted. But it's not too late. We can still do everything exactly as we planned. If I . . . if somehow I . . .'

'But that's what I'm trying to tell you,' Callum said, creeping forward. 'This *is* exactly what we planned.'

And that's when Ben felt the knife against his throat.

Sunday 27 October, 10.19 a.m.

They were halfway to Beaconsfield when they heard the emergency call being reported on the radio.

Fleet was sitting up front beside the driver. DC Bevan was in the back. As the news came in, Fleet and the driver exchanged a glance. They already had the lights going. Without needing to be told, the driver hit the siren.

The PC drove fast and smoothly, but even so Fleet gripped the handle above the door. *Start praying we're not already too late*, he'd told Bevan, but the emergency call suggested the killer's endgame was already in motion. Fleet couldn't bring himself to think about what that might mean for Nicky.

As the buildings around them began to thin, the traffic eased slightly as well, and when they finally escaped the city, the roads opened up completely. The PC had muted the siren when they'd made it out into the countryside, and now Fleet could hear other sirens in the distance. It was hard to tell whether the sounds were coming from up ahead or from somewhere behind them.

Two minutes out from the school, the traffic began to pick up again, but all the cars were heading in the opposite direction.

'How many officers were already at the school for the memorial service?' Fleet asked Bevan.

'Six,' Bevan replied, a phone in his left hand and a radio in his right. He'd been talking into one or the other – occasionally both at the same time – for most of the journey. 'But it sounds as though they've all got their hands full. No one's managed to find Callum Richardson. He was seen arriving – he was caught on camera outside the gates – but from the sound of it his bodyguards have lost track of him, too.'

Fleet cursed. 'How the hell did they manage to do that?'

'Apparently Richardson instructed them to wait outside the chapel during the service. They were still outside when everything kicked off.'

Scowling, Fleet turned back to face the road. As he did so, the PC was forced to brake sharply. The road had tightened, and a car that was heading their way was drifting into the oncoming lane. The man driving, Fleet saw, had been adjusting his rear-view mirror, presumably to try to get a peek at what was going on behind him.

'Sorry, sir,' the PC said, once they'd threaded their way past.

'Not your fault,' Fleet told him. He rearranged himself in his seat, tugging at his seatbelt where it had half garrotted him.

They rounded another bend, and this time the PC had to slow the car to a crawl. The entrance to Beaconsfield's driveway was just ahead, and as well as a queue of cars trying to get out, there was an ambulance trying to get in. The gates were wide enough to allow two vehicles to fit side by side, but beyond the gatehouse the drive itself immediately tapered. Fleet knew from his past visits that there were laybys every hundred metres or so further up, but there was otherwise only space for one car at a time.

'Will you look at that idiot?' said Bevan.

Other than a select group of reporters, the press had been banned from school grounds during the memorial service, but that hadn't stopped half a dozen news vans clustering on the verge opposite the gatehouse. And now one of the vans was trying to tailgate the ambulance and follow it up the driveway to the school. A second news van was halfway across the road, as though the driver were contemplating a similar move, and the result was a total logjam. The PC allowed the siren to admit another wail, but it was as effective as hurling abuse at a frozen computer screen. They were clearly as close to the school as they would be able to get.

Before they'd even come to a complete stop, Fleet opened his door and swung his feet on to the tarmac. Bevan was half a second behind him.

They squeezed through the gap between the news vans, and hurried towards the gates. When they reached the gate-house, Fleet saw two of the PCs who'd been detailed to the event waving their hands around uselessly. One was trying to clear a path for the ambulance, even though there was nowhere for the cars in front of it to go. The other PC appeared to be berating the driver of the SUV that was leading the procession from the grounds.

'You two!' Fleet yelled. 'Stop flapping around like headless chickens, and concentrate on clearing the road. Get those news vans back on to the verge. Or even better, tell them to sling their hook!'

Without pausing to hear a response, Fleet began racing up the driveway towards the school. As well as meandering through the trees, the road was on an incline, and it wasn't long before Fleet was cursing himself for not having stuck to his diet. Bevan wasn't moving any faster, though. He was still clutching his phone and radio, and was doing his best to monitor the chatter as they went. He seemed to be in direct contact with one of the officers inside the grounds, but his frown told Fleet all he needed to know. Apart from anything, Fleet could see with his own eyes that the situation was a mess. There were cars queued nose-to-tail the entire length of the driveway.

'Christ,' he muttered to Bevan. 'How the hell are the emergency vehicles supposed to make it through?'

They reached a point near the top of the drive where the road swept back on itself, and Fleet pulled Bevan towards the trees. 'Shortcut.'

With Fleet leading the way, they scrambled over the ditch at the side of the road and into the thick line of trees. They battled through the branches, the ground beneath their feet sodden from the recent rain, and moments later emerged into the car park.

If the situation in the driveway was a mess, the scene outside the school was one of total chaos.

The main building was directly across from them, and the central clock tower was dwarfed by a vast plume of smoke, coal black against the pale blue sky. Parents were scrambling to get their sons and daughters to safety, while scores of others – adults, children, even the yellow-vested officials who Fleet presumed were teachers who'd been press-ganged into acting as marshals – simply stood around staring, clogging the spaces between the vehicles. Drivers yelled at each other through tightly wound windows, their words drowned out by the blare of horns. A film crew had somehow made it up the drive, and at least half a dozen photographers were jostling for the best spots to take pictures from. There was even a drone hovering in the air not far from the column of smoke.

'Who's in charge here?' Fleet yelled, and the marshal standing closest turned his way.

'You,' said Fleet, marching up to him. The man looked barely old enough to drive, let alone teach, but at least he'd been showing enough sense to try to herd a group of pupils away from the building, rather than just gawping at the smoke.

'Round up your colleagues,' Fleet told him. 'Start heading down the driveway towards the gates. As you go, get the cars into the lay-bys. Force them into the ditch if you have to. You need to clear a path for the emergency vehicles.'

The teacher nodded tightly and set to his task.

Fleet and Bevan continued through the crowd, towards the rear of the building. They rounded the corner – and for the first time got an idea of exactly what they were up against.

Not only was the school on fire, the chapel was, too.

For an instant, Fleet thought of the picture in the book the headmaster had given him in Beaconsfield's library. The image had been vivid enough, but looking at the scene before him, he recognised how far the artist's rendering had fallen short of reality. The air shimmered in the heat, and smoke swirled around them in a bitter fog. And the fire itself was just a backdrop to the pandemonium caused by the blaze. Despite all the people who had made it to their cars, there were still hundreds of pupils, parents and other guests caught between the chapel and the school. Some were simply clustered in groups, weeping and coughing in the smoke. Assuming all six-hundred-odd pupils had been in the chapel, and estimating the additional visitors based on the number of cars, there must have been almost a thousand people either in the chapel or the school when the fire started.

'Tell me the fire engines are on their way,' Fleet said to Bevan. He had to shout to make himself heard above the yells and the crackling of the flames.

'They're two minutes out,' Bevan replied, his radio to his ear. He didn't need to add what Fleet was already thinking:

that even when the rest of the emergency vehicles arrived, they would still need to find a way up that drive.

Fleet looked around. One of the PCs who'd been assigned to the memorial service was weaving her way towards them up the hill. Like Bevan, she had her radio in her hand, and Fleet presumed she was one of the officers the detective constable had been communicating with.

'Sir,' the PC puffed, saluting loosely. Her yellow jacket was streaked with black, and there was soot on her cheeks and forehead.

'Where are the other officers?' Fleet asked. 'Are any of you hurt?'

Still out of breath, the PC shook her head. 'No, sir. We . . . we're all OK. But the chapel . . . it just went up. One moment everyone was singing, the next they were screaming. But we think . . . we think everybody's out. Shari, Frank, Charlie . . . they're just making sure it's clear.'

She pointed back down the hill, and Fleet saw the three officers he'd yet to account for emerging from the chapel. One was helping an older man who was doubled over, coughing. There was no telling if he was the last of the congregation to emerge, but Fleet had to hope there was nobody else trapped inside.

'Good work,' Fleet told the PC, 'all of you. But no one's to go back inside that building. Is that understood?' Even as he spoke, there was a sound like distant thunder, and when Fleet, Bevan and the PC turned back to face the chapel, they were just in time to see a section of the roof near the base of the spire cave in. More than a few people in the crowd screamed.

The PC swallowed. 'That's affirmative, sir.'

The other officers were drawing closer, and Bevan waved them over.

Fleet looked behind him at the school, and though the fire in the main building still seemed to be contained to the southern wing, if the chapel was anything to go by, it wouldn't take long for the flames to spread.

He turned back to the uniforms as they fell in before him. 'You two,' he said, gesturing to the first PC he'd spoken to and the woman beside her, 'head round to the front of the main building. Make sure everyone gets back beyond the trees. And you two' – he indicated the remaining two officers – 'focus on trying to clear this side of the grounds.'

Faces blackened by the smoke from the chapel, and with sweat pouring down their brows, the officers nodded their understanding. The man one of them had been helping was managing to make his own way towards the front of the school. Most of the other civilians seemed to be drifting in the same direction, but there were still far too many people caught between the chapel and the main building.

Fleet clapped his hands. 'Let's get moving.'

Bevan spun away as the PCs did, clearly meaning to help corral the crowd, but Fleet grabbed his arm and pulled him back.

'Not you, Sean.' Fleet cast around, scanning the faces around him. 'You and I are going to find the man who did this.'

Ben – May 1997
(The day of his death)

Ben froze.

Cold at first, the initial sensation of the blade against his neck was soon displaced by the warmth of a trickle of blood.

'What . . . what are you doing?' Ben said. 'Callum, please . . . I said I'd do it! I'll do anything you want!'

Lance was the one holding the knife, and his other hand had seized Ben's shoulder. In front of him, Callum was taking something from his pocket. It looked like a rolled-up piece of fabric, and slowly he began to unwind it.

'You still don't understand, do you?' Callum said. 'This *is* what we want. It's what we've wanted from the start.'

Melissa had edged into Ben's eyeline, but when he turned pleadingly towards her, she looked away.

Callum, meanwhile, took a step closer, and Ben finally recognised what he was holding. It was a stole – a priest's scarf – like one of the ones Father Steiner sometimes wore when he was conducting a service. Not just *like* Father Steiner's, in fact. It *was* Father Steiner's, and that was when Ben finally understood.

'No,' he said. 'No! Please, don't do this!' He shook his head, forgetting about the knife, and the tip of the blade once again pierced his skin. He hardly felt it, but he sensed Lance flinch slightly, as though he were the one who'd been hurt.

Callum continued moving forward. The white and gold fabric of the stole was stretched tightly between his hands.

'It's perfect,' he said. 'Don't you see? Last time it was Melissa's word against a teacher's. Which might have been enough if Father Steiner hadn't interfered. And if Melissa had held her nerve.'

He didn't so much as glance Melissa's way, but her eyes dropped towards the ground.

'This time, the evidence will be laid out for everyone to see,' Callum went on. 'It will be as simple as reading a picture book. Father Steiner lured you in, giving you gifts and pretending to be your friend. He tricked you into having a relationship with him, and when you decided you wanted to end it, and threatened to expose him for what he was, he lost his temper. Maybe he didn't mean to hurt you. Maybe it was the only way he could be certain you'd stay quiet.'

Callum wrapped the ends of the stole around his fingers.

'And the best part is,' he said, 'nobody will have the slightest clue that any of *us* were involved. Nobody really thinks we're your friends. Even if somebody saw us come out here into the woods with you, we'll claim you went off on your own, and chances are they won't find your body for days anyway. Not until they think to drain the lake.'

Ben's eyes flicked involuntarily to the steel-grey water, which continued to boil under the strengthening rain. 'But *why*?' he pleaded. 'Why are you doing this?'

He jerked again, and Lance responded by moving the knife to the front of his throat. It was a letter opener, Ben realised, glancing down. Did it belong to Father Steiner, too? Was that what Lance had been looking for when he'd been searching Father Steiner's desk? Maybe not for the letter opener specifically, but for *something* that could be used to bolster the evidence against him.

'Keep him still!' Callum barked, glowering at Lance, and

then he fixed his glare on Ben. 'We're doing this because it's *right*,' he said. 'And all good causes require sacrifice, Ben. My father taught me that, though I'm sure he never meant to. He's never intentionally taught me anything – other than that his own good causes are more important to him than his only son. That a *school* is.' Callum sneered and shook his head. 'Do you know what my father told me before he sent me here? He said he *knew* I'd never live up to the Richardson name. That I've been a disappointment to him – a *distraction* – since the day I was born. He said he could only hope that his alma mater would teach me something about what it means to be a man.'

Callum smiled again, bitterly. 'Well, it's taught me plenty. More than my father could have imagined. *He's* the one who still has something to learn. So I'm going to help him. I'm going to show him what happens when hypocrites and frauds get found out – starting with everyone connected to his precious school. Because, once we're done, Beaconsfield's reputation will be in ruins, and people will start to realise who my father *really* is. They'll look more closely at all the places he sends his money, and they'll see that they're all as corrupt and hypocritical as he is; that everything about him is just a *front*.'

A fleck of spittle had caught on the corner of Callum's mouth, and he wiped it away.

'They call him a philanthropist,' he scoffed. 'They say he *helps* people. But the only person my father has ever cared about is *himself*.'

Ben was watching in horrified silence, any hope he'd had of reasoning with Callum ebbing away. He looked again at Melissa, who was watching Callum as intently as Ben had been, her expression caught somewhere between fear and despair. She didn't want to be part of this. Ben *knew* she didn't, not really.

'Melissa,' he begged. '*Please*. You don't have to do what he says! We can just . . . we can forget any of this ever happened!'

'Melissa will do as she's told!' Callum snapped. 'And anyway, she feels exactly the same way I do.'

Melissa's nod was automatic, as though she were responding to something that had been drummed into her, over and over. Maybe she didn't want to be part of this, but she was clearly too scared to back out.

'Lance,' said Ben, trying to turn. '*You* don't want to do this. I know you don't. I heard you. In the darkroom. You didn't even know what was going to happen! So that's . . . what I'll tell everyone! If you help me, if you let me go, I'll say—'

'Shut up!' Lance hissed in Ben's ear. 'Just . . . just shut the fuck up, will you? It's too late. Don't you get it? I *tried* to make you understand, but you were too stupid to see. How many times does someone have to insult you before you realise they don't want you around?' Ben felt rather than saw him shake his head. 'Why did you have to be so gullible? So fucking *desperate*! Right from the start! Do you think it was an accident we were there to meet you the day you arrived? That we happened to be there whenever you needed help? It wasn't one of your roommates who put piss on your bunk! It wasn't always the other kids who stole your stuff! It's *your* fault what's about to happen, not mine!'

Now Ben was the one to shake his head. He felt despair as the truth finally sank in. He and Callum were almost toe to toe now, the stole in Callum's outstretched hands the only thing between them.

'They . . . they won't believe you!' Ben said. 'Kill me if you

282

like, but they'll catch you! They'll figure out it was you! They won't believe Father Steiner was capable!'

'I'm afraid they will,' Callum responded, almost consolingly. 'That's partly why we chose Father Steiner in the first place. There are *always* rumours about people like him. It hardly matters if we started them or not. And unfortunately, he won't have an alibi. He's alone in his room right now. I checked just before we came to find you. And the laxative I slipped into his tea this morning should keep him there for a few hours yet.' He smiled as he registered the confusion on Ben's face. 'Every Saturday morning, he has one of the catering staff deliver a pot of Earl Grey to his door. And he tends to leave it sitting in the corridor long enough for it to grow cold – or for someone passing to slip a little something into the pot.'

Callum's smile vanished, and he raised the stole, clearly preparing to loop it around Ben's neck. At the same time, Lance tightened his hold on Ben's arm. But as he did so, he lowered the letter opener slightly, and Ben realised this was his one and only chance.

He stamped down on Lance's foot, and simultaneously grabbed for the stole. It was so tightly wound around Callum's hands, there was no way he could have wrenched it free, but he managed to pull Callum off balance. All three of them toppled to the floor, and Ben registered the letter opener spilling from Lance's hand. Lance cried out, a mixture of surprise and pain, while Callum roared in frustration. Ben was the first on to his feet, but when he spun to try to get his bearings, Callum was crouched in front of him, the blade somehow in his grip. He swiped, and instinctively Ben raised his hands to deflect the blow. There was no pain, not yet, but he knew from the blood that he'd been cut. He

283

staggered backwards, and tripped over Lance. He heard Lance swear, flailing with his fists and landing a blow on Ben's stomach. Ben lashed out himself, his elbow clashing with Lance's jaw – and then he was up and running.

He barely registered the direction. Away from the lake, was all he could think. Away from Callum and the monsters he'd thought of as his friends. He veered, darting first one way and then the other, hoping to lose them amid the trees.

The school. He needed to get back to the school.

But the faster he ran, the more the branches seemed to want to hold him back. They snatched at him, snagging his clothes and tugging his hair. It was almost as though the forest itself was on Callum's side.

As if to prove it, a root hooked around Ben's toes, and he tumbled, rolling in a tangle as he landed and then slamming into a tree. For a second, two, he couldn't breathe. The wind had been knocked out of him – all of his energy, too.

'Where's he gone?' said a voice. Lance's. 'He was right up ahead!'

'Don't you lose him!' came Callum's reply. 'It's your fault he got away in the first place!'

Ben didn't dare try to get up. The others were metres away at most, but they'd obviously lost sight of him when he'd fallen.

'*My* fault?' Lance replied. 'You're the one who was standing there gloating! You can never resist bragging about how clever you are, can you?'

'Lance, don't . . .' said Melissa, and to Ben it sounded as though she were right on top of him.

'You *let* him get away, I bet!' Callum said, ignoring Melissa's interjection. 'The same way you tried to drive him away before! And *you*,' he added, and Ben got the sense he'd rounded on Melissa. 'You're just as bad. Why didn't you try to stop him?'

'I did, I—'

'Don't even bother! Just *find* him. Go that way, both of you! Cut him off. Don't let him get back to the school!'

There was a crash of footsteps in the undergrowth, and Ben found himself screwing up his eyes, the way he did sometimes when he was lying in bed and there were shapes in the dark closing in.

But the footsteps seemed to be moving away: Callum in one direction, Lance and Melissa in the other. Tentatively, Ben raised his head. He got to his feet, ready to run but unsure which way to go. From the sound of it, Callum was focusing on the area around the lake. Melissa and Lance were heading uphill, just as Callum had instructed, meaning to block his way back to the school. But if Ben followed behind them, maybe he could make it to the chapel . . .

He moved as stealthily as he could. It felt like twilight beneath the canopy and the thickening rain, and Melissa and Lance were no more than shadows up ahead. Ben kept as close as he dared, his stomach aching from where Lance had punched him, a sharper pain in the palms of his hands. His tears were mingling with the rain, and it felt like he was stumbling around blind.

But then he saw the chapel through the trees. The main entrance faced the school, but there was another door at the rear, pointing towards the abandoned graveyard. It was never locked. For Father Steiner, it was a source of pride that the chapel's doors were always kept open.

Ben changed direction, his pace quickening as the trees around him began to thin. The door was just ahead of him now, and he didn't even pause to make sure none of the others were following him. He burst through the entrance at a run, emerging into one of the aisles beside the vestry.

'Father Steiner!' he called, not caring now about how much noise he made. 'Father Steiner, *please*. Help me!'

But when Ben staggered from the aisle into the nave, he saw that the chapel was empty. Of *course* it was empty. It was Saturday, and Callum had *told* Ben that the chaplain was in his room.

'Father Steiner!' Ben called again, not yet ready to give up hope. His eyes fixed on the door to the vestry. It was the only other place the chaplain might be. He crossed the nave and threw open the door – but the vestry was as empty as the rest of the chapel.

Ben could have howled with disappointment. He thought he might actually be sick. Yet before he could do either of those things, he heard what sounded like the main door into the church creaking open. And then there were footsteps on the cold stone floor, steadily making their way towards him.

Ben panicked. Shutting himself in the vestry, his first thought was to find somewhere to hide. But there was nowhere in the narrow chamber where he wouldn't be spotted within seconds. What he needed was a weapon. Something to swing, or hurl, or *stab* with. He began to search – quietly at first, but with increasing desperation. It sounded like a single set of footsteps, meaning either Lance and Melissa had split up, or Callum had guessed where Ben might be. Maybe he'd been following Ben the entire way, biding his time until Ben was cornered . . .

There was a sideboard behind him, but the first drawer he opened contained nothing but candles. Another was stuffed with notebooks and sheets of paper, the next with linen for the altar. Ben began to pull it all out on to the floor, frantically searching for something, *anything*, that might help him. But there was nothing, just useless bits of old . . .

A stack of papers had spilled from one of the drawers, and when Ben happened to look down, his entire body seized up in horror.

The photographs. The pictures of *him*. Somehow they were scattered around his feet. But that was impossible! Callum had given them back to him. Ben could feel them in his pocket. Meaning . . . meaning . . .

Meaning they'd made copies. Ben almost groaned at his own stupidity. *Of course* they would have made copies. And after Ben had failed to hide the first set in Father Steiner's room, one of the others had put another set in the next best place. Probably at the same time as they'd taken one of Father Steiner's stoles.

Ben let his hands drop to his sides, and slowly he backed away from the sideboard. He had nothing to fight with, nowhere to hide. Callum had thought of *everything*.

Unless . . .

The footsteps had stopped.

The door into the vestry was swinging open.

Ben was trapped, precisely as Callum wanted him to be – but there was one other place he could go.

Without stopping to think, he charged shoulder first at the door. He clattered into it with all his might, and heard Callum cry out as the door impacted against him. Ben didn't pause to check how badly he was hurt. He just hurdled Callum's legs where he had fallen, sprinting back towards the door that would take him outside and to the graveyard.

He should have gone there from the off. He'd wanted a hiding place, and he had one. Once he was down in the crypt, he would be safe. Nobody would ever find him there!

The rain was coming down in ropes now, lashing the leaves in the trees and filling the air with a sound like static. Even though Ben knew exactly where he was going, he almost overshot the graveyard, and had to veer to his left at the last moment. He heard Callum raging somewhere behind him, but from the sound of it he was back amid the trees. Ben, on the other hand, had reached the clearing – and the crypt itself was just . . . *there*.

He was going to make it!

As Ben started down the steps, the blackness of the crypt seemed to swallow him. At first he could see where he was treading, but in the dark, and with water cascading down the stairs, he lost his footing. He slipped, and gave a cry, and landed with his arm trapped beneath him. There was a crack, and his cry of surprise turned into one of pain.

He rolled, and felt his back lodge against the base of the steps. He knew he should try to crawl deeper into the darkness, but he couldn't bring himself to move. His fragile hope had shattered at the same time as his arm, replaced instead by despair.

He wasn't ready to die.

He knew he'd done some bad things. Some very bad things. But surely he didn't deserve *this*.

It was only supposed to have been a game – a stupid game he hadn't even wanted to play.

And now he was lying here bleeding, scrunching up his eyes at the pain in his arm.

He wanted to wail, to call for help, but he couldn't be sure who would reach him first. And there were footsteps close by. He could hear them. Meaning it was crucial he didn't make a sound. He couldn't run any more either, not in the state he was in, and not without drawing attention to himself.

His only chance was to squash in tight, and to hope that the monsters passed him by. To trust the shadows, and to pray. *Please God, if you're really out there, keep me hidden. Keep me safe.*

Please let me never be found.

Sunday 27 October, 10.41 a.m.

There was no sign of Callum Richardson anywhere. There were two men in identikit suits scouring the hillside, and Fleet guessed they were Richardson's bodyguards. But with the smoke billowing from the chapel, and the crowd all around them just as thick, it was obvious they were having about as much luck locating their employer as Fleet was.

There was another scream, and Fleet whipped his head around just in time to see a second section of the chapel's roof begin to cave in. A flaming piece of debris broke loose, and when it landed on the ground in front of the chapel doors, it exploded in a shower of sparks. As far as Fleet could tell, nobody was hurt, but as he checked around to make sure, he spotted a figure standing alone amid the turmoil. It was the headmaster, Adrian Harris. He seemed mesmerised by the flames, and was clearly far too close to the burning chapel. His robes were twisted and misaligned, as though he'd been caught in the press of people as they'd rushed to escape the burning building. And though he stood as tall and straight as he always did, there seemed something about him that was broken.

With Bevan beside him, Fleet set off towards him, weaving his way through the throng. Even though he was heading downhill, it felt like he was wading upstream.

'Mr Harris!' Fleet called as they drew near. This close to the chapel, the heat was like a physical mass. The flames crackled and roared, completely smothering the shouts and yells of the people who were stumbling up the hill.

'*Mr Harris!*'

It was only when Fleet was right on top of him that the headmaster finally turned. He appeared dazed, like someone who wasn't sure whether he was awake or asleep.

'Detective Inspector? What . . . what's happening? The chapel . . . the school . . .'

Harris turned, shifting his glassy gaze from the pyre before him to the main building, ablaze at the top of the slope. Fleet hauled him back from the flames to a safer distance further up the hill. The headmaster was still trying to look at the chapel, and Fleet spun him round.

'Where is he, Mr Harris? Look at me, Mr Harris! *You need to tell me where he is.*'

'But . . . I don't . . . I don't know who—'

'I know you lied,' said Fleet, cutting the headmaster off. 'You lied to me about not knowing about the crypt. And you lied to Father Steiner. Nobody ever came to inspect the site, did they? You didn't want anyone investigating the subsidence in the chapel because you were scared about what they might find.'

The headmaster could only stare, and it was all Fleet could do to resist seizing the man by his lapels and giving him a shake.

Instead, he edged closer. 'When Father Steiner first came to you about the cracks, you told him someone had looked into it before he'd even joined the school. And then, when he pushed for the matter to be investigated again years later, you pretended to take care of it. But you never arranged for either survey, did you? You didn't dare. Because by the time the chaplain first came to you, *you'd already helped bury Ben's body.*'

Now Harris's eyes widened. 'What? No! That's . . . that's

not true!' But behind the outrage in his expression, there was an unmistakable flicker of fear.

'I know who killed Ben, Mr Harris. I know who killed Melissa Haynes, and Lance Wheeler, and I know who set fire to the school. And I think you do, too.'

Now the headmaster was shaking his head. He'd started backing away, but Bevan had moved behind him, and Harris had nowhere to go.

Fleet closed the gap between them. 'So I'm going to ask you one more time, Mr Harris. Where is he? Where's your *son*?'

Isaac – May 1997
(The day of Ben's death)

When the door slammed into him, Isaac was knocked from his feet. He hit his head on the wall behind him, and landed heavily on the hard stone floor. And then someone was vaulting over him, hurdling his legs and sprinting for the exit.

It was the shock as much as the bump to the head that left Isaac stunned. The chapel was supposed to have been empty. Father Steiner was sick in his room – Isaac had seen him there himself. That was why he was here in the first place, to collect the notes the chaplain had prepared for his morning sermon, and had left in the chapel when he'd started feeling ill.

Groggily, Isaac raised his head, and caught sight of the figure running for the door. A boy. A pupil. And if Isaac wasn't mistaken . . .

He forced himself to get up, ignoring the throbbing in his skull. The door into the vestry had swung almost closed, and he pulled it wide – and when he saw what lay before him, it was like being knocked off his feet all over again.

The vestry had been ransacked. The chaplain's papers were all over the floor, as well as the candles, and the linen, and everything else the sideboard had contained. The cupboard doors hung open, and the drawers had been wrenched from their runners.

And that wasn't all. At Isaac's feet there was a face gazing up at him. Smiling, *leering*.

Isaac bent and picked up the photograph. Was he . . . he *was*. He was *naked*.

Isaac's confusion soured instantly into disgust. He let go of the photograph as though it had burned him, but as it fell he realised there was another one lying on the floor. And another, and another – a whole load of them scattered about like a spilled deck of cards. A disgusting, depraved deck of cards, like the novelty pack Isaac had seen other boys playing with after lights out in his dorm.

What were the photographs doing here? Who had taken them? *Why?*

Isaac was only sure of one thing.

Ben.

Ben had done this.

Isaac had seen him running. And though at first he'd struggled to understand, all of a sudden it made perfect sense.

Isaac had *known* Ben was up to no good. He'd challenged him on it the first time Ben had volunteered to help in the chapel, all those weeks ago when the two of them had been alone together in this very room. And since that day, Isaac had been watching. He'd tried to be kind; to think generously, the way Father Steiner always did. Maybe Ben truly believed in God – or wanted to, at least. Maybe he hated boarding school as much as Isaac did, and – exactly as it had for Isaac – the chapel had become a sort of haven, a place he didn't feel quite so alone. But every time Isaac tried to give Ben the benefit of the doubt, something would happen that would revive his initial instincts. Isaac had seen Ben sneaking out of the dorm in the middle of the night, clearly up to no good. He'd watched the way Ben talked to Father Steiner, pretending to hang on to the chaplain's every word, when it was perfectly obvious he was faking. Like the time he'd asked Father Steiner to sign that stupid book. Isaac had seen that, too, peering out from behind the vestry door.

And he knew Ben's type. One of the benefits of not having any friends himself – other than Father Steiner – was that Isaac had plenty of time to watch everyone else, and he'd come to learn *everybody's* type. Ben was a misfit. A troublemaker. Someone who caused nothing but mayhem wherever he went. You only had to look at the state of the vestry.

So what was he up to? Was he stealing? Or was it something worse? Was he trying to get Father Steiner in trouble? Was that why the vestry had been ransacked, and the photographs left on the floor? So that the police would be called to investigate a burglary, but when they came they would discover something else?

The very thought made Isaac boil with anger. Father Steiner was the only good thing about this place. Isaac would never have admitted it, least of all to Father Steiner himself, but the chaplain had become like a father to him. A *real* father. Not like his actual dad, who went out of his way to act as though Isaac didn't exist. Who'd even made Isaac enrol at Beaconsfield under his mother's name, to ensure none of the other pupils found out they were related!

Thinking about his father twisted Isaac's stomach into knots, but it was nothing compared to how he felt at that moment about Ben. Whatever he was up to, he wouldn't get away with it. Not if Isaac could help it.

He spun away from the vestry.

He'd heard the chapel door slam shut, meaning Ben was already outside. But Isaac would catch him. He would make him admit what he had done. And then Father Steiner would see that Isaac had been right about Ben all along, and it would go back to the way it was before, when Isaac had the chaplain all to himself.

He threw open the door Ben had fled through, and

immediately had to brace himself against the weather. It was raining just as heavily as it had been when he'd crossed from the school, but now the wind had picked up, too, making the trees buckle and writhe. And although it shouldn't have been getting dark for hours yet, it was as gloomy as dusk in mid-November.

At first, he thought he'd lost Ben already. But . . . *there*. A figure had reached the tree line further down the hill. Isaac yelled Ben's name, but his shout was doused by the rain. Ben kept moving, and Isaac set off after him.

The ground was boggy underfoot. The going was easier once Isaac reached the woods, but then it became even harder to see, and more than once he lost sight of Ben amid the trees. But then Ben abruptly veered left, and it became obvious to Isaac what he was doing. He was only pretending to head into the woods, when really he meant to double back, and leave Isaac floundering in the forest.

Well, Isaac was smarter than that. He veered left himself, knowing that – if he was quick enough – he could cut Ben off in the clearing.

Yet Isaac struggled to keep up. They were moving parallel, Ben about thirty metres deeper into the woods. The trees were thicker where he was, but somehow he was managing to pull ahead. By the time Isaac reached the clearing, Ben was already past the graves and near the tree line on the opposite side. If Isaac wasn't careful, he would lose him completely.

He called out again, and to his ear he sounded like an angry parent chasing an errant child. This time he thought maybe Ben had heard him, because he came to a halt just before he reached the trees. But then, suddenly, he vanished.

One moment he'd been standing there, the next he was gone.

Isaac stopped in his tracks. He wiped the rain from his eyes, and squinted through the gloom to try to see.

'Ben?' he said, but his voice wouldn't have carried even if there'd been anyone there to hear it.

He started across the abandoned graveyard, raising a hand to his forehead so that it was like a visor. He continued to squint, but more in confusion now than because of the rain. Had his eyes deceived him? Had Ben been closer to the woods than he'd thought? But he could have sworn Ben had been standing right beside that pile of stones. If he'd made it all the way across the clearing, Isaac would surely have caught sight of him dashing between the trees.

And then he spotted it.

Right there, amid the stones.

There was a hole.

More than a hole, it was an *entrance*. There were steps, just visible, leading down.

'What the . . . ?'

Isaac moved closer, but there was no way to see beyond the gloom. It was like peering into a cavity filled with tar. He placed his foot on the topmost step, and this time, instead of looking, he angled his ear. He thought he heard . . . crying. Or moaning. Or . . .

He stepped lower, trying to ignore the feeling that he was descending into an open grave. 'Be—' he started to say, and that's when a hand shot out and grabbed his ankle.

Isaac gave a cry of shock. He felt his leg being pulled from under him, and he landed heavily on the base of his spine. The steps were as slippery as a water slide, and there was no way to stop himself falling. He jolted, jarred, his way to the bottom, every step delivering another blow. When he finally hit the ground, his head rocked back against the earth, and for a moment all he could focus on was the pain. He tried to move, just to see if he still could – but then something landed on top of him, and the hand that had grabbed his ankle closed instead around his throat.

Isaac couldn't see, couldn't think, couldn't *breathe*. There was a noise as though from a wounded animal, and it took him a moment to realise it was coming from Ben.

Isaac tried to speak, to say Ben's name, but his hand was like a clamp, his ferocity like nothing Isaac had ever known. It was as though he thought Isaac were trying to attack *him*.

Slowly Ben's outline began to emerge, but even as the darkness all around them faded to grey, another, deeper black began to creep in. It was like being in a tunnel that was slowly constricting, and Isaac knew he was on the brink of passing out. He tried pulling at Ben's fingers, but it was like trying to prise apart a vice. Instead Isaac flailed, feeling for something, *anything*, that might help. His hand closed around something hard – a rock? a piece of rubble? – but as he struggled, he lost his grip. He found it again, dropped it, and the third time he clasped it tight. And then he swung – once, twice – with everything he had, aiming the stone at Ben's head.

The sound it made was sickeningly soft, like a melon being hit by a hammer.

Ben immediately rocked backwards, and for a moment Isaac thought he was free. Yet before he could even draw breath, Ben was on him again, impossibly, and clawing once more at Isaac's neck. This time Isaac reached out as well. His fingers found purchase, and he latched on tight, squeezing with all his might. And he kept on squeezing, *squeezing*, until he realised he was breathing freely, and the hand that had tightened around his own throat had long since fallen away.

It was the mention of his son that finally roused the headmaster from his stupor.

'Isaac?' he said. '*Isaac* did this?' He looked around at the burning buildings. 'But . . . *why*?'

'To get to Richardson,' Fleet replied. 'He wants to punish him, the way he punished Melissa and Lance.' Quite why, Fleet wasn't sure yet, but it was clear that Isaac blamed them for what had happened.

'I know you loved Isaac, Mr Harris,' Fleet said. 'I know you never stopped loving him. That's why you've been here for as long as you have. Isn't that right?' He had the headmaster's complete attention now, but he didn't wait for him to answer. 'I thought at first that it was just about protecting the school for you. I even wondered if you might have been covering for Richardson, safeguarding his family's donations. But it was never about either of those things, was it?'

From Fleet's very first encounter with Adrian Harris, the man had stood as proud and unyielding as an oak tree, his demeanour a parody, almost, of how a head teacher at an elite private boarding school was *supposed* to present himself. Amid the smoke and the heat from the burning chapel, the facade he presented had begun to crack, but there was a flash of the old headmaster in his reaction to what Fleet had said.

'You thought I would cover for Callum Richardson? That I ever gave a *damn* about this school?' Harris turned from the chapel and looked up the hill to the main building, where the fire was steadily beginning to spread. He was clearly still in shock, but for the first time there was a hint of bitter satisfaction in his eyes – as though he was finally beginning to comprehend what was happening.

'My *son* came to me for help, Detective Inspector,' he said, turning back. 'Tell me, what would *you* have done?'

And there it was. Fleet met Bevan's eye, as both men grasped the subtext of what Harris had said: the confession he had implicitly conveyed.

The headmaster appeared to register it himself.

'He . . . he was hurt,' Harris said. 'And he never came to me for *anything*. It was always *Father Steiner* he went to.' He spoke the chaplain's name like a jealous child. 'He . . . he acted like he resented me. Like he *hated* me. He never seemed to understand that I was only ever trying to protect him! If the other pupils had found out he was my son, they would have made his life hell. I've *seen* what children are capable of, Detective Inspector. I *know*!'

Anger flared in his voice – but it faded just as rapidly.

'It was the middle of the night when he came to my room,' he went on. 'He'd been sitting down in that hole for *hours*. And when he told me what had happened, I . . . I was *appalled*, obviously, but I . . . I loved him, and . . . and so I helped him. I washed him, just like I used to do when he was a baby. I cleared up the vestry, and covered up the crypt. I made sure it would never be found.' He was shaking his head as he spoke, looking down at the ground, and abruptly he raised his head. 'He didn't *mean* to kill anyone. Benjamin Draper was the one to attack *him*! And I couldn't let an *accident* ruin my son's life. Benjamin was just a . . . a . . . I mean, compared to Isaac, he . . . he would never have amounted to—'

'His name was Ben, Mr Harris,' Fleet interrupted, any

sympathy he'd been starting to feel for Harris quickly evaporating. 'And whatever justification you've been clinging on to for all these years, the reality is you're an accessory to murder. You will be arrested, and charged – but in the meantime you need to do the right thing. You need to help us find your son.'

Harris started shaking his head again, whether as a refusal or a denial about what was happening, Fleet wasn't sure.

'There are *lives* at stake, Mr Harris! *Tell me where he is.*'

'But . . . I don't know! I swear! The last time I spoke to him, he was nineteen years old. After what happened, he . . . he blamed me. For *everything*. For the break-up with his mother, for my insisting on bringing him *here*. I only know what he looks like now from the picture on his website!'

Another chunk of the chapel's roof caved in, and there was a *whump* as the debris hit the floor. Fleet focused on the headmaster, searching his face for another lie, but he could sense that Harris, this time, was telling the truth.

'Show me,' Fleet said.

Harris's expression creased in confusion.

'The picture. Show it to me!'

Bevan was already holding out his phone for Harris to take. With fumbling fingers, Harris tried typing in the address of the website he'd mentioned, but he was clearly struggling to complete the task. Bevan was watching over Harris's shoulder, his eyes progressively narrowing, and after a moment he took the phone back and started tapping on the screen himself, evidently finishing whatever Harris had started.

He flipped the phone to allow Fleet to see.

On the screen was a picture of a man who could have been anything from Fleet's age to a decade younger. And immediately Fleet spotted the resemblance between Isaac and his father. They had the same high cheekbones and angled jaw. On Isaac, however, they looked less severe, and with his neatly combed hair, and his jumper and tie, he looked more like a bank clerk than a killer.

And then Fleet noticed the URL.

'This is him?' he said to Harris, jabbing a finger towards the screen. '*This* is your son?'

Harris nodded – and another piece of the puzzle slotted into place.

Bevan was already raising the phone to his ear, angling himself away from the roar of the flames. Fleet was left staring at the headmaster, cursing his own stupidity. They'd found their killer days ago. Nicky had, rather, and Fleet had been too slow to see it.

Shining Light. Isaac was the manager at Shining Light.

'He . . . he calls himself Zack now,' Harris said. 'He doesn't even use his mother's surname any more. He hates her almost as much as he hates me – blames her for letting me bring him *here*. He goes by Lawrence. It was his grandfather's name. His mother's father. He was the only person in the family Isaac ever got along with.'

Fleet was scouring the crowd on the hill, squinting to try to peer through the smoke. From the look of it, about half of the attendees of the memorial service had already made it around to the front of the building, but that still left hundreds of people between the chapel and the school.

Think, Fleet urged himself. He had to presume Isaac had been waiting to pounce on Richardson the moment the panic in the chapel set in. So what then? Would he have dealt with Richardson at the first opportunity, left his body to be consumed by the flames? But if so, why set *two* fires? If it was just to ensure the school burned down as well, why not start the blaze more centrally, rather than in the wing of the building where the fire would be slowest to spread?

As if in answer, the bell in the clock tower at the front of the school began its hourly toll, the chimes resonating above the noise of the flames like a fire warning in a medieval village. Between the gongs there was a wail of approaching sirens. The fire engines had got past those news crews, then, as well as the cars clogging the drive. Now they just needed to negotiate the crowd at the front of the building.

The crowd . . . the news crews . . .

Fleet's gaze snapped to the stream of people being herded by his colleagues towards the car park. He thought of Isaac gazing up into the CCTV camera in Richardson's living room, his look an obvious challenge. *Your turn to hide*, his note had read – suggesting he didn't just want to punish Richardson. He wanted to scare him. To humiliate him. And all at once Fleet thought he knew how.

He turned, grabbing Bevan by the sleeve. The DC still had his phone to his ear.

'Talk as we go!' Fleet instructed.

'But . . . what about him?' Bevan signalled with his chin towards the headmaster.

Harris was rooted to the spot, his robes hanging off him like a broken sail, the fire flickering weakly in his tear-filled eyes. It was obvious he wasn't going anywhere.

'We'll deal with him later,' Fleet replied. Harris looked at him pleadingly, and Fleet turned his back, unsure whether to feel pity or disgust.

The fire in the main building was gathering momentum. Fleet made directly for the flames.

'Sir?' said Bevan, running to keep pace. 'Where are we going?' The anxiety was palpable in his voice.

As they diverged from the main stream of people, the space around them began to open up, but the wind was funnelling thick grey plumes into their eyes. Fleet had to pause and wait for the smoke to clear. 'There,' he said. 'That way.' He pointed to the archway on the southern side of the building that would lead them into the quad.

They had to wrap their arms across their mouths against the smoke. When they entered the short stone tunnel, there was a noise like the sound the roof of the chapel had made just before it began to cave in. For a moment Fleet was sure the entire archway was going to fall on their heads. But they made it through, and when they emerged into the central courtyard, the air was immediately clearer. Even the heat was less intense.

The eye of the storm, Fleet thought to himself grimly.

He looked around – and saw a body on the ground beside the fountain.

He thought at first that it was Richardson. Either Fleet had been wrong about what Isaac meant to do, or Richardson had forced a change of plan.

But as Fleet rushed to the man's side, he realised it was one of the bodyguards he'd seen hunting for Richardson in the grounds. The man's suit jacket was heavy with blood, but he was alive.

'That way,' the bodyguard growled, as Fleet bent close. 'They went . . . that way.' One hand was holding his stomach. The other pointed across the quad.

Fleet helped Bevan to get the man sitting up. He looked the way they'd come, and saw flames were already spouting from the windows above the archway. The bodyguard's colleague had appeared on the other side of the tunnel, his finger pressed to his earpiece, but Fleet waved him back. Bevan was radioing for medical assistance, but it was clear the fire would be all around them by the time an ambulance crew arrived.

'Help me get him to his feet,' Fleet instructed.

The bodyguard roared in pain as Fleet and Bevan hauled him upright, but the fact that he was able to scream at all told Fleet there was still some strength left in him.

'Go,' said Bevan. 'I've got him.'

Fleet looked across doubtfully, but Bevan nodded his insistence. The bodyguard was clutching the stab wound in his belly, blood leaking through his fingers, but he was able to support most of his own weight.

The bodyguard raised his head. 'If you hurry, you'll . . . catch them,' he said through his grimace.

Fleet pointed to a door in the north-west corner of the quad. 'Go that way. Head right once you get inside, and don't stop. The corridor will take you to the entrance hall.'

Bevan started off, the bodyguard's arm slung around his shoulders. Fleet watched to make sure they could manage, then turned the way the bodyguard had directed him. There was a small wooden door hanging open in a wall that jutted into the quad. Fleet's gaze drifted up, and he saw the clock tower looming overhead.

He swore inwardly, realising his instincts about Isaac's intentions had been right.

He ran for the door. The only way forward beyond the threshold was the staircase leading up. It wound around the inside of the tower in an angled spiral, with only a flimsy-looking wooden handrail separating the stairs from the central bore. The platform at the top of the tower must have been at least forty metres in the air. Just the thought of being up so high made Fleet feel dizzy.

'Christ,' he muttered. 'As if a burning building weren't enough.'

He started to climb, and as he did so he heard a yell from above. He leaned out across the handrail as far as he dared, and caught a flash of movement somewhere near the top. There were two people pressed close together, and as the man at the rear happened to glance down, Fleet caught sight of his face. It was Isaac – *Zack* – and he was holding a knife that was still bloody from the wound he'd inflicted on Richardson's bodyguard. When he saw Fleet following them, he shouted again, driving Callum Richardson on. It struck Fleet that it was probably only because the bodyguard had got in Zack's way that Callum Richardson wasn't already dead. Fleet had to hope that Bevan had got the man to safety, and that the stab wound wasn't as serious as it had looked.

The higher Fleet climbed, the tighter he clung to the wall. He tried to ignore the void beyond the handrail, as well as his lungs clamouring for air.

Nicky, he reminded himself. *You're doing this for Nicky. And you're going to make sure she realises what you went through just as soon as you know she's safe.*

There was an opening at the top of the staircase, and Fleet made it to the final flight of steps just in time to see a trailing foot disappear on to the platform beyond. He clambered up the last few stairs and out on to the platform himself.

'Stay back!' roared a voice. 'One more step and I'll cut his throat! I swear to God, I'll do it!'

Fleet rocked back on his heels. It wasn't just a response to Zack's command and the knife pressed to Callum Richardson's neck; it was the scene that had opened up before him. They must have been the equivalent of five or six storeys in the air, on a platform maybe seven metres square, the clock tower's bell like a chandelier above their heads. All four sides of the platform were completely open, save for a stone pillar at each corner, and a perimeter wall that was knee height at best. Fleet had emerged on to the platform barely a metre from the edge. The front entrance to the school was directly below, all the people who'd escaped the chapel gathering together at the top of the driveway in a writhing mass.

Fleet had to grab the nearest pillar to steady himself. As he did, Zack began yelling to the crowd.

'Hey! Up here!'

He shoved Richardson towards the edge of the platform, in the corner opposite Fleet. Richardson was more dishevelled than Fleet had ever seen him. His suit was ripped at the shoulder, and his tie knot was halfway around his neck. His cheeks were crimson, whether from anger or because the tie was throttling him, Fleet wasn't able to tell.

'Hey!' Zack yelled again, and then he angled his mouth to Richardson's ear. 'There's your audience, Callum. Why not give them a wave?'

Richardson bared his teeth in response, and Zack raised the knife and grabbed his tie, tugging at it as though he were a dog on a lead.

'I said, *wave*.'

Richardson slowly raised his hand, and people down below began to point. Exactly as Zack had wanted, he and Richardson were centre stage. The fire in the chapel had been a distraction: a chance for Zack to get to Richardson without being caught. The fire in the southern wing of the school had been to drive everyone to the front of the building, so that Zack could parade Richardson before them, and finish what he'd started.

'Zack,' Fleet said, edging forward. 'You don't need to do this!'

'Get *back*!'

Zack tightened his grip on Richardson's tie, drawing him closer to the tip of the knife. Richardson's eyes were fixed on the blade.

'You have no idea what I need to do!' said Zack. 'You have no idea how long I've been made to wait!'

'Twenty-two years,' Fleet said. 'I do know, Zack. I work with Nicky. I'm Detective Inspector Fleet. *Rob*. And I want to help you. But first you need to give me the knife.'

The mention of Nicky gave Zack pause.

'Where is she, Zack? My friend, Nicky. What did you do to her?'

Zack's jaw bulged as he bit down. 'She shouldn't have interfered. She shouldn't have kept *pressing*. I didn't *want* to hurt her! It was her fault for getting in the way!'

Fleet felt his stomach lurch, and this time it was nothing to do with his fear of heights.

There was a commotion below, and Fleet and Zack both turned. A fire crew had arrived on the scene, and the crowd was parting to let them through. The news teams had made it up the drive as well, and several had already begun filming. From being focused on the flames, however, the cameras were now pointing at the top of the clock tower, and the drone Fleet had spotted earlier was hovering level with the platform. Zack unpeeled his lips into a hate-filled grin.

Fleet stole a glance in the opposite direction, back across the courtyard. The southern wing of the building had been completely engulfed by the fire. The wind was blowing the smoke away from them, down the hill towards the chapel, but the flames were creeping around the quad. The northern wing of the building was now the only section of the school that wasn't ablaze, yet if they stayed in the clock tower much longer, the fire would consume them from the bottom up.

'Zack, listen to me. Whatever you want those people down there to know, you can tell them from a place of safety. You've got everybody's attention. I guarantee they'll listen to what you say.'

'They'll listen,' Zack agreed. 'But it's not from me they need to hear.' He shoved Richardson even closer to the edge, and someone down below let out a scream. 'Go on,' Zack spat. '*Tell them.* Tell the world what kind of person you really are!'

Richardson bucked against Zack's grip. He was furious, Fleet could see, but that didn't stop the terror from showing in his eyes. He focused his anger on Fleet. 'For Christ's sake, *do* something, will you?'

Zack jerked Richardson around, moving the knife to his kidneys and forcing him to face the crowd.

'Tell them!' Zack roared. 'Tell everybody what you did!'

'I didn't *do* anything!' Richardson shot back. 'Whatever you think you know, nothing *happened*! It was just talk, that's all. A stupid game!'

'A *game*?' Zack spluttered, and Fleet saw spit speckle Richardson's cheek. 'You tried to murder Ben Draper! You planned to frame Father Steiner! Your *game* ruined my *life*!'

His voice carried out across the crowd, and Fleet registered the gasps.

'You didn't know *that* part, did you, Detective Inspector?' said Zack. 'What did you think, that I *meant* to kill Ben? I shouldn't have even been there! *Ben* shouldn't have been there! He was only out in the woods that day because Callum and the others meant to throttle him and toss his body in the lake!'

Fleet's eyes locked on to Richardson's, and he knew immediately that Zack was telling the truth. *That* was the scheme Richardson and the others had come up with: their plan to destroy the school. Father Steiner was the target, just as Fleet had suspected, but the reason they'd involved Ben was because he was a target, too. An allegation of a sexual relationship, this time, was only supposed to have been the beginning – a prelude to something far worse.

But how did it get to the point that Zack had killed Ben instead? An *accident*, the headmaster had called it. *Benjamin Draper was the one to attack* him.

'He thought you were one of them?' Fleet said to Zack. 'Is that how it happened?'

'I found Ben in the vestry,' Zack said. 'He swung the door at me and ran off towards the crypt. I didn't even know the crypt was there! I tried to catch him, because . . . because I thought he was up to something. I thought he was trying to get Father Steiner in trouble, when Father Steiner had never been anything but kind to him. To *anyone*. He was the closest thing to a real father I ever had! But when I chased Ben into the graveyard, I fell. He pulled me, rather. Down into the hole with him. And then *he* tried to strangle *me*!'

Once again Fleet looked at Richardson. 'Because he was scared,' he said. 'Because he was already running for his life.'

Richardson's features were contorted with rage. His gaze flicked between Zack and the people watching down below, before finally settling on Fleet. 'It's not true. None of what he's saying is true! Just look at what he's doing, for Christ's sake! He's a lunatic. A *freak show*! Just like he was when he was a kid!'

'That's why you pointed us to Melissa and Lance,' Fleet said, ignoring Richardson's denials. 'To the scandal involving Richard Hewitt. You knew we'd find out about it eventually, and that we'd begin to suspect Ben's death was connected to something similar. So you tried to distance yourself from the others. Because *you* were never implicated in the sexual assault charge, were you? Only Father Steiner suspected you were involved.'

Fleet edged slightly further along the platform.

'What happened, Richardson? Did the three of you split up in the woods when Ben got away from you? But you had no idea what happened after that, did you? You couldn't have known, because Ben never turned up. Maybe, at the time, you assumed he must have run away, just like everybody said, because you knew more than anyone that he had reason to. But when his body was discovered twenty-two years later, you decided Melissa and Lance must have killed him after all. There was no other conclusion you could have drawn.'

And it would have been the same for Melissa and Lance, Fleet realised. Richardson had assumed the others had killed Ben; Melissa and Lance would have thought it was Richardson. Maybe, unlike Richardson, they'd feared Ben was dead right from the beginning. That Richardson had gone through with it without telling them, and hadn't trusted them with the truth. Maybe they'd suspected he'd abandoned the original plan for the same reason – because he didn't trust them to stick to their story.

Except they had. All three of them. They'd told the police the same lie about playing hide-and-seek they'd agreed on from the beginning. And Melissa and Lance had lived with their guilt – and the uncertainty about what had really happened – ever since.

'Did Melissa tell you all of this?' Fleet asked Zack. 'Is that how you found out?'

'She didn't need to tell me. When she first turned up at the shelter six months ago, she didn't even know who I was. But I recognised *her*. So I . . . I listened in when she was talking to the counsellor. The sessions take place in the room right next door to my office. At first it was just curiosity,' Zack added almost defensively, as though eavesdropping were the crime he was most ashamed of. 'I wanted to know what had happened to her. How, from being Little Miss Perfect, her life had gone so wrong. She didn't tell the counsellor everything. She *couldn't* have, because she didn't know how Ben's story ended.' He turned back to Richardson, and raised the tip of the knife level with his eye. 'But *I* did. I knew exactly what happened to Ben – and thanks to Melissa I found out the reasons why.'

'And so you killed her,' said Fleet. 'Lance Wheeler, too.'

Zack rounded on Fleet. 'They deserved it! And anyway, they had their chances! I *knew* Callum was the one behind it, and I wanted them both to help me prove it. But Melissa was a drug addict. Even if she'd agreed to help me, nobody would have believed a word she said. And in the end Lance was no more use to me than she was. When I approached him, he threatened to tell on *me*!'

'So you fought. And you made his death look like suicide to buy yourself time. Time enough to get to Richardson.'

'I could have got to him whenever I wanted!' Zack retorted. 'I broke into his house, didn't I? And I proved it today. But hurting him wouldn't have been enough. I wanted him to suffer the way I've suffered. To feel the same terror Ben did!' He shook his head incredulously. 'He wanted to be *prime minister*. For *years* he's been sitting there in front of the cameras calling *other people* hypocrites. And while he was living in a mansion, being driven around in limousines, my life was in *pieces*!' Once again Zack shook his head, more bitterly this time. 'I wasn't going to let him get away with it, not after I found out the truth.'

Your turn to hide. All of a sudden the note he'd left made a twisted kind of sense.

'And the email?' said Fleet. 'The tip-off that led us to Ben's body? That was to get us sniffing around Richardson, too? To build up to something like this?' He spread his arms to indicate the scene around them. The fire was close enough now that smoke was drifting across the platform and the air was beginning to shimmer in the heat.

Zack smiled again, the same embittered grin he'd shown before. 'I told you, I wanted to see him squirm. To watch as his reputation fell apart. I knew all the evidence pointed his way, and I knew that even if *you* didn't convict him, the enemies he'd made would. The press, the politicians: all the people who hated him as much as I did.'

Immediately Fleet thought of Webb and Manish Apte. About how smug Webb in particular must have been feeling at the idea that *he* was the one pulling the strings.

'But then,' said Zack, 'when my father announced the memorial service, I knew this was how it was supposed to end.' He looked around at the burning building and the crowd watching on below. 'It's perfect. Don't you see? It's exactly the type of tribute Ben deserves. Not just a remembrance. A *reckoning*.'

Fleet edged another step closer. 'Do you really think this is what Ben would have wanted? For you to lose your life as well? Look around you, Zack! If we stay up here much longer, we're *all* going to die!'

'Don't you get it yet?' Zack snapped. 'I don't *care* what happens to me! Do you think I would have told you where Ben's body was if I did? My life was over the minute I told you about the crypt. It was over twenty-two years ago!'

Fleet heard boot-steps on the stairwell below, and when he glanced he saw firefighters on the penultimate flight of steps. They yelled up to him, frantically urging him down.

Zack, meanwhile, had turned back to Richardson, his hand still gripping Richardson's tie and the knife pointing at his throat.

'Say it!' Zack commanded, forcing Richardson forward. 'The cameras are rolling, Callum. All the eyes of the audience are on you. Admit that you were going to kill him! That Ben only died because of you!'

'OK!' Richardson bleated. 'I admit it! I—'

But that was as far as he got. As he'd started speaking, Zack had withdrawn the knife. Just a fraction – but Richardson must have realised it was the only opportunity he was going to get.

He whipped himself around, and though the knife slashed across his arm, it was obvious he barely felt it. He let out a roar, his rage all at once matching Zack's. Richardson, though, was taller, and he was able to make his size count. They spun, and suddenly Zack was the one leaning into space, the hand around Richardson's tie his only tether. In his other hand, he continued to clutch the knife, but Richardson was battling for it, too. They were so fixated on the tussle, neither man appeared to notice how close they were to losing their balance.

Fleet dived, catching Richardson around the midriff just in time. Richardson had one hand around Zack's throat, driving him backwards across the wall. But Richardson's tie bound them together, and the closer Zack came to tipping over the edge, the further Richardson was forced to lean, too. Fleet had his feet braced against the wall, and it was taking all of his strength to keep both men from falling.

'Pull him up!' he yelled. 'For Christ's sake, Richardson!'

But Richardson paid no notice. Every sinew in his neck was straining against the loop of silk that was tugging him forwards.

Suddenly he let go of Zack's throat, and focused on the knife instead. But he was no longer trying to wrench it from Zack's grip. Instead he was drawing it across his body.

'No!' Fleet roared, but he was powerless to intervene. If he let go of Richardson, *both* men would die.

With two hands now to Zack's one, Richardson forced the knife closer to his own throat. Zack's eyes narrowed in confusion – and then widened as he realised what was happening. He tried to fight it, but like Fleet there was nothing he could do. The knife was moving in slow motion, but when the blade touched the edge of the outstretched tie, the material was severed in a blink.

And then it was over. Fleet and Richardson were toppling backwards, and Zack was screaming as he plummeted towards the ground.

Sunday 27 October, 12.14 p.m.

'Nicky? *Nicky*. Where is she? Is she—'

'Rob, don't.' Randy was at the doorway trying to hold him back. There were other police officers on the scene as well, and the entire building had already been cordoned off. When Fleet and Bevan had seen the photograph of Zack on the DC's phone, Bevan had immediately called it in, directing a team of officers to Shining Light. But they'd been too late. It was obvious they'd been too late. If Nicky were still alive, she would already be in the ambulance at the front of the building. And the fact that Randy was here at all told Fleet everything he needed to know.

'I want to see her, Randy!' He struggled to break Randy's hold on his arm.

'Rob. *Rob*. Just wait a minute, will you?'

Fleet was trying to get through the main door into the building, and for a moment he stopped struggling. 'Wait for *what*? Is she in there? Why haven't they brought her out yet?'

'That's what I've been trying to tell you. You're going the wrong way.'

Randy pulled him towards the alleyway at the side of the building.

'They found her out back. In a part of the building that's sealed off from the rest. I'm assuming whoever owns the place ran out of money before they could complete the renovations.' He looked Fleet up and down. 'You know, you really should get yourself checked out first. At least clean

316

yourself up a bit. What's Nicky going to think when she sees you?'

Fleet felt the glitch in his own movements. 'You mean . . .'

Randy stopped and turned. The confusion on his face turned to understanding. 'Christ on a tricycle. Did no one tell you she was alive? And then you saw me here, the angel of death himself . . .' He broke into a smile. 'Nicky's fine, Rob. At least, she's going to be. I'm here for the same reason you are. And they only haven't moved her yet because she's refusing to let them carry her on a stretcher.'

Fleet's relief burst out of him as laughter. 'She's really OK? She's not hurt, or . . .'

Randy's smile broadened. 'Come and see for yourself.'

There was a separate entrance to the disused wing of the building – a door that appeared to have been boarded up until relatively recently. In place of the planks that had been sealing it shut, a pair of heavy-duty bolts were screwed to the outside. Two padlocks lay broken on the floor, presumably where Fleet's colleagues had forced them open to gain access.

He and Randy stepped into a room that stank of mildew and dust, the only light coming from the gaps around the plywood that had been nailed over the windows.

Randy led Fleet to the other side of the room and through the broken shell of a corridor – cracked ceiling tiles scattered all over the floor, and electrical wires dangling from gaps in the plaster. There was another door at the end of the passageway, and as before there was a pair of broken padlocks on the floor.

There were two paramedics crouching down just beyond the threshold. Nicky had clearly lost her battle over the stretcher, because she was lying on a gurney between them.

317

When Fleet approached and said her name, she opened her eyes.

She smiled at him weakly. 'Have you . . . solved this thing yet?' she managed to say. She swallowed. 'Because I'm pretty sure I know who did it.'

It was hours before they were able to talk to each other properly.

They were at the hospital. Fleet was fine: a few scratches and bruises he didn't even remember getting, and a cough from all the smoke he'd managed to inhale, but otherwise he'd been given a clean bill of health. As clean a bill of health as an overweight man approaching forty who smoked a dozen cigarettes a day could hope to receive, anyway.

Nicky was in a bed in a private room, and would remain there for a couple of nights at least. She was suffering from exhaustion, and dehydration, and there was a nasty ring of bruises around her neck, as well as a bump the size of a tennis ball on the back of her head. Zack may not have wanted her dead, but he'd made sure she would remain unconscious long enough to allow him to move her from the house in the docks to the shelter in Blackhawk without any chance of her waking up. He'd locked her in the derelict section of the building with no food or water, and although Nicky had already made it perfectly clear that she didn't want Fleet – or anyone – making a fuss, the reality was she probably wouldn't have survived another day if they hadn't got to her when they did. Apart from anything, it seemed patently obvious that when Zack had set his stage at Beaconsfield, he'd had no intention of coming back.

'I feel like such an idiot,' Nicky was saying. Her voice remained croaky, and the doctor had warned her to limit how much she tried to talk.

Fleet passed her the cup of ice chips one of the nurses had left for her.

'We *chatted*,' Nicky went on, disgustedly. 'Zack actually told me to my face how much he hated Richardson. I even flirted with him a bit, because I thought I could get him to help me.' She shook her head, and winced at the pain it seemed to cause her. 'And then I trailed him around the building like a puppy, for pity's sake, and all the while Melissa was locked up in the same place you found me.'

When their colleagues had searched the disused part of Shining Light more thoroughly, they'd seen clear evidence that Nicky wasn't the first person Zack had kept imprisoned there. Although they would never know for sure, it seemed likely that Zack had abducted Melissa at some point after he'd settled on his plan, which began with the anonymous message to the police. He'd told Fleet that Melissa had refused to help him, but whatever had happened between them, it was clear Zack needed her out of the way. He'd supplied her with heroin, perhaps as a way to keep her compliant, and also to get her to cooperate when he used her to lure Nicky to the docks. As well as the fresh track marks Randy had spotted on Melissa's body, there'd been needles and various other paraphernalia on the floor in the room where she'd apparently been held.

It made Fleet wonder whether Zack had really intended to kill Melissa – or even Lance – from the start. Or whether it was all about Richardson for him, and he'd only resorted to killing the others when he'd felt he had no choice: Lance, when he threatened to betray him; Melissa, when Zack was so close to realising his goal, he didn't want to risk her ruining things at the last. He'd kidnapped Nicky for the very same reason, and probably decided that moving two bodies from the docks to Shining Light would be taking too much of a chance. He'd told himself afterwards that both Melissa and Lance deserved to die, but perhaps only because it's what he needed to believe.

'Melissa never really tried to locate Lance, did she?' said Nicky. 'Do you think she even knew Ben's body had been found?'

'It seems unlikely,' Fleet replied. 'We only had Zack's word about when Melissa actually went missing, after all. He told you it was the same day the rumours about Ben first started appearing online, but I'd imagine that was for our benefit. To encourage us to draw our own conclusions.'

'And he wrote Lance's address on the notepad in Melissa's room for the same reason,' put in Nicky. 'Used the residents' computer to search for Lance rather than his own. He knew we'd come looking for Melissa, and he wanted to keep us focused on Richardson and his friends. To deflect attention away from *him*.' Nicky exhaled. 'Not that he needed to worry. I didn't even come close to suspecting him.'

'You had no cause to,' Fleet reassured her. 'Not at that point.'

'That doesn't make me feel any less of an idiot. And then, after I got the call from Melissa, I walked straight into Zack's trap.'

'If it makes you feel any better,' said Fleet, 'I would have done the same thing. And you're not the only one feeling like a fool, you know.'

'You?' said Nicky, showing her surprise. 'You're the hero of the hour. What have you got to feel foolish about? I saw what happened up on that tower. The footage has been play-ing non-stop on the news.'

Fleet had seen it, too, in the hospital waiting room. The

clip had cut away just at the moment Zack started to fall, but that hadn't made it any easier for Fleet to watch.

'I didn't save him. Zack. *Isaac.* I wasn't able to talk him down.'

'You saved Richardson,' Nicky countered. 'Which, OK, I can understand might not be something you feel like getting printed on a T-shirt, but you saved my life, too, you know. And from what I've heard, it was largely thanks to you that no one was seriously hurt in the fire. The situation was a mess until you and Sean got there.'

Fleet wasn't convinced he could take any credit, but it was indeed a miracle that nobody had been killed in the blaze. By the time the fire was brought under control, however, Beaconsfield had been completely gutted. Fleet had his doubts the school would ever open again, not after everything that had happened: with Ben, with Zack, and after its headmaster had been charged as an accessory to murder. The irony that Richardson and the others had ultimately achieved what they set out to wasn't lost on Fleet. And there was another irony, too: that Zack, by the end, had wanted the same thing they did. Maybe the fire itself hadn't been his primary goal, but he wouldn't have set the blaze in the first place if he hadn't been happy to see Beaconsfield burn.

Fleet wondered if Father Steiner might be secretly thankful, too. He would never have approved of the means, Fleet knew, but he'd never approved of Beaconsfield either. And now he was free to move on.

'I'll be putting DC Bevan forward for a commendation,' Fleet told Nicky. 'He saved Richardson's bodyguard's life.'

'You both did,' Nicky insisted. 'And don't forget Ben, boss. This case was about getting justice for *him*. It may not feel like much of a success at the moment, but I'd say it definitely goes down as a win.'

Fleet smiled wryly. 'Well, rather than being so hard on yourself, you might want to tell yourself the same thing.'

Nicky looked down. She swirled the ice chips around in her cup.

'It was like a penance for Zack, wasn't it?' she said, after a moment. 'The shelter. Helping people like Melissa. It was a way for him to try to make up for what he did.'

And that was another irony: the fact that, if Zack hadn't set up Shining Light, and if Melissa hadn't gone there for help, he would never have found out what had led him down that path in the first place.

Nicky raised her head. 'Do we know what happened to him yet?' she asked Fleet. 'After Ben, and after Harris helped him cover his tracks . . .'

'Harris has been filling in some of the gaps, and Sean's been keeping me up to date,' Fleet said. 'Apparently nobody at Beaconsfield ever saw Isaac again. With the fuss around Ben, and the fact that no one had ever really paid any attention to Isaac anyway, him leaving school went completely unnoticed.'

'Father Steiner must have noticed, surely?'

'He did, but he also knew how unhappy Beaconsfield had made Isaac, and Harris fed him some story that Ben's disappearance had left his son too upset to stay. It seems that at some point Isaac went to live with his mother, but he never forgave her for letting his father take him to Beaconsfield, and in the end he turned his back on her as well. He lived on the streets for a while, became an addict himself, before someone connected to a church – someone very much like Father Steiner, I would imagine – involved him in setting up the shelter.'

Nicky took a moment to consider. 'I wonder why he went

to Harris in the first place,' she said. 'You know, after what happened in the crypt. If he was so close to Father Steiner, why didn't he go to the chaplain for help instead?'

Fleet had pondered the same thing himself. 'Because he would have been too ashamed to, I think. Because he *cared* about Father Steiner's opinion of him – whereas, in Isaac's mind at least, his father couldn't think any less of him than he already did. Plus, Isaac probably realised that Harris would be more able to help him. What was it Harris said when we spoke to him? Something about a crisis . . .'

Nicky recalled the words before Fleet could. '*It takes more than a crisis to prevent the wheels at this school from continuing to turn.*'

'Right,' Fleet said. He recalled something else Harris had said to them. The headmaster had insisted that his son had always been treated like any other Beaconsfield pupil, without fear or favour. He'd said it with pride, but Fleet could only imagine how hurtful that must have been. It was one thing to be sent away from your parents. It must surely have been far harder to see your father every day, and watch him pretend you didn't exist.

Nicky gave a sniff, and Fleet raised an eyebrow.

'I'm not laughing,' Nicky explained. 'If anything it makes you want to cry. You know, when you think about how similar they all were. Ben, Zack, Callum Richardson. Not their personalities, obviously. But the stuff they were dealing with. The things that made them who they were.'

Fleet had been thinking about that part, too. More than Nicky could have realised.

'Richardson in particular was ready to commit *murder*, for Christ's sake,' Nicky went on. 'It was more important to him that his father should be made to suffer than an innocent boy should be allowed to live.'

323

Now Fleet shifted uncomfortably. This was the man he had saved: a murderer in all but deed. Although maybe that was no longer accurate. Richardson hadn't *needed* to let Zack die. He'd chosen to – and Fleet had no doubt he would make the same decision all over again.

'It's pretty obvious he's been driven by rage his entire life,' Fleet said. 'I'm not just talking about his time at Beaconsfield, or even the way he acted after he left school. Because it didn't stop when his father died. If anything, his father's death only spurred him on, probably because for Richardson it would have felt like his father had won. That he'd died without ever having to pay for what he'd done.'

'So Richardson reinvented himself, and turned against the rest of the world instead. The establishment, in particular.'

'Right,' said Fleet. 'Whatever that means. Although I doubt Richardson's any clearer in his mind than I am. For him, anyone with power is the enemy. The police, politicians, you name it. The man's never done anything constructive in his life. For him, it's all about tearing things down.'

'Can you imagine what he would have been like as prime minister?' Nicky said. 'Then again, maybe it's not so hard to picture. A narcissistic former TV star given the keys to a nuclear silo . . . It's not like it hasn't happened before.' She looked at Fleet anxiously. 'There's no way that's actually going to happen, is there? I take it Richardson's under arrest?'

'For the time being,' Fleet said. 'But I have my doubts any charges will stick.'

'You've got to be kidding me,' said Nicky. 'He admitted he tried to kill Ben! I realise the cameras didn't pick up every word, but they caught enough.'

'He had a knife to his throat,' Fleet countered. 'He wouldn't even need a solicitor to help him wriggle out of that one. And there's no actual proof of what went on – not any more. And without Melissa or Lance to give their side of the story . . .'

Nicky shook her head in disbelief. 'Why is it that people like Richardson always seem to wriggle away scot-free? They use people like Ben – people like Lance and Melissa, too, who were probably just as vulnerable in their own way as Ben was – and then toss them aside like pieces of rubbish. I bet, in spite of everything that's happened, Richardson doesn't feel an ounce of regret.'

'Oh, I don't know about that. Maybe he won't be sorry for any of the hurt he caused, but I'm sure he'll be feeling plenty sorry for himself. His career's over. His political ambitions are, too. Millions of people watched him being accused of murder, and then saw him force a man to his death. Maybe, when it comes to Zack, self-defence will hold up in court, but not when it comes to public opinion. Richardson's finished and he knows it.'

Nicky didn't appear quite satisfied. 'Even so – and I realise I probably shouldn't say this – but I can't help thinking it would have been better if Richardson had been the one to fall from that clock tower.'

As ever, Nicky had put her finger on it: the source of Fleet's discomfort. Because no matter how much he tried to ignore it, a little voice inside him kept whispering exactly the same thing.

'Was that what Zack intended, do you think?' Nicky asked. 'I mean, even if Richardson had admitted everything Zack wanted him to . . . would Zack have pushed him?'

'Honestly?' said Fleet. 'I think he meant to jump and take Richardson with him.'

For a moment, neither of them spoke. Nicky was the one to break the silence.

'Christ,' she said. 'That was one seriously screwed-up group of kids.'

Again, it was precisely what Fleet had been thinking himself. He turned his gaze towards the window. The hospital wasn't far from the water, and the view, fittingly or not, was of the docks.

'Boss?' said Nicky, eventually. 'Are you OK? What's on your mind?'

'Nothing, I . . .' Fleet turned back and gave his best impression of a smile. 'I'm just thinking about a conversation I had with Holly, that's all. One we need to finish.'

Nicky nodded politely. She sucked her ice chips, clearly not wanting to pry.

Then: 'She's pregnant,' Fleet announced, surprising even himself. Nicky coughed into her straw.

'It's not mine,' Fleet added quickly. 'She and I aren't . . . I mean, we haven't . . .' He allowed the sentence to tail off, and finished with a sigh. 'The point is, she's planning to have it on her own, and the last time we spoke, I think I gave her the impression—' He interrupted himself. 'No. I *know* I gave her the impression that I didn't approve. That I didn't think she could manage on her own.'

'What did you say to her?' There was a trace of judgement in Nicky's tone.

'Nothing! That is, I didn't say what I'd intended to say. It came out wrong, that's all, and I . . . Well. I need to set things right.' Once again, Fleet sighed. 'Nicky, listen . . . can I ask you something?'

As close as he and Nicky were, they rarely spoke about anything that wasn't linked to work, and Fleet was expecting it to feel awkward. But Nicky smiled at him as though having a conversation about their private lives was the most natural thing in the world. Which, probably, it should have been.

'Sure,' she said. 'Anything.'

'Those kids,' said Fleet. 'Ben, Isaac. Melissa and Lance. Even Richardson. Do you think if . . . I don't know. If Isaac had known his father loved him . . . Or if Ben's family had given the kid a proper chance . . .' He trailed off, aware he hadn't finished his question, but not quite sure how to end it.

Nicky answered him anyway, and Fleet had a sense she was drawing on her own experiences as well. 'I think it would have made all the difference,' she said.

Fleet found himself smiling. He was on the verge of telling Nicky what he had in mind, when there was a tap at the window in the door.

Fleet turned, and saw – of all people – Manish Apte. The man Fleet knew only as Webb was lurking in the background, transfixed as ever by his phone. Apte beamed, as though he and Fleet were old friends, and waved for him to come outside.

'Christ,' Fleet muttered. 'What are they doing here?'

Nicky was trying to see past Fleet.

'Is that the PCC? Who's the scruffy bloke behind him?'

'That's our friend from the Home Office. I'm not even sure he's fully human. At a guess, I'd put him as one part snake and two parts iPhone.' He smiled at Nicky's snigger. 'I'd better go and see what they want.'

'Boss . . .' said Nicky, and Fleet turned back.

'I know, I know,' he said, sounding even to his ear like a surly teenager. '*Play nice.*'

Nicky smiled mischievously. 'Actually, boss – and given that you've got licence to say whatever you want right now – I was going to suggest you tell them to go to hell.'

One week later

Sunday 3 November, 10.55 a.m.

Fleet stood facing the familiar blue door, his hand raised to ring the bell. He'd come this far, and still he hesitated, succumbing to a nervousness he hadn't anticipated.

The surroundings, oddly, didn't help. He knew this street like he knew the one on which he'd grown up, and aside from a few trees that had been planted where others had been cut down, and a car or two he didn't recognise in the neighbours' driveways, it was barely any different from the last time he'd been here. The house was unaltered, too. Again, it was as familiar to him as his childhood home. He'd dug the flowerbeds beside him, laid the slabs in the path below his feet, put the paint on the door in front of him himself. Although, it was beginning to flake, he noticed. A physical sign of how, even though he might have belonged here once, enough time had passed that he might as well be a stranger.

Which made him question – again – what he was doing here in the first place. He'd had his chance and he'd blown it. Except . . . things had changed. Hadn't they? *He* had.

He pressed the bell. The chime took him by surprise. That had changed as well, and he tried not to read it as an omen.

He waited, until from somewhere inside he heard the sound of footsteps. The glass in the front door darkened, and then the door itself was opening wide.

'Rob?'

Holly was wearing sweats, a faded T-shirt and a pair of

gardening gloves. She looked more beautiful than Fleet had ever seen her.

'Hello, Sprig.'

Holly served coffee in the back garden. It was one part of the house that was totally transformed. When Fleet had lived here, they'd never quite got around to tidying it up, save for mowing the lawn every couple of weeks in the summer, and repairing the fence at the rear of the plot. Holly, though, had gone to town. She'd put up a trellis and coaxed a clematis through the gaps, and tamed the rest of the plants into order – so much so that the garden appeared twice as wide as it once had. A little jasmine Fleet remembered Holly buying had graduated from its sad little plastic tub into a huge clay pot on one side of the patio, from which it had wallpapered the entire seating area.

'You've been working hard,' Fleet said admiringly.

Holly shaded her eyes against the low autumn sun. She looked around the garden, as though seeing it for the first time. 'I have,' she declared, before adding, with a little smile, 'You see? I'm not totally helpless.'

Not for one moment had Fleet ever thought she was, but it was a clear reference to the discussion they'd had the last time they'd spoken to each other face-to-face, just before DS Bevan had interrupted them on the rooftop. They'd exchanged a handful of texts since, and Nicky had filled Holly in on everything that had happened with the case, but that still left the conversation she and Fleet had been having unfinished.

'So apparently Roger's taking early retirement,' Fleet said.

'Roger Burton?' Holly was sitting on the chair nearest to Fleet, and she set her mug down on the little round table. 'Really? I always figured he'd work into his grave.'

Something must have shown on Fleet's face.

'Oh, no. He isn't—'

'Cancer,' said Fleet. 'Stage three, apparently.'

'*No.* Poor Roger! And poor Marian. And their kids . . . They must be, what? Eighteen and twenty?'

Holly had a better memory for such things than Fleet did, and he trusted that she was almost certainly right. But however old Roger's kids were, it was a shitty thing for any family to have to deal with. Fleet's own father had died of cancer when Fleet was just thirteen, and it was a battle he wouldn't have wished on anybody. And while he and Burton may have had their quarrels, they'd also known each other for years.

'It's in his lungs, if you can believe it. The man's never smoked a cigarette in his life. He runs the London Marathon every year, not to mention all those hours he puts in on the squash court.' Fleet glanced at Holly. 'Sorry. I realise it's not the most cheerful news to bring you on a Sunday morning.'

'Don't be silly,' Holly replied. 'I don't suppose there's ever really a good time for news like that.'

Fleet bobbed his head. 'Anyway. With Roger stepping down, people are being shuffled up the ladder. And, well . . . They offered me DCI.'

'Detective chief inspector? That's great!' Holly hesitated, as again she seemed to register something in Fleet's expression. 'Isn't it?'

'It would mean more money, obviously.'

'But you don't want to take it?'

'I'm not saying that. I just . . . They want a stooge, Sprig. Another yes-man among the brass to replace Roger. They weren't very happy with him in the end, you know, which was mainly my fault. To be honest, I'm not sure the cancer by itself would have been enough to convince Roger to hang up his uniform.'

'You mean they forced him out?'

'Suggestions were made, from what I can gather,' Fleet replied. 'But while they weren't best pleased with Roger, they were delighted by how things turned out with Callum Richardson. So they swung by Nicky's hospital room to offer me a pat on the head.'

'And what did you tell them?'

Fleet's first instinct had been to follow Nicky's advice. Her very words had been right there on the tip of his tongue. But he'd managed to hold himself back.

Fleet put down his cup of coffee and looked Holly in the eye. 'I told them I needed to discuss it with my ex-wife,' he said.

Holly frowned. 'With me? But . . . why?'

Fleet took a deep breath. He'd messed this up once already, and he was determined not to do so again.

'Sprig, I . . .' Fleet's eyes went to Holly's belly. 'I want to help. If you'll let me. With the baby. With everything. And I wondered . . . That is, I thought . . . I wondered if the extra money might come in useful.'

Something changed in Holly's expression, and Fleet pressed on before she could misinterpret what he was saying.

'It's not because I think you *need* my help,' he insisted. 'Or because I think you can't manage on your own. I've *never* thought that, Sprig. Not once.' He cast his gaze around the rejuvenated garden. 'I mean, Jesus. You'd cope with twins if you had to. With triplets.'

Holly gave something like a laugh. 'Dear God,' she said. 'Don't even go there.'

Fleet tested a smile. Holly didn't quite show one back.

'The thing is, Sprig,' he went on, 'I've had time to think.

For the past couple of years, it feels as though that's *all* I've been doing. And then there was Sadie. And now Ben. Not just Ben, in fact. Callum Richardson. Isaac. All the others. They all . . . all they needed . . . I mean, I don't *know*, obviously, but the thing that was missing from their lives . . . from *all* their lives—'

Fleet shook his head, cutting himself off. He was in danger of falling into the same trap he had last time.

He started again. 'Whatever happens, whatever you decide to do, and however you decide to raise your baby, I know for a fact it couldn't be any luckier. Ben, Isaac – they had no one. Not a single person who loved them, not in the way they needed. And one person, I think, is all it takes. Especially if it's someone like you.'

Fleet took a breath, acutely aware of how closely Holly was scrutinising what he was saying.

'So it's not about that,' he went on. 'I just . . . *I was wrong*, Sprig. That's what I came here to tell you. I thought I couldn't ever be a father, but when you came to me and told me you were pregnant, all I could think was . . . was how stupid I'd been to let you go. To let *us* go. And I wished . . . I wished more than anything we were having this baby together.'

He paused, trying to read Holly's expression. She rolled her lips, and Fleet couldn't tell if she was upset or trying to contain her anger.

He held up his palms. 'Which isn't to say I'm trying to muscle in on your situation. If you want me to leave – to leave you alone, I mean – then all you have to do is say. And I will. I'll go. I promise.'

He left a pause, praying that Holly wouldn't fill it.

'But if you decide you can forgive me,' he went on, tentatively, 'and there's anything I can do to make up for my mistake . . . anything at all, I mean. Like . . . like money, if you need it, obviously, but also, I don't know. Babysitting. Just for example. Or . . . or someone to talk to. A friend. Someone who . . . who cares about you. Then . . . then that's what I'm offering. To be there for you. In whatever way you'll let me. *If* you'll let me.' Once again he took a deep breath. 'Because I love you, Holly. I've always loved you. And although part of me has changed, that's the one thing about me that never will.'

Once again Fleet waited. Once again he had no idea what Holly would say.

'Don't take the job.'

Now Fleet was the one to frown. 'Sorry?'

'The job. The promotion. Don't take it. You'd hate it, Rob. You know you would.'

Fleet wriggled in his seat. 'That's not necessarily—'

'You would. We both know you would. Tell me honestly,' Holly pressed, 'if you had the choice, what would you want to do next?'

Fleet opened his mouth to argue again, to insist that being a yes-man wouldn't be *that* bad. But Holly knew him at least as well as he knew himself.

He sighed. 'Honestly? I'd do what I'm doing now. We could use one or two extra bodies, a few more resources here and there – but I think Roger actually did me a favour when he stuck me in that room with those stacks of files.'

'You mean you'd want to stay on missing persons?'

Fleet shrugged, as though it weren't quite so important to him as it felt. 'The way I see it, they're only missing for as long as someone's looking for them. After that, they're essentially lost. And, well . . . just recently I've come to know what that feels like.'

Now, finally, Holly smiled. 'So there you go then. Decision made. And if you're sensible, you'll cash in some of those Brownie points you've earned in exchange for those extra resources.'

Fleet couldn't help but laugh. It was a release of tension as much as anything, but as quickly as it went away, it began to build again.

'And . . . the other thing?' he said. 'What about . . . what about the rest of it, Sprig?'

It was strange: from being so unsure he was doing the right thing, or even if he was entitled to ask, there was suddenly nothing in the world Fleet wanted more than for Holly to let him back in; to give him the chance to show her, not just tell her, how sorry he was.

He leaned forward.

Holly did, too. A tear fell from her eye . . . and then she smiled again as she took hold of Fleet's hands.

'You realise . . . you realise it wouldn't be straightforward. Don't you? I'm not just talking about the baby. There's . . . us. And the baby's father . . .'

Fleet raised Holly's hands to his lips. She was right: wherever they went from here, it wouldn't be easy. But Fleet wasn't worried. He knew things rarely went according to plan, and that fate had a tendency to pull the rug from beneath your feet. Yet if he'd learned anything recently, it was that the hardest part of life was working out what was most important – and in that moment, it had never felt so simple.

Acknowledgements

The Hiding Place is my tenth published novel – something that dawned on me as I was writing it, and that still catches me by surprise. My agent, Caroline Wood, has been with me since the beginning, and I can only hope I will have the privilege of working with her for the next ten novels and more. Likewise the entire team at Felicity Bryan Associates: thank you all for your enthusiasm, dedication and support.

I also want to thank my incredibly talented publishing team at Penguin: my wonderful editor, Katy Loftus, as well as Vikki Moynes, Georgia Taylor, Chloe Davies, Ellie Hudson and Natalie Wall, as well as Gemma Wain for her exceptional copy-editing skills and the entire art team for their fabulous cover design.

A huge thank-you as well to all my fellow writers who have been generous enough to offer their support and words of encouragement over the years. There have been so many, I would be bound to overlook someone if I attempted to list them all, but hopefully you know who you are – I cannot express my gratitude enough. The same applies to all the bloggers, reviewers, booksellers and librarians who have helped to champion my books – and of course to you, the reader, for taking a chance on my writing in the first place.

Finally, thank you to my friends and family. Again, you know who you are, and hopefully you also know how much you mean to me. My wife, Sarah, is my first and most dedicated reader, and if it wasn't for her I probably wouldn't be writing at all. The book is dedicated to her, as well as to our three children, Barnaby, Joey and Anja. Much of *The Hiding Place* was written during lockdown, so I feel I owe you all an extra special thank-you for your astonishing feats of flexibility and forbearance during what was unquestionably the most challenging year of your young lives. I couldn't be prouder of you.

SIMON LELIC
THE SEARCH PARTY

The killer isn't out there. It's one of you.

Sixteen-year-old Sadie Saunders is missing.
Five friends set out into the woods to find her.
But they're not just friends . . .
THEY'RE SUSPECTS.
You see, this was never a search party.
It's a witch hunt.

And not everyone will make it home alive . . .

'Clever and atmospheric'
Mark Edwards

'A brilliantly tense tale'
Araminta Hall

'A bloody good read'
John Marrs

SIMON LELIC

THE HOUSE

The perfect couple. The perfect house . . . The perfect crime.

Londoners Jack and Syd moved into the house a year ago. It seemed like their dream home: tons of space, the perfect location and a friendly owner who wanted a young couple to have it.

So when they made a grisly discovery in the attic, Jack and Syd chose to ignore it. That was a mistake.

Because someone has just been murdered outside their back door.

AND NOW THE POLICE ARE WATCHING THEM.

SIMON LELIC
THE LIAR'S ROOM

One room. Two liars. No way out.

Susanna Fenton has a secret. Fourteen years ago she left her identity behind, reinventing herself as a counsellor and starting a new life. It was the only way to keep her daughter safe.

But everything changes when Adam Geraghty walks into her office. She's never met this young man before – so why does she feel like she knows him?

Then Adam starts to tell her about a girl. A girl he wants to hurt. And Susanna realizes she was wrong.
She doesn't know him.

BUT HE KNOWS HER.

'It will have you up all hours of the night'
Kathryn Croft

'Taut, unsettling and brilliantly done'
T. M. Logan

'A wonderfully claustrophobic read'
Cath Staincliffe